Praise for the novels of Jeffery Deaver

'The most creative, skilled and intriguing thriller writer in the world . . . [Deaver] has produced a stunning series of bestsellers with unique characterisation, intelligent characters, beguiling plots and double-barrelled and sometimes triple-barrelled solutions' *Sunday Telegraph*

'The best psychological thriller writer around' *The Times*

'The pace is terrific, the suspense inexorable, and there is an excellent climax . . . If you want thrills, Deaver is your man.' *Guardian*

'One of the finest crime writers in the world . . . grabs the reader by the throat from the beginning . . . Superb.' *Independent on Sunday*

'Jeffery Deaver is grand master of the ticking-clock thriller.' Kathy Reichs

'The twists and turns from devilish Deaver will have you burning the midnight oil, then using it to set fire to the candle you'll be burning at both ends until you finish . . . the perfect accompaniment on a winter's night, curled up on the sofa with a glass of your favourite tipple.' *Sun*

'There is no one better at wrong-footing the reader.' *Evening Standard*

'One of the world's best plotters – his intricate twists and turns catch out even the hardened thriller reader . . . This is a true master at work – elegant, assured, supremely crafted thriller writing at its very best' *Daily Mail*

Also by Jeffery Deaver

*Mistress of Justice*
*The Lesson of Her Death*
*Praying for Sleep*
*Speaking in Tongues*
*A Maiden's Grave*
*The Devil's Teardrop*
*The Blue Nowhere*
*Garden of Beasts*
*The Bodies Left Behind*
*Edge*
*The October List*

The Rune Series
*Manhattan is My Beat*
*Death of a Blue Movie Star*
*Hard News*

The Location Scout Series
*Shallow Graves*
*Bloody River Blues*
*Hell's Kitchen*

The Lincoln Rhyme Thrillers
*The Bone Collector*
*The Empty Chair*
*The Stone Monkey*
*The Vanished Man*
*The Twelfth Card*
*The Cold Moon*
*The Broken Window*
*The Burning Wire*
*The Kill Room*

The Kathryn Dance Thrillers
*The Sleeping Doll*
*Roadside Crosses*
*XO*

A James Bond Novel
*Carte Blanche*

Short Stories
*Twisted*
*More Twisted*

# JEFFERY
# DEAVER

# THE COFFIN
# DANCER

**HODDER**

First published in the United States of America in 1998 by Simon & Schuster

First published in Great Britain in 1998 by Hodder & Stoughton
An Hachette UK company

This Hodder paperback edition published 2014

1

A CIP catalogue record for this title is available from the British Library

Paperback ISBN 978 1 444 79156 3
Ebook ISBN 978 1 848 94169 4

Printed and bound by Clays Ltd, St Ives plc

Hodder & Stoughton policy is to use papers that are natural, renewable
and recyclable products and made from wood grown in sustainable forests.
The logging and manufacturing processes are expected to conform to the
environmental regulations of the country of origin.

Hodder & Stoughton Ltd
338 Euston Road

To the memory of my grandmother
Ethel May Rider

# TOO MANY WAYS TO DIE

No hawk can be a pet. There is no senti-
mentality. In a way, it is the psychiatrist's art.
One is matching one's mind against another
mind with deadly reason and interest.

*THE GOSHAWK*, T. H. WHITE

# Chapter
# ONE

When Edward Carney said good-bye to his wife, Percey, he never thought it would be the last time he'd see her.

He climbed into his car, which was parked in a precious space on East Eighty-first Street in Manhattan, and pulled into traffic. Carney, an observant man by nature, noticed a black van parked near their town house. A van with mud-flecked, mirrored windows. He glanced at the battered vehicle and recognized the West Virginia plates, realizing he'd seen the van on the street several times in the past few days. But then the traffic in front of him sped up. He caught the end of the yellow light and forgot the van completely. He was soon on the FDR Drive, cruising north.

Twenty minutes later he juggled the car phone and called his wife. He was troubled when she didn't answer. Percey'd been scheduled to make the flight with him – they'd flipped a coin last night for the left-hand seat and she'd won, then given him one of her trademark victory grins. But then she'd wakened at 3 A.M. with a blinding migraine, which had stayed with her all day. After a few phone calls they'd found a substitute copilot and Percey'd taken a Fiorinal and gone back to bed.

A migraine was the only malady that would ground her.

Lanky Edward Carney, forty-five years old and still wearing a military hairstyle, cocked his head as he listened to the phone ringing miles away. Their answering machine clicked on and he returned the phone to the cradle, mildly concerned.

He kept the car at exactly sixty miles per hour, centered perfectly in the right lane; like most pilots he was conservative behind the wheel. He trusted other airmen but thought most drivers were crazy.

In the office of Hudson Air Charters, on the grounds of Mamaroneck Regional Airport, in Westchester, a cake awaited. Prim and assembled Sally Anne, smelling like the perfume department at Macy's, had baked it herself to commemorate the company's new contract. Wearing the ugly rhinestone biplane brooch her grandchildren had given her last Christmas, she scanned the room to make sure each of the dozen or so employees had a piece of devil's food sized just right for them. Ed Carney ate a few bites of cake and talked about tonight's flight with Ron Talbot, whose massive belly suggested he loved cake, though he survived mostly on cigarettes and coffee. Talbot wore the dual hats of operations and business manager and he worried out loud if the shipment would be on time, if the fuel usage for the flight had been calculated correctly, if they'd priced the job right. Carney handed him the remains of his cake and told him to relax.

He thought again about Percey and stepped away into his office, picked up the phone.

Still no answer at their town house.

Now concern became worry. People with children and people with their own business always pick up a ringing phone. He slapped the receiver down, thought about calling a neighbor to check up on her. But then the large white truck pulled up in front of the hangar next to the office and it was time to go to work.

Talbot gave Carney a dozen documents to sign just as young Tim Randolph arrived, wearing a dark suit, white shirt, and narrow black tie. Tim referred to himself as a 'copilot' and Carney liked that. 'First officers' were company people, airline creations, and while Carney respected any man who was competent in the right-hand seat, pretension put him off.

Tall, brunette Lauren, Talbot's assistant, had worn her lucky dress, whose blue color matched the hue of the Hudson Air logo – a silhouette of a falcon flying over a gridded globe. She leaned close to Carney and whispered, 'It's going to be okay now, won't it?'

'It'll be fine,' he assured her. They embraced for a moment. Sally Anne hugged him too and offered him some cake for the flight. He demurred. Ed Carney wanted to be gone. Away from the sentiment, away from the festivities. Away from the ground.

And soon he was. Sailing three miles above the earth, piloting a Lear 35A, the finest private jet ever made, clear of markings or insignia except for its $N$ registration number, polished silver, sleek as a pike.

They flew toward a stunning sunset – a perfect orange disk easing into big, rambunctious clouds, pink and purple, leaking bolts of sunlight.

Only dawn was as beautiful. And only thunderstorms more spectacular.

It was 723 miles to O'Hare and they covered that distance in less than two hours. Air Traffic Control's Chicago Center politely asked them to descend to fourteen thousand feet, then handed them off to Chicago Approach Control.

Tim made the call. 'Chicago Approach. Lear Four Niner *Charlie Juliet* with you at one four thousand.'

'Evening, Niner *Charlie Juliet*,' said yet another placid air traffic controller. 'Descend and maintain eight thousand. Chicago altimeter thirty point one one. Expect vectors to twenty-seven L.'

'Roger, Chicago. Niner *Charlie Juliet* out of fourteen for eight.'

O'Hare is the busiest airport in the world and ATC put them in a holding pattern out over the western suburbs of the city, where they'd circle, awaiting their turn to land.

Ten minutes later the pleasant, staticky voice requested, 'Niner *Charlie Juliet*, heading zero nine zero over the numbers downwind for twenty-seven L.'

'Zero nine zero. Niner *Charlie Juliet*,' Tim responded.

Carney glanced up at the bright points of constellations in the stunning gunmetal sky and thought, Look, Percey, it's all the stars of evening . . .

And with that he had what was the only unprofessional urge of perhaps his entire career. His concern for Percey arose like a fever. He needed desperately to speak to her.

'Take the aircraft,' he said to Tim.

'Roger,' the young man responded, hands going unquestioningly to the yoke.

Air Traffic Control crackled, 'Niner *Charlie Juliet*, descend to four thousand. Maintain heading.'

'Roger, Chicago,' Tim said. 'Niner *Charlie Juliet* out of eight for four.'

Carney changed the frequency of his radio to make a unicom call. Tim glanced at him. 'Calling the Company,' Carney explained. When he got Talbot he asked to be patched through the telephone to his home.

As he waited, Carney and Tim went through the litany of the pre-landing check.

'Flaps approach . . . twenty degrees.'

'Twenty, twenty, green,' Carney responded.

'Speed check.'

'One hundred eighty knots.'

As Tim spoke into his mike – 'Chicago, Niner *Charlie Juliet*, crossing the numbers; through five for four' – Carney heard the phone start to ring in their Manhattan town house seven hundred miles away.

Come on, Percey. Pick up! Where *are* you?

Please . . .

ATC said, 'Niner *Charlie Juliet*, reduce speed to one eight zero. Contact tower. Good evening.'

'Roger, Chicago. One eight zero knots. Evening.'

Three rings.

Where the hell is she? What's wrong?

The knot in his gut grew tighter.

The turbofan sang, a grinding sound. Hydraulics moaned. Static crackled in Carney's headset.

Tim sang out, 'Flaps thirty. Gear down.'

'Flaps, thirty, thirty, green. Gear down. Three green.'

And then, at last – in his earphone – a sharp click.

His wife's voice saying, 'Hello?'

He laughed out loud in relief.

Carney started to speak but, before he could, the aircraft gave a huge jolt – so vicious that in a fraction of a second the force of the explosion ripped the bulky headset from his ears and the men were flung forward into the control panel. Shrapnel and sparks exploded around them.

Stunned, Carney instinctively grabbed the unresponsive yoke with his left hand; he no longer had a right one. He turned toward Tim just as the man's bloody, rag-doll body disappeared out of the gaping hole in the side of the fuselage.

'Oh, God. No, no . . .'

Then the entire cockpit broke away from the disintegrating plane and rose into the air, leaving the fuselage and wings and engines of the Lear behind, engulfed in a ball of gassy fire.

'Oh, Percey,' he whispered, 'Percey . . .' Though there was no longer a microphone to speak into.

# Chapter
# TWO

Big as asteroids, bone yellow.

The grains of sand glowed on the computer screen. The man was sitting forward, neck aching, eyes in a hard squint – from concentration, not from any flaw in vision.

In the distance, thunder. The early morning sky was yellow and green and a storm was due at any moment. This had been the wettest spring on record.

Grains of sand . . .

'Enlarge,' he commanded, and dutifully the image on the computer doubled in size.

Strange, he thought.

'Cursor down . . . stop.'

Leaning forward again, straining, studying the screen.

Sand, Lincoln Rhyme reflected, is a criminalist's delight: bits of rock, sometimes mixed with other material, ranging from .05 to 2 millimeters (larger than that is gravel, smaller is silt). It adheres to a perp's clothing like sticky paint and conveniently leaps off at crime scenes and hideouts to link murderer and murdered. It also can tell a great deal about where a suspect has been. Opaque sand means he's been in the desert. Clear means beaches. Hornblende means Canada.

Obsidian, Hawaii. Quartz and opaque igneous rock, New England. Smooth gray magnetite, the western Great Lakes.

But where this particular sand had come from, Rhyme didn't have a clue. Most of the sand in the New York area was quartz and feldspar. Rocky on Long Island Sound, dusty on the Atlantic, muddy on the Hudson. But this was white, glistening, ragged, mixed with tiny red spheres. And what are those rings? White stone rings like microscopic slices of calamari. He'd never seen anything like this.

The puzzle had kept Rhyme up till 4 A.M. He'd just sent a sample of the sand to a colleague at the FBI's crime lab in Washington. He'd had it shipped off with great reluctance – Lincoln Rhyme hated someone else answering his own questions.

Motion at the window beside his bed. He glanced toward it. His neighbors – two compact peregrine falcons – were awake and about to go hunting. Pigeons beware, Rhyme thought. Then he cocked his head, muttering, 'Damn,' though he was referring not to his frustration at identifying this uncooperative evidence but at the impending interruption.

Urgent footsteps were on the stairs. Thom had let visitors in and Rhyme didn't want visitors. He glanced toward the hallway angrily. 'Oh, not now, for God's sake.'

But they didn't hear, of course, and wouldn't have paused even if they had.

Two of them . . .

One was heavy. One not.

A fast knock on the open door and they entered.

'Lincoln.'

Rhyme grunted.

Lon Sellitto was a detective first grade, NYPD, and the one responsible for the giant steps. Padding along beside him was his slimmer, younger partner, Jerry Banks, spiffy in his pork gray suit of fine plaid. He'd doused his cowlick with spray – Rhyme could smell propane, isobutane, and vinyl acetate – but the charming spike still stuck up like Dagwood's.

The rotund man looked around the second-floor bedroom, which measured twenty by twenty. Not a picture on the wall. 'What's different, Linc? About the place?'

'Nothing.'

'Oh, hey, I know – it's clean,' Banks said, then stopped abruptly as he ran into his faux pas.

'Clean, sure,' said Thom, immaculate in ironed tan slacks, white shirt, and the flowery tie that Rhyme thought was pointlessly gaudy though he himself had bought it, mail order, for the young man. The aide had been with Rhyme for several years now – and though he'd been fired by Rhyme twice, and quit once, the criminalist had rehired the unflappable nurse/assistant an equal number of times. Thom knew enough about quadriplegia to be a doctor and had learned enough forensics from Lincoln Rhyme to be a detective. But he was content to be what the insurance company called a 'caregiver,' though both Rhyme and Thom disparaged the term. Rhyme called him, variously, his 'mother hen' or 'nemesis', both of which delighted the aide no end. He now maneuvered around the visitors. 'He didn't like it but I hired Molly Maids and got the place scrubbed down. Practically needed to be fumigated. He wouldn't talk to me for a whole day afterwards.'

'It didn't need to be cleaned. I can't find anything.'

'But then he doesn't *have* to find anything, does he?' Thom countered. 'That's what *I'm* for.'

No mood for banter. 'Well?' Rhyme cast his handsome face toward Sellitto. 'What?'

'Got a case. Thought you might wanta help.'

'I'm busy.'

'What's all that?' Banks asked, motioning toward a new computer sitting beside Rhyme's bed.

'Oh,' Thom said with infuriating cheer, 'he's state-of-the-art now. Show them, Lincoln. Show them.'

'I don't *want* to show them.'

More thunder but not a drop of rain. Nature, as often, was teasing today.

Thom persisted. 'Show them how it works.'

'Don't want to.'

'He's just embarrassed.'

'Thom,' Rhyme muttered.

But the young aide was as oblivious to threats as he was to recrimination. He tugged his hideous, or stylish, silk tie. 'I don't know why he's behaving this way. He seemed very proud of the whole setup the other day.'

'Did not.'

Thom continued. 'That box there' – he pointed to a beige contraption – 'that goes to the computer.'

'Whoa, two hundred megahertz?' Banks asked, nodding at the computer. To escape Rhyme's scowl he'd grabbed the question like an owl snagging a frog.

'Yep,' Thom said.

But Lincoln Rhyme was not interested in computers. At the moment Lincoln Rhyme was interested only in microscopic rings of sculpted calamari and the sand they nestled in.

Thom continued. 'The microphone goes into the computer. Whatever he says, the computer recognizes. It took the thing a while to learn his voice. He mumbled a lot.'

In truth Rhyme was quite pleased with the system – the lightning-fast computer, a specially made ECU box – environmental control unit – and voice-recognition software. Merely by speaking he could command the cursor to do whatever a person using a mouse and keyboard could do. And he could dictate too. Now, with words, he could turn the heat up or down and the lights on or off, play the stereo or TV, write on his word processor, make phone calls, and send faxes.

'He can even write music,' Thom said to the visitors. 'He tells the computer what notes to mark down on the staff.'

'Now that's useful,' Rhyme said sourly. 'Music.'

For a C4 quad – Rhyme's injury was at the fourth cervical vertebra – nodding was easy. He could also shrug, though not as dismissingly as he'd have liked. His other circus trick was moving his left ring finger a few millimeters in any direction he chose. That had been his entire physical repertoire for the past several years; composing a sonata for the violin was probably not in the offing.

'He can play games too,' Thom said.

'I hate games. I don't play games.'

Sellitto, who reminded Rhyme of a large unmade bed, gazed at the computer and seemed unimpressed. 'Lincoln,' he began gravely. 'There's a task-forced case. Us 'n' the feds. Ran into a problem last night.'

'Ran into a brick wall,' Banks ventured to say.

'We thought . . . well, *I* thought you'd want to help us out on this one.'

*Want* to help them out?

'I'm working on something now,' Rhyme explained. 'For Perkins, in fact.' Thomas Perkins, special agent in charge of the Manhattan office of the FBI. 'One of Fred Dellray's boys is missing.'

Special Agent Fred Dellray, a longtime veteran with the Bureau, was a handler for most of the Manhattan office's undercover agents. Dellray himself had been one of the Bureau's top undercover ops. He'd earned commendations from the director himself for infiltrating everything from Harlem drug lords' headquarters to black militant organizations. One of Dellray's agents, Tony Panelli, had gone missing a few days earlier.

'Perkins told us,' Banks said. 'Pretty weird.'

Rhyme rolled his eyes at the unartful phrase. Though he

couldn't dispute it. The agent had disappeared from his car across from the Federal Building in downtown Manhattan around 9 P.M. The streets weren't crowded but they weren't deserted either. The engine of the Bureau's Crown Victoria was running, the door open. There was no blood, no gunshot residue, no scuff marks indicating struggle. No witnesses – at least no witnesses willing to talk.

Pretty weird indeed.

Perkins had a fine crime scene unit at his disposal, including the Bureau's Physical Evidence Response Team. But it had been Rhyme who'd set up PERT and it was Rhyme whom Dellray had asked to work the scene of the disappearance. The crime scene officer who worked as Rhyme's partner had spent hours at Panelli's car and had come away with no unidentified fingerprints, ten bags of meaningless trace evidence, and – the only possible lead – a few dozen grains of this very odd sand.

The grains that now glowed on his computer screen, as smooth and huge as heavenly bodies.

Sellitto continued. 'Perkins's gonna put other people on the Panelli case, Lincoln, if you'll help us. Anyway, I think you'll want this one.'

That verb again – *want*. What was this all about?

Rhyme and Sellitto had worked together on major homicide investigations some years ago. Hard cases – and public cases. He knew Sellitto as well as he knew any cop. Rhyme generally distrusted his own ability to read people (his ex-wife, Blaine, had said – often, and heatedly – that Rhyme could spot a shell casing a mile away and miss a human being standing in front of him), but he could see now that Sellitto was holding back.

'Okay, Lon. What is it? Tell me.'

Sellitto nodded toward Banks.

'Phillip Hansen,' the young detective said significantly, lifting a puny eyebrow.

Rhyme knew the name only from newspaper articles. Hansen – a large, hard-living businessman originally from Tampa, Florida – owned a wholesale company in Armonk, New York. It was remarkably successful and he'd become a multimillionaire thanks to it. Hansen had a good deal for an entrepreneur. He never had to look for customers, never advertised, never had receivables problems. In fact, if there was any downside to PH Distributors, Inc., it was that the federal government and New York State were expending great energy to shut it down and throw its president in jail. Because the product Hansen's company sold was not, as he claimed, secondhand military surplus vehicles but weaponry, more often than not stolen from military bases or imported illegally. Earlier in the year two army privates had been killed when a truckload of small arms was hijacked near the George Washington Bridge on its way to New Jersey. Hansen was behind it – a fact the U.S. attorney and the New York attorney general knew but couldn't prove.

'Perkins and us're hammering together a case,' Sellitto said. 'Working with the army CID. But it's been a bitch.'

'And nobody ever dimes him,' said Banks. 'Ever.'

Rhyme supposed that, no, no one would dare snitch on a man like Hansen. The young detective continued. 'But finally, last week, we got a break. See, Hansen's a pilot. His company's got warehouses at Mamaroneck Airport – that one near White Plains? A judge issued paper to check 'em out. Naturally we didn't find anything. But then last week, it's midnight? The airport's closed but there're some people there, working late. They see a guy fitting Hansen's description drive out to this private plane, load some big duffel bags into it, and take off. Unauthorized. No flight plan, just takes off. Comes back forty minutes later, lands, gets back into his car, and burns rubber out of there. No duffel bags. The witnesses give the registration number to the

FAA. Turns out it's Hansen's private plane, not his company's.'

Rhyme said, 'So he knew you were getting close and he wanted to ditch something linking him to the killings.' He was beginning to see why they wanted him. Some seeds of interest here. 'Air Traffic Control track him?'

'LaGuardia had him for a while. Straight out over Long Island Sound. Then he dropped below radar for ten minutes or so.'

'And you drew a line to see how far he could get over the Sound. There're divers out?'

'Right. Now, we knew that soon as Hansen heard we had the three witnesses he was gonna rabbit. So we managed to put him away till Monday. Federal Detention.'

Rhyme laughed. 'You got a judge to buy probable cause on that?'

'Yeah, with the risk of flight,' Sellitto said. 'And some bull-shit FAA violations and reckless endangerment thrown in. No flight plan, flying below FAA minimums.'

'What'd Mister Hansen say?'

'He knows the drill. Not a word to the arrestings, not a word to the prosecutors. Lawyer denies everything and's preparing suit for wrongful arrest, yadda, yadda, yadda . . . So if we find the fucking bags we go to the grand jury on Monday and, bang, he's away.'

'Provided,' Rhyme pointed out, 'there's anything incriminating in the bags.'

'Oh, there's something incriminating.'

'How do you know?'

'Because Hansen's scared. He's hired somebody to kill the witnesses. He's already got one of 'em. Blew up his plane last night outside of Chicago.'

And, Rhyme thought, they want me to find the duffel bags . . . Fascinating questions were now floating into his mind. Was it possible to place the plane at a particular location over the water because of a certain type of precipitation or saline deposit or insect found crushed on the leading edge of the wing? Could one calculate the time of death of an insect? What about salt concentrations and pollutants in the water? Flying that low to the water, would the engines or wings pick up algae and deposit it on the fuselage or tail?

'I'll need some maps of the Sound,' Rhyme began. 'Engineering drawings of his plane—'

'Uhm, Lincoln, that's not why we're here,' Sellitto said.

'Not to find the bags,' Banks added.

'No? Then?' Rhyme tossed an irritating tickle of black hair off his forehead and frowned the young man down.

Sellitto's eyes again scanned the beige ECU box. The wires that sprouted from it were dull red and yellow and black and lay curled on the floor like sunning snakes.

'We want you to help us find the killer. The guy Hansen hired. Stop him before he gets the other two wits.'

'And?' For Rhyme saw that Sellitto still had not mentioned what he was holding in reserve.

With a glance out the window the detective said, 'Looks like it's the Dancer, Lincoln.'

'The Coffin Dancer?'

Sellitto looked back and nodded.

'You're sure?'

'We heard he'd done a job in D.C. a few weeks ago. Killed a congressional aide mixed up in arms deals. We got pen registers and found calls from a pay phone outside Hansen's house to the hotel where the Dancer was staying. It's gotta be him, Lincoln.'

On the screen the grains of sand, big as asteroids, smooth as a woman's shoulders, lost their grip on Rhyme's interest.

'Well,' he said softly, 'that's a problem now, isn't it?'

# Chapter
# THREE

She remembered:

Last night, the cricket chirp of the phone intruding on the drizzle outside their bedroom window.

She'd looked at it contemptuously as if NYNEX were responsible for the nausea and the suffocating pain in her head, the strobe lights flashing behind her eyelids.

Finally she'd rolled to her feet and snagged the receiver on the fourth ring.

'Hello?'

Answered by the empty-pipe echo of a unicom radio-to-phone patch.

Then a voice. Perhaps.

A laugh. Perhaps.

A huge roar. A click. Silence.

No dial tone. Just silence, shrouded by the crashing waves in her ears.

*Hello? Hello? . . .*

She'd hung up the phone and returned to the couch, watched the evening rain, watched the dogwood bend and straighten in the spring storm's breeze. She'd fallen asleep again. Until the phone rang again a half hour later with the news about Lear Niner *Charlie Juliet* going down on approach and carrying her husband and young Tim Randolph to their deaths.

Now, on this gray morning, Percey Rachael Clay knew that the mysterious phone call last night had been from her husband. Ron Talbot – the one who'd courageously called to deliver the news of the crash – had explained he'd patched a call through to her at around the time the Lear had exploded.

Ed's laugh . . .

*Hello? Hello?*

Percey uncorked her flask, took a sip. She thought of the windy day years ago when she and Ed had flown a pontoon equipped Cessna 180 to Red Lake, Ontario, setting down with about six ounces of fuel left in the tank, and celebrated their arrival by downing a bottle of label-less Canadian whiskey, which turned out to give them both the most dire hangovers of their lives. The thought brought tears to her eyes now, as the pain had then.

'Come on, Perce, enough of that, okay?' said the man sitting on the living room couch. 'Please.' He pointed to the flask.

'Oh, right,' her gravelly voice responded with controlled sarcasm. 'Sure.' And she took another sip. Felt like a cigarette but resisted. 'What the hell was he doing calling me on final?' she asked.

'Maybe he was worried about you,' Brit Hale suggested. 'Your migraine.'

Like Percey, Hale hadn't slept last night. Talbot had called him too with the news of the crash and he'd driven down from his Bronxville apartment to be with Percey. He'd stayed with her all night, helped her make the calls that had to be made. It was Hale, not Percey, who'd delivered the news to her own parents in Richmond.

'He had no business doing that, Brit. A call on final.'

'That had nothing to do with what happened,' Hale said gently.

'I know,' she said.

They'd known each other for years. Hale had been one of Hudson Air's first pilots and had worked for free for the first four months until his savings ran out and he had to approach Percey reluctantly with a request for some salary. He never knew that she'd paid it out of her own savings, for the company didn't turn a profit for a year after incorporation. Hale resembled a lean, stern schoolteacher. In reality he was easygoing – the perfect antidote to Percey – and a droll practical joker who'd been known to roll a plane into inverted flight if his passengers were particularly rude and unruly and keep it there until they calmed down. Hale often took the right seat to Percey's left and was her favorite copilot in the world. 'Privilege to fly with you, ma'am,' he'd say, offering his imperfect Elvis Presley impersonation. 'Thank you very much.'

The pain behind her eyes was nearly gone now. Percey had lost friends – to crashes mostly – and she knew that psychic loss was an anesthetic to physical pain.

So was whiskey.

Another hit from the flask. 'Hell, Brit.' She slumped into the couch beside him. 'Oh, hell.'

Hale slipped his strong arm around her. She dropped her head, covered with dark curls, to his shoulder. 'Be okay, babe,' he said. 'Promise. What can I do?'

She shook her head. It was an answerless question.

A sparse mouthful of bourbon, then she looked at the clock. Nine A.M. Ed's mother would be here any minute. Friends, relatives . . . There was the memorial service to plan . . .

So much to do.

'I've got to call Ron,' she said. 'We've got to do something. The Company . . .'

In airlines and charters the word 'company' didn't mean

the same as in any other business. The Company, cap C, was an entity, a living thing. It was spoken of with reverence or frustration or pride. Sometimes with sorrow. Ed's death had inflicted a wound in many lives, the Company's included, and the injury could very well be lethal.

So much to do . . .

But Percey Clay, the woman who never panicked, the woman who'd calmly controlled deadly Dutch rolls, the nemesis of Lear 23s, who'd recovered from graveyard spirals that would have sent many seasoned pilots into spins, now sat paralyzed on the couch. Odd, she thought, as if from a different dimension, I can't move. She actually looked at her hands and feet to see if they were bone white and bloodless.

Oh, Ed . . .

And Tim Randolph too, of course. As good a copilot as you'd ever find, and good first officers were rare. She pictured his young, round face, like a younger Ed's. Grinning inexplicably. Alert and obedient but firm – giving no-nonsense orders, even to Percey herself, when he had command of the aircraft.

'You need some coffee,' Hale announced, heading for the kitchen. 'I'll getcha a whipped double mochaccino latte with steamed skim.'

One of their private jokes was about sissy coffees. Real pilots, they both felt, drink only Maxwell House or Folgers.

Today, though, Hale, bless his heart, wasn't really talking about coffee. He meant: Lay off the booze. Percey took the hint. She corked the flask and dropped it on the table with a loud clink. 'Okay, okay.' She rose and paced through the living room. She caught sight of herself in the mirror. The pug face. Black hair in tight, stubborn curls. In her tormented adolescence, during a moment of despair, she'd given herself a crew cut. That'll show 'em. Though all this act of defiance did was to give the chamin' girls of the Lee School in Richmond even more ammunition against her. Percey had a slight figure and marbles of black eyes that her mother repeatedly said were her finest quality. Meaning her only quality. And a quality that men, of course, didn't give a shit about.

Dark lines under those eyes today and hopeless matte skin – smoker's skin, she remembered from the years she went through two packs of Marlboros a day. The earring holes in her lobes had long ago grown closed.

A look out the window, past the trees, into the street in front of the town house. She caught sight of the traffic and something tugged at her mind. Something unsettling.

What? What is it?

The feeling vanished, pushed away by the ringing of the doorbell.

Percey opened the door and found two burly police officers in the entryway.

'Mrs Clay?'

'Yes.'

'NYPD.' Showing IDs. 'We're here to keep an eye on you until we get to the bottom of what happened to your husband.'

'Come in,' she said. 'Brit Hale's here too.'

'Mr Hale?' one of the cops said, nodding. 'He's here? Good. We sent a couple of Westchester County troopers to his place too.'

And it was then that she looked past one of the cops, into the street, and the elusive thought popped into her mind.

Stepping around the policemen onto the front stoop.

'We'd rather you stayed inside, Mrs Clay . . .'

Staring at the street. What was it?

Then she understood.

'There's something you should know,' she said to the officers. 'A black van.'

'A . . . ?'

'A black van. There was this black van.'

One of the officers took out a notebook. 'You better tell me about it.'

'Wait,' Rhyme said.

Lon Sellitto paused in his narration.

Rhyme now heard another set of footsteps approaching, neither heavy nor light. He knew whose they were. This was not deduction. He'd heard this particular pattern many times.

Amelia Sachs's beautiful face, surrounded by her long red hair, crested the stairs, and Rhyme saw her hesitate for a moment, then continue into the room. She was in full navy blue patrol uniform, minus only the cap and tie. She carried a Jefferson Market shopping bag.

Jerry Banks flashed her a smile. His crush was adoring and obvious and only moderately inappropriate – not many patrol officers have a history of a Madison Avenue modeling career behind them, as did tall Amelia Sachs. But the gaze, like the attraction, was not reciprocated, and the young man, a pretty boy himself despite the badly shaved face and cowlick, seemed resigned to carrying his torch a bit longer.

'Hi, Jerry,' she said. To Sellitto she gave another nod and a deferential 'sir'. (He was a detective lieutenant and a legend in Homicide. Sachs had cop genes in her and had been taught over the dinner table as well as in the academy to respect elders.)

'You look tired,' Sellitto commented.

'Didn't sleep,' she said. 'Looking for sand.' She pulled a dozen Baggies out of the shopping bag. 'I've been out collecting exemplars.'

'Good,' Rhyme said. 'But that's old news. We've been reassigned.'

'Reassigned?'

'Somebody's come to town. And we have to catch him.'

'Who?'

'A killer,' Sellitto said.

'Pro?' Sachs asked. 'OC?'

'Professional, yes,' Rhyme said. 'No OC connection that we know about.' Organized crime was the largest purveyor of for-hire killers in the country.

'He's freelance,' Rhyme explained. 'We call him the Coffin Dancer.'

She lifted an eyebrow, red from worrying with a fingernail. 'Why?'

'Only one victim's ever got close to him and lived long enough to give us any details. He's got – or had, at least – a tattoo on his upper arm: the Grim Reaper dancing with a woman in front of a coffin.'

'Well, *that's* something to put in the "Distinguishing Marks" box on an incident report,' she said wryly. 'What else you know about him?'

'White male, probably in his thirties. That's it.'

'You traced the tattoo?' Sachs asked.

'Of course,' Rhyme responded dryly. 'To the ends of the earth.' He meant this literally. No police department in any major city around the world could find any history of a tattoo like his.

'Excuse me, gentlemen and lady,' Thom said. 'Work to do.' Conversation came to a halt while the young man went through the motions of rotating his boss. This helped clear his lungs. To quadriplegics certain parts of their body become personified; they develop special relationships with them. After his spine was shattered while searching a crime scene some years ago Rhyme's arms and legs had become his cruelest enemies and he'd spent desperate energy trying to force them to do what he wanted. But they'd won, no contest, and stayed as still as wood. Then he'd confronted the racking spasms that shook his body unmercifully. He'd tried to force them to stop. Eventually they had – on their own, it seemed. Rhyme couldn't exactly claim victory though he did accept their surrender. Then he'd turned to lesser challenges and had taken on his lungs. Finally, after a year of rehab, he weaned himself off the ventilator. Out came the trachea tube and he could breathe on his own. It was his only victory against his body and he harbored a dark superstition that the lungs were biding their time to get even. He figured he'd die of pneumonia or emphysema in a year or two.

Lincoln Rhyme didn't necessarily mind the idea of dying. But there were too many ways to die; he was determined not to go unpleasantly.

Sachs asked, 'Any leads? LKA?'

'Last known was down in the D.C. area,' Sellitto said in his Brooklyn drawl. 'That's it. Nothin' else. Oh, we hear about him some. Dellray more'n us, with all his skels and CIs, you know. The Dancer, he's like he's ten different people. Ear jobs, facial implants, silicon. Adds scars, removes scars. Gains weight, loses weight. Once he skinned this corpse – took some guy's hands off and wore 'em like gloves to fool CS about the prints.'

'Not me, though,' Rhyme reminded. 'I wasn't fooled.'

Though I still didn't get him, he reflected bitterly.

'He plans everything,' the detective continued. 'Sets up diversions then moves in. Does the job. And he fucking cleans up afterwards real efficient.' Sellitto stopped talking, looking strangely uneasy for a man who hunts killers for a living.

Eyes out the window, Rhyme didn't acknowledge his ex-partner's reticence. He merely continued the story. 'That case – with the skinned hands – was the Dancer's most recent job in New York. Five, six years ago. He was hired by one Wall Street investment banker to kill his partner. Did the job nice and clean. My CS team got to the scene and started to walk the grid. One of them lifted a wad of paper out of the trash can. It set off a load of PETN. About eight ounces, gas enhanced. Both techs were killed and virtually every clue was destroyed.'

'I'm sorry,' Sachs said. There was an awkward silence between them. She'd been his apprentice and his partner for more than a year – and had become his friend too. Had even spent the night here sometimes, sleeping on the couch or even, as chaste as a sibling, in Rhyme's half-ton Clinitron bed. But the talk was mostly forensic, with Rhyme's lulling her to sleep with tales of stalking serial killers and brilliant cat burglars. They generally steered clear of personal issues. Now she offered nothing more than 'It must have been hard.'

Rhyme deflected the taut sympathy with a shake of his head. He stared at the empty wall. For a time there'd been art posters taped up around the room. They were long gone but his eyes played a game of connect-the-dots with the bits of tape still stuck there. A lopsided star was the shape they traced, while within him somewhere, deep, Rhyme felt an empty despair, replaying the horrid crime scene of the explosion, seeing the burnt, shattered bodies of his officers.

Sachs asked, 'The guy who hired him, he was willing to dime the Dancer?'

'Was willing to, sure. But there wasn't much he could say. He delivered cash to a drop box with written instructions. No electronic transfers, no account numbers. They never met in person.' Rhyme inhaled deeply. 'But the worst part was that the banker who'd paid for the hit changed his mind. He lost his nerve. But he had no way to get in touch with the Dancer. It didn't matter anyway. The Dancer's told him right up front: "Recall is not an option."'

Sellitto briefed Sachs about the case against Phillip Hansen, the witnesses who'd seen his plane make its midnight run, and the bomb last night.

'Who are the other wits?' she asked.

'Percey Clay, the wife of this Carney guy killed last night

in the plane. She's the president of their company, Hudson Air Charters. Her husband was VP. The other wit's Britton Hale. He's a pilot works for them. I sent baby-sitters to keep an eye on 'em both.'

Rhyme said, 'I've called Mel Cooper in. He'll be working the lab downstairs. The Hansen case is task-forced so we're getting Fred Dellray to represent the feds. He'll have agents for us if we need them and's clearing one of U.S. Marshal's wit-protection safe houses for the Clay woman and Hale.'

Lincoln Rhyme's opulent memory intruded momentarily and he lost track of what Sellitto was saying. An image of the office where the Dancer had left the bomb five years ago came to mind again.

Remembering: The trash can, blown open like a black rose. The smell of the explosive – the choking chemical scent, nothing at all like wood-fire smoke. The silky alligatoring on the charred wood. The seared bodies of his techs, drawn into the pugilistic attitude by the flames.

He was saved from this horrid reverie by the buzz of the fax machine. Jerry Banks snagged the first sheet. 'Crime scene report from the crash,' he announced.

Rhyme's head snapped toward the machine eagerly. 'Time to go to work, boys and girls!'

Wash 'em. Wash 'em off.

Soldier, are those hands clean?

Sir, they're getting there, sir.

The solid man, in his mid-thirties, stood in the washroom of a coffee shop on Lexington Avenue, lost in his task.

Scrub, scrub, scrub . . .

He paused and looked out the men's room door. Nobody seemed interested that he'd been in here for nearly ten minutes.

Back to scrubbing.

Stephen Kall examined his cuticles and big red knuckles.

Lookin' clean, lookin' clean. No worms. Not a single one.

He'd been feeling fine as he moved the black van off the street and parked it deep in an underground garage. Stephen had taken what tools he needed from the back of the vehicle and climbed the ramp, slipping out onto the busy street. He'd worked in New York several times before but he could never get used to all the people, a thousand people on this block alone.

Makes me feel cringey.

Makes me feel *wormy*.

And so he stopped here in the men's room for a little scrub.

Soldier, aren't you through with that yet? You've got two targets left to eliminate.

Sir, almost, sir. Have to remove the risk of any trace evidence prior to proceeding with the operation, sir.

Oh, for the luva Christ . . .

The hot water pouring over his hands. Scrubbing with a brush he carried with him in a plastic Baggie. Squirting the pink soap from the dispenser. And scrubbing some more.

Finally he examined the ruddy hands and dried them under the hot air of the blower. No towels, no telltale fibers.

No worms either.

Stephen wore camouflage today, though not military olive drab or Desert Storm beige. He was in jeans, Reeboks, a work shirt, a gray windbreaker speckled with paint drips. On his belt was his cell phone and a large tape measure. He looked like any other contractor in Manhattan and was wearing this outfit today because no one would think twice about a workman wearing cloth gloves on a spring day.

Walking outside.

Still lots of people. But his hands were clean and he wasn't cringey anymore.

He paused at the corner and looked down the street at the building that had been the Husband's and Wife's town house but was the Wife's alone now because the Husband had been neatly blown into a million small pieces over the Land of Lincoln.

So, two witnesses were still alive and they both had to be dead before the grand jury convened on Monday. He glanced at his bulky stainless-steel watch. It was nine-thirty Saturday morning.

Soldier, is that enough time to get them both?

Sir, I may not get them both now but I still have nearly forty-eight hours, sir. That is more than sufficient time to locate and neutralize both targets, sir.

But, Soldier, do you mind challenges?

Sir, I *live for* challenges, sir.

There was a single squad car in front of the town house. Which he'd expected.

All right, we have a known kill zone in front of the house, an unknown one inside . . .

He looked up and down the street, then started along the sidewalk, his scrubbed hands tingling. The backpack weighed close to sixty pounds but he hardly felt it. Crew-cut Stephen was mostly muscle.

As he walked he pictured himself as a local. Anonymous. He didn't think of himself as Stephen or as Mr Kall or Todd Johnson or Stan Bledsoe or any of the dozens of other aliases he'd used over the past ten years. His real name was like a rusty gym set in the backyard, something you were aware of but didn't really see.

He turned suddenly and stepped into the doorway of the building opposite the Wife's town house. Stephen pushed open the front door and looked out at the large glass windows across the street, partially obscured by a flowering dogwood tree. He put on a pair of expensive yellow-tinted shooting glasses and the glare from the window vanished. He could see figures moving around inside. One cop . . . no, two cops. A man with his back to the window. Maybe the Friend, the other witness he'd been hired to kill. And . . . yes! There was the Wife. Short. Homely. Boyish. She was wearing a white blouse. It made a good target.

She stepped out of view.

Stephen bent down and unzipped his backpack.

# Chapter
# FOUR

A sitting transfer into the Storm Arrow wheelchair. Then Rhyme took over, gripping the plastic straw of the sip-and-puff controller in his mouth, and he drove into the tiny elevator, formerly a closet, that carried him unceremoniously down to the first floor of his town house.

In the 1890s, when the place had been built, the room into which Lincoln Rhyme now wheeled had been a parlor off the dining room. Plaster-and-lath construction, fleur-de-lis crown molding, domed icon recesses, and solid oak floorboards joined as tight as welded steel. An architect, though, would have been horrified to see that Rhyme had had the wall separating the two rooms demolished and large holes dug into the remaining walls to run additional electrical lines. The combined rooms were now a messy space filled not with Tiffany's stained glass or moody landscapes by George Innes but with very different objets d'art: density-gradient tubes, computers, compound microscopes, comparison 'scopes, a gas chromatograph/mass spectrometer, a PoliLight alternative light source, fuming frames for raising friction ridge prints. A very expensive scanning electron microscope hooked to an energy dispersive X-ray unit sat prominently in the corner. Here too were the mundane tools of the criminalist's trade: goggles, latex and cut-resistant gloves, beakers, screwdrivers and pliers, postmortem finger spoons, tongs, scalpels, tongue depressors, cotton swabs, jars, plastic bags, examining trays, probes. A dozen pairs of chopsticks (Rhyme ordered his assistants to lift evidence the way they picked up dim sum at Ming Wa's).

Rhyme steered the sleek, candy-apple red Storm Arrow into position beside the worktable. Thom placed the microphone over his head and booted up the computer.

A moment later Sellitto and Banks appeared in the doorway, joined by another man who'd just arrived. He was tall and rangy, with skin dark as tires. He was wearing a green suit and an unearthly yellow shirt.

'Hello, Fred.'

'Lincoln.'

'Hey.' Sachs nodded to Fred Dellray as she entered the room. She'd forgiven him for arresting her not long ago – an interagency squabble – and they now had a curious affinity, this tall, beautiful cop and the tall, quirky agent. They were both, Rhyme had decisively concluded, *people* cops (he himself being an *evidence* cop). Dellray trusted forensics as little as Rhyme trusted the testimony of witnesses. As for former beat cop Sachs, well, there was nothing Rhyme could do about her natural proclivities but he was determined that she push those talents aside and become the best criminalist in New York, if not the country. A goal that was easily within her grasp, even if she herself didn't know it.

Dellray loped across the room, stationed himself beside the window, crossed his lanky arms. No one – Rhyme included – could peg the agent exactly. He lived alone in a small apartment in Brooklyn, loved to read literature and philosophy, and loved even more to play pool in tawdry bars. Once the jewel in the crown of the FBI's undercover agents, Fred Dellray was still referred to occasionally by the nickname he'd had

when he was in the field: 'the Chameleon'. He'd been a renegade, everybody knew that, but his handlers in the Bureau
gave him plenty of slack; Dellray had over a thousand arrests
to his credit. But he'd spent too much time undercover and
despite his considerable skill at being who he was not, he'd
become 'overextended', as the Bureau-ese went. It was only
a matter of time before he'd be recognized and killed, so he'd
reluctantly agreed to take an administrative job running other
undercovers and CIs – confidential informants.

'So, mah boys tell me we got us the Dancer hisself,' the
agent muttered, the patois less Ebonics than, well . . . pure
Dellray. His grammar and vocabulary, like his life, were largely
improvised.

'Any word on Tony?' Rhyme asked.

'My boy gone missing?' Dellray asked, his face screwing
up angrily. 'Not. A. Thing.'

Tony Panelli, the agent who'd disappeared from the Federal
Building several days before, had left behind a wife at home,
a gray Ford with a running engine, and a number of grains
of infuriatingly mysterious sand – the sensuous asteroids that
promised answers but had so far delivered none.

'When we catch the Dancer,' Rhyme said, 'we'll get back
on it, Amelia and me. Full-time. Promise.'

Dellray angrily tapped the unlit tip of a cigarette nestling
behind his left ear. 'The Dancer . . . Shit. Better nail his ass
this time. Shit.'

'What about the hit?' Sachs asked. 'The one last night.
Have any details?'

Sellitto read through the wad of faxes and some of his
own handwritten notes. He looked up. 'Ed Carney took off
from Mamaroneck Airport around seven-fifteen last night.
The company – Hudson Air – they're a private charterer. They
fly cargo, corporate clients, you know. Lease out planes. They'd
just gotten a new contract to fly – get this – body parts for

transplants to hospitals around the Midwest and East Coast. Hear it's a real competitive business nowadays.'

'Cutthroat,' Banks offered and was the only one who smiled at his joke.

Sellitto continued. 'The client was U.S. Medical and Healthcare. Based up in Somers. One of those for-profit hospital chains. Carney had a real tight schedule. Was supposed to fly to Chicago, Saint Louis, Memphis, Lexington, Cleveland, then lay over in Erie, Pennsylvania. Come back this morning.'

'Any passengers?' Rhyme asked.

'Not whole ones,' Sellitto muttered. 'Just the cargo. Everything's routine about the flight. Then about ten minutes out of O'Hare, a bomb goes off. Blows the shit out of the plane. Killed both Carney and his copilot. Four injuries on the ground. His wife, by the way, was supposed to be flying with him but she got sick and had to cancel.'

'There an NTSB report?' Rhyme asked. 'No, of course not, there wouldn't be. Not yet.'

'Report won't be ready for two, three days.'

'Well, we can't *wait* two or three days!' Rhyme griped loudly. 'I need it now!'

A pink scar from the ventilator hose was visible on his throat. But Rhyme had weaned himself off the fake lung and could breathe like nobody's business. Lincoln Rhyme was a C4 quad who could sigh, cough, and shout like a sailor. 'I need to know everything about the bomb.'

'I'll call a buddy in the Windy City,' Dellray said. 'He owes me major. Tell 'im what's what and have 'im ship us whatever they got pronto.'

Rhyme nodded to the agent, then considered what Sellitto had told him. 'Okay, we've got two scenes. The crash site in Chicago. That one's too late for you, Sachs. Contaminated as hell. We'll just have to hope the folks in Chicago do a halfway decent job. The other scene's the airport in Mamaroneck – where the Dancer got the bomb on board.'

'How do we know he did it at the airport?' Sachs said. She was rolling her brilliant red hair in a twist, then pinning it on top of her head. Magnificent strands like these were a liability at crime scenes; they threatened to contaminate the evidence. Sachs went about her job armed with a Glock 9 and a dozen bobby pins.

'Good point, Sachs.' He loved her outguessing him. 'We *don't* know and we won't until we find the seat of the bomb. It might've been planted in the cargo, in a flight bag, a coffeepot.'

Or a wastebasket, he thought grimly, again recalling the Wall Street bombing.

'I want every single bit of that bomb here as soon as possible. We have to have it,' Rhyme said.

'Well, Linc,' Sellitto said slowly, 'the plane was a mile up when it blew. The wreckage's scattered over a whole fucking subdivision.'

'I don't care,' Rhyme said, neck muscles aching. 'Are they still searching?'

Local rescue workers searched crash sites but investigations were federal so it was Fred Dellray who placed a call to the FBI special agent at the site.

'Tell him we need every piece of wreckage that tests positive for explosive. I'm talking nanograms. I want that bomb.'

Dellray relayed this. Then he looked up, shook his head. 'Scene's released.'

'What?' Rhyme snapped. 'After twelve hours? Ridiculous. Inexcusable!'

'They had to get the streets open. He said—'

'Fire trucks!' Rhyme called.

'What?'

'Every fire truck, ambulance, police car . . . every emergency vehicle that responded to the crash. I want the tires scraped.'

Dellray's long, black face stared at him. 'You wanna repeat that? For my ex-good friend here?' The agent pushed the phone at him.

Rhyme ignored the receiver and said to Dellray, 'Emergency vehicle tires're one of the best sources for good evidence at contaminated crime scenes. They were first on the scene, they usually have new tires with deep tread grooves, and they probably didn't drive anywhere but to and from the site. I want all the tires scraped and the trace sent here.'

Dellray managed to get a promise from Chicago that the tires of as many emergency vehicles as they could get to would be scraped.

'Not "as many as",' Rhyme called. '*All* of them.'

Dellray rolled his eyes and relayed that information too, then hung up.

Suddenly Rhyme cried, 'Thom! Thom, where are you?'

The belabored aide appeared at the door a moment later. 'In the laundry room, that's where.'

'Forget laundry. We need a time chart. Write, write . . .'

'Write *what*, Lincoln?'

'On that chalkboard, right there. The big one.' Rhyme looked at Sellitto. 'When's the grand jury convening?'

'Nine on Monday.'

'The prosecutor'll want them there a couple hours early – the van'll pick 'em up between six and seven.' He looked at the wall clock. It was now 10 A.M. Saturday.

'We've got exactly forty-five hours. Thom, write, "Hour 1 of 45".'

The aide hesitated.

'Write!'

He did.

Rhyme glanced at the others in the room. He saw their eyes flickering uncertainly, a skeptical frown on Sachs's face. Her hand rose to her scalp and she scratched absently.

'Think I'm being melodramatic?' he asked. 'Think we don't need a reminder?'

No one spoke for a moment. Finally Sellitto said, 'Well, Linc, I mean, it's not like anything's going to happen by then.'

'Oh, yes, something's going to happen,' Rhyme said, eyes on the male falcon as the muscular bird launched himself effortlessly into the air over Central Park. 'By seven o'clock on Monday morning, either we'll've nailed the Dancer, or both our witnesses'll be dead. There're no other options.'

Thom hesitated then picked up the chalk and wrote.

The dense silence was broken by the chirp of Banks's cell phone. He listened for a minute, then looked up. 'Here's something,' he said.

'What?' Rhyme asked.

'Those uniforms guarding Mrs Clay and the other witness, Britton Hale?'

'What about them?'

'They're at her town house. One of 'em just called in. Seems Mrs Clay says there was a black van she'd never seen before parked on the block outside the house for the last couple days. Out-of-state plates.'

'She get the tag? Or state?'

'No,' Banks responded. 'She said it was gone for a while last night after her husband left for the airport.'

Sellitto stared at him.

Rhyme's head eased forward. 'And?'

'She said it was back this morning for a little while. It's gone now. She was—'

'Oh, Jesus,' Rhyme whispered.

'What?' Banks asked.

'Central!' the criminalist shouted. 'Get on the horn to Central. Now!'

\*    \*    \*

A taxi pulled up in front of the Wife's town house.

An elderly woman got out and walked unsteadily to the door.

Stephen watching, vigilant.

Soldier, is this an easy shot?

Sir, a shooter never thinks of a shot as easy. Every shot requires maximum concentration and effort. But, sir, I can make this shot and inflict lethal wounds, sir. I can turn my targets into jelly, sir.

The woman climbed up the stairs and disappeared into the lobby. A moment later Stephen saw her appear in the Wife's living room. There was a flash of white cloth – the Wife's blouse again. The two of them hugged. Another figure stepped into the room. A man. A cop? He turned around. No, it was the Friend.

Both targets, Stephen thought excitedly, only thirty yards away.

The older woman – mother or mother-in-law – remained in front of the Wife as they talked, heads down.

Stephen's beloved Model 40 was in the van. But he wouldn't need the sniper rifle for this shot, only the long-barrel Beretta. It was a wonderful gun. Old, battered, and functional. Unlike many mercenaries and pros, Stephen didn't make a fetish out of his weapons. If a rock was the best way to kill a particular victim, he'd use a rock.

He assessed his target, measuring angles of incidence, the window's potential distortion and deflection. The old woman stepped away from the Wife and stood directly in front of the glass.

Soldier, what is your strategy?

He'd shoot through the window and hit the elderly woman high. She'd fall. The Wife would instinctively step forward toward her and bend over her, presenting a fair target. The Friend would run into the room too and would profile just fine.

And what about the cops?

A slight risk. But uniformed patrolmen were modest shots at best and had probably never been fired on in the line of duty. They'd be sure to panic.

The lobby was still empty.

Stephen pulled back the slide to cock the weapon and give himself the better control of squeezing the trigger in the gun's single-action mode. He pushed the door open and blocked it with his foot, looked up and down the street.

No one.

Breathe, soldier. Breathe, breathe, breathe . . .

He lowered the gun to his palm, the butt resting heavy in his gloved hand. He began applying imperceptible pressure to the trigger.

Breathe, breathe.

He stared at the old woman, and forgot completely about squeezing, forgot about aiming, forgot about the money he was making, forgot everything in the universe. He simply held the gun steady as a rock in his supple, relaxed hands and waited for the weapon to fire itself.

# Chapter
# FIVE

The elderly woman wiping tears, the Wife standing behind her, arms crossed.

They were dead, they were—

Soldier!

Stephen froze. Relaxed his trigger finger.

Lights!

Flashing lights, silently zooming along the street. The turret lights on a police cruiser. Then two more cars, then a dozen, and an Emergency Services van bounding over the potholes. Converging on the Wife's town house from both ends of the street.

Safety your weapon, Soldier.

Stephen lowered the gun, stepped back into the dim lobby.

Police ran from the cars like spilt water. They spread out along the sidewalk, gazing outward and up at the rooftops. They flung open the doors to the Wife's town house, shattering the glass and pushing inside.

The five ESU officers, in full tactical gear, deployed along the curb, covering exactly the spots that ought to be covered, eyes vigilant, fingers curled loosely on the black triggers of their black guns. Patrol officers might be glorified traffic cops but there were no better soldiers than New York's ESU. The Wife and the Friend had disappeared, probably flung to the floor. The old lady too.

More cars, filling the street and pulling up onto the sidewalks.

Stephen Kall, feeling cringey. Wormy. Sweat dotted his palms and he flexed his fist so the glove would soak it up.

Evacuate, Soldier . . .

With a screwdriver he pried open the lock to the main door and pushed inside, walking fast but not running, head down, making for the service entrance that led to the alley. No one saw him, and he slipped outside. Was soon on Lexington Avenue, walking south through the crowds toward the underground garage where he'd parked the van.

Looking ahead.

Sir, trouble here, sir.

More cops.

They'd closed down Lexington Avenue about three blocks south and were setting up a perimeter around the town house, stopping cars, looking over pedestrians, moving door to door, shining their long flashlights into parked cars. Stephen saw two cops, hands twitching on the butts of their Glocks, ask one man to step out of his car while they searched under a pile of blankets in the backseat. What troubled Stephen was that the man was white and about Stephen's age.

The building where he'd parked the van was within the search perimeter. He couldn't drive out without being stopped. The line of cops moved closer. He walked quickly back to the garage and pulled open the van door. Quickly he changed clothes – ditching the contractor outfit and dressing in blue jeans, work shoes (no telltale tread marks), a black T-shirt, a dark green windbreaker (no lettering of any kind), and a baseball cap (free of team insignia). The backpack contained his laptop, several cellular phones, his small-arms weapons, and ammunition from the van. He got more bullets, his binoculars, the night vision scope, tools, several packages of explosives, and various detonators. Stephen put the supplies in the large backpack.

The Model 40 was in a Fender bass guitar case. He lifted this out of the back of the van and set it with the backpack on the garage floor. He considered what to do about the van. Stephen had never touched any part of the vehicle without wearing gloves and there was nothing inside that would give away his identity. The Dodge itself was stolen and he'd removed both the dash VIN and the secret VINs. He'd made the license plates himself. He'd planned on abandoning it sooner or later and could finish the job without the vehicle. He decided to leave it now. He covered the boxy Dodge with a blue Wolf car tarp, slipped his k-bar knife into the tires, flattening them, to make it look like the van had been there for months. He left the garage through the elevator to the building.

Outside, he slipped into the crowd. But there were police everywhere. His skin started to crawl. It felt wormy, moist. He stepped up to a phone booth and pretended to make a call, lowered his head to the metal plate of the phone, felt the sweat prickle on his forehead, under his arms. Thinking, They're *everywhere*. Looking for him, looking *at* him. From cars. From the street.

From *windows* . . .

The memory came back again . . .

The face in the window.

He took a deep breath.

The face in the window . . .

It had happened recently. Stephen'd been hired for a hit in Washington, D.C. The job was to kill a congressional aide selling classified military arms information to – Stephen assumed – a competitor of the man who'd hired Stephen. The aide had been understandably paranoid and kept a safe house in Alexandria, Virginia. Stephen had learned where it was and finally managed to get close enough for a pistol shot – although it would be a tricky one.

*Once chance, one shot . . .*

Stephen had waited for four hours, and when the victim arrived and darted toward his town house Stephen had managed to fire a single shot. Hit him, he believed, but the man had fallen out of sight in a courtyard.

Listen to me, boy. You listening?

Sir, yessir.

You track down every wounded target and finish the job. You follow the blood spoor to hell and back, you have to.

Well—

No well about it. You confirm *every* kill. You understand me? This's not an option.

Yessir.

Stephen had climbed over the brick wall into the man's courtyard. He found the aide's body sprawled on the cobble-stones, beside a goat-head fountain. The shot had been fatal after all.

But something odd had happened. Something that sent a shiver through him and very few things in life had ever made him shiver. Maybe it was just a fluke, the way the aide had fallen or the way the bullet hit him. But it appeared that someone had carefully untucked the victim's bloody shirt and pulled it up to see the tiny entrance wound above the man's sternum.

Stephen had spun around, looking for whoever had done this. But, no, there was no one nearby.

Or so he thought at first.

Then Stephen happened to look across the courtyard. There was an old carriage house, its windows smeared and dirty, lit from behind with failing sunset light. In one of those windows he saw – or imagined he saw – a face looking out at him. He couldn't see the man – or woman – clearly. But whoever it was didn't seem particularly scared. They hadn't ducked or tried to run.

A witness, you left a witness, Soldier!

Sir, I will eliminate the possibility of identification immediately, sir.

But when he kicked in the door of the carriage house he found it was empty.

Evacuate, Soldier . . .

*The face in the window* . . .

Stephen had stood in the empty building, overlooking the courtyard of the aide's town house, lit with bold western sunlight, and turned around and around in slow, manic circles.

Who was it? What had he been doing? Or was it just Stephen's imagination? The way his stepfather used to see snipers in the hawk nests of West Virginia oak trees.

The face in the window had gazed at him the way his stepfather would look at him sometimes, studying him, inspecting. Stephen, remembering what young Stephen had often thought: Did I fuck up? Did I do good? What's he *thinking* about me?

Finally he couldn't wait any longer and he'd headed back to his hotel in Washington.

Stephen had been shot at and beaten and stabbed. But nothing had shaken him as much as that incident in Alexandria. He'd never once been troubled by the faces of his victims, dead or alive. But the face in the window was like a worm crawling up his leg.

Cringey . . .

Which was exactly what he felt now, seeing the lines of officers moving toward him from both directions on Lexington. Cars were honking, drivers were angry. But the police paid no mind; they continued their dogged search. It was just a matter of minutes until they spotted him – an athletic white man by himself, carrying a guitar case that might easily contain the best sniper rifle God put on this earth.

His eyes went to the black, grimy windows overlooking the street.

He prayed he wouldn't see a face looking out.

*Soldier, the fuck you talking about?*

*Sir, I—*

*Reconnoiter, Soldier.*

*Sir, yessir.*

A burnt, bitter smell came to him.

He turned around and found he was standing outside a Starbucks. He walked in and while he pretended to read the menu in fact he surveyed the customers.

At a table by herself a large woman sat in one of the flimsy, uncomfortable chairs. She was reading a magazine and nursing a tall cup of tea. She was in her early thirties, dumpy, with a broad face and a thick nose. Starbucks, he free-associated . . . Seattle . . . dyke?

But, no, he didn't think so. She pored over the *Vogue* in her hands with envy, not lust.

Stephen bought a cup of Celestial Seasonings tea, chamomile. He picked up the container and started to walk toward a seat at the window. Stephen was just passing the woman's table when the cup slipped from his hand and dropped onto the chair opposite her, spraying the hot tea all over the floor. She slid back in surprise, looking up at the horrified expression on Stephen's face.

'Oh, my goodness,' he whispered, 'I am sooo sorry.' He lunged for a handful of napkins. 'Tell me I didn't get any on you. *Please!*'

Percey Clay pulled away from the young detective who held her pinned to the floor.

Ed's mother, Joan Carney, lay a few feet away, her face frozen in shock and bewilderment.

Brit Hale was up against the wall, covered by two strong cops. It looked as if they were arresting him.

'I'm sorry, ma'am, Mrs Clay,' one cop said. 'We—'

'What's going on?' Hale seemed mystified. Unlike Ed and Ron Talbot and Percey herself, Hale had never been military, never come close to combat. He was fearless – he always wore long sleeves instead of a pilots' traditional short-sleeve white shirt to hide the leathery burn scars on his arms from the time a few years ago he'd climbed into a flaming Cessna 150 to rescue a pilot and passenger. But the idea of crime – intentional harm – was wholly alien to him.

'We got a call from the task force,' the detective explained. 'They think the man who killed Mr Carney has been back. Probably to come after you two. Mr Rhyme thinks the killer was the one driving that black van you saw today.'

'Well, we have *those* men to guard us,' Percey snapped, tossing her head to the cops who'd arrived earlier.

'Jesus,' Hale muttered, looked outside. 'There must be twenty cops out there.'

'Away from the window, please, sir,' the detective said firmly. 'He could be on a rooftop. The site's not secure yet.'

Percey heard footsteps running up the stairs. 'The roof?' she asked sourly. 'Maybe he's tunneling into the basement.' She put her arm around Mrs Carney. 'You all right, Mother?'

'What's going on, what is all this?'

'They think you might be in danger,' the officer said. 'Not you, ma'am,' he added to Ed's mother. 'Mrs Clay and Mr Hale here. Because they're witnesses in that case. We were told to secure the premises and take them to the command post.'

'They talk to him yet?' Hale asked.

'Don't know who that'd be, sir.'

The lean man answered, 'The guy we're witnesses *against*. Hansen.' Hale's world was the world of logic. Of reasonable people. Of machines and numbers and hydraulics. His three marriages had failed because the only place where his heart poked out was in the science of flight and the irrefutable sense of the cockpit. He now swiped his hair off his fore-head and said, 'Just ask him. He'll tell you where the killer is. *He* hired him.'

'Well, I don't think it's quite as easy as that.'

Another officer appeared in the doorway. 'Street's secure, sir.'

'If you'll come with us, please. Both of you.'

'What about Ed's mother?'

'Do you live in the area?' the officer asked.

'No. I'm staying with my sister,' Mrs Carney answered. 'In Saddle River.'

'We'll drive you back there, have a New Jersey trooper stay outside the house. You're not involved in this, so I'm sure there's nothing to worry about.'

'Oh, Percey.'

The women hugged. 'It'll be okay, Mother.' Percey struggled to hold back the tears.

'No, it won't,' the frail woman said. 'It'll never be okay . . .'

An officer led her off to a squad car.

Percey watched the car drive off, then asked the cop beside her, 'Where're we going?'

'To see Lincoln Rhyme.'

Another officer said, 'We're going to walk out together, an officer on either side of you. Keep your heads down and don't look up under any circumstance. We're going to walk fast to that second van there. See it? You jump in. Don't look out the windows, and get your belts on. We'll be driving fast. Any questions?'

Percey opened the flask and took a sip of bourbon. 'Yeah, who the hell is Lincoln Rhyme?'

'You sewed that? Yourself?'

'I did,' the woman said, tugging at the embroidered denim vest, which, like the plaid skirt she wore, was slightly too large, calculated to obscure her substantial figure. The stitching reminded him of the rings around a worm's body. He shivered, felt sick.

But he smiled and said, 'That's amazing.' He'd sopped up the tea and apologized like the gentleman his stepfather could sometimes be.

He asked if she minded if he sat down with her.

'Uhm . . . no,' she said and hid the *Vogue* in her canvas bag as if it were porn.

'Oh, by the way,' Stephen said, 'I'm Sam Levine.' Her eyes flickered at his surname and took in his Aryan features. 'Well, it's Sammie mostly,' he added. 'To Mom I'm Samuel but only if I've done something wrong.' A chuckle.

'I'll call you "friend",' she announced. 'I'm Sheila Horowitz.'

He glanced out the window to avoid having to shake her moist hand, tipped with five white, squooshy worms.

'Pleased to meet you,' he said, turning back, sipping his new cup of tea, which he found disgusting. Sheila noticed that two of her stubby nails were dirty. She tried unobtrusively to dig the crud from under them.

'It's relaxing,' she explained. 'Sewing. I have an old Singer. One of those old black ones. Got it from my grams.' She tried to straighten her shiny, short hair, wishing undoubtedly that today of all days she'd washed it.

'I don't know any girls who sew anymore,' Stephen said. 'Girl I dated in college did. Made most of her own clothes. Was *I* impressed.'

'Uhm, in New York, like, nobody, and I mean nobody, sews.' She sneered emphatically.

'My mother used to sew all the time, hours on end,' Stephen said. 'Every stitch had to be just perfect. I mean perfect. A thirty-second of an inch apart.' This was true. 'I still have some of the things she made. Stupid, but I kept 'em just 'cause she made them.' This was not.

Stephen could still hear the start and stop of the Singer motor coming from his mother's tiny, hot room. Day and night. Get those stitches right. One thirty-second of an inch. Why? Because it's *important*! Here comes the ruler, here comes the belt, here comes the cock . . .

'Most men' – the stress she put on the word explained a deal about Sheila Horowitz's life – 'don't care doodles for sewing. They want girls to do sports or know movies.' She added quickly, 'And I do. I mean, I've been skiing. I'm not as good as you, I'll bet. And I like to go to the movies. Some movies.'

Stephen said, 'Oh, I don't ski. I don't like sports much.' He looked outside and saw the cops everywhere. Looking in every car. A swarm of blue worms . . .

Sir, I don't understand why they're mounting this offensive, sir.

Soldier, your job is not to understand. Your job is to infiltrate, evaluate, delegate, isolate, and eliminate. That is your only job.

'Sorry?' he asked, missing what she'd said.

'I said, oh, don't give me that. I mean, I'd have to work out for, like, months to get in shape like you. I'm going to join the Health & Racquet Club. I've been planning to. Only, I've got back problems. But I really, really am going to join.'

Stephen laughed. 'Aw, I get so tired of – geez, all these girls look so sick. You know? All thin and pale. Take one of those skinny girls you see on TV and send her back to King Arthur's day and, bang, they'd call for the court surgeon and say, "She must be dying, m'lord."'

Sheila blinked, then roared with laughter, revealing unfortunate teeth. The joke gave her an excuse to rest her hand on his arm. He felt the five worms kneading his skin and fought down the nausea. 'My daddy,' she said, 'he was a career army officer, traveled a lot. He told me in other countries they think American girls are way skinny.'

'He was a soldier?' Sam Sammie Samuel Levine asked, smiling.

'Retired colonel.'

'Well . . .'

Too much? he wondered. No. He said, 'I'm service. Sergeant. Army.'

'No! Where you stationed?'

'Special Operations. In New Jersey.' She'd know enough not to ask any more about Special Ops activities. 'I'm glad you've got a soldier in the family. I sometimes don't tell people what I do. It's not too cool. 'Specially around here. New York, I mean.'

'Don't you worry about that. I think it's *very* cool, friend.' She nodded at the Fender case. 'And you're a musician, too?'

'Not really. I volunteer at a day care center. Teach kids music. It's something the base does.'

Looking outside. Flashing lights. Blue white. A squad car streaked past.

She scooted her chair closer and he detected a repulsive scent. It made him go cringey again and the image came to mind of worms oozing through her greasy hair. He nearly vomited. He excused himself for a moment and spent three minutes scrubbing his hands. When he returned he noticed two things: that the top button of her blouse had been undone and that the back of her sweater contained about a thousand cat hairs. Cats, to Stephen, were just four-legged worms.

He looked outside and saw that the line of cops was getting closer. Stephen glanced at his watch and said, 'Say, I've gotta pick up my cat. He's at the vet—'

'Oh, you have a cat? What's his name?' She leaned forward. 'Buddy.'

Her eyes glowed. 'Oh, cutey cutey cute. You have a picture?' Of a fucking cat?

'Not on me,' Stephen said, clicked his tongue regretfully.

'Is poor Buddy sicky-wicky?'

'Just a checkup.'

'Oh, good for you. Watch out for those worms.'

'How's that?' he asked, alarmed.

'You know, like heartworm.'

'Oh. Right.'

'Uhm, if you're good, friend,' Sheila said, singsongy again, 'maybe I'll introduce you to Garfield, Andrea, and Essie. Well, it's *really* Esmeralda but she'd never approve of that, of course.'

'They sound so wonderful,' he said, gazing at the pictures Sheila'd dug from her wallet. 'I'd love to meet them.'

'You know,' she blurted, 'I only live three blocks away. On Eighty-first.'

'Hey, got an idea.' He looked bright. 'Maybe I could drop this stuff off and meet your babies. Then you could help me collect Buddy.'

'Neat-o,' Sheila said.

'Let's go.'

Outside, she said, 'Ooo, look at all the police. What's going on?'

'Wow. Dunno.' Stephen slung the backpack over his shoulder. Something metal clinked. Maybe a flash grenade banged against his Beretta.

'What's in there?'

'Musical instruments. For the kids.'

'Oh, like triangles?'

'Yeah, like triangles.'

'You want me to carry your guitar?'

'You mind?'

'Uhm, I think it'd be neat.'

She took the Fender case and slipped her arm through his and they walked past a cluster of cops, who were blind to the loving couple, and continued down the street, laughing and talking about those crazy cats.

# Chapter
# SIX

Thom appeared in Lincoln Rhyme's doorway and motioned someone inside.

A trim, crew-cut man in his fifties. Captain Bo Haumann, head of the NYPD's Emergency Services Unit – the police's SWAT team. Grizzled and tendony, Haumann looked like the drill sergeant he'd been in the service. He spoke slowly and reasonably, and he looked you dead in the eye, with a faint smile, when he talked. In tactical operations he was often suited up in flak jacket and Nomex hood and was usually one of the first officers through the door in a dynamic barricade entry.

'It's really him?' the captain asked. 'The Dancer?'

'S'what we heard,' Sellitto said.

The slight pause, which from the gray-haired cop was like a loud sigh from anyone else. Then he said, 'I've got a couple of Thirty-two-E teams dedicated.'

Thirty-two-E officers, nicknamed after their operations room at Police Plaza, were an unkept secret. Officially called Special Procedures Officers of the Emergency Services Unit, the men and women were mostly ex-military and had been relentlessly instructed in full S&S procedures – search and surveillance – as well as assault, sniping, and hostage rescue. There weren't many of them. The city's tough reputation notwithstanding, there were relatively few tactical operations in New York and the city's hostage negotiators – considered the best in the country – usually resolved standoffs before an assault was necessary. Haumann's committing two teams, which totaled ten officers, to the Dancer would have used up most of the 32-Es.

A moment later a slight, balding man wearing very unstylish glasses entered the room. Mel Cooper was the best lab man in IRD, the department's Investigation and Resources Division, which Rhyme used to head. He'd never searched a crime scene, never arrested a perp, had probably forgotten how to fire the slim pistol he grudgingly wore on the back of his old leather belt. Cooper had no desire to be anywhere in the world except sitting on a lab stool, peering into microscopes and analyzing friction ridge prints (well, there and on the ballroom dance floor, where he was an award-winning tango dancer).

'Detective,' Cooper said, using the title that Rhyme had carried when he'd hired Cooper away from Albany PD some years ago, 'thought I was going to be looking at sand. But I hear it's the Dancer.' There's only one place the word travels faster than on the street, Rhyme reflected, and that's inside the Police Department itself. 'We'll get him this time, Lincoln. We'll get him.'

As Banks briefed the newcomers Rhyme happened to look up. He saw a woman in the doorway of the lab. Dark eyes scanning the room, taking it all in. Not cautious, not uneasy.

'Mrs Clay?' he asked.

She nodded. A lean man appeared in the doorway beside her. Britton Hale, Rhyme assumed.

'Please come in,' the criminalist said.

She stepped into the middle of the room, glancing at

Rhyme, then at the wall of forensic equipment near Mel Cooper.

'Percey,' she said. 'Call me Percey. You're Lincoln Rhyme?'

'That's right. I'm very sorry about your husband.'

She nodded briskly, seemed uncomfortable with the sympathy.

Just like me, Rhyme thought.

He asked the man standing beside Percey, 'And you're Mr Hale?'

The lanky pilot nodded and stepped forward to shake hands, then noticed Rhyme's arms were strapped to the wheelchair. 'Oh,' he muttered, then blushed. He stepped back.

Rhyme introduced them to the rest of the team, everyone except Amelia Sachs, who – at Rhyme's insistence – was changing out of her uniform and putting on the jeans and sweatshirt that happened to be hanging upstairs in Rhyme's closet. He'd explained that the Dancer often killed or wounded cops as a diversion; he wanted her to look as civilian as possible.

Percey pulled a flask from her slacks pocket, a silver flask, and took a short sip. She drank the liquor – Rhyme smelled expensive bourbon – as if it were medicine.

Betrayed by his own body, Rhyme rarely paid attention to the physical qualities in others, except victims and perps. But Percey Clay was hard to ignore. She wasn't much over five feet tall. Yet she radiated a distilled intensity. Her eyes, black as midnight, were captivating. Only after you managed to look away from them did you notice her face, which was unpretty – pug and tomboyish. She had a tangle of black curly hair, cropped short, though Rhyme thought that long tresses would soften the angular shape of her face. She didn't adopt the cloaking mannerisms of some short people – hands on hips, crossed arms, fingers stationed in front of the mouth. She offered as few gratuitous gestures as Rhyme did, he realized.

A sudden thought came to him: She's like a Gypsy.

He realized that she was studying him too. And hers seemed to be a curious reaction. Seeing him for the first time, most people slap a dumb grin on their faces, blush red as fruit, and force themselves to stare fixedly at Rhyme's forehead so their eyes won't drop accidentally to his damaged body. But Percey looked once at his face – handsome with its trim lips and Tom Cruise nose, a face younger than its forty-some years – and once at his motionless legs and arms and torso. But her attention focused immediately on the crip equipment – the glossy Storm Arrow wheelchair, the sip-and-puff controller, the headset, the computer.

Thom entered the room and walked up to Rhyme to take his blood pressure.

'Not now,' his boss said.

'Yes now.'

'No.'

'Be quiet,' Thom said and took the pressure reading anyway. He pulled off the stethoscope. 'Not bad. But you're tired and you've been way too busy lately. You need some rest.'

'Go away,' Rhyme grumbled. He turned back to Percey Clay. Because he was a crip, a quad, because he was merely a portion of a human being, visitors often seemed to think he couldn't understand what they were saying; they spoke slowly or even addressed him through Thom. Percey now spoke to him directly and earned many points from him for doing this. 'You think we're in danger, Brit and me?'

'Oh, you are. Serious danger.'

Sachs walked into the room and glanced at Percey and Rhyme.

He introduced them.

'Amelia?' Percey asked. 'Your name's *Amelia*?'

Sachs nodded.

A faint smile passed over Percey's face. She turned slightly and shared it with Rhyme.

'I wasn't named after her – the flier,' Sachs said, recalling, Rhyme guessed, that Percey was a pilot. 'One of my grandfather's sisters. Was Amelia Earhart a hero?'

'No,' Percey said. 'Not really. It's just kind of a coincidence.'

Hale said, 'You're going to have guards for her, aren't you? Full-time?' He nodded at Percey.

'Sure, you bet,' Dellray said.

'Okay,' Hale announced. 'Good . . . One thing. I was thinking you really ought to have a talk with that guy. Phillip Hansen.'

'A talk?' Rhyme queried.

'With Hansen?' Sellitto asked. 'Sure. But he's denying everything and won't say a word more'n that.' He looked at Rhyme. 'Had the Twins on him for a while.' Then back to Hale. 'They're our best interrogators. And he stonewalled completely. No luck so far.'

'Can't you threaten him . . . or something?'

'Uhm, no,' the detective said. 'Don't think so.'

'Doesn't matter,' Rhyme continued. 'There's nothing Hansen could tell us anyway. The Dancer never meets his clients face-to-face and he never tells them how he's going to do the job.'

'The Dancer?' Percey asked.

'That's the name we have for the killer. The Coffin Dancer.'

'*Coffin* Dancer?' Percey gave a faint laugh, as if the phrase meant something to her. But she didn't elaborate.

'Well, that's a little spooky,' Hale said dubiously, as if cops shouldn't have eerie nicknames for their bad guys. Rhyme supposed he was right.

Percey looked into Rhyme's eyes, nearly as dark as hers. 'So what happened to you? You get shot?'

Sachs – and Hale too – stirred at these blunt words but Rhyme didn't mind. He preferred people like himself – those with no use for pointless tact. He said equably, 'I was searching a crime scene at a construction site. A beam collapsed. Broke my neck.'

'Like that actor. Christopher Reeve.'

'Yes.'

Hale said, 'That was tough. But, man, he's brave. I've seen him on TV. I think I would've killed myself if that'd happened.'

Rhyme glanced at Sachs, who caught his eye. He turned back to Percey. 'We need your help. We have to figure out how he got that bomb on board. Do you have any idea?'

'None,' Percey said then looked at Hale, who shook his head.

'Did you see anyone you didn't recognize near the plane before the flight?'

'I was sick last night,' Percey said. 'I didn't even go to the airport.'

Hale said, 'I was upstate, fishing. I had the day off. Didn't get home till late.'

'Where exactly was the plane before it took off?'

'It was in our hangar. We were outfitting it for the new charter. We had to take seats out, install special racks with heavy-duty power outlets. For the refrigeration units. You know what the cargo was, don't you?'

'Organs,' Rhyme said. 'Human organs. Do you share the hangar with any other company?'

'No, it's ours. Well, we lease it.'

'How easy is it to get inside?' Sellitto asked.

'It's locked if nobody's around but the past couple days we've had crews working twenty-four hours to outfit the Lear.'

'You know the crews?' Sellitto asked.

'They're like family,' Hale said defensively.

Sellitto rolled his eyes at Banks. Rhyme supposed that the detective was thinking that family members were always the first suspects in a murder case.

'We'll take the names anyway, you don't mind. Check 'em out.'

'Sally Anne, she's our office manager, 'll get you a list.'

'You'll have to seal the hangar,' Rhyme said. 'Keep every-body out.'

Percey was shaking her head. 'We can't—'

'Seal it,' he repeated. 'Everybody out. Every . . . body.'

'But—'

Rhyme said, 'We have to.'

'Whoa,' Percey said, 'hold up there.' She looked at Hale. '*Foxtrot Bravo*?'

He shrugged. 'Ron said it'll take another day at least.'

Percey sighed. 'The Learjet that Ed was flying was the only one outfitted for the charter. There's another flight sched-uled for tomorrow night. We'll have to work nonstop to get the other plane ready for that flight. We can't close the hangar.'

Rhyme said, 'I'm sorry. This isn't an option.'

Percey blinked. 'Well, I don't know who you are to give me options . . .'

'I'm somebody trying to save your life,' Rhyme snapped.

'I can't risk losing this contract.'

'Hold up, miss,' Dellray said. 'You're not understandin' this bad guy . . .'

'He killed my husband,' she responded in a flinty voice. 'I understand him perfectly. But I'm not being bullied into losing this job.'

Sachs's hands went to her hips. 'Hey, hold up there. If there's anybody who can save your skin, it's Lincoln Rhyme. I don't think we need an attitude here.'

Rhyme's voice broke into the argument. He asked calmly, 'Can you give us an hour for the search?'

'An hour?' Percey considered this.

Sachs gave a laugh and turned her surprised eyes on her boss. She asked, 'Search a hangar in an hour? Come on,

Rhyme.' Her face said: Here I am defending you, and now you're pulling this? Whose side are you on?

Some criminalists assigned teams to search crime scenes. But Rhyme always insisted that Amelia Sachs search alone, just as he'd done. A single CS searcher had a focus that couldn't be achieved with other people on the scene. An hour was an extraordinarily brief time for a single person to cover a large scene. Rhyme knew this but he didn't respond to Sachs. He kept his eyes on Percey. She said, 'An hour? All right. I can live with that.'

'Rhyme,' Sachs protested, 'I'll need more time.'

'Ah, but you're the best, Amelia,' he joshed. Which meant the decision had already been made.

'Who can help us up there?' Rhyme asked Percey.

'Ron Talbot. He's a partner in the company and our operations manager.'

Sachs jotted the name in her watch book. 'Should I go now?' she asked.

'No,' Rhyme responded, 'I want you to wait until we have the bomb from the Chicago flight. I need you to help me analyze it.'

'I only have an hour,' she said testily. 'Remember?'

'You'll have to wait,' he grumbled, then asked Fred Dellray, 'What about the safe house?'

'Oh, we got a place you'll like,' the agent said to Percey. 'In Manhattan. Your taxpayer dollars be working hard. Yep, yep. U.S. marshals use it for the crème de la crème in witness protection. Only thing is, we need somebody from NYPD for baby-sitting detail. Somebody knows and appreciates the Dancer.'

And just then Jerry Banks looked up, wondering why everybody was staring at him. 'What?' he asked. *'What?'* And tried in vain to pat down his persistent cowlick.

\* \* \*

Stephen Kall, talker of soldier talk, shooter of soldier guns, had never in fact been a soldier.

But he now said to Sheila Horowitz, 'I'm proud of my military heritage. And that's the truth.'

'Some people don't—'

'No,' he interrupted, 'some people don't respect you for it. But that's their problem.'

'It *is* their problem,' Sheila echoed.

'You have a nice place here.' He looked around the dump, filled with Conran's markdowns.

'Thank you, friend. Uhm, you, like, want something to drink? Oopsie, there I go using that old preposition the wrong way. Mom's always after me. Watching too much TV. Like, like, like. Shamie shamie.'

What the fuck is she talking about?

'You live here alone?' he asked with a pleasant smile of curiosity.

'Yep, just me and the dynamic trio. I don't know why they're hiding. Those silly-billy scamps.' Sheila nervously pinched the fine hem of her vest. And because he hadn't answered, she repeated, 'So? Something to drink?'

'Sure.'

He saw a single bottle of wine, dust encrusted, sitting on top of her refrigerator. Saved for that special occasion. Was this it?

Apparently not. She broke out the diet Dr Pepper.

He strolled to the window and looked out. No police on the street here. And only a half block to a subway stop. The apartment was on the second floor, and though she had grates on the back windows, they were un-locked. If he had to he could climb down the fire escape and disappear onto Lexington Avenue, which was always crowded . . .

She had a telephone and a PC. Good.

He glanced at a wall calendar – pictures of angels. There were a few notations but nothing for this weekend.

'Hey, Sheila, would you—' He caught himself and shook his head, fell silent.

'Uhm, what?'

'Well, it's . . . I know it's stupid to ask. I mean, it's such short notice and everything. I was just wondering if you had plans for the next couple of days.'

Cautious here. 'Oh, I, uhm, I was supposed to see my mother.'

Stephen wrinkled his face in disappointment. 'Too bad. See, I have this place in Cape May—'

'The Jersey shore!'

'Right. I'm going out there—'

'After you get Buddy?'

Who the fuck was Buddy?

Oh, the cat. 'Right. If you weren't doing anything, I thought you might like to come out.'

'You have . . . ?'

'My mom's going to be there, some of her girlfriends.'

'Well, golly. I don't know.'

'So, why don't you call your mother and tell her she'll have to live without you for the weekend?'

'Well . . . I don't really have to call. If I don't show up it's, like, no big deal. It was like, maybe I'll go, maybe I won't.'

So she'd been lying. An empty weekend. Nobody'd miss her for the next few days.

A cat jumped up next to him, stuck her face into his. He pictured a thousand worms spraying over his body. He pictured the worms squirming through Sheila's hair. Her wormy fingers. Stephen began to detest this woman. He wanted to scream.

'Ooo, say hello to our new friend, Andrea. She likes you, Sam.'

He stood up, looking around the apartment. Thinking:

Remember, boy, anything can kill.

Some things kill fast and some things kill slow. But anything can kill.

'Say,' he asked, 'you have any packing tape?'

'Uhm, for . . . ?' Her mind raced. 'For . . . ?'

'The instruments I have in the bag? I need to tape one of the drums back together.'

'Oh, sure, I've got some in here.' She walked into the hallway. 'I send my aunties packages every Christmas. I always buy a new roll of tape. I can never remember if I've bought one before so I end up with a ton of them. Aren't I a silly-billy?'

He didn't answer because he was surveying the kitchen and decided that was the best kill zone in the apartment.

'Here you go.' She tossed him the roll of tape playfully. He instinctively caught it. He was angry because he hadn't had the chance to put his gloves on. He knew he'd left prints on the roll. He shivered in rage and when he saw Sheila grinning, saying, 'Hey, good catch, friend,' what he was really looking at was a huge worm moving closer and closer. He set the tape down and pulled on his gloves.

'Gloves? You cold? Say, friend, what're you . . . ?'

He ignored her and opened the refrigerator door, began removing the food.

She stepped farther into the room. Her giddy smile started to fade. 'Uhm, you hungry?'

He began removing the shelves.

A look passed between them and suddenly, from deep within her throat, came a faint '*Eeeeeeee.*'

Stephen got the fat worm before she made it halfway to the front door.

Fast or slow?

He dragged her back into the kitchen. Toward the refrigerator.

# Chapter
# SEVEN

Threes.

Percey Clay, honors engineering major, certified airframe and power plant mechanic, and holder of every license the Federal Aviation Agency could bestow on pilots, had no time for superstition.

Yet as she drove in a bulletproof van through Central Park on the way to the federal safe house in Midtown, she thought of the old adage that superstitious travelers repeat like a grim mantra. Crashes come in threes.

Tragedies too.

First, Ed. Now, the second sorrow: what she was hearing over the cell phone from Ron Talbot, who was in his office at Hudson Air.

She was sandwiched between Brit Hale and that young detective, Jerry Banks. Her head was down. Hale watched her, and Banks looked vigilantly out the window at traffic, passersby, and trees.

'U.S. Med agreed to give us one more shot.' Talbot's breath wheezed in and out alarmingly. One of the best pilots she'd ever known, Talbot hadn't driven an aircraft for years – grounded because of his precarious health. Percey considered this a horrifyingly unjust punishment for his sins of liquor, cigarettes, and food (largely because she shared them). 'I mean, they *can* cancel the contract. Bombs aren't force majeure. They don't excuse us from performance.'

'But they're letting us make the flight tomorrow.'

A pause.

'Yeah. They are.'

'Come on, Ron,' she snapped. 'No bullshit between us.' She heard him light another cigarette. Big and smokey – the man she'd bum Camels from when she was quitting smoking – Talbot was forgetful of fresh clothing and shaves. And inept at delivering bad news.

'It's *Foxtrot Bravo*,' he said reluctantly.

'What about her?'

N695FB was Percey Clay's Learjet 35A. Not that the paperwork indicated this. Legally the twin-engine jet was leased to Clay-Carney Holding Corporation Two, Inc., a wholly owned subsidiary of Hudson Air Charters, Ltd., by Morgan Air Leasing Inc., which in turn leased it from La Jolla Holding Two's wholly owned subsidiary Transport Solutions Incorporated, a Delaware company. This byzantine arrangement was legal and common, given the fact that both airplanes and airplane crashes are phenomenally expensive.

But everyone at Hudson Air Charters knew that November Six Nine Five *Foxtrot Bravo* was Percey's. She'd logged thousands of hours in the airplane. It was her pet. It was her children. And on the too-many nights Ed was gone just the thought of the aircraft would take the sting out of the loneliness. A sweet stick, the aircraft could cruise at forty-five thousand feet at speeds of 460 knots – over 500 miles per hour. She personally knew it could fly higher and faster, though that was a secret kept from Morgan Air Leasing, La Jolla Holding, Transport Solutions, and the FAA.

Talbot finally said, 'Getting her outfitted – it's going to be trickier than I thought.'

'Go on.'

'All right,' he said finally. 'Stu quit.' Stu Marquard, their chief mechanic.

'*What?*'

'The son of a bitch quit. Well, he hasn't yet,' Talbot continued. 'He called in sick but it sounded funny, so I made some calls. He's going over to Sikorsky. Already took the job.'

Percey was stunned.

This was a major problem. Lear 35As came equipped as eight-seat passenger jets. To make the aircraft ready for the U.S. Medical run, most of the seats had to be stripped out, shock-absorbed, refrigerated bays had to be installed, and extra power outlets had to be run from the engine's generators. This meant major electrical and airframe work.

There were no mechanics better than Stu Marquard and he'd outfitted Ed's Lear in record time. But without him Percey didn't know how they could finish in time for tomorrow's flight.

'What is it, Perce?' Hale asked, seeing her grimacing face.

'Stu quit,' she whispered.

He shook his head, not understanding. 'Quit what?'

'He left,' she muttered. 'Quit his job. Going to work on fucking choppers.'

Hale gazed at her in shock. 'Today?'

She nodded.

Talbot continued. 'He's scared, Perce. They know it was a bomb. The cops aren't saying anything but everybody knows what happened. They're nervous. I was talking to John Ringle—'

'Johnny?' A young pilot they'd hired last year. 'He's not leaving too?'

'He was just asking if we're closing down for a while. Until this all blows over.'

'No, we're not closing down,' she said firmly. 'We're not canceling a single goddamn job. It's business as usual. And if anybody else calls in sick, fire them.'

'Percey . . .'

Talbot was dour but everybody knew he was the company's soft touch.

'All right,' she snapped, '*I'll* fire them.'

'Look, about *Foxtrot Bravo*, I can do most of the work myself,' said Talbot, a certified airframe mechanic himself.

'Do what you can. But see if you can find another mechanic,' she told him. 'We'll talk later.'

She hung up.

'I can't believe it,' Hale said. 'He quit.' The pilot was bewildered.

Percey was furious. People were bailing out – the worst sin there was. The Company was dying. Yet she didn't have a clue how to save it.

Percey Clay had no monkey skills for running a business. *Monkey skills* . . .

A phrase she'd heard when she was a fighter pilot. Coined by a navy flier, an admiral, it meant the esoteric, unteachable talents of a natural-born pilot.

Well, sure, Percey had monkey skills when it came to flying. Any type of aircraft, whether she'd flown it previously or not, under any weather conditions, VFR or IFR, day or night. She could drive the plane flawlessly and set it down on that magic spot pilots aimed for – exactly 'a thousand past the numbers' – a thousand feet down the landing strip past the white runway designation. Sailplanes, biplanes, Hercs, seven three sevens, MiGs – she was at home in any cockpit.

But that was about as far as Percey Rachael Clay's monkey skills extended.

She had none at family relations, that was for sure. Her tobacco society father had refused to speak to her for years – had actually disinherited her – when she'd dropped out of his alma mater, UVA, to attend aviation school at Virginia Tech. (Even though she told him that the departure from Charlottesville was inevitable – six weeks into the first semester Percey'd KO'd a sorority president after the lanky blond commented in an overloud whisper that the troll girl might want to pledge at the ag school and not on Greek Row.)

Certainly no monkey skills at navy politics. Her awe-inspiring flight performance in the big Tomcats didn't quite tip the balance against her unfortunate habit of speaking her mind when everyone else was keeping mum about certain events.

And no skills at running the very charter company she was president of. It was mystifying to her how Hudson Air could be so busy yet continue to skirt bankruptcy. Like Ed and Brit Hale and the other staff pilots, Percey was constantly working (one reason she shunned scheduled airlines was the asinine FAA pronouncement that pilots fly no more than eighty hours a month). So why were they constantly broke? If it hadn't been for charming Ed's ability to get clients, and grumpy Ron Talbot's to cut costs and juggle creditors, they never would have survived for the past two years.

The Company had nearly gone under last month but Ed managed to snare the contract from U.S. Medical. The hospital chain made an astonishing amount of money doing transplants, which she learned was a business far bigger than just hearts and kidneys. The major problem was getting the donor organ to the appropriate recipient within hours of its availability. Organs were often flown on commercial flights (carried in coolers in the cockpit), but transporting them was dictated by commercial airline scheduling and routing. Hudson Air didn't have those restrictions. The Company agreed to dedicate one aircraft to U.S. Medical. It would fly a counterclockwise route throughout the East Coast and Midwest to six or eight of the company's locations, circulating organs wherever they were needed. Delivery was guaranteed. Rain, snow, wind shear, conditions at minimum — as long as the airport was open and it was legal to fly, Hudson Air would deliver the cargo on time.

The first month was to be a trial period. If it worked out they'd get an eighteen-month contract that would be the backbone for the Company's survival.

Apparently Ron had charmed the client into giving them another chance, but if *Foxtrot Bravo* wasn't ready for tomorrow's flight . . . Percey didn't even want to think about that possibility.

As she rode in the police car through Central Park Percey Clay looked over the early spring growth. Ed had loved the park and had run here frequently. He'd do two laps around the reservoir and return home looking bedraggled, his grayish hair hanging in strands around his face. And me? Percey laughed sadly to herself now. He'd find her sitting at home, poring over a nav log or an advanced turbofan repair manual, maybe smoking, maybe drinking a Wild Turkey. And, grinning, Ed would poke her in the ribs with a strong finger and ask if she could do anything *else* unhealthy at the same time. And while they laughed, he'd sneak a couple of swigs of the bourbon.

Remembering then how he'd bend down and kiss her shoulder. When they made love it was that juncture where he'd rest his face, bent forward, locked against her skin, and Percey Clay believed that there, where her neck flared onto her delicate shoulders, if only there, she was a beautiful woman.

Ed . . .

*All the stars of evening . . .*

Tears again filling her eyes, she glanced up into the gray sky. Ominous. She estimated the ceiling at one five hundred feet, winds 090 at fifteen knots. Wind shear conditions. She shifted in the seat. Brit Hale's strong fingers were encircling her forearm. Jerry Banks was chatting about something. She wasn't listening.

Percey Clay came to a decision. She unfolded the cell phone again.

# Chapter
# EIGHT

The siren wailed.

Lincoln Rhyme expected to hear the Doppler effect as the emergency vehicle cruised past. But right outside his front door the siren gave a brief chirrup and went silent. A moment later Thom let a young man into the first-floor lab. Crowned with a spiffy crew cut, the Illinois state trooper wore a blue uniform, which had probably been immaculate when he put it on yesterday but was now wrinkled and streaked with soot and dirt. He'd run an electric razor over his face but had made only faint inroads into the dark beard that contrasted with his thin yellow hair. He was carrying two large canvas satchels and a brown folder, and Rhyme was happier to see him than he'd been to see anybody in the past week.

'The bomb!' he shouted. 'Here's the bomb!'

The officer, surprised at the odd collection of law enforcers, must have wondered what hit him as Cooper scooped the bags away and Sellitto scrawled a signature on the receipt and chain-of-custody card and shoved them back into his hand. 'Thanks so long see you,' the detective exhaled, turning back to the evidence table.

Thom smiled politely to the trooper and let him out of the room.

Rhyme called, 'Let's go, Sachs. You're just standing around! What've we got?'

She offered a cold smile and walked over to Cooper's table, where the tech was carefully laying out the contents of the bags.

What *was* her problem today? An hour was plenty of time to search a scene, if that's what she was upset about. Well, he liked her feisty. He himself was always at his best that way. 'Okay, Thom, help us out here. The blackboard. We need to list the evidence. Make us some charts. "CS-One". The first heading.'

'C, uhm, S?'

'"Crime scene",' the criminalist snapped. 'What else would it be? "CS-One, Chicago".'

In a recent case, Rhyme had used the back of a limp Metropolitan Museum poster as an evidence profiling chart. He was now state-of-the-art – several large chalkboards were mounted to the wall, redolent with scents that took him back to humid spring school days in the Midwest, living for science class and despising spelling and English.

The aide, casting an exasperated glance toward his boss, picked up the chalk, brushed some dust from his perfect tie and knife-crease slacks, and wrote.

'What do we have, Mel? Sachs, help him.'

They began unloading the plastic bags and plastic jars of ash and bits of metal and fiber and wads of plastic. They assembled contents in porcelain trays. The crash site searchers – if they were on a par with the men and women Rhyme had trained – would have used roller-mounted magnets, large vacuum cleaners, and a series of fine mesh screens to locate debris from the blast.

Rhyme, expert in most areas of forensics, was an authority

on bombs. He'd had no particular interest in the subject until the Dancer left his tiny package in the wastebasket of the Wall Street officer where Rhyme's two techs were killed. After that Rhyme had taken it on himself to learn everything he could about explosives. He'd studied with the FBI's Explosives Unit, one of the smallest – but most elite – in the federal lab, composed of fourteen agent-examiners and technicians. They didn't find IEDs – improvised explosive devices, the law enforcement term for bombs – and they didn't render them safe. Their job was to analyze bombs and bomb crime scenes and to trace and categorize the makers and their students (bomb manufacture was considered an art in certain circles and apprentices worked hard to learn the techniques of famous bomb makers).

Sachs was poking over the bags. 'Doesn't a bomb destroy itself?'

'Nothing's ever completely destroyed, Sachs. Remember that.' Though as he wheeled closer and examined the bags, he admitted, 'This was a bad one. See those fragments? That pile of aluminum on the left? The metal's shattered, not bent. That means the device had a high brisance—'

'High . . . ?' Sellitto asked.

'Brisance.' Rhyme explained: 'Detonation rate. But even so, sixty to ninety percent of a bomb survives the blast. Well, not the explosive, of course. Though there's always enough residue to type it. Oh, we've got plenty to work with here.'

'Plenty?' Dellray snorted a laugh. 'Bad as puttin' Humpty-Dumpty together again.'

'Ah, but that's not our job, Fred,' Rhyme said briskly. 'All we need to do is catch the son of a bitch who pushed him off the wall.' He wheeled further down the table. 'What's it look like, Mel? I see battery, I see wire, I see timer. What else? Maybe bits of the container or packing?'

Suitcases have convicted more bombers than timers and

detonators. It's not talked about but unclaimed baggage is often donated to the FBI by airlines and blown up in an attempt to duplicate explosions and provide standards for criminalists. In the Pan Am flight 103 bombing, the FBI identified the bombers not through the explosive itself but through the Toshiba radio it had been hidden in, the Samsonite suitcase containing the radio, and the clothes packed around it. The clothing in the suitcase was traced back to a store in Sliema, Malta, whose owner identified a Libyan intelligence agent as the person who'd bought the garments.

But Cooper shook his head. 'Nothing near the seat of detonation except bomb components.'

'So it wasn't in a suitcase or flight bag,' Rhyme mused. 'Interesting. How the hell did he get it on board? Where'd he plant it? Lon, read me the report from Chicago.'

'"Difficult to determine exact blast location",' Sellitto read, '"because of extensive fire and destruction of aircraft. Site of device seems to be underneath and behind the cockpit."'

'Underneath and behind. I wonder if a cargo bay's there. Maybe . . .' Rhyme fell silent. His head swiveled back and forth, gazing at the evidence bags. 'Wait, wait!' he shouted. 'Mel, let me see those bits of metal there. Third bag from the left. The aluminum. Put it under a 'scope.'

Cooper had connected the video output of his compound microscope to Rhyme's computer. What Cooper saw, Rhyme could see. The tech began mounting samples of the minuscule bits of debris on slides and running them under the 'scope.

A moment later Rhyme ordered, 'Cursor down. Double click.'

The image on his computer screen magnified.

'There, look! The skin of the plane was blown inward.'

'Inward?' Sachs asked. 'You mean the bomb was on the *outside*?'

'I think so, yes. What about it, Mel?'

'You're right. Those polished rivet heads are all bent inward. It was outside, definitely.'

'A rocket maybe?' Dellray asked. 'SAM?'

Reading from the report Sellitto said, 'No radar blips consistent with missiles.'

Rhyme shook his head. 'No, everything points to a bomb.'

'But on the *outside*?' Sellitto asked. 'Never heard of that before.'

'That explains this,' Cooper called. The tech, wearing magnifying goggles and armed with a ceramic probe, was looking over bits of metal as fast as a cowboy counts heads in a herd. 'Fragments of ferrous metal. Magnets. Wouldn't stick to the aluminum skin but there was steel under it. And I've got bits of epoxy resin. He stuck the bomb on the outside with the magnets to hold it until the glue hardened.'

'And look at the shock waves in the epoxy,' Rhyme pointed out. 'The glue wasn't completely set, so he planted it not long before takeoff.'

'Can we brand the epoxy?'

'Nope. Generic composition. Sold everywhere.'

'Any hope of prints? Tell me true, Mel.'

Cooper's answer was a faint, skeptical laugh. But he went through the motions anyway and scanned the fragments with the PoliLight wand. Nothing was evident except the blast residue. 'Not a thing.'

'I want to smell it,' Rhyme announced.

'Smell it?' Sachs asked.

'With the brisance, we know it's high explosive. I want to know exactly what kind.'

Many bombers used low explosives – substances that burn quickly but don't explode unless confined in, say, a pipe or box. Gunpowder was the most common of these. High explosives – like plastic or TNT – detonate in their natural state and don't need to be packed inside anything. They were expensive and hard to come by. The type and source of explosive could tell a lot about the bomber's identity.

Sachs brought a bag to Rhyme's chair and opened it. He inhaled.

'RDX,' Rhyme said, recognizing it immediately.

'Consistent with the brisance,' Cooper said. 'You thinking C three or C four?' Cooper asked. RDX was the main component of these two plastic explosives, which were military; they were illegal for a civilian to possess.

'Not C three,' Rhyme said, again smelling the explosive as if it were a vintage Bordeaux. 'No sweet smell . . . Not sure. And strange . . . I smell something else . . . GC it, Mel.'

The tech ran the sample through the gas chromatograph/mass spectrometer. This machine isolated elements in compounds and identified them. It could analyze samples as small as a millionth of a gram and, once it had determined what they were, could run the information through a database to determine, in many cases, brand names.

Cooper examined the results. 'You're right, Lincoln. It's RDX. Also oil. And this is weird – starch . . .'

'Starch!' Rhyme cried. 'That's what I smelled. It's guar flour . . .'

Cooper laughed as those very words popped up on the computer screen. 'How'd you know?'

'Because it's military dynamite.'

'But there's no nitroglycerine,' Cooper protested. The active ingredient in dynamite.

'No, no, it's not real dynamite,' Rhyme said. 'It's a mixture of RDX, TNT, motor oil, and the guar flour. You don't see it very often.'

'Military, huh?' Sellitto said. 'Points to Hansen.'

'That it does.'

The tech mounted samples on his compound 'scope's stage.

The images appeared simultaneously on Rhyme's computer screen. Bits of fiber, wires, scraps, splinters, dust.

He was reminded of a similar image from years ago, though in circumstances very different. Looking through a heavy brass kaleidoscope he'd bought as a birthday present for a friend. Claire Trilling, beautiful and stylish. Rhyme had found the kaleidoscope in a store in SoHo. The two of them had spent an evening sharing a bottle of merlot and trying to guess what kind of exotic crystals or gemstones were making the astonishing images in the eyepiece. Finally, Claire, nearly as scientifically curious as Rhyme, had unscrewed the bottom of the tube and emptied the contents onto a table. They'd laughed. The objects were nothing more than scraps of metal, wood shavings, a broken paper clip, torn shreds from the Yellow Pages, thumbtacks.

Rhyme pushed those memories aside and concentrated on the objects he was seeing on the screen: A fragment of waxed manila paper – what the military dynamite had been wrapped in. Fibers – rayon and cotton – from the detonating cord the Dancer had tied around the dynamite, which would crumble too easily to mold around the cord. A fragment of aluminum and a tiny colored wire – from the electric blasting cap. More wire and an eraser-size piece of carbon from the battery.

'The timer,' Rhyme called. 'I want to see the timer.'

Cooper lifted a small plastic bag from the table.

Inside was the still, cold heart of the bomb.

It was in nearly perfect shape, surprising Rhyme. Ah, your first slipup, he thought, speaking silently to the Dancer. Most bombers will pack explosives around the detonating system to destroy clues. But here the Dancer had accidentally placed the timer behind a thick steel lip in the metal housing that held the bomb. The lip had protected the timer from the blast.

Rhyme's neck stung as he strained forward, looking at the bent clock face.

Cooper scrutinized the device. 'I've got the model number and manufacturer.'

'Run everything through ERC.'

The FBI's Explosives Reference Collection was the most extensive database on explosive devices in the world. It included information on all bombs reported in the United States, as well as actual physical evidence from many of them. Certain items in the collection were antiques, dating back to the 1920s.

Cooper typed on his computer keyboard. A moment later his modem whistled and crackled.

Two minutes later the results of the request came back.

'Not good,' the bald man said, grimacing slightly, about as emotional as the technician ever got. 'No specific profiles match this particular bomb.'

Nearly all bombers fall into a pattern when they make their devices – they learn a technique and stick pretty close to it. (Given the nature of their product it's a good idea not to experiment too much.) If the parts of the Dancer's bomb matched an earlier IED in, say, Florida or California, the team might be able to pick up additional clues from those bomb sites that could lead them to the man's whereabouts. The rule of thumb is that if two bombs share at least four points of construction – soldered leads instead of taped, for instance, or analog versus digital timers – they were probably made by the same person or under his tutelage. The Dancer's bomb several years ago in Wall Street was different from this one. But, Rhyme knew, this was intended to serve a different purpose. That bomb was planted to hamper a crime scene investigation; this one, to blow a large airplane out of the sky.

And if Rhyme knew anything about the Coffin Dancer, it was that he tailored his tools to the job.

'Gets worse?' Rhyme asked, reading Cooper's face as the tech stared at the computer screen.

'The timer.'

Rhyme sighed. He understood. 'How many billions and billions in production?'

'The Daiwana Corporation in Seoul sold a hundred and forty-two thousand of them last year. To retail stores, OEMs, and licensees. There's no coding on them to tell where they were shipped.'

'Great. Just great.'

Cooper continued to read the screen. 'Hm. The folks at ERC say they're very interested in the device and hope we'll add it to their database.'

'Oh, our number one priority,' Rhyme grumbled.

His shoulder muscles suddenly cramped and he had to lean back into the headrest of the wheelchair. He breathed deeply for a few minutes until the nearly unbearable pain subsided, then vanished. Sachs, the only one who noticed, stepped forward, but Rhyme shook his head toward her, said, 'How many wires you make out, Mel?'

'Just two, it looks like.'

'Multichannel or fiber optic?'

'Nope. Just average-ordinary bell wire.'

'No shunts?'

'None.'

A shunt is a separate wire, that completes the connection if a battery or timer wire is cut in an attempt to render the bomb safe. All sophisticated bombs have shunting mechanisms.

'Well,' Sellitto said, 'that's good news, isn't it? Means he's getting careless.'

But Rhyme believed just the opposite. 'Don't think so,

Lon. The only point of a shunt is to make rendering safe tougher. Not having a shunt means he was confident enough the bomb wouldn't be found and would blow up just like he'd planned – in the air.'

'This thing,' Dellray asked contemptuously, looking over the bomb components. 'What kind of people'd our boy have to rub shoulders with to make something like this? I got good CIs knowing 'bout bomb suppliers.'

Fred Dellray too had learned more about bombs than he'd ever intended. His longtime partner and friend, Toby Doolittle, had been on the ground floor of the Oklahoma City federal building several years ago. He'd been killed instantly in the fertilizer bomb explosion.

But Rhyme shook his head. 'It's all off-the-shelf stuff, Fred. Except for the explosives and the detonator cord. Hansen probably supplied them. Hell, the Dancer could've gotten everything he needed at Radio Shack.'

'What?' Sachs asked, surprised.

'Oh, yeah,' Cooper said, adding, 'We call it the Bomber's Store.'

Rhyme wheeled along the table over to a piece of steel housing twisted like crumpled paper, stared at it for a long moment.

Then he backed up and looked at the ceiling. 'But why plant it outside?' he pondered. 'Percey said there were always lots of people around. And doesn't the pilot walk around the plane before they take off, look at the wheels and things?'

'I think so,' Sellitto said.

'Why didn't Ed Carney or his copilot see it?'

'Because,' Sachs said suddenly, 'the Dancer couldn't put the bomb on board until he knew for sure who was going to be in the plane.'

Rhyme swiveled around to her. 'That's it, Sachs! He was there watching. When he saw Carney get on board he knew he had at least one of the victims. He slipped it on somewhere after Carney got on board and before the plane took off. You've got to find out where, Sachs. And search it. Better get going.'

'Only have an hour – well, less now,' said cool-eyed Amelia Sachs as she started toward the door.

'One thing,' Rhyme said.

She paused.

'The Dancer's a little different from everybody else you've ever been up against.' How could he explain it? 'With him, what you see isn't necessarily what is.'

She cocked an eyebrow, meaning, Get to the point.

'He's probably not up there, at the airport. But if you see anyone make a move for you, well . . . shoot first.'

'What?' She laughed.

'Worry about yourself first, the scene second.'

'I'm just CS,' she answered, walking through the door. 'He's not going to care about me.'

'Amelia, listen . . .'

But he heard her footsteps receding. The familiar pattern: the hollow thud on the oak, the mute steps as she crossed the Oriental carpet, then the tap on the marble entryway. Finally, the coda – as the front door closed with a snap.

# Chapter
# NINE

The best soldiers are patient soldiers.

Sir, I'll remember that, sir.

Stephen Kall was sitting at Sheila's kitchen table, deciding how much he disliked Essie, the mangy cat, or whoever the fuck it was, and listening to a long conversation on his tape recorder. At first he'd decided to find the cats and kill them but he'd noticed that they occasionally gave an unearthly howl. If neighbors were used to the sound they might become suspicious if they heard only silence from Sheila Horowitz's apartment.

Patience . . . Watching the cassette roll. Listening.

It was twenty minutes later that he heard what he'd been hoping for on the tape. He smiled. Okay, good. He collected his Model 40 in the Fender guitar case, snug as a baby, and walked to the refrigerator. He cocked his head. The noises had stopped. It didn't shake any longer. He felt a bit of relief, less cringey, less *crawly*, thinking of the worm inside, now cold and still. It was safe to leave. He picked up his back-pack and left the dim apartment with its pungent cat musk, dusty wine, and a million trails of disgusting worms.

\* \* \*

Into the country.

Amelia Sachs sped though a tunnel of spring trees, rocks on one side, a modest cliff on another. A dusting of green, and everywhere the yellow starbursts of forsythia.

Sachs was a city girl, born in Brooklyn General Hospital, and was a lifetime resident of that borough. Nature, for her, was Prospect Park on Sundays or, on weekday evenings, Long Island forest preserves, where she'd hide her black sharklike Dodge Charger from the patrol cruisers prowling for her and her fellow racers.

Now, at the wheel of an Investigation and Resources Division rapid response vehicle – a crime scene station wagon – she punched the accelerator, swerved onto the shoulder, and passed a van that sported an upside-down Garfield cat suctioned to the rear window. She made the turnoff that took her deep into Westchester County.

Lifting her hand off the wheel she compulsively poked her finger into her hair and worried her scalp. Then she gripped the plastic wheel of the RRV once again and shoved the accelerator down until she burst into the suburban civilization of strip malls, sloppy commercial buildings, and fast food franchises.

She was thinking about bombs, about Percey Clay.

And about Lincoln Rhyme.

Something was different about him today. Something significant. They'd been working together for a year now, ever since he'd shanghaied her away from a coveted assignment with Public Affairs to help him catch a serial kidnapper. At the time Sachs had been at a low point in her life – an affair gone bad and a corruption scandal in the department that disillusioned her so much that she wanted out of Patrol altogether. But Rhyme wouldn't let her. Simple as that. Even though he was a civilian consultant he'd arranged for her transfer to Crime Scene. She protested some but soon gave up the pretense of reluctance; the fact was that she loved the work. And she loved working with Rhyme, whose brilliance was exhilarating and intimidating and – an admission she made to no one – goddamn sexy.

Which wasn't to say that she could read him perfectly. Lincoln Rhyme played life close to his chest and he wasn't revealing all to her.

*Shoot first* . . .

What was that all about? You *never* discharged a weapon at a crime scene if there was any way to avoid it. A single gunshot would contaminate a scene with carbon, sulfur, mercury, antimony, lead, copper, and arsenic, and the discharge and blowback could destroy vital trace evidence. Rhyme himself told her of the time he'd had to shoot a perp hiding at a scene, his biggest concern being that the shots had ruined much of the evidence. (And when Sachs, believing she'd at last outthought him, said, 'But what did it matter, Rhyme? You got the perp, right?' he'd pointed out acerbically, 'But what if he'd had *partners,* hmm? What *then*?')

What was so different about the Coffin Dancer, other than the stupid name and the fact he seemed marginally smarter than the typical mafioso or Westie triggerman?

And working the scene at the hangar in an *hour*? It seemed to Sachs that he'd agreed to that as a favor for Percey. Which was completely unlike him. Rhyme would keep a scene sealed for days if he thought it was necessary.

These questions nagged and Amelia Sachs didn't like unanswered questions.

Though she had no more time for speculation. Sachs spun the wheel of the RRV and turned into the wide entrance to the Mamaroneck Regional Airport. It was a busy place, nestled into a woody area of Westchester County, north of Manhattan. The big airlines had affiliated companies with service here – United Express, American Eagle – but most of the planes parked here were corporate jets, all of them unmarked, for security reasons, she guessed.

At the entrance were several state troopers, checking IDs. They did a double take when she pulled up – seeing the beautiful redhead driving an NYPD crime scene RRV and wearing blue jeans, a windbreaker, and a Mets cap. They waved her through. She followed signs to Hudson Air Charters and found the small cinder-block building at the end of a row of commercial airline terminals.

She parked in front of the building and leapt out. She introduced herself to two officers who were standing guard over the hangar and the sleek, silver airplane that was inside. She was pleased that the local cops had run police tape around the hangar and the apron in front of it to secure the scene. But she was dismayed by the size of the area.

An hour to search? She could've spent an entire day here.

Thanks loads, Rhyme.

She hurried into the office.

A dozen men and women, some in business suits, some in overalls, stood in clusters. They were mostly in their twenties and thirties. Sachs supposed they'd been a young and enthusiastic group until last night. Now their faces revealed a collective sorrow that had aged them quickly.

'Is there someone named Ron Talbot here?' she asked, displaying her silver shield.

The oldest person in the room – a woman in her fifties, with spun and sprayed hair and wearing a frumpy suit – walked up to Sachs. 'I'm Sally Anne McCay,' she said. 'I'm the office manager. Oh, how's Percey?'

'She's all right,' Sachs said guardedly. 'Where's Mr Talbot?'

A brunette in her thirties wearing a wrinkled blue dress stepped out of an office and put her arm around Sally Anne's shoulders. The older woman squeezed the younger's hand. 'Lauren, you okay?'

Lauren, her puffy face a mask of shock, asked Sachs, 'Do they know what happened yet?'

'We're just starting the investigation . . . Now, Mr Talbot?'

Sally Anne wiped tears then glanced toward an office in the corner. Sachs walked to the doorway. Inside was a bearish man with a stubbled chin and tangle of uncombed black-and-gray hair. He was poring over computer printouts, breathing heavily. He looked up, a dismal expression on his face. He'd been crying too, it seemed.

'I'm Officer Sachs,' she said. 'I'm with the NYPD.'

He nodded. 'You have him yet?' he asked, looking out the window as if he expected to see Ed Carney's ghost float past. He turned back to her. 'The killer?'

'We're following up on several leads.' Amelia Sachs, second-generation cop, had the art of evasion down cold.

Lauren appeared in Talbot's doorway. 'I can't believe he's gone,' she gasped, an edgy panic in her voice. 'Who'd do something like that? *Who?*' As a patrol officer – a beat cop – Sachs had delivered her share of bad news to loved ones. She never got used to the despair she heard in the voices of surviving friends and family.

'Lauren.' Sally Anne took her colleague's arm. 'Lauren, go on home.'

'No! I don't want to go home. I want to know who the hell did it? Oh, Ed . . .'

Stepping farther into Talbot's office, Sachs said, 'I need your help. It looks like the killer mounted the bomb outside the plane underneath the cockpit. We have to find out where.'

'Outside?' Talbot was frowning. 'How?'

'Magnetized and glued. The glue wasn't completely set before the blast so it had to've been not long before takeoff.'

Talbot nodded. 'Whatever I can do. Sure.'

She tapped the walkie-talkie on her hip. 'I'm going to go on-line with my boss. He's in Manhattan. We're going to ask you some questions.' Hooked up the Motorola, headset, and stalk mike.

'Okay, Rhyme, I'm here. Can you hear me?'

Though they were on an areawide Special Ops frequency and should have been ten-fiveing and K'ing, according to Communications Department procedures, Sachs and Rhyme rarely bothered with radioese. And they didn't now. His voice grumbled through the earphone, bouncing off who knew how many satellites. 'Got it. Took you long enough.'

Don't push it, Rhyme.

She asked Talbot, 'Where was the plane before it took off? Say, an hour, hour and a quarter?'

'In the hangar,' Talbot said.

'You think he could've gotten to the plane there? After the – what do you call it? When the pilot inspects the plane?'

'The walkaround. I suppose it's possible.'

'But there were people around all the time,' Lauren said. The crying fit was over and she'd wiped her face. She was calmer now and determination had replaced despair in her eyes.

'Who are you, please?'

'Lauren Simmons.'

'Lauren's our assistant operations manager,' Talbot said. 'She works for me.'

Lauren continued. 'We'd been working with Stu – our chief mechanic, our *former* chief mechanic – to outfit the aircraft, working round the clock. We would've seen anybody near the plane.'

'So,' Sachs said, 'he mounted the bomb after the plane left the hangar.'

'Chronology!' Rhyme's voice crackled through the headset. 'Where was it from the moment it left the hangar until takeoff?'

When she relayed this question Talbot and Lauren led her into a conference room. It was filled with charts and scheduling boards, hundreds of books and notebooks and stacks of papers. Lauren unrolled a large map of the airport. It contained a thousand numbers and symbols Sachs didn't understand, though the buildings and roadways were clearly outlined.

'No plane moves an inch,' Talbot explained in a gruff baritone, 'unless Ground Control gives the okay. *Charlie Juliet* was—'

'What? *Charlie* . . . ?'

'The number of the plane. We refer to planes by the last two letters on the registration number. CJ. So we called it *Charlie Juliet*.' It was parked in the hangar here . . .' He tapped the map. 'We finished loading—'

'When?' Rhyme called, so loud she wouldn't have been surprised if Talbot had heard. 'We need times! Exact times.'

The logbook in *Charlie Juliet*'d been burned to a cinder and the time-stamped FAA tape hadn't been transcribed yet. But Lauren examined the company's internal records. 'Tower gave 'em push-back clearance at seven-sixteen. And they reported wheels up at seven-thirty.'

Rhyme had heard. 'Fourteen minutes. Ask them if the plane was ever both out of sight and stopped during that time.'

Sachs did and Lauren answered, 'Probably there.' She pointed.

A narrow portion of taxiway about two hundred feet long. The row of hangars hid it from the rest of the airport. It ended at a T intersection.

Lauren said, 'Oh, and it's an ATC No Vis area.'

'That's right,' Talbot said, as if this were significant.

'Translation!' Rhyme called.

'Meaning?' Sachs asked.

'Out of visibility from Air Traffic Control,' Lauren answered. 'A blind spot.'

'Yes!' came the voice through her earphone. 'Okay, Sachs. Seal and search. Release the hangar.'

To Talbot she said, 'We're not going to bother with the hangar. I'm releasing it. But I want to seal off that taxiway. Can you call the tower? Have them divert traffic?'

'I *can*,' he said doubtfully. 'They aren't going to like it.'

She said, 'If there's any problem have them call Thomas Perkins. He's head of the FBI's Manhattan office. He'll clear it with FAA HQ.'

'FAA? In Washington?' Lauren asked.

'That's the one.'

Talbot gave a faint smile. 'Well, okay.'

Sachs started for the main door then paused, looking out at the busy airport. 'Oh, I've got a car,' she called to Talbot. 'Is there anything special you do when you drive around an airport?'

'Yeah,' he said, 'try not to run into any airplanes.'

# THE KILL ZONE

A falconer's bird, however tame and affectionate, is as close to a wild animal in condition and habit as an animal that lives with man can be. Above all, it hunts.

*A RAGE FOR FALCONS*, STEPHEN BODIO

# Chapter
# TEN

'I'm here, Rhyme,' she announced.

Sachs climbed out of the RRV wagon and pulled latex gloves on her hands and wound rubber bands around her shoes – to make certain her footprints wouldn't be confused with the perp's, as Rhyme had taught her.

'And where, Sachs,' he asked, 'is *here*?'

'At the intersection of taxiways. Between a row of hangars. It's where Carney's plane would've stopped.'

Sachs glanced uneasily at a line of trees in the distance. It was an overcast, dank day. Another storm was threatening. She felt exposed. The Dancer might be here now – maybe he'd returned to destroy evidence he'd left behind, maybe to kill a cop and slow down the investigation. Like the bomb in Wall Street a few years ago, the one that killed Rhyme's techs.

*Shoot first . . .*

Damn it, Rhyme, you're spooking me! Why're you acting like this guy walks through walls and spits poison?

Sachs took the PoliLight box and large suitcase from the back of the RRV. She opened the suitcase. Inside were a hundred tools of the trade: screwdrivers, wrenches, hammers, wire cutters, knives, friction ridge collection equipment, ninhydrin, tweezers, brushes, tongs, scissors, flex-claw pick-ups, a gunshot residue kit, pencils, plastic and paper bags, evidence collection tape . . .

*One, establish the perimeter.*

She ran yellow police line tape around the entire area.

*Two, consider media and range of camera lenses and microphones.*

No media. Not yet. Thank you, Lord.

'What's that, Sachs?'

'I'm thanking God there're no reporters.'

'A fine prayer. But tell me what you're doing.'

'Still securing the scene.'

'Look for the—'

'Entrance and exit,' she said.

*Step three, determine the perpetrator's entrance and exit routes – they will be secondary crime scenes.*

But she didn't have a clue as to where they might be. He could've come from anywhere. Snuck around the corners, driven here in a luggage cart, a gas truck . . .

Sachs donned goggles and began sweeping the PoliLight wand over the taxiway. It didn't work as well outside as in a dark room, but with the heavy overcast she could see flecks and streaks glowing under the eerie green-yellow light. There were, however, no footprints.

'Sprayed her down last night,' the voice called behind her.

Sachs spun around, hand on her Glock, a half draw from the holster.

I'm *never* this edgy, Rhyme. It's all your fault.

Several men in coveralls were standing at the yellow tape. She walked up to them cautiously and checked their picture IDs. They matched the men's faces. Her hand slipped off the gun.

'They hose the place down every night. If you're looking for something. Thought you were.'

'High-pressure hose,' the second one added.

Great. Every bit of trace, every footprint, every fiber sloughed off the Dancer was gone.

'You see anybody here last night?'

'This have to do with the bomb?'

'Around seven-fifteen?' she persisted.

'Nope. Nobody comes up here. These hangars're deserted. Probably gonna tear 'em down someday.'

'What're you doing here now?'

'Saw a cop. You are a cop, right? And just thought we'd have a look-see. This *is* about that bomb, right? Who did it? Arabs? Or them militia shits?'

She shooed them off. Into the microphone she said, 'They cleaned the taxiway last night, Rhyme. High-pressure water, looks like.'

'Oh, no.'

'They—'

'Hey there.'

She sighed, turning again, expecting to find the two workmen back. But the new visitor was a cocky county trooper, wearing a blocked Smokey the Bear hat and razor-creased gray slacks. He ducked under the tape.

'Excuse me,' she protested. 'This is a secure area.'

He slowed but didn't stop. She checked his ID. It matched. The picture showed him looking off slightly, a cover boy on a men's fashion magazine.

'You're that officer from New York, right?' He laughed generously. 'Nice uniforms they have down there.' Eyeing her tight jeans.

'This area's sealed off.'

'I can help. I took the forensics course. Mostly I'm highway detail but I've got major crimes experience. You have *some* hair. Bet you've heard that before.'

'I really will have to ask you—'

'Jim Everts.'

Don't go into first-name territory; it sticks like flypaper. 'I'm Officer Sachs.'

'Big hubbub, this. A bomb. Messy.'

'See, Jim, this tape here's to keep people *out* of the scene. Now, you gonna be helpful and step back behind it?'

'Wait. You mean officers too?'

'That I do, yes.'

'You mean me too?'

'Exactly.'

There were five classic crime scene contaminators: weather, relatives of the victim, suspects, souvenir collectors, and – the all-time worst – fellow cops.

'I won't touch a thing. Cross my heart. Just be pleasure to watch you work, honey.'

'Sachs,' Rhyme whispered, 'tell him to get the fuck out of your crime scene.'

'Jim, get the fuck out of my crime scene.'

'Or you'll report him.'

'Or I'll report you.'

'Oooo, gonna be *that* way, is it?' He held his hands up in surrender. The last of the flirt drained from his slick grin.

'Get *going*, Sachs.'

The trooper ambled away slowly enough to drag some of his pride with him. He looked back once but a scathing retort eluded him.

Amelia Sachs began to walk the grid.

There were several different ways to search crime scenes. A strip search – walking in a serpentine pattern – was usually used for outdoor scenes because it covered the most ground quickly. But Rhyme wouldn't hear of that. He used the grid pattern – covering the entire area back and forth in one direction, walking one foot at a time, then turning perpendicular and walking back and forth the other way. When he was running IRD, 'walking the grid' became synonymous with searching a crime scene, and heaven help any cops Rhyme caught taking shortcuts or daydreaming when they were on the grid.

Sachs now spent a half hour moving back and forth. While the spray truck might've eliminated prints and trace evidence, it wouldn't destroy anything larger that the Dancer might've dropped, nor would it ruin footprints or body impressions left in the mud beside the taxiway.

But she found nothing.

'Hell, Rhyme, not a thing.'

'Ah, Sachs, I'll bet there is. I'll bet there's plenty. Just takes a little bit more effort than most scenes. The Dancer's not like other perps, remember.'

Oh, *that* again.

'Sachs.' His voice low and seductive. She felt a shiver. 'Get into him,' Rhyme whispered. 'You know what I mean.'

She knew exactly what he meant. Hated the thought. But, oh, yes, Sachs knew. The best criminalists were able to find a place in their minds where the line between hunter and hunted was virtually nonexistent. They moved through the crime scene not as cops tracking down clues but as the perp himself, feeling his desires, lusts, fears. Rhyme had this talent. And though she tried to deny it, Sachs did too. (She'd searched a scene a month ago – a father had murdered his wife and child – and managed to find the murder weapon when no one else had. After the case she hadn't been able to work for a week and had been plagued by flashbacks that *she'd* been the one who stabbed the victims to death. Saw their faces, heard their screams.)

Another pause. 'Talk to me,' he said. And finally the edginess in his voice was gone. 'You're him. You're walking where he's walked, you're thinking the way he thinks . . .'

He'd said words like these to her before, of course. But

now – as with everything else about the Dancer – it seemed to her that Rhyme had more in mind than just finding obscure evidence. No, she sensed that he was desperate to know about this perp. Who he was, what made him kill.

Another shiver. An image in her thoughts: Back to the other night. The lights of the airfield, the sound of airplane engines, the smell of jet exhaust.

'Come on, Amelia . . . You're him. You're the Coffin Dancer. You know Ed Carney's on the plane, you know you have to get the bomb on board. Just think about it for a minute or two.'

And she did, summoning up from somewhere a need to kill.

He continued, speaking in an eerie, melodic voice. 'You're brilliant,' he said. 'You have no morals whatsoever. You'll kill *anyone*, you'll do *anything* to get to your goal. You divert attention, you use people . . . Your deadliest weapon is deception.'

I lay in wait.

*My deadliest weapon* . . .

She closed her eyes.

*. . . is deception.*

Sachs felt a dark hope, a vigilance, a hunt lust.

'I—'

He continued softly. 'Is there any distraction, any diversion you can try?'

Eyes open now. 'The whole area's empty. Nothing to distract the pilots with.'

'Where are you hiding?'

'The hangars're all boarded up. The grass is too short for cover. There're no trucks or oil drums. No alleys. No nooks.'

In her gut: desperation. What'm I going to do? I've *got* to plant the bomb. I don't have any time. Lights . . . there're lights everywhere. What? What should I do?

She said, 'I can't hide around the other side of the hangars. There're lots of workers. It's too exposed. They'll see me.'

For a moment, Sachs herself floated back into her mind and she wondered, as she often did, why Lincoln Rhyme had the power to conjure her into someone else. Sometimes it angered her. Sometimes it thrilled.

Dropping into a crouch, ignoring the pain in her knees from the arthritis that had tormented her off and on for the past ten of her thirty-three years. 'It's all too open here. I feel exposed.'

'What're you thinking?'

There're people looking for me. I can't let them find me. I can't!

This is risky. Stay hidden. Stay down.

Nowhere to hide.

If I'm seen, everything's ruined. They'll find the bomb, they'll know I'm after all three witnesses. They'll put them in protective custody. I'll *never* get them then. I *can't* let that happen.

Feeling his panic she turned back to the only possible place to hide. The hangar beside the taxiway. In the wall facing her was a single broken window, about three by four feet. She'd ignored it because it was covered with a sheet of rotting plywood, nailed to the frame on the inside.

She approached it slowly. The ground in front was gravel; there were no footprints.

'There's a boarded-up window, Rhyme. Plywood on the inside. The glass is broken.'

'Is it dirty, the glass that's still in the window?'

'Filthy.'

'And the edges?'

'No, they're clean.' She understood why he'd asked the question. 'The glass was broken recently!'

'Right. Push the board. Hard.'

It fell inward without any resistance and hit the floor with a huge bang.

'What was that?' Rhyme shouted. 'Sachs, are you all right?'

'Just the plywood,' she answered, once more spooked by his uneasiness.

She shone her halogen flashlight through the hangar. It was deserted.

'What do you see, Sachs?'

'It's empty. A few dusty boxes. There's gravel on the floor—'

'That was him!' Rhyme answered. 'He broke in the window and threw gravel inside, so he could stand on the floor and not leave footprints. It's an old trick. Any footprints in front of the window? Bet it's more gravel,' he added sourly.

'Is.'

'Okay. Search the window. Then climb inside. But be sure to look for booby traps first. Remember the trash can a few years ago.'

Stop it, Rhyme! Stop it.

Sachs shined the light around the space again. 'It's clean, Rhyme. No traps. I'm examining the window frame.'

The PoliLight showed nothing other than a faint mark left by a finger in a cotton glove. 'No fiber, just the cotton pattern.'

'Anything in the hangar? Anything worth stealing?'

'No. It's empty.'

'Good,' Rhyme said.

'Why good?' she asked. 'I said there's no print.'

'Ah, but it means it's *him*, Sachs. It's not logical for someone to break in wearing cotton gloves when there's nothing to steal.'

She searched carefully. No footprints, no fingerprints, no visible evidence. She ran the Dustbuster and bagged the trace.

'The glass and gravel?' she asked. 'Paper bag?'

'Yes.'

Moisture often destroyed trace and though it looked unprofessional, certain evidence was best transported in brown paper bags rather than in plastic.

'Okay, Rhyme. I'll have it back to you in forty minutes.'

They disconnected.

As she packed the bags carefully into the RRV, Sachs felt edgy, as she often did just after searching a scene where she'd found no obvious evidence – guns or knives or the perp's wallet. The trace she'd collected *might* have a clue as to who the Dancer was and where he was hiding. But the whole effort could have been a bust too. She was anxious to get back to Rhyme's lab and see what he could find.

Sachs climbed into the station wagon and sped back to the Hudson Air office. She hurried into Ron Talbot's office. He was talking to a tall man whose back was to the door. Sachs said, 'I found where he was, Mr Talbot. The scene's released. You can have the tower—'

The man turned around. It was Brit Hale. He frowned, trying to think of her name, remembered it. 'Oh. Officer Sachs. Hey. How you doing?'

She started to nod an automatic greeting, then stopped.

What was he doing here? He was supposed to be in the safe house.

She heard a soft crying and looked into the conference room. There was Percey Clay sitting next to Lauren, the pretty brunette who Sachs remembered was Ron Talbot's assistant. Lauren was crying and Percey, resolute in her own sorrow, was trying to comfort her. She glanced up, saw Sachs, and nodded to her.

No, no, no . . .

Then the third shock.

'Hi, Amelia,' Jerry Banks said cheerfully, sipping coffee and standing by a window, where he'd been admiring the Learjet parked in the hangar. 'That plane's something, isn't it?'

'What're they doing here?' Sachs snapped, pointing at Hale and Percey, forgetting that Banks outranked her.

'They had some problem or other about a mechanic,' Banks said. 'Percey wanted to stop by here. Try to find—'

'Rhyme,' Sachs shouted into the microphone. 'She's here.'

'Who?' he asked acerbically. 'And *where* is there?'

'Percey. And Hale too. At the airport.'

'No! They're supposed to be at the safe house.'

'Well, they're not. They're right here in front of me.'

'No, no, no!' Rhyme raged. A moment passed. Then he asked, 'Ask Banks if they followed evasive driving procedures.'

Banks, uncomfortable, responded that they hadn't. 'She was real insistent that they stop here first. I tried to talk her—'

'Jesus, Sachs. He's there someplace. The Dancer. I know he's there.'

'How could he be?' Sachs's eyes strayed to the window.

'Keep 'em down,' Rhyme said. 'I'll have Dellray get an armored van from the Bureau's White Plains field office.'

Percey heard the commotion. 'I'll go to the safe house in an hour or so. I have to find a mechanic to work on—'

Sachs waved her silent, then said, 'Jerry, keep them here.' She ran to the door and looked out over the gray expanse of the airfield as a noisy prop plane charged down the runway. She pulled the stalk mike closer to her mouth. 'How, Rhyme?' she asked. 'How'll he come at us?'

'I don't have a clue. He could do anything.'

Sachs tried to reenter the Dancer's mind, but couldn't. All she thought was, *Deception* . . .

'How secure is the area?' Rhyme asked.

'Pretty tight. Chain-link fence. Troopers at a roadblock at the entrance, checking tickets and IDs.'

Rhyme asked, 'But they're not checking IDs of police, right?'

Sachs looked at the uniformed officers, recalling how casually they'd waved her through. 'Oh, hell, Rhyme, there're a dozen marked cars here. A couple unmarkeds too. I don't know the troopers or detectives . . . He could be any one of them.'

'Okay, Sachs. Listen, find out if any local cops're missing. In the past two or three hours. The Dancer might've killed one and stolen their ID and uniform.'

Sachs called a state trooper up to the door, examined him and his ID closely, and decided he was the real article. She said, 'We think the killer may be nearby, maybe impersonating an officer. I need you to check out everybody here. If you don't recognize 'em, let me know. Also, find out from your dispatcher if any cops from around the area've gone missing in the past few hours.'

'I'm on it, Officer.'

She returned to the office. There were no blinds on the windows and Banks had moved Percey and Hale into an interior office.

'What's going on?' Percey asked.

'You're out of here in five minutes,' Sachs said, glancing out the window, trying to guess how the Dancer would attack. She had no idea.

'Why?' the flier asked, frowning.

'We think the man who killed your husband's here. Or on his way here.'

'Oh, come on. There's cops all over the field. It's perfectly safe. I need to—'

Sachs snapped to her, 'No arguments.'

But argue she did. 'We can't leave. I've just had my chief mechanic quit. I have to—'

'Perce,' Hale said uneasily, 'maybe we ought to listen to her.'

'We've got to get that aircraft—'

'Get back. In there. And be quiet.'

Percey's mouth opened wide in shock. 'You can't talk to me that way. I'm not a prisoner.'

'Officer Sachs? Hellooo?' The trooper she'd spoken to outside stepped into the doorway. 'I've done a fast visual of everybody here in uniform and the detectives too. No unknowns. And no reports of any state or Westchester officers missing. But our Central Dispatch told me something maybe you oughta know about. Might be nothing, but—'

'Tell me.'

Percey Clay said, 'Officer, I have to talk to you . . .'

Sachs ignored her and nodded to the trooper. 'Go on.'

'Traffic Patrol in White Plains, about two miles away. They found a body in a Dumpster. Think he was killed about an hour ago, maybe less.'

'Rhyme, you hear?'

'Yes.'

Sachs asked the cop, 'Why d'you think that's important?'

'It's the way he was killed. Was a hell of a mess.'

'Ask him if the hands and face were missing,' Rhyme asked.

'What?'

'Ask him!'

She did, and everyone in the office stopped talking and stared at Sachs.

The trooper blinked in surprise and said, 'Yes, ma'am, Officer. Well, the hands at least. The dispatcher didn't say anything about the face. How'd you know . . . ?'

Rhyme blurted, 'Where's it now? The body?'

She relayed the question.

'In a coroner's bus. They're taking it to the county morgue.'

'No,' Rhyme said. 'Have them get it to you, Sachs. I want you to examine it.'

'The—'

'Body,' he said. 'It's got the answer to how he's going to come at you. I don't want Percey and Hale moved until we know what we're up against.'

She told the cop Rhyme's request.

'Okay,' he said. 'I'll get on it. That's . . . You mean you want the body *here*.'

'Yes. Now.'

'Tell 'em to get it there fast, Sachs,' Rhyme said. He sighed. 'Oh, this is bad. Bad.'

And Sachs had the uneasy thought that Rhyme's urgent grief was not only for the man who had just died so violently, whoever he was, but for those who, maybe, were about to.

People believe that the rifle is the important tool for a sniper, but that's wrong. It's the telescope.

What do we call it, Soldier? Do we call it a *telescopic sight*? Do we call it a *'scope?'*

Sir, we do not. It's a *telescope*. This one is a Redfield, three-by-nine variable, with crosshair reticles. There is none better, sir.

The telescope Stephen was mounting on top of the Model 40 was twelve and three-quarters inches long and weighed just over twelve ounces. It had been matched to this particular rifle with corresponding serial numbers and had been painstakingly adjusted for focus. The parallax had been fixed by the optical engineer in the factory so that the crosshairs resting on the lip of a man's heart five hundred yards away would not move perceptibly when the sniper's head eased from left to right. The eye relief was so accurate that the recoil would knock the eyepiece back to within one millimeter of Stephen's eyebrow and yet never touch a hair.

The Redfield telescope was black and sleek, and Stephen kept it draped in velvet and nestled in a Styrofoam block in his guitar case.

Now, hidden in a nest of grass some three hundred yards from the Hudson Air hangar and office, Stephen fitted the black tube of the telescope into its mount, perpendicular to the gun (he always thought of his stepfather's crucifix when he mounted it), then he swung the heavy tube into position with a satisfying click. He screwed down the lug nuts.

Soldier, are you a competent sniper?

Sir, I am the best, sir.

What are your qualifications?

Sir, I am in excellent physical shape, I am fastidious, I am right-handed, I have 20/20 vision, I do not smoke or drink or take any kind of drugs, I can lie still for hours at a time, and I live to send bullets up the ass of my enemy.

He nestled further into the pile of leaves and grass.

There might be worms here, he thought. But he wasn't feeling cringey at the moment. He had his mission and that was occupying his mind completely.

Stephen cradled the gun, smelling the machine oil from the bolt-action receiver and the neat's-foot oil from the sling, so worn and soft it was like angora. The Model 40 was a 7.62 millimeter NATO rifle and weighed eight pounds, ten ounces. The trigger pull generally ranged from three to five pounds, but Stephen set it a bit higher because his fingers were very strong. The weapon had a rated effective range of a thousand yards, though he had made kills at more than thirteen hundred.

Stephen knew this gun intimately. In sniper teams, his stepfather had told him, the snipers themselves have no disassemble authority, and the old man wouldn't let him strip the weapon himself. But that was one rule of the man's that hadn't seemed right to Stephen and so, in a moment of uncharacteristic defiance, he'd secretly taught himself how to dismantle the rifle, clean it, repair it, and even machine parts that needed adjustment or replacement.

Through the telescope he scanned Hudson Air. He couldn't see the Wife, though he knew she was there or soon would be. Listening to the tape of the phone tap on the Hudson Air office lines, Stephen had heard her tell someone named Ron that they were changing their plans; rather than going to the safe house they were driving to the airport to find some mechanics who could work on the airplane.

Using the low crawl technique, Stephen now moved forward until he was on a slight ridge, still hidden by trees and grass but with a better view of the hangar, the office, and the parking lot in front of it, separated from him by flat grass fields and two runways.

It was a glorious kill zone. Wide. Very little cover. All entrances and exits easily targeted from here.

Two people stood outside at the front door. One was a county or state trooper. The other was a woman – red hair dipping beneath a baseball cap. Very pretty. She was a cop, plainclothes. He could see the boxy outline of a Glock or Sig-Sauer high on her hip. He lifted his range finder and put the split image on the woman's red hair. He twisted a ring until the images moved together seamlessly.

Three hundred and sixteen yards.

He replaced the range finder, lifted the rifle, and sighted on the woman, centering the reticles on her hair once more. He glanced at her beautiful face. It troubled him, her attractiveness. He didn't like it. Didn't like *her*. He wondered why.

The grass rustled around him. He thought: Worms.

Was starting to feel cringey.

*The face in the window* . . .

He put the crosshairs on her chest.

The cringey feeling went away.

Soldier, what is the sniper's motto?

Sir, it is 'One chance, one shot, one kill.'

The conditions were excellent. There was a slight right-to-left crosswind, which he guessed was four miles an hour. The air was humid, which would buoy the slug. He was shooting over unvaried terrain with only moderate thermals.

He slid back down the knoll and ran a cleaning rod, tipped

with a soft cotton cloth, through the Model 40. You always cleaned your weapon before firing. The slightest bit of moisture or oil could put a shot off by an inch or so. Then he made a loop sling and lay down in his nest.

Stephen loaded five rounds into the chamber. They were M-118 match-quality rounds, manufactured at the renowned Lake City arsenal. The bullet itself was a 173-grain boattail and it struck its target at a speed of a half mile a second. Stephen had altered the slugs somewhat, however. He'd drilled into the core and filled them with a small explosive charge and replaced the standard jacket with a ceramic nose that would pierce most kinds of body armor.

He unfolded a thin dish towel and spread it out on the ground to catch the ejected cartridges. Then he doubled the sling around his left biceps and planted that elbow firmly on the ground, keeping the forearm absolutely perpendicular to the ground – a bone support. He 'spot-welded' his cheek and right thumb to the stock above the trigger.

Then slowly he began scanning the kill zone.

It was hard to see inside the offices but Stephen thought he caught a glimpse of the Wife.

Yes! It was her.

She was standing behind a big curly-haired man in a wrinkled white shirt. He held a cigarette. A young blond man in a suit, a badge on his belt, ushered them back out of sight.

Patience . . . she'll present again. They don't have a clue that you're here. You can wait all day. As long as the worms—

Flashing lights again.

Into the parking lot sped a county ambulance. The red-haired cop saw it. Her eyes grew excited. She ran toward the vehicle.

Stephen breathed deeply.

*One chance* . . .

Zero your weapon, Soldier.

Normal come-up elevation at 316 yards is three minutes, sir. He clicked the sight so that the barrel would be pointed upward slightly to take gravity into account.

*One shot . . .*

Calculate the crosswind, Soldier.

Sir, the formula is range in hundreds of yards times velocity divided by fifteen. Stephen's mind thought instantly: Slightly less than one minute of windage. He adjusted the telescope accordingly.

Sir, I am ready, sir.

*One kill . . .*

A shaft of light streamed from behind a cloud and lit the front of the office. Stephen began to breathe slowly and evenly.

He was lucky; the worms stayed away. And there were no faces watching him from the windows.

# Chapter
# ELEVEN

The medic rolled out of the ambulance.

She nodded to him. 'I'm Officer Sachs.'

He aimed his rotund belly her way and, straight-faced, said, 'So. You ordered the pizza?' Then giggled.

She sighed. 'What happened?' Sachs said.

'What happened? T'him? He got himself dead's what happened.' He looked her over, shook his head. 'What kinda cop are you? I never seen you up here.'

'I'm from the city.'

'Oh, the city. She's from the city. Well, better ask,' he added gravely. 'You ever see a body before?'

Sometimes you bend just a little. Learning how and how far takes some doing but it's a valuable lesson. Sometimes more than valuable, sometimes necessary. She smiled. 'You know, we've got a real critical situation here. I'd sure appreciate your help. Could you tell me where you found him?'

He studied her chest for a moment. 'Reason I ask about seeing bodies is this one's gonna bother you. I could do what needs to be done, searching it or whatever.'

'Thanks. We'll get to that. Now, again, where'd you find him?'

'Dumpster in a parking lot 'bout two clicks—'

'That's miles,' another voice added.

'Hey, Jim,' the medic said.

Sachs turned. Oh, great. It was the *GQ* cop. The one who'd been flirting with her on the taxiway. He strode up to the ambulance.

'Hi, honey. Me again. How's your police tape holdin' up? Whatcha got, Earl?'

'One body, no hands.' Earl yanked the door open, reached in, and unzipped the body bag. Blood flowed out onto the floor of the ambulance.

'Ooops.' Earl winked. 'Say, Jim, after you're through here, wanna get some spaghetti?'

'Mebbe pig's knuckles.'

'There's a thought.'

Rhyme interrupted. 'Sachs, what's going on there? You got the body?'

'I've got it. Trying to figure out the story.' To the medic she said, 'We've gotta *move* on this. Anybody have any idea who he is?'

'Wasn't anything around to ID him. No missing persons reported. Nobody saw nothing.'

'Any chance he's a cop?'

'Naw. Nobody I know,' Jim said. 'You, Earl?'

'Nup. Why?'

Sachs didn't answer. She said, 'I need to examine him.'

'Okay, miss,' Earl said. 'How 'bout I give you a hand?'

'Hell,' the trooper said, 'sounds like *he's* the one needs a hand.' He chuckled; the medic gave another of his piggy giggles.

She climbed up in the back of the ambulance and unzipped the body bag completely.

And because she wasn't going to tug off her jeans and have intercourse with them or at the very least flirt back, they had no choice but to torment her further.

'The thing is, this isn't the kind of traffic detail you're probably used to,' Earl said to her. 'Hey, Jim, this as bad as the one you saw last week?'

'That head we found?' The cop mused, 'Hell, I'd rather have a fresh head any day than a month-er. You ever seen a month-er, honey? Now, they're about as unpleasant as can be. Give a body three, four months in the water, hey, not a problem – mostly just bones. But you get one's been simmering for a month . . .'

'Nasty,' Earl said. 'Uck-o.'

'You ever seen a month-er, honey?'

''Preciate your not saying that, Jim,' she said absently to the cop.

'"Month-er"?'

'"Honey".'

'Sure, sorry.'

'Sachs,' Rhyme snapped, 'what the hell is going on?'

'No ID, Rhyme. Nobody's got a clue as to who it is. Hands removed with a fine-bladed razor saw.'

'Is Percey safe? Hale?'

'They're in the office. Banks's with them. Away from the windows. What's the word on the van?'

'Should be there in ten minutes. You've got to find out about that body.'

'You talking to yourself, hon – Officer?'

Sachs studied the poor man's body. She guessed the hands had been removed just after he'd died, or as he was dying, because of the copious amount of blood. She pulled on her latex examining gloves.

'It's strange, Rhyme. Why's he only partially ID-proofed?'

If killers don't have time to dispose of a body completely they ID-proof it by removing the main points of identification: the hands and the teeth.

'I don't know,' the criminalist responded. 'It's not like the

Dancer to be careless, even if he was in a hurry. What's he wearing?'

'Just skivvies. No clothes or other ID found at the scene.'

'Why,' Rhyme mused, 'did the Dancer pick him?'

'*If* it was the Dancer did this.'

'How many bodies turn up like that in Westchester?'

'To hear the locals tell it,' she said ruefully, 'every other day.'

'Tell me about the corpse. COD?'

'You determine the cause of death?' she called to chubby Earl.

'Strangled,' the tech said.

But Sachs noticed right away there were no petechial hemorrhages on the inner surface of the eyelids. No damage to the tongue either. Most strangulation victims bite their tongue at some point during the attack.

'I don't think so.'

Earl cast another glance at Jim and snorted. 'Sure, he was. Lookit that red line on his neck. We call that a ligature mark, honey. You know, we can't keep him here forever. They start going ripe, days like this. Now, *that's* a smell you haven't lived till you smelt.'

Sachs frowned. 'He wasn't strangled.'

They double-teamed her. 'Hon – Officer, that's a ligature mark,' Jim, the trooper, said. 'I seen hundreds of 'em.'

'No, no,' she said. 'The perp just ripped a chain off him.'

Rhyme broke in. 'That's probably it, Sachs. First thing you do when you're ID-proofing a corpse, get rid of the jewelry. It was probably a Saint Christopher, maybe inscribed. Who's there with you?'

'A pair of cretins,' she said.

'Oh. Well, what *is* the COD?'

After a brief search she found the wound. 'Ice pick or narrow-bladed knife in the back of the skull.'

The medic's round form eased into the doorway. 'We woulda found that,' he said defensively. 'I mean, we were in such an all-fire hurry to get here, thanks to you folks.'

Rhyme said to Sachs, 'Describe him.'

'He's overweight, big gut. Lotta flab.'

'Tan or sunburn?'

'On his arms and torso only. Not legs. He's got untrimmed toenails and a cheap earring – steel posts, not gold. His briefs are Sears and they've got holes in them.'

'Okay, he's looking blue collar,' Rhyme said. 'Workman, deliveryman. We're closing in. Check his throat.'

'What?'

'For his wallet or papers. If you want to keep a corpse anonymous for a few hours you shove their IDs down their throat. It doesn't get spotted till the autopsy.'

A chortle of laughter from outside.

Which Sachs ended quickly when she grabbed the man's jaws, pulled wide, and started reaching inside.

'Jesus,' Earl muttered. 'What're you doing?'

'Nothing there, Rhyme.'

'You better cut. The throat. Go deeper.'

Sachs had bridled at some of Rhyme's more macabre requests in the past. But today she glanced at the grinning boys behind her and lifted her illegal but cherished switchblade from her jeans pocket, clicked it open.

Took the grins off both faces.

'Say, honey, what're you doing?'

'Little surgery. Gotta look inside.' Like she did this every day.

'I mean, I can't deliver no corpse to the coroner cut up by some New York City cop.'

'Then *you* do it.'

She offered him the handle of the knife.

'Aw, she's shitting us, Jim.'

She lifted an eyebrow and slipped the knife into the man's Adams' apple like a fisherman gutting a trout.

'Oh, Jesus, Jim, lookit what she's doing. Stop her.'

'I'm outa here, Earl. I didn't see that.' The trooper walked off.

She finished the tidy incision and gazed inside, sighed. 'Nothing.'

'What the hell is he up to?' Rhyme asked. 'Let's think . . . What if he isn't ID-proofing the body? If he'd wanted to he would've taken the teeth. What if there's something else he's trying to hide from us?'

'Something on the vic's hands?' Sachs suggested.

'Maybe,' Rhyme responded. 'Something that he couldn't wash off the corpse easily. And something that'd tell us what he was up to.'

'Oil? Grease?'

'Maybe he was delivering jet fuel,' Rhyme said. 'Or maybe he was a caterer – maybe his hands smelled of garlic.'

Sachs looked around the airport. There were dozens of gasoline deliverymen, ground crews, repairmen, construction workers building a new wing on one of the terminals.

Rhyme continued, 'He's a big guy?'

'Yep.'

'He was probably sweating today. Maybe he wiped his head. Or scratched it.'

*I*'ve been doing that all day myself, Sachs thought, and felt an urge to dig into her hair, hurt her skin as she always did when she felt frustrated and tense.

'Check his scalp, Sachs. Behind the hairline.'

She did.

And there she found it.

'I see streaks of color. Blue. Bits of white too. On the hair and skin. Oh, hell, Rhyme. It's paint! He's a painting contractor. And there're about twenty construction workers on the grounds.'

'The line on the neck,' Rhyme continued. 'The Dancer pulled off his necklace ID.'

'But the picture'd be different.'

'Hell, the ID's probably covered with paint or he faked it somehow. He's on the field somewhere, Sachs. Get Percey and Hale down on the floor. Put a guard on 'em and get everybody else out, looking for the Dancer. SWAT's on its way.'

Problems.

He was watching the red-haired cop in the back of the ambulance. Through the Redfield telescope he couldn't see clearly what she was doing. But he suddenly felt uneasy.

He felt she was doing something to *him*. Something to expose him, to tie him down.

The worms were getting closer. The face at the window, the wormy face, was looking for him.

Stephen shuddered.

She jumped out of the ambulance, looking around the field.

Something's happening, Soldier.

Sir, I am aware of that, sir.

The redhead began shouting orders to other cops. Most of them looked at her, took her news grimly, then looked around. One ran to his car, then a second.

He saw the redhead's pretty face and her wormy eyes scanning the airport grounds. He rested the reticles on her perfect chin. What had she found? What was she looking for?

She paused and he saw her talking to herself.

No, not herself. She was talking into a headset. The way she'd listen, then nod, it seemed that she was taking orders from someone.

Who? he wondered.

Someone who'd figured out that I'm here, Stephen thought.

Someone looking for me.

Someone who can watch me through windows and disappear instantly. Who can move through walls and holes and tiny cracks to sneak up and find me.

A chill down his back – he actually shivered – and for a moment the reticles of the telescope danced away from the redheaded cop and he lost acquisition of a target completely.

What the fuck was that, Soldier?

Sir, I don't know, sir.

When he reacquired the redhead he saw how bad things were. She was pointing right at the painting contractor's van he'd just stolen. It was parked about two hundred feet from him, in a small parking lot reserved for construction trucks.

Whoever the redhead was talking to had found the painter's body and discovered how he'd gotten onto the airport grounds.

The worm moved closer. He felt its shadow, its cold slime.

The cringey feeling. Worms crawling up his legs . . . worms crawling down his neck . . .

What should I do? he wondered

One chance . . . one shot . . .

They're so close, the Wife and the Friend. He could finish everything right now. Five seconds was all it would take. Maybe those were their outlines he could see in the window. That shadowy form. Or *that* one . . . But Stephen knew that if he fired through the glass, everyone would drop to the floor. If he didn't kill the Wife with the first shot, he'd ruin the chance.

I need her outside. I need to draw them out of cover into the kill zone. I can't miss there.

He had no time. No time! Think!

*If you want a doe, endanger the calf.*

Stephen began breathing slowly. In, out, in, out. He drew his target. Began applying pressure, imperceptible, to the trigger. The Model 40 fired.

The *ka-boom* rolled over the field and all the cops hit the ground, drawing their weapons.

Another shot, and a second puff of smoke flew from the tail-mounted engine of the silver jet in the hangar.

The redheaded cop, her own gun in hand, was crouching, scanning for location. She glanced at the two smoking holes in the skin of the plane, then looked out over the field once more, pointing a stubby Glock out in front of her.

Take her out?

Yes? No?

Negative, Soldier. Stay fixed on your target.

He fired again. The puff of explosion tore another tiny chunk out of the side of the airplane.

Calm. Another shot. The kick in the shoulder, the sweet smell of the burnt powder. A windshield in the cockpit exploded.

This was the shot that did it.

Suddenly there she was – the Wife – forcing her way through the office door, grappling with the young blond cop who tried to hold her back.

No target yet. Keep her coming.

Squeeze. Another bullet tore through the engine.

The Wife, her face horrified, broke free and ran down the stairs toward the hangar to close the doors, to protect her child.

Reload.

He laid the reticles on her chest as she stepped to the ground and started to run.

Full target lead of four inches, Stephen calculated automatically. He moved the gun ahead of her and squeezed the trigger. It fired just as the blond cop tackled her and they went down below a slight dip in the earth. A miss. And they had just enough cover to keep him from skimming slugs into their backs.

They're moving in, Soldier. They're flanking you.

Yessir, understood.

Stephen glanced over the runways. Other police had appeared. They were crawling toward their cars. One car was speeding directly toward him, only fifty yards away. Stephen used one shot to take out the engine block. Steam spraying from the front end, the car eased to a stop.

Stay calm, he told himself.

We're prepared to evacuate. We just need one clear shot.

He heard several fast pistol shots. He looked back at the redhead. She was in a competition combat stance, pointing the stubby pistol in his direction, looking for his muzzle flash. The sound of the shot wouldn't do her any good, of course; it was why he never bothered with silencers. Loud noises are as hard to pinpoint as soft ones.

The redheaded cop was standing tall, squinting as she gazed.

Stephen closed the bolt of the Model 40.


Amelia Sachs saw a faint glimmer and she knew where the Coffin Dancer was.

In a small grove of trees about three hundred yards away. His telescopic sight caught the reflected glint of the pale clouds overhead.

'Over there,' she cried, pointing, to two county cops huddling in their cruiser.

The troopers rolled into their car and took off, skidding behind a nearby hangar to flank him.

'Sachs,' Rhyme called through her headset. 'What's—'

'Jesus, Rhyme, he's on the field, shooting at the plane.'

'What?'

'Percey's trying to get to the hangar. He's shooting explosive slugs. He's shooting to draw her out.'

'You stay down, Sachs. If Percey's going to kill herself, let her. But you stay down!'

She was sweating furiously, hands shaking, heart pounding. She felt the quiver of panic run down her back.

'Percey!' Sachs cried.

The woman had broken free from Jerry Banks and rolled to her feet. She was speeding toward the hangar door.

'No!'

Oh, hell.

Sachs's eyes were on the spot where she'd seen the flare of the Dancer's scope.

Too far, it's too far, she thought. I can't hit anything at that distance.

If you stay calm, you can. You've got eleven rounds left. There's no wind. Trajectory's the only problem. Aim high and work down.

She saw several leaves fly outward as the Dancer fired again.

An instant later a bullet passed within inches of her face. She felt the shock wave and heard the snap as the slug, traveling twice the speed of sound, burned the air around her.

She uttered a faint whimper and dropped to her stomach, cowering.

No! You had a chance to shoot. Before he rechambered. But it's too late now. He's locked and loaded again.

She looked up fast, lifted her gun, then lost her nerve. Head down, the Glock pointed generally in the direction of the trees, she fired five fast shots.

But she might as well have been shooting blanks.

Come on, girl. Get up. Aim and shoot. You got six left and two clips on your belt.

But the thought of the near miss kept her pinned to the ground.

Do it! she raged at herself.

But she couldn't.

All Sachs had the courage for was to raise her head a few

inches – just far enough to see Percey Clay, sprinting, race to the hangar door just as Jerry Banks caught up with her. The young detective shoved her down to the ground behind a generator cart. Almost simultaneously with the rolling boom of the Coffin Dancer's rifle there came the sickening crack of the bullet striking Banks, who spun about like a drunk as blood puffed into a cloud around him.

And on his face, first a look of surprise, then of bewilderment, then of nothing whatsoever as he spiraled down to the damp concrete.

# Chapter
# TWELVE

'Well?' Rhyme asked.

Lon Sellitto folded up his phone. 'They still don't know.' Eyes out the window of Rhyme's town house, tapping the glass compulsively. The falcons had returned to the ledge but kept their eyes vigilantly on Central Park, uncharacteristically oblivious to the noise.

Rhyme had never seen the detective this upset. His doughy, sweat-dotted face was pale. A legendary homicide investigator, Sellitto was usually unflappable. Whether he was reassuring victims' families or relentlessly punching holes in a suspect's alibi, he always concentrated on the job before him. But at the moment his thoughts seemed miles away, with Jerry Banks, in surgery – maybe dying – in a Westchester hospital. It was now three on Saturday afternoon and Banks had been in the operating room for an hour.

Sellitto, Sachs, Rhyme, and Cooper were on the ground floor of Rhyme's town house, in the lab. Dellray had left to make sure the safe house was ready and to check out the new baby-sitter the NYPD was providing to replace Banks.

At the airport they'd loaded the wounded young detective into the ambulance – the same one containing the dead, handless painting contractor. Earl, the medic, had stopped being an asshole long enough to work feverishly to stop Banks's torrential bleeding. Then he'd sped the pale, unconscious detective to the emergency room several miles away.

FBI agents from White Plains got Percey and Hale into an armored van and started south to Manhattan, using evasive driving techniques. Sachs worked the new crime scenes: the sniper nest, the painter's van, and the Dancer's gateway wheels – a catering van. It was found not far from where he'd killed the contractor and where, they guessed, he'd have hidden the car he'd driven to Westchester in.

Then she'd sped back to Manhattan with the evidence.

'What've we got?' Rhyme now asked her and Cooper. 'Any rifle slugs?'

Worrying a tattered bloody nail, Sachs explained, 'Nothing left of them. They were explosive rounds.' She seemed very spooked, eyes flitting like birds.

'That's the Dancer. Not only deadly but his evidence self-destructs.'

Sachs prodded a plastic bag. 'Here's what's left of one. I scraped it off a wall.'

Cooper spilled the contents into a porcelain examining tray. He stirred them. 'Ceramic tipped too. Vests're pointless.'

'Grade-A asshole,' Sellitto offered.

'Oh, the Dancer knows his tools,' Rhyme said.

There was a bustle of activity at the doorway and Thom let two suited FBI agents into the room. Behind them were Percey Clay and Brit Hale.

Percey asked Sellitto, 'How's he doing?' Her dark eyes looked around the room, saw the coolness that greeted her. Didn't seem fazed. 'Jerry, I mean.'

Sellitto didn't answer.

Rhyme said, 'He's still in surgery.'

Her face was fretted, hair more tangled than this morning. 'I hope he'll be all right.'

Amelia Sachs turned to Percey and said coldly, 'You what?'

'I said, I hope he'll be all right.'

'You *hope*?' The policewoman towered over her, stepped closer. The squat woman stood her ground as Sachs continued. 'Little late for that, isn't it?'

'What's your problem?'

'That's what I oughta be asking you. You got him shot.'

'Hey, Officer,' Sellitto said.

Composed, Percey said, 'I didn't ask him to run after me.'

'You'd be dead if it wasn't for him.'

'Maybe. We don't know that. I'm sorry he was hurt. I—'

'And how sorry are you?'

'Amelia,' Rhyme said sharply.

'No, I want to know *how* sorry. Are you sorry enough to give blood? To wheel him around if he can't walk? Give his eulogy if he dies?'

Rhyme snapped, 'Sachs, take it easy. It's not her fault.'

Sachs slapped her hands, tipped in chewed nails, against her thighs. 'It's not?'

'The Dancer outthought us.'

Sachs continued, gazing down into Percey's dark eyes. 'Jerry was baby-sitting you. When you ran into the line of fire, what'd you think he was going to do?'

'Well, I didn't think, okay? I just reacted.'

'Jesus.'

'Hey, Officer,' Hale said, 'maybe you act a lot cooler under pressure than some of us. But we're not used to getting shot at.'

'Then she should've stayed down. In the office. Where I told her to stay.'

There seemed to be a slight drawl in Percey's voice when

she continued. 'I saw my aircraft endangered. I reacted. Maybe for you it's like seeing your partner wounded.'

Hale said, 'She just did what any pilot would've done.'

'Exactly,' Rhyme announced. 'That's what I'm saying, Sachs. That's the way the Dancer works.'

But Amelia Sachs wasn't letting go. 'You should've been in the safe house in the first place. You never should have gone to the airport.'

'That was Jerry's fault,' said Rhyme, growing angrier. 'He had no authority to change the route.'

Sachs glanced at Sellitto, who'd been Banks's partner for two years. But apparently he wasn't about to stand up for the young man.

'This's been a real pleasure,' Percey Clay said dryly, turning toward the door. 'But I've got to get back to the airport.'

'What?' Sachs almost gasped. 'Are you crazy?'

'That's impossible,' Sellitto said, emerging from his gloom.

'It was bad enough just trying to get my aircraft outfitted for the flight tomorrow. Now we've got to repair the damage too. And since it looks like every certified mechanic in Westchester's a damn coward I'm going to have to do the work myself.'

'Mrs Clay,' Sellitto began, 'not a good idea. You'll be okay in the safe house but there's no way we can guarantee your safety anywhere else. You stay there until Monday, you'll be—'

'Monday,' she blurted. 'Oh, no. You don't understand. I'm driving that aircraft tomorrow night – the charter for U.S. Medical.'

'You can't—'

'A question,' asked the icy voice of Amelia Sachs. 'Could you tell me exactly who else you want to kill?'

Percey stepped forward. She snapped, 'Goddamn it, I lost my husband and one of my best employees last night. I'm not losing my company too. You can't tell me where I'm going or not. Not unless I'm under arrest.'

'Okay,' Sachs said, and in a flash the cuffs were ratcheted onto the woman's narrow wrists. 'You're under arrest.'

'Sachs,' Rhyme called, enraged. 'What are you doing? Uncuff her. Now!'

Sachs swung to face him, snapped back, 'You're a civilian. You can't order me to do a *thing*!'

'*I* can,' Sellitto said.

'Uh-un,' she said adamantly. 'I'm the arresting, Detective. You can't stop me from making a collar. Only the DA can throw a case out.'

'What is this bullshit?' Percey spat out, the vestigial drawl returning full force. 'What're you arresting me for? Being a witness?'

'The charge is reckless endangerment, and if Jerry dies then it'll be criminally negligent homicide. Or maybe manslaughter.'

Hale worked up some courage and said, 'Look now. I don't really like the way you've been talking to her all day. If you arrest her, you're going to have to arrest me . . .'

'Not a problem,' Sachs said, then asked Sellitto, 'Lieutenant, I need your cuffs.'

'Officer, enougha this crap,' he grumbled.

'Sachs,' Rhyme called, 'we don't have time for this! The Dancer's out there, planning another attack right now.'

'You arrest me,' Percey said, 'I'll be out in two hours.'

'Then you'll be dead in two hours and ten minutes. Which would be your business—'

'Officer,' Sellitto snapped, 'you're on real thin ice here.'

'—if you didn't have this habit of taking other people with you.'

'Amelia,' Rhyme said coldly.

She swung to face him. He called her 'Sachs' most of the time; using her first name now was like a slap in the face.

The chains on Percey's bony wrists clinked. In the window the falcon fluttered its wings. No one said a word.

Finally, in a reasonable voice, Rhyme asked, 'Please take the cuffs off and let me have a few minutes alone with Percey.'

Sachs hesitated. Her face was an expressionless mask.

'Please, Amelia,' Rhyme said, struggling to be patient.

Without a word she unhooked the cuffs.

Everyone filed out.

Percey rubbed her wrists then pulled her flask from her pocket and took a sip.

'Would you mind closing the door?' Rhyme asked Sachs.

But she merely glanced toward him and then continued into the corridor. It was Hale who swung the heavy oak door shut.

Outside in the hallway Lon Sellitto called again about Banks. He was still in surgery and the floor nurse would say nothing else about him.

Sachs took this news with a faint nod. She walked to the window overlooking the alley behind Rhyme's town house. The oblique light fell onto her hands and she looked at her torn nails. She'd put bandages on two of the most damaged fingers. Habits, she thought. Bad habits . . . Why can't I stop?

The detective walked up beside her, looked up at the gray sky. More spring storms were promised.

'Officer,' he said, speaking softly so none of the others could hear. 'She fucked up, that lady did, okay. But you gotta understand – she's not a pro. Our mistake was *letting* her fuck up and, yeah, Jerry should've known better. It hurts me more than I can even think about to say it. But he blew it.'

'No,' she said through clenched teeth. 'You don't understand.'

'Whatsat?'

Could she say it? The words were so hard.

'*I* blew it. It's not Jerry's fault.' She tossed her head toward Rhyme's room. 'Or Percey's. It's mine.'

'You? Fuck, you 'n' Rhyme're the ones figured out he was at the airport. He mighta nailed everybody, it wasn't for you.'

She was shaking her head. 'I saw . . . I saw the Dancer's position before he capped Jerry.'

'And?'

'I knew exactly where he was. I drew a target. I . . .'

Oh, hell. This was hard.

'What're you sayin', Officer?'

'He let off a round at me . . . Oh, Christ. I clenched. I hit the ground.' Her finger disappeared into her scalp and she scratched until she felt slick blood. Stop it. Shit.

'So?' Sellitto didn't get it. 'Everybody hit the deck, right? I mean, who wouldn't?'

Staring out the window, face burning with shame. 'After he fired and missed, I'd've had at least three seconds to fire – I knew he was shooting bolt action. I could've lost a whole clip at him. But I tongued dirt. Then I didn't have the balls to get up again because I knew he'd rechambered.'

Sellitto scoffed. 'What? You're worried 'cause you didn't stand up, without cover, and give a sniper a nice fat target? Come on, Officer . . . And, hey, wait a minute, you had your service weapon?'

'Yeah, I—'

'Three hundred yards with a Glock nine? In your dreams.'

'I might not have hit him but I could've parked enough nearby to keep him pinned down. So he wouldn't've got that last shot in and hit Jerry. Oh, hell.' She clenched her hands, looked at her index-finger nail again. It was dark with blood. She scratched again.

The brilliant red reminded her of the dust cloud of blood rising around Jerry Banks and so she scratched harder still.

'Officer, I wouldn't lose any sleep over that one.'

How could she explain? What was eating at her now was more complex than the detective knew. Rhyme was the best criminalist in New York, maybe in the country. Sachs aspired, but she'd never match him at that. But shooting – like driving fast – was one of *her* gifts. She could outshoot most of the men and women on the force, either-handed. She'd prop dimes up on the fifty-yard range and shoot for the glare, making presents of the bent coins for her goddaughter and her friends. She *could* have saved Jerry. Hell, she might even have hit the son of a bitch.

She was furious with herself, furious with Percey for putting her in this position.

And furious with Rhyme too.

The door swung open and Percey appeared in the door. With a cold look at Sachs she asked Hale to join them. He disappeared into the room and a few minutes later it was Hale who opened the door and said, 'He'd like everyone back inside.'

Sachs found them this way: Percey was sitting next to Rhyme in a battered old armchair. She had this ridiculous image of them as a married couple.

'We're compromising,' Rhyme announced. 'Brit and Percey'll go to Dellray's safe house. They'll have somebody else do the repairs on the plane. Whether we find the Dancer or not, though, I've agreed to let her make the flight tomorrow night.'

'And if I just arrest her?' Sachs said heatedly. 'Take her to detention?'

She'd thought Rhyme would explode at this – she was ready for it – but he said reasonably, 'I thought about that, Sachs. And I don't belive it's a good idea. There'd be more exposure – court, detention, transport. The Dancer'd have more of a chance to get them.'

Amelia Sachs hesitated then gave in, nodded. He was

right; he usually was. But right or not, he'd have things his way. She was his assistant, nothing more. An employee. That's all she was to him.

Rhyme continued. 'Here's what I've got in mind. We're going to set a trap. I'll need your help, Lon.'

'Talk to me.'

'Percey and Hale'll go to the safe house. But I want to make it look like they're going someplace else. We'll make a big deal out of it. Very visible. I'd pick one of the precincts, pretend they're going into the lockup there for security. We'll put out a transmission or two on citywide, unscrambled, that we're closing the street in front of the station house for security and transporting all booked suspects down to detention to keep the facility clear. If we're lucky the Dancer'll be listening on a scanner. If not, the media'll pick it up and he might hear about it that way.'

'How 'bout the Twentieth?' Sellitto suggested.

The Twentieth Precinct, on the Upper West Side, was only a few blocks from Lincoln Rhyme's town house. He knew many of the officers there.

'Okay, good.'

Sachs then noticed some uneasiness in Sellitto's eyes. He leaned forward toward Rhyme's chair, sweat dripping down his broad, creased forehead. In a voice only Rhyme and Sachs could hear, he whispered, 'You're sure about this, Lincoln. I mean, you thought about it?'

Rhyme's eyes swiveled toward Percey. A look passed between the two of them. Sachs didn't know what it meant. She knew only that she didn't like it.

'Yes,' Rhyme said. 'I'm sure.'

Though to Sachs he didn't seem very sure at all.

# Chapter
# THIRTEEN

'Lots of trace, I see.'

Rhyme looked approvingly at the plastic bags Sachs had brought back from the airport crime scenes.

Trace evidence was Rhyme's favorite – the bits and pieces, sometimes microscopic, left by perps at crime scenes, or picked up there by them unwittingly. It was trace evidence that even the cleverest of perps didn't think to alter or plant and it was trace that even the most industrious couldn't dispose of altogether.

'The first bag, Sachs? Where did it come from?'

She flipped angrily through her notes.

What was eating at her? he wondered. Something was wrong, Rhyme could see. Maybe it had to do with her anger at Percey Clay, maybe her concern for Jerry Banks. But maybe not. He could tell from the cool glances that she didn't want to talk about it. Which was fine with him. The Dancer had to be caught. It was their only priority at the moment.

'This's from the hangar where the Dancer waited for the plane.' She held up two of the bags. She nodded at three others. 'This's from the sniper's nest. This's from the painting van. This's from the catering van.'

'Thom . . . Thom!' Rhyme shouted, startling everyone in the room.

The aide appeared in the doorway. He asked a belabored 'Yes? I'm trying to fix some food here, Lincoln.'

'Food?' Rhyme asked, exasperated. 'We don't need to eat. We need more charts. Write: "CS-Two, Hangar." Yes, "CS-Two, Hangar." That's good. Then another one. "CS-Three." That's where he fired from. His grassy knoll.'

'I should write that? "Grassy Knoll"?'

'Of course not. It's a joke. I *do* have a sense of humor, you know. Write: "CS-Three, Sniper's Nest." Now, let's look at the hangar first. What do you have?'

'Bits of glass,' Cooper said, spilling the contents out on a porcelain tray like a diamond merchant. Sachs added, 'And some vacuumed trace, a few fibers from the windowsill. No FR.'

Friction ridge prints, he meant. Finger or palm.

'He's too careful with prints,' Sellitto said glumly.

'No, that's *encouraging*,' Rhyme said, irritated – as he often was – that no one else drew conclusions as quickly as he could.

'Why?' the detective asked.

'He's careful because he's on file somewhere! So when we *do* find a print we'll stand a good chance of ID'ing him. Okay, okay, cotton glove prints, they're no help . . . No boot prints because he scattered gravel on the hangar floor. He's a smart one. But if he were stupid, nobody's need us, right? Now, what does the glass tell us?'

'What could it tell us,' Sachs asked shortly, 'except he broke in the window to get into the hangar?'

'I wonder,' Rhyme said. 'Let's look at it.'

Mel Cooper mounted several shards on a slide and placed it under the lens of the compound 'scope at low magnification. He clicked the video camera on to send the image to Rhyme's computer.

Rhyme motored back to it. He instructed, 'Command mode.' Hearing his voice, the computer dutifully slipped a menu onto the glowing screen. He couldn't control the microscope itself but he could capture the image on the computer screen and manipulate it – magnify or shrink it, for instance. 'Cursor left. Double click.'

Rhyme strained forward, lost in the rainbow auras of refraction. 'Looks like standard PPG single-strength window glass.'

'Agreed,' Cooper said, then observed, 'No chipping. It was broken by a blunt object. His elbow maybe.'

'Uh-huh, uh-huh. Look at the conchoidal, Mel.'

When someone breaks a window the glass shatters in a series of conchoidal breaks – curved fracture lines. You can tell from the way they curve which direction the blow came from.

'I see it,' the tech said. 'Standard fractures.'

'Look at the dirt,' Rhyme said abruptly. 'On the glass.'

'See it. Rainwater deposits, mud, fuel residue.'

'What *side* of the glass is the dirt on?' Rhyme asked impatiently. When he was running IRD, one of the complaints of the officers under him was that he acted like a schoolmarm. Rhyme considered it a compliment.

'It's . . . oh.' Cooper caught on. 'How can that be?'

'What?' Sachs asked.

Rhyme explained. The conchoidal fractures began on the clean side of the glass and ended on the dirty side. 'He was *inside* when he broke the window.'

'But he couldn't've been,' Sachs protested. 'The glass was inside the hangar. He—' She stopped and nodded. 'You mean he broke it out, then scooped the glass up and threw it inside with the gravel. But why?'

'The gravel wasn't to prevent shoe prints. It was to fool us into thinking he broke *in*. But he was already *inside* the hangar and broke *out*. Interesting.' The criminalist considered this for a moment, then shouted, 'Check that trace. There any brass in it? Any brass with *graphite* on it?'

'A key,' Sachs said. 'You're thinking somebody gave him a key to get into the hangar.'

'That's exactly what I'm thinking. Let's find out who owns or leases the hangar.'

'I'll call,' Sellitto said and flipped open his cell phone.

Cooper looked through the eyepiece of another microscope. He had it on high magnification. 'Here we go,' he said. 'Lot of graphite and brass. What I'd guess is some 3-In-One oil too. So it was an old lock. He had to fiddle with it.'

'Or?' Rhyme prompted. 'Come on, think!'

'Or a new-made key!' Sachs blurted.

'Right! A sticky one. Good. Thom, the chart, please! Write: "Access by key."'

In his precise handwriting the aide wrote the words.

'Now, what else do we have?' Rhyme sipped and puffed and swung closer to the computer. He misjudged and slammed into it, nearly knocking over his monitor.

'Goddamn,' he muttered.

'You all right?' Sellitto asked.

'Fine, I'm fine,' he snapped. 'Anything *else*? I was asking – anything else?'

Cooper and Sachs brushed the rest of the trace onto a large sheet of clean newsprint. They put on magnifying goggles and went over it. Cooper lifted several flecks with a probe and placed them on a slide.

'Okay,' Cooper said. 'We've got fibers.'

A moment later Rhyme was looking at the tiny strands on his computer screen.

'What do you think, Mel? Paper, right?'

'Yep.'

Speaking into his headset, Rhyme ordered his computer

to scroll through the microscopic images of the fibers. 'Looks like two different kinds. One's white or buff. The other's got a green tint.'

'Green? Money?' Sellitto suggested.

'Possibly.'

'You have enough to gas a few?' Rhyme asked. The chromatograph would destroy the fibers.

Cooper said they had and proceeded to test several of them.

He read the computer screen. 'No cotton and no soda, sulfite, or sulfate.'

These were chemicals added to the pulping process in making high-quality paper.

'It's cheap paper. And the dye's water soluble. There's no oil-based ink.'

'So,' Rhyme announced, 'it's not money.'

'Probably recycled,' Cooper said.

Rhyme magnified the screen again. The matrix was large now and the detail lost. He was momentarily frustrated and wished that he was looking through a real compound 'scope eyepiece. There was nothing like the clarity of fine optics.

Then he saw something.

'Those yellow blotches, Mel? Glue?'

The tech looked through the microscope's eyepiece and announced, 'Yes. Envelope glue, looks like.'

So possibly the key had been delivered to the Dancer in an envelope. But what did the green paper signify? Rhyme had no idea.

Sellitto folded up his phone. 'I talked to Ron Talbot at Hudson Air. He made a few calls. Guess who leases that hangar where the Dancer waited.'

'Phillip Hansen,' Rhyme said.

'Yep.'

'We're making a good case,' Sachs said.

True, Rhyme thought, though his goal was not to hand the Dancer over to the AG with a watertight case. No, he wanted the man's head on a pike.

'Anything else there?'

'Nothing.'

'Okay, let's move on to the other scene. The sniper's nest. He was under a lot of pressure there. Maybe he got careless.'

But, of course, he hadn't been careless.

There were no shell casings.

'Here's why,' Cooper said, examining the trace through the scope. 'Cotton fibers. He used a dish towel to catch the casings.'

Rhyme nodded. 'Footprints?'

'Nope.' She explained that the Dancer'd worked his way around the patches of exposed mud, staying on the grass even when he was racing to the catering van to escape.

'How many FRs you find?'

'None at the sniper's nest,' Sachs explained. 'Close to two hundred in the two vans.'

Using AFIS – the automated fingerprint identification system that linked digitalized criminal, military, and civil service fingerprint databases around the country – a coldsearch of this many prints would be possible (though very time consuming). But as obsessed as Rhyme was with finding the Dancer, he didn't bother with an AFIS request. Sachs reported that she'd found his glove prints in the vans too; the friction ridge prints inside the vehicles wouldn't be the Dancer's.

Cooper emptied the plastic bag onto an examining tray. He and Sachs looked over it. 'Dirt, grass, pebbles . . . Here were go. Can you see this, Lincoln?' Cooper mounted another slide.

'Hairs,' Cooper said, bent over his own 'scope. 'Three, four, six, nine . . . a dozen of 'em. It looks like a continuous medulla.'

The medulla is a canal running through the middle of a strand of some types of hair. In humans, the medulla is either nonexistent or fragmented. A continuous medulla meant the hair was animal. 'What do you think, Mel?'

'I'll run them through the SEM.' The scanning electron microscope. Cooper ran the scale up to fifteen-hundred-times magnification and adjusted dials until one of the hairs was centered in the screen. It was a whitish stalk with sharp-edged scales resembling a pineapple's skin.

'Cat,' Rhyme announced.

'Cats, plural,' Cooper corrected, looking into the compound 'scope again. 'Looks like we've got a black and a calico. Both shorthairs. Then a tawny, long and fine. Persian, something like that.'

Rhyme snorted. 'Don't think the Dancer's profile's that he's an animal lover. He's either passing for somebody with cats or's staying with somebody who's got 'em.'

'More hair,' Cooper announced and mounted a slide on the compound 'scope. 'Human. It's . . . wait, two strands about six inches long.'

'He's shedding, huh?' Sellitto asked.

'Who knows?' Rhyme said skeptically. Without the bulb attached, it's impossible to determine the sex of the person who lost the strand. Age, except with an infant's hair, was also impossible to tell. Rhyme suggested, 'Maybe it's the paint truck driver's. Sachs? He have long hair?'

'No. Crew cut. And it was blond.'

'What do you think, Mel?'

The tech scanned the length of the hair. 'It's been colored.'

'The Dancer's known for changing his appearance,' Rhyme said.

'Don't know, Lincoln,' Cooper said. 'The dye's similar to the natural shade. You'd think he'd go for something real different if he wanted to change his identity. Wait, I see two colors of dye. The natural shade is black. It's had some auburn added, and then more recently a dark purple wash. About two to three months apart.'

'I'm also picking up a lot of residue here, Lincoln. I ought to gas one of the hairs.'

'Do it.'

A moment later Cooper was reading the chart on the computer connected to the GC/MS. 'Okay, we've got some kind of cosmetic.'

Makeup was very helpful to the criminalist; cosmetic manufacturers were notorious for changing the formulation of their products to take advantage of new trends. Different compositions could often be pinpointed to different dates of manufacture and distribution locations.

'What do we have?'

'Hold on.' Cooper was sending the formula to the brand name database. A moment later he had an answer. 'Slim-U-Lite. Swiss made, imported by Jencon, outside of Boston. It's a regular detergent-based soap with oils and amino acids added. It was in the news – the FTC's on their case for claiming that it takes off fat and cellulite.'

'Let's profile,' he announced. 'Sachs, what do you think?'

'About him?'

'About *her*. The one aiding and abetting him. Or the one he killed to hide out in her apartment. And maybe steal her car.'

'You're sure it's a woman?' wondered Lon Sellitto.

'No. But we don't have time to be timid in our speculations. More women are worried about cellulite than men. More women color their hair than men. Bold propositions! Come on!'

'Well, overweight,' Sachs said. 'Self-image problem.'

'Maybe punky, New Wave, or whatever the fuck the weirdos call 'emselves nowadays,' Sellitto suggested. 'My daughter turned her hair purple. Pierced some stuff too, which I don't want to talk about. How 'bout the East Village?'

'I don't think she's going for a rebel image,' Sachs said. 'Not with those colors. They're not different enough. She's trying to be stylish and nothing she's doing is working. I say she's fat, with short hair, in her thirties, professional. Goes home alone to her cats at night.'

Rhyme nodded, staring at the chart. 'Lonely. Just the sort to get suckered in by somebody with a glib tongue. Let's check veterinarians. We know she's got three cats, three different colors.'

'But where?' Sellitto asked. 'Westchester? Manhattan?'

'Let's first ask,' Rhyme mulled, 'why would he hook up with this woman in the first place?'

Sachs snapped her fingers. 'Because he *had* to! Because we nearly trapped him.' Her face had lit up. Some of the old Amelia was back.

'Yes!' Rhyme said. 'This morning, near Percey's town house. When ESU moved in.'

Sachs continued. 'He ditched the van and hid out in her apartment until it was safe to move.'

Rhyme said to Sellitto, 'Get some people calling vets. For ten blocks around the town house. No, make it the whole Upper East Side. Call, Lon, call!'

As the detective punched numbers into his phone, Sachs asked gravely, 'You think she's all right? The woman?'

Rhyme answered from his heart though not with what he believed to be the truth. 'We can hope, Sachs. We can hope.'

# Chapter
# FOURTEEN

To Percey Clay the safe house didn't appear particularly safe.

It was a three-story brownstone structure like many others along this block near the Morgan Library.

'This's it,' an agent said to her and Brit Hale, nodding out the window of the van. They parked in the alley and she and Hale were hustled through a basement entrance. The steel door slammed shut. They found themselves staring at an affable man in his late thirties, lean and with thinning brown hair. He grinned.

'Howdy,' he said, showing his NYPD identification and gold shield. 'Roland Bell. From now on you meet anybody, even somebody charming as me, ask 'em for an ID and make sure it's got an i-dentical picture on it.'

Percey listened to his relentless drawl and asked, 'Don't tell me . . . you're a Tarheel?'

'That I am.' He laughed. 'Lived in Hoggston – not a joke, no – until I escaped to Chapel Hill for four years. Understand you're a Richmond gal.'

'Was. Long time ago.'

'And you, Mr Hale?' Bell asked. 'You flying the Stars and Bars too?'

'Michigan,' Hale said, shaking the detective's vigorous hand. 'Via Ohio.'

'Don't you worry, I'll forgive you for that little mistake of yours in the eighteen sixties.'

'I myself would've surrendered,' Hale joked. 'Nobody asked me.'

'Hah. Now, I'm a Homicide detective but I keep drawing this witness protection detail 'cause I have this knack of keeping people alive. So my dear friend Lon Sellitto asked me to help him out. I'll be baby-sitting y'all for a spell.'

Percey asked, 'How's that other detective?'

'Jerry? What I hear, he's still in the operating room. No news yet.'

His speech may have been slow but his eyes were very fast, scooting over their bodies. Looking for what? Percey wondered. To see if they were armed? Had microphones hidden on them? Then he'd scan the corridor. Then the windows.

'Now,' Bell said, 'I'm a nice fellow but I can be a bit muley when it comes to looking after who I'm s'posed to.' He gave Percey a faint smile. 'You look a bit muley yourself, but just remember that everything I tell you t'do's for your own good. All right? All right. Hey, I think we're going to get along just fine. Now lemme show you our grade-A accommodations.'

As they walked upstairs he said, 'Y'all're probably dead to know how safe this place is . . .'

Hale asked uncertainly, 'What was that again? "Dead to know"?'

'Means, uhm, eager. I guess I talk a bit South still. Boys down in the Big Building – that's headquarters – fool with me some. Leave messages saying they've collared themselves a redneck and want me to translate for 'em. Anyway, this place is good 'n' safe. Our friends in Justice, oh, they know what they're doing. Bigger'n it looks from the outside, right?'

'Bigger than a cockpit, smaller than an open road,' Hale said.

Bell chuckled. 'Those front windows? Didn't look too secure when you were driving up?'

'That *was* one thing . . . ,' Percey began.

'Well, here's the front room. Take a peek.' He pushed open a door.

There *were* no windows. Sheets of steel had been bolted over them. 'Curtains're on the other side,' Bell explained. 'From the street it looks just like dark rooms. All the other windows're bulletproof glass. But you stay away from 'em all the same. And keep the shades drawn. The fire escape and roof're loaded with sensors and we've got tons of video cameras hidden around the place. Anybody comes near we check 'em clip and clean 'fore they get to the front door. It'd take a ghost with anorexia to get in here.' He walked down a wide corridor. 'Follow me down this dogtrot here . . . Okay, that's your room there, Mrs Clay.'

'Long as we're living together, you may's well call me Percey.'

'Done deal. And you're over here . . .'

'Brit.'

The rooms were small and dark and very still – very different from Percey's office in the corner of the hangar at Hudson Air. She thought of Ed, who preferred to have an office in the main building, his desk organized, pictures of B17s and P-51s on the wall, Lucite paperweights on every stack of documents. Percey liked the smell of jet fuel, and for a sound track to her workday the buzz saw of pneumatic wrenches. She thought of them together, him perched on her desk, sharing coffee. She managed to push the thought away before the tears started again.

Bell called onto his walkie-talkie. 'Principals in position.' A moment later two uniformed policemen appeared in the corridor. They nodded and one of them said, 'We'll be out here. Full-time.' Curiously, their New York twang didn't seem that different from Bell's resonant drawl.

'That was good,' Bell said to Percey.

She raised an eyebrow.

'You checked his ID. Nobody's gonna get the bulge on you.'

She smiled wanly.

Bell said to Percey, 'Now, we've got two men with your mother-in-law in New Jersey. Any other family needs watching?'

Percey said she didn't, not in the area.

He repeated the question to Hale, who answered, with a rueful grin, 'Not unless an ex-wife's considered family. Well, wives.'

'Okay. Cats'r dogs need watering?'

'Nope,' Percey said. Hale shook his head.

'Then we may's well just ree-lax. No phone calls from cell phones if you've got one. Only use that line there. Remember the windows and curtains. Over there, that's a panic button. Worse comes to worst, and it won't, you hit it and drop to the ground. Now, you need anything, just give me a holler.'

'As a matter of fact, I do,' Percey said. She held up the silver flask.

'Well, now,' Bell drawled, 'you want me to help you empty it, I'm afraid I'm still on duty. But 'preciate the offer. You want me to help you *fill* it, why, that's a done deal.'

Their scam didn't make the five o'clock news.

But three transmissions went out unscrambled on a citywide police channel, informing the precincts about a 10–66 secure operation at the Twentieth Precinct and broadcasting a 10–67 traffic advisory about street closures on the Upper West Side. All suspects apprehended within the borders of the Twentieth were to be taken directly to Central Booking and the Men's or Women's Detention Center downtown. No one would be allowed in or out of the precinct without a special okay from the FBI. Or the FAA – Dellray's touch.

As this was being broadcast, Bo Haumann's 32-E teams went into position around the station house.

Haumann was now in charge of that portion of the operation. Fred Dellray was putting together a federal hostage rescue team in case they discovered the cat lady's identity and her apartment. Rhyme, along with Sachs and Cooper, continued to work the evidence from the crime scenes.

There were no new clues, but Rhyme wanted Sachs and Cooper to reexamine what they'd already found. This was criminalistics – you looked and looked and looked, and then, when you couldn't find anything, you looked some more. And when you hit another brick wall, you kept right on looking.

Rhyme had wheeled up close to his computer and was ordering it to magnify images of the timer found in the wreckage of Ed Carney's plane. The timer itself might have been useless, because it was so generic, but Rhyme wondered if it might not contain a little trace or even a partial latent print. Bombers often believe that fingerprints are destroyed in the detonation and will shun gloves when working with the tinier components of the devices. But the blast itself will not necessarily destroy prints. Rhyme now ordered Cooper to fume the timer in the SuperGlue frame and, when that revealed nothing, to dust it with the Magna-Brush, a technique for raising prints that uses fine magnetic powder. Once again he found nothing.

Finally he ordered that the sample be bombarded by the nit-yag, slang for a garnet laser that was state-of-the-art in raising otherwise invisible prints. Cooper was looking at the image under the 'scope while Rhyme examined it on his computer screen.

Rhyme gave a short laugh, squinted, then looked again, wondering if his eyes were playing tricks on him.

'Is that? . . . Look. Lower right-hand corner!' Rhyme called.

But Cooper and Sachs could see nothing.

His computer-enhanced image had found something that Cooper's optical 'scope had missed. On the lip of metal that had protected the timer from being blown to smithereens was a faint crescent of ridge endings, crossings and bifurcations. It was no more than a sixteenth of an inch wide and maybe a half inch long.

'It's a print,' Rhyme said.

'Not enough to compare,' Cooper said, gazing at Rhyme's screen.

There are a total of about 150 individual ridge characteristics in a single fingerprint but an expert can determine a match with only eight to sixteen ridge matches. Unfortunately this sample didn't even provide half that.

Still, Rhyme was excited. The criminalist who couldn't twist the focus knob of a compound 'scope had found something that the others hadn't. Something he probably would have missed if he'd been 'normal'.

He ordered the computer to load a screen capture program and he saved the print as a .bmp file, not compressing it to .jpg, to avoid any risk of corrupting the image. He printed out a hard copy on his laser printer and had Thom tape it up next to the crash-site-scene evidence board.

The phone rang and, with his new system, Rhyme tidily answered the call and turned on the speakerphone.

It was the Twins.

Also known by the affectionate handle 'the Hardy Boys', this pair of Homicide detectives worked out of the Big Building, One Police Plaza. They were interrogators and canvassers – the cops who interview residents, bystanders, and witnesses after a crime – and these two, who bore a vague resemblance to each other, were considered the best in the city. Even Lincoln Rhyme, with his distrust of the powers of human observation and recall, respected them.

Despite their delivery.

'Hey, Detective. Hey, Lincoln,' said one of them. Their names were Bedding and Saul. In person, you could hardly tell them apart. Over the phone, Rhyme didn't even try.

'What've you got?' he asked. 'Find the cat lady?'

'This one was easy. Seven veterinarians, two boarding services—'

'Made sense to hit them too. And—'

'We did three pet walking companies too. Even though—'

'Who walks cats, right? But they also feed and water and change the litter when you're away. Figured it couldn't hurt.'

'Three of the vets had a maybe, but they weren't sure. They were pretty big operations.'

'Lotsa animals on the Upper East Side. You'd be surprised. Maybe you wouldn't.'

'And so we had to call employees at home. You know, doctors, assistants, washers—'

'That's a job. Pet washer. Anyway, a receptionist at a vet on Eighty-second was thinking it might be this customer, Sheila Horowitz. She's mid-thirties, short dark hair, heavyset. Has three cats. One black and the other blond. They don't know the color on the third one. She lives on Lexington between Seventy-eighth and Seventy-ninth.'

Five blocks from Percey's town house.

Rhyme thanked them and told them to stay on call, then barked, 'Get Dellray's teams over there now! You too, Sachs. Whether he's there or not, we'll have a scene to search. I think we're getting close. Can you feel it, everybody? We're getting close!'

\*    \*    \*

Percey Clay was telling Roland Bell about her first solo flight.

Which didn't go quite as she planned.

She'd taken off from the small grass strip four miles outside of Richmond, feeling the familiar *ka-thunk ka-thunk* as the Cessna's gear bounded over the rough spots just before she hit V1 speed. Then back on the yoke and the crisp little 150 took to the air. A humid spring afternoon, just like this one.

'Must've been exciting,' Bell offered, with a curiously dubious look.

'Got more so,' Percey said, then took a hit from the flask.

Twenty minutes later the engine quit over the Wilderness in eastern Virginia, a nightmare of brambles and loblolly pine. She set the staunch plane down on a dirt road, cleared the fuel line herself, and took off once again, returning home without incident.

There was no damage to the little Cessna – so the owner never found out about the joyride. In fact the only fallout from the incident was the whipping she got from her mother because the principal at the Lee School had reported Percey'd been in yet another fight and had punched Susan Beth Halworth in the nose and fled after fifth period.

'I had to get away,' Percey explained to Bell. 'They were picking on me. I think they were calling me "troll". I got called that a lot.'

'Kids can be cruel,' Bell said. 'I'd tan my boys' hide, they ever did anything like – Wait, how old were you?'

'Thirteen.'

'Can you do that? I mean, don't you need to be eighteen to fly?'

'Sixteen.'

'Oh. Then . . . how'd it work that you were flyin'?'

'They never caught me,' Percey said. 'That's how it worked.'

'Oh.'

She and Roland Bell were sitting in her room in the safe

house. He'd refilled her flask with Wild Turkey – a bread-and-butter present from a mob informant who'd lived here for five weeks – and they were sitting on a green couch, the squelch mercifully turned down on his walkie-talkie. Percey sat back, Bell forward – his posture due not to the uncomfortable furniture but to his extraordinary mindfulness. His eye would catch the motion of a fly zipping past the door, a breath of air pushing a curtain, and his hand would stray to one of the two large guns he carried.

At his prompting she continued the story of her flying career. She got her student pilot certificate at age sixteen, her private pilot certificate a year later, and at eighteen she had her commercial ticket.

To her parents' horror, she fled the tobacco business circuit (Father didn't work for a 'company' but for a 'grower', though it was a $6 billion corporation to everyone else) and went for her engineering degree. ('Dropping out of UVA was the first sensible thing she's done,' her mother pointed out to Percey's father, the only time the girl could remember her mother taking her side. The woman had added, 'It'll be easier to find a husband at Virginia Tech.' Meaning the boys won't have such high standards.)

But it wasn't parties or boys or sororities she was interested in. It was one thing and one thing only. Aircraft. Every day that it was physically and financially possible, she flew. She got her flight instructor's cert and started teaching. She didn't like the job particularly, but she persisted for a very savvy reason: the hours you spent flight-instructing went in your logbook as pilot-in-command time. Which would look good on the résumé when she went knocking on airline doors.

After graduation she began the life of an unemployed pilot. Lessons, air shows, joyrides, an occasional left-hand seat assignment for a delivery service or small charter company. Air taxis, seaplanes, crop dusting, even stunts, flying old

Stearman and Curtis Jenny biplanes on Sunday afternoons at roadside carnivals.

'It was tough, real tough,' she said to Roland Bell. 'Maybe like getting started in law enforcement.'

'Not a world of difference, I'd guess. I was running speed traps and overseeing crossing guard detail as sheriff of Hoggston. We had three consecutive years with no homicides, even accidental. Then I started moving up – got a job as a deputy with the county, working Highway Patrol. But that was mostly picking folk outa moonshine wrecks. So I went back to UNC for a criminology/sociology degree. Then I moved to Winston-Salem and got myself a gold shield.'

'A what?'

'Detective. Course, I got beat up twice and shot at three times before my first review . . . Hey, be careful what you ask for; you may get it. You ever hear that?'

'But you were doing what you wanted.'

'I was that. You know, my aunt who raised me'd always say, "You walk the direction God points you." Think there's something to that. I'm keen to know, how'd you start your own company?'

'Ed – my husband – and Ron Talbot and I did that. About seven, eight years ago. But I had a stopover first.'

'How's that?'

'I enlisted.'

'No fooling?'

'Yep. I was desperate to fly and nobody was hiring. See, before you can get a job with a big charter or an airline you have to be rated on the kind of planes they fly. And in order to get rated you've got to pay for training and simulator time – out of your own pocket. Can cost you ten thousand bucks to get a ticket to fly a big jet. I was stuck flying props 'cause I couldn't afford any training. Then it occurred to me: I could enlist and get paid to fly the sexiest aircraft on earth. So I signed up. Navy.'

'Why them?'

'Carriers. Thought it'd be fun to land on a moving runway.'

Bell winced. She cocked her eyebrow and he explained. 'In case you didn't guess, I'm not a huge fan of your business.'

'You don't like pilots?'

'Oh, no, don't mean that. It's flying I don't like.'

'You'd rather be shot at than go flying?'

Without consideration, he nodded emphatically, then asked, 'You see combat?'

'Sure did. Las Vegas.'

He frowned.

'Nineteen ninety-one. The Hilton Hotel. Third floor.'

'Combat? I don't get it.'

Percey asked, 'You ever hear about Tailhook?'

'Oh, wasn't that the navy convention or something? Where a bunch of male pilots got all drunk and attacked some women? You were *there*?'

'Got groped and pinched with the best of 'em. Decked one lieutenant and broke the finger of another, though I'm sorry to say he was too drunk to feel the pain till the next day.' She sipped some more bourbon.

'Was it as bad as they said?'

After a moment she said, 'You're used to expecting some North Korean or some Iranian in a MiG to drop out of the sun and lock on. But when the people supposed to be on your side do it, well, it really throws you. Makes you feel dirty, betrayed.'

'What happened?'

'Aw, kind of a mess,' she muttered. 'I wouldn't roll over. I named names and put some folks out of business. Some pilots, but some high-up folks too. That didn't sit well in the briefing room. As you can imagine.'

Monkey skills or no monkey skills, you don't fly with wingmen you don't trust. 'So I left. It was all right. I'd had fun with the 'Cats, fun flying sorties. But it was time to leave. I'd met Ed – my husband – and we'd decided to open up this charter. I kissed and made up with Daddy – sort of – and he lent me most of the money for the Company.' She shrugged. 'Which I paid back at prime plus three, never late a day on a payment. The son of a gun . . .'

This brought back a dozen memories of Ed. Helping her negotiate the loan. Shopping together for aircraft at the skeptical leasing companies. Renting hangar space. Arguing as they struggled to fix a nav-com panel at three in the morning, trying to get ready for a 6 A.M. flight. The images hurt as bad as her ferocious migraines. Trying to deflect her thoughts, she asked, 'So what brings you to parts north?'

'Wife's family's up here. On Long Island.'

'You gave up North Carolina for in-laws?' Percey nearly made a comment about how'd his wife lasso him into that but was glad she hadn't. Bell's hazel eyes easily held hers as he said, 'Beth was pretty sick. Passed away nineteen months ago.'

'Oh, I'm so sorry.'

'Thank you. They had Sloan-Kettering up here and her folks and sister too. The fact is I needed some help with the kids. I'm fine pitching the football and making chili but they need other stuff than that. Like, I shrunk most of their sweaters first time I dried 'em. That sort of thing. I wasn't averse to a move anyway. Wanted to show the kids there's more to life than silos and harvesters.'

'You got pictures?' Percey asked, tipping back the flask. The hot liquor burned for a brief exquisite moment. She decided she'd quit drinking. Then decided not to.

''Deed I do.' He fished a wallet from his baggy slacks and displayed the children. Two blond boys, around five and seven. 'Benjamin and Kevin,' Bell announced.

Percey also caught a glimpse of another photo – a pretty, blond woman, short hair in bangs.

'They're adorable.'

'You have any kids?'

'No,' she answered, thinking, I always had my reasons. There was always next year or the next. When the company was doing better. When we'd leased that 737. After I got my DC-9 rating ... She gave him a stoic smile. 'Yours? They want to be cops when they grow up?'

'Soccer players's what they want to be. Not much of a market for that in New York. Unless the Mets keep playing the way they've been.'

Before the silence grew too thick, Percey asked, 'Is it okay if I call the Company? I've got to see how my aircraft's coming.'

'You bet. I'll leave you be. Just make sure you don't give our number or address to a soul. It's the one thing I'm gonna be real muley about.'

# Chapter
# FIFTEEN

'Ron. It's Percey. How is everyone?'

'Shook up,' he answered. 'I sent Sally home. She couldn't—'

'How is she?'

'Just couldn't deal with it. Carol too. And Lauren. Lauren was out of control. I've never seen anybody that upset. How're you and Brit?'

'Brit's mad. I'm mad. What a mess this is. Oh, Ron . . .'

'And that detective, the cop who got shot?'

'I don't think they know yet. How's *Foxtrot Bravo*?'

'It's not as bad as it could be. I've already replaced the cockpit window. No breaches in the fuselage. Number two engine . . . that's a problem. We've got to replace a lot of the skin. We're trying to find a new fire extinguisher cartridge. I don't think it'll be a problem . . .'

'But?'

'But the annular has to be replaced.'

'The combustor? Replace it? Oh, Jesus.'

'I've already called the Garrett distributor in Connecticut. They agreed to deliver one tomorrow, even though it's Sunday. I can have it installed in a couple, three hours.'

'Hell,' she muttered, 'I should be there . . . I told them I'd stay put but, damn it, I should be there.'

'Where are you, Percey?'

And Stephen Kall, listening to this conversation as he sat in Sheila Horowitz's dim apartment, was ready to write. He pressed the receiver closer to his ear.

But the Wife said only, 'In Manhattan. About a thousand cops around us. I feel like the pope or the president.'

Stephen had heard on his police scanner reports of some curious activity around the Twentieth Precinct, which was on the Upper West Side. The station house was being closed and suspects were being relocated. He wondered if that was where the Wife was right now – at the precinct house.

Ron asked, 'Are they going to stop this guy? Do they have any leads?'

Yes, do they? Stephen wondered.

'I don't know,' she said.

'Those gunshots,' Ron said. 'Jesus, they were scary. Reminded me of the service. You know, that sound of the guns.'

Stephen wondered again about this Ron fellow. Could he be useful?

Infiltrate, evaluate . . . *interrogate*.

Stephen considered tracking him down and torturing him to get him to call Percey back and ask where the safe house was . . .

But although he probably could get through the airport security again it would be a risk. And it would take too much time.

As he listened to their conversation Stephen gazed at the laptop computer in front of him. A message saying, *Please wait*, kept flashing. The remote tap was connected to a NYNEX relay box near the airport and had been transmitting their conversations to Stephen's tape recorder for the past week. He was surprised the police hadn't found it yet.

A cat – Esmeralda, *Essie,* the worm sack – climbed onto the table and arched her back. Stephen could hear the irritating purring.

He began to feel cringey.

He elbowed the cat roughly to the floor and enjoyed her pained bleat.

'I've been looking for more pilots,' Ron said uncomfortably. 'I've got—'

'We just need one. Right-hand seat.'

A pause. 'What?' Ron asked.

'I'm taking the flight tomorrow. All I need is an FO.'

'You? I don't think that's a good idea, Perce.'

'You have anybody?' she asked shortly.

'Well, the thing is—'

'Do you *have* anyone?'

'Brad Torgeson's on the call list. He said he had no problem helping us out. He knows about the situation.'

'Good. A pilot with balls. How's his Lear time?'

'Plenty . . . Percey, I thought you were hiding out until the grand jury.'

'Lincoln agreed to let me take the flight. If I stayed here until then.'

'Who's Lincoln?'

Yes, Stephen thought. Who *is* Lincoln?

'Well, he's this weird man . . .' The Wife hesitated, as if she wanted to talk about him but wasn't sure what to say. Stephen was disappointed when she said only, 'He's working with the police, trying to find the killer. I told him I'd stay here until tomorrow but I was definitely making the flight. He agreed.'

'Percey, we can delay it. I'll talk to U.S. Medical. They know we're going through some—'

'No,' she said firmly. 'They don't want excuses. They want wheels-up on schedule. And if we can't do it they'll find somebody else. When are they delivering the cargo?'

'Six or seven.'

'I'll be there late afternoon. I'll help you finish with the annular.'

'Percey,' he wheezed, 'everything's going to be fine.'

'We get that engine fixed on time, everything'll be *great*.'

'You must be going through hell,' Ron said.

'Not really,' she said.

Not yet, Stephen corrected silently.


Sachs skidded the RRV station wagon around the corner at forty miles per hour. She saw a dozen tactical agents trotting along the street.

Fred Dellray's teams were surrounding the building where Sheila Horowitz lived. A typical Upper East Side brownstone, next door to a Korean deli, in front of which an employee squatted on a milk crate, peeling carrots for the salad bar and staring with no particular curiosity at the machine-gun-armed men and women surrounding the building.

Sachs found Dellray, weapon unholstered, in the foyer, examining the directory.

*S.Horowitz. 204.*

He tapped his radio. 'We're on four eight three point four.'

The secure federal tactical operations frequency. Sachs adjusted her radio as Dellray peered into the Horowitz woman's mailbox with a small black flashlight. 'Nothin' picked up today. Got a feeling that girl's gone.' He then said, 'We got our folk on the fire escape and floor above and below with a SWAT cam and some mikes. Haven't seen anybody inside. But we're pickin' up some scratching and purring. Nothing sounds human, though. She got cats, remember. That was a feather in his cap, thinking of the vets. Our man Rhyme, I mean.'

I know who you mean, she thought.

Outside, the wind was howling and another line of black

clouds was trooping over the city. Big slabs of bruise-colored cloud.

Dellray snarled into his radio. 'All teams. Status?'

'Red Team. We're on the fire escape.'

'Blue Team. First floor.'

'Roger,' Dellray muttered. 'Search and Surveillance. Report.'

'Still not sure. We're getting faint infrared readings. Whoever or whatever's in there isn't moving. Could be a sleeping cat. Or a wounded victim. Or might be a pilot light or lamp that's been burning for a while. Could be the subject, though. In an interior part of the apartment.'

'Well, what do you *think*?' Sachs asked.

'Who's that?' the agent asked over the radio.

'NYPD, Portable Five Eight Eight Five,' Sachs responded, giving her badge number. 'I want to know what your opinion is. Do you think the suspect is inside?'

'Why you askin'?' Dellray wanted to know.

'I want an uncontaminated scene. I'd like to go in alone if they think he's not there.' A dynamic entry by a dozen tactical officers was probably the most efficient way to utterly decimate a crime scene.

Dellray looked at her for a moment, his dark face creased, then said into his stalk mike, 'What's your opinion, S&S?'

'We just can't say for sure, sir,' the disembodied agent reported.

'Know you can't, Billy. Just gimme what your gut's telling you.'

A pause, then: 'I *think* he's rabbited. Think it's clean.'

'Hokay.' To Sachs he said, 'But you take one officer with you. That's an order.'

'I go in first, though. He can cover me from the door. Look, this guy just isn't leaving *any* evidence anywhere. We need a break.'

'All right, Officer.' Dellray nodded to several of the federal SWAT agents. 'Entry approved,' he muttered, slipping out of hipster as he spoke words of law enforcement art.

One of the tactical agents had the lobby door lock disassembled in thirty seconds.

'Hold up,' Dellray said, cocking his head. 'It's a call from Central.' He spoke into the radio. 'Give 'em the frequency.' He looked at Sachs. 'Lincoln's calling you.'

A moment later the criminalist's voice intruded. 'Sachs,' he said, 'what're you doing?'

'I'm just—'

'Listen,' he said urgently. 'Don't go in alone. Let them secure the scene first. You know the rule.'

'I've got backup—'

'No, let SWAT secure it first.'

'They're sure he's not there,' she lied.

'That's not good enough,' he shot back. 'Not with the Dancer. Nobody's ever sure with him.'

*This* again. I don't need it, Rhyme. Exasperated, she said, 'This's the sort of scene he's not expecting us to find. He probably hasn't hosed it. We could find a fingerprint, a shell casing. Hell, we could find his credit card.'

No response. It wasn't often that Lincoln Rhyme was rendered silent.

'Quit spooking me, Rhyme. Okay?'

He didn't respond and she had a strange feeling that he wanted her to be spooked. 'Sachs . . . ?'

'What?'

'Just be careful' was his only advice and the words were offered tentatively.

Then suddenly five tactical agents appeared, wearing Nomex gloves and hoods, blue flak jackets, and holding black H&K's.

'I'll call you from inside,' she said.

She started up the stairs after them, her thoughts more on the heavy crime scene suitcase she held in her weak hand, her left, than on the black pistol in her right.

In the old days, in the Before days, Lincoln Rhyme had been a walker.

There was something about motion that soothed him. A stroll through Central or Washington Square Park, a brisk walk through the Fashion District. Oh, he'd pause often – maybe to collect a bit of evidence for the databases at the IRD lab – but once the bits of dirt or the plants or the samples of building materials were safely stowed and their sources jotted in his notebook, he'd continue on his way again. Miles and miles he'd walk.

One of the most frustrating things about his present condition was the inability to let off tension. He now had his eyes closed and he rubbed the back of his head into the headrest of the Storm Arrow, grinding his teeth together.

He asked Thom for some scotch.

'Don't you need to be clearheaded?'

'No.'

'I think you do.'

Go to hell, Rhyme thought, and ground his teeth harder. Thom would have to clean off a bloody gum, have to arrange for the dentist to come over. And I'll be a prick with *him* too.

Thunder rolled in the distance and the lights dimmed.

He pictured Sachs at the front of the tactical force. She was right, of course: an ESU team doing a full secure of the apartment would contaminate it badly. Still, he was worried sick for her. She was too reckless. He'd seen her scratching her skin, pulling eyebrows, chewing nails. Rhyme, ever skeptical of the psychologist's black arts, nonetheless knew self-destructive behavior when he saw it. He'd also been for a drive with her – in her souped-up sports car. They'd hit speeds over 150 miles per hour and she seemed frustrated that the rough roads on Long Island wouldn't let her do twice that.

He was startled to hear her whispering voice. 'Rhyme, you there?'

'Go ahead, Amelia.'

A pause. 'No first names, Rhyme. It's bad luck.'

He tried to laugh. Wished he hadn't used the name, wondered why he had.

'Go ahead.'

'I'm at the front door. They're going to take it down with a battering ram. The other team reported in. They really don't think he's there.'

'You wearing your armor?'

'Stole a feebie's flak jacket. Looks like I'm wearing black cereal boxes for a bra.'

'On three,' Rhyme heard Dellray's voice, 'all teams, take out door and windows, cover all areas, but hold short of entry. One . . .'

Rhyme was so torn. How badly he wanted the Dancer – he could taste it. But, oh, how frightened he was for her.

'Two . . .'

Sachs, damn it, he thought. I don't want to worry about you . . .

'Three . . .'

He heard a soft snap, like a teenager cracking his knuckles, and found himself leaning forward. His neck quivered with a huge cramp and he leaned back. Thom appeared and began to massage it.

'It's all right,' he muttered. 'Thank you. Could you just get the sweat? Please.'

Thom looked at him suspiciously – at the word 'please' – then wiped his forehead.

What're you doing, Sachs?

He wanted to ask but wouldn't think of distracting her just now.

Then he heard a gasp. The hairs on the back of his neck stirred. 'Jesus, Rhyme.'

'What? Tell me.'

'The woman . . . the Horowitz woman. The refrigerator door's open. She's inside. She's dead but it looks like . . . Oh, God, her eyes.'

'Sachs . . .'

'It looks like he put her inside when she was still alive. Why the hell would he—'

'Think past it, Sachs. Come on. You can do it.'

'Jesus.'

Rhyme knew Sachs was claustrophobic. He imagined the terror she'd be feeling, looking at the terrible mode of death.

'Did he tape her or tie her?'

'Tape. Some kind of clear packing tape on her mouth. Her eyes, Rhyme. Her eyes . . .'

'Don't get shook, Sachs. The tape'll be a good surface for prints. What're the floor surfaces?'

'Carpet in the living room. And linoleum in the kitchen. And—' A scream. 'Oh God!'

'*What?*'

'Just one of the cats. It jumped in front of me. Little shit . . . Rhyme?'

'What?'

'I'm smelling something. Something funny.'

'Good.' He'd taught her always to smell the air at a crime scene. It was the first fact a CS officer should note. 'But what does "funny" mean?'

'A sour smell. Chemical. Can't place it.'

Then he realized that something didn't make sense.

'Sachs,' he asked abruptly. 'Did *you* open the refrigerator door?'

'No. I found it that way. It's propped open with a chair, looks like.'

Why? Rhyme wondered. *Why'd* he do that? He thought furiously.

'That smell, it's stronger. Smokey.'

The woman's a distraction! Rhyme thought suddenly. He left the door open to make sure the entry team would focus on it!

Oh, no, not again!

'Sachs! That's fuse you're smelling. A time-delay fuse. There's another bomb! Get out now! He left the refrigerator door open to lure us inside.'

'What?'

'It's a fuse! He's set a bomb. You've got seconds. Get out! Run!'

'I can get the tape. On her mouth.'

'Get the fuck out!'

'I can get it . . .'

Rhyme heard a rustle, a faint gasp, and seconds later, the ringing bang of the explosion, like a sledgehammer on a boiler.

It stunned his ear.

'No!' he cried. 'Oh, no!'

He glanced at Sellitto, who was staring at Rhyme's horrified face. 'What happened, what happened?' the detective was calling.

A moment later Rhyme could hear through the earpiece a man's voice, panicky, shouting, 'We've got a fire. Second floor. The walls're gone. They're gone . . . We got injuries . . . Oh, God. What happened to her? Look at the blood. All the blood! We need help. Second floor! Second floor . . .'

Stephen Kall walked a circle around the Twentieth Precinct on the Upper West Side.

The station house wasn't far from Central Park and he caught a glimpse of the trees.

The cross street the precinct house was located on was guarded, but security wasn't too bad. There were three cops in front of the low building, looking around nervously. But there were none on the east side of the station house, where a thick steel grille covered the windows. He guessed that this was the lockup.

Stephen continued around the corner and then walked south to the next cross street. There were no blue sawhorses closing off this street, but there were guards – two more cops. They eyed every car and pedestrian that passed. He studied the building briefly then continued yet another block south and circled around the west side of the precinct. He slipped through a deserted alley, took his binoculars from his backpack, and gazed at the station house.

Can you *use* this, Soldier?

Sir, yes, I can, sir.

In a parking lot beside the station house was a gas pump. An officer was filling his squad car with gas. It never occurred to Stephen that police cars wouldn't buy their gas at Amoco or Shell stations.

For a long moment he gazed at the pumps through his small, heavy Leica binoculars, then put them back into the bag and hurried west, conscious, as always, of people on the lookout for him.

# Chapter
# SIXTEEN

'Sachs!' Rhyme cried again.

Damnit, what was she *thinking* of? How could she be so careless?

'What happened?' Sellitto asked again. 'What's going on?'

*What happened to her?*

'A bomb in the Horowitz apartment,' Rhyme said hopelessly. 'Sachs was inside when it went off. Call them. Find out what happened. On the speakerphone.'

*All the blood . . .*

An interminable three minutes later Sellitto was patched through to Dellray.

'Fred,' Rhyme shouted, 'how is she?'

A harrowing pause before he answered.

'Ain't good, Lincoln. We're just gettin' the fire out now. It was an AP of some kind. Shit. We shoulda looked first. Fuck.'

Antipersonnel booby traps were usually plastic explosive or TNT and often contained shrapnel or ball bearings – to inflict the most damage they could.

Dellray continued. 'Took a coupla walls down and burned mosta the place out.' A pause. 'I have to tell you, Lincoln.

We . . . found . . .' Dellray's voice – usually so steady – now waffled uneasily.

'What?' Rhyme demanded.

'Some body parts . . . A hand. Part of an arm.'

Rhyme closed his eyes and felt a horror he hadn't felt in years. An icy stab through his insentient body. His breath came out in a low hiss.

'Lincoln—' Sellitto began.

'We're still searching,' Dellray continued. 'She might not be dead. We'll find her. Get her to the hospital. We'll do everything we can. You know we will.'

Sachs, why the hell did you do it? Why did I let you?

I should never—

Then a crackle sounded in his ear. A pop loud as a firecracker. 'Could somebody . . . I mean, Jesus, could somebody get this off me?'

'Sachs?' Rhyme called into the microphone. He was sure the voice was hers. Then it sounded like she was choking and retching.

'Uck,' she said. 'Oh, boy . . . This's gross.'

'Are you all right?' He turned to the speakerphone. 'Fred, where is she?'

'Is that you, Rhyme?' she asked. 'I can't hear anything. Somebody talk to me!'

'Lincoln,' Dellray called. 'We got her! She's A-okay. She's all right.'

'Amelia?'

He heard Dellray shouting for medics. Rhyme, whose body hadn't shivered for some years, noted that his left ring finger was trembling fiercely.

Dellray came back on. 'She can't hear too good, Lincoln. What happened was . . . looks like what happened was it was the *woman's* body we saw. Horowitz. Sachs pulled it out of the fridge just 'fore the bang. The corpse took mosta the blast.'

Sellitto said, 'I see that look, Lincoln. Give her a break.'

But he didn't.

In a fierce growl he said, 'What the hell were you thinking of, Sachs? I told you it was a bomb. You should've *known* it was a bomb and bailed out.'

'Rhyme, is that you?'

She was faking. He knew she was.

'Sachs—'

'I had to get the tape, Rhyme. Are you there? I can't hear you. It was plastic packing tape. We need to get one of his prints. You said so yourself.'

'Honestly,' he snapped, 'you're impossible.'

'Hello? Hello-o? Can't hear a word you're saying.'

'Sachs, don't give me any crap.'

'I'm going to check something, Rhyme.'

There was silence for a moment.

'Sachs? . . . Sachs, you there? What the hell . . . ?'

'Rhyme, listen – I just hit the tape with the PoliLight. And guess what? There's a partial on it! I've got one of the Dancer's prints!'

That stopped him for a moment, but he soon resumed his tirade again. He was well into his lecture before he realized that he was reading the riot act to an empty line.

She was sooty and had a stunned look about her.

'No dressing-down, Rhyme. It was stupid but I didn't think about it. I just moved.'

'What happened?' he asked. His stern visage had fallen away momentarily, he was so happy to see her alive.

'I was halfway inside. I saw the AP charge behind the door and didn't think I could make it out in time. I grabbed the woman's body out of the fridge. I was going to pull her to the kitchen window. It blew before I got halfway there.'

Mel Cooper looked over the bag of evidence Sachs handed

him. He examined the soot and fragments from the bomb. 'M forty-five charge. TNT, with a rocker switch and forty-five-second fuse delay. The entry team knocked it over when they rammed the door; that ignited the fuse. There's graphite, so it's newer-formulation TNT. Very powerful, very bad.'

'Fucker,' Sellitto spat out. 'Time delay . . . He wanted to make sure as many people got into the room as possible 'fore it blew.'

Rhyme asked, 'Anything traceable?'

'Off-the-shelf military. Won't lead us anywhere except—'

'To the asshole gave it to him,' Sellitto muttered. 'Phillip Hansen.' The detective's phone rang and he took the call, lowered his head as he listened, nodding.

'Thank you,' he said finally, shut off the phone.

'What?' Sachs asked.

The detective's eyes were closed.

Rhyme knew it was about Jerry Banks.

'Lon?'

'It's Jerry.' The detective looked up. Sighed. 'He'll live. But he lost his arm. They couldn't save it. Too much damage.'

'Oh, no,' Rhyme whispered. 'Can I talk to him?'

'No,' the detective said. 'He's asleep.'

Rhyme thought of the young man, pictured him saying the wrong thing at the wrong time, poking at his cowlick, rubbing a razor cut on his smooth, pink chin. 'I'm sorry, Lon.'

The detective shook his head, much the same way Rhyme deflected bouquets of sympathy. 'We got other things to worry about.'

Yes, they did.

Rhyme noticed the plastic packing tape – the gag the Dancer had used. He could see, as could Sachs, a faint lipstick mark on the adhesive side.

Sachs was staring at the evidence, but it wasn't a clinical look. Not a *scientist's* gaze. She was troubled.

'Sachs?' he asked.

'Why'd he do that?'

'The bomb?'

She shook her head. 'Why'd he put her in the refrigerator?' She lifted a finger to her mouth and chewed a nail. Of
her ten fingers, only one nail – the little finger of her left
hand – was long and shapely. The others were chewed. Some
were brown with dried blood.

The criminalist answered, 'I think it was because he wanted
to distract us so we wouldn't focus on the bomb. A body in
a refrigerator – that got our attention.'

'I don't mean that,' she answered. 'COD was suffocation.
He put her in there *alive*. Why? Is he a sadist or something?'

Rhyme answered, 'No, the Dancer's not a sadist. He can't
afford to be. His only urge is to complete the job, and he's
got enough willpower to keep his other lusts under control.
Why'd he suffocate her when he could have used a knife or
rope? . . . I'm not exactly sure, but it could be good for us.'

'How's that?'

'Maybe there was something about her that he hated, and
he wanted to kill her in the most unpleasant way he could.'

'Yeah, but why's that good for us?' Sellitto asked.

'Because' – it was Sachs who answered – 'it means maybe
he's losing his cool. He's getting careless.'

'Exactly,' Rhyme called, proud of Sachs for making the
connection. But she didn't notice his smile of approval. Her
eyes dipped closed momentarily and she shook her head,
probably replaying the image of the dead woman's horrified
eyes. People thought criminalists were cold (how often had
Rhyme's wife leveled that charge at him?), but in fact the
best ones had a heartbreaking empathy for the victims of
the scenes they searched. Sachs was one of these.

'Sachs,' Rhyme whispered gently, 'the print?'

She looked at him.

'You found a print, you said. We have to move fast.'

Sachs nodded. 'It's a partial.' She held up the plastic bag. 'Could it be hers?'

'No, I printed her. Took a while to find her hands. But the print definitely isn't hers.'

'Mel,' Rhyme said.

The tech put the bit of packing tape in a SuperGlue frame and heated some glue. Immediately a tiny portion of the print became evident.

Cooper shook his head. 'I don't believe it,' he muttered.

'What?'

'He wiped the tape, the Dancer. He must've known he touched it without a glove on. There's only a bit of one partial left.'

Like Rhyme, Cooper was a member of the International Association for Identification. They were experts at identifying people from fingerprints, DNA, and odontology – dental remains. But this particular print – like the one on the metal lip of the bomb – was beyond their power. If any experts could find and classify a print, it would be the two of them. But not this print.

'Shoot it and mount it,' Rhyme muttered. 'Up on the wall.' They'd go through the motions because it was what you had to do in this business. But he was very frustrated. Sachs had nearly died for nothing.

Edmond Locard, the famous French criminalist, developed a principle named after him. He said that in every encounter between criminal and victim there is an exchange of evidence. It might be microscopic, but a transfer takes place. Yet it seemed to Rhyme that if anyone could disprove Locard's Principle, it was the ghost they called the Coffin Dancer.

Sellitto, seeing the frustration on Rhyme's face, said, 'We've got the trap at the station house. If we're lucky we'll get him.'

'Let's hope. We could use some goddamn luck.'

He closed his eyes, rested his head on the pillow. A moment later he heard Thom saying, 'It's nearly eleven. Time for bed.'

At times it's easy to neglect the body, to forget we even *have* bodies – times like these, when lives are at stake and we have to step out of our physical beings and keep working, working, working. We have to go far beyond our normal limitations. But Lincoln Rhyme had a body that wouldn't tolerate neglect. Bedsores could lead to sepsis and blood poisoning. Fluid in the lungs, to pneumonia. Didn't catheterize the bladder? Didn't massage the bowels to encourage a movement? Spenco boots too tight? Dysreflexia was the consequence and that could mean a stroke. Exhaustion alone could bring on an attack.

*Too many ways to die . . .*

'You're going to bed,' Thom said.

'I have to—'

'Sleep. You have to sleep.'

Rhyme acquiesced; he was tired, very tired.

'All right, Thom. All right.' He wheeled toward the elevator. 'One thing.' He looked back. 'Could you come up in a few minutes, Sachs?'

She nodded, watching the tiny elevator door swing shut.

She found him in the Clinitron.

Sachs had waited ten minutes to give him time to take care of bedtime functions – Thom had applied the catheter and brushed his boss's teeth. She knew Rhyme talked tough – he had a crip's disregard for modesty. But she knew too that there were personal routines he didn't want her to witness.

She used the time to take a shower in the downstairs bathroom, dressed in clean clothes – hers – which Thom happened to have in the laundry room in the basement.

The lights were dim. Rhyme was rubbing his head against the pillow like a bear scratching his back on a tree. The Clinitron was the most comfortable bed in the world. Weighing a half ton, it was a massive slab containing glass beads through which flowed heated air.

'Ah, Sachs, you did good today. You outthought him.'

Except thanks to me Jerry Banks lost his arm.

And I let the Dancer get away.

She walked to his bar and poured a glass of Macallan, lifted an eyebrow.

'Sure,' he said. 'Mother's milk, the dew of nepenthe . . .'

She kicked her issue shoes off, pulled up her blouse to look at the bruise.

'Ouch,' Rhyme said.

The bruise was the shape of Missouri and dark as an eggplant.

'I don't like bombs,' she said. 'Never been that close to one. And I don't like them.'

Sachs opened her purse, found and swallowed three aspirin dry (a trick arthritics learn early). She walked to the window. There were the peregrines. Beautiful birds. They weren't large. Fourteen, sixteen inches. Tiny for a dog. But for a bird . . . utterly intimidating. Their beaks were like the claws on a creature from one of those *Alien* movies.

'You all right, Sachs? Tell me true?'

'I'm okay.'

She returned to the chair, sipped more of the smokey liquor.

'You want to stay tonight?' he asked.

On occasion she'd spend the night here. Sometimes on the couch, sometimes in bed next to him. Maybe it was the fluidized air of the Clinitron, maybe it was the simple act of lying next to another human being – she didn't know the reason – but she never slept better than when she slept here. She hadn't enjoyed being close to another man since her most recent boyfriend, Nick. She and Rhyme would lie together and talk. She'd tell him about cars, about her pistol matches, about her mother and her goddaughter. About her father's full life and sad, protracted death. She'd ante up far more personal information than he. But that was all right. She loved listening to him say whatever he wanted to. His mind was astonishing. He'd tell her about old New York, about Mafia hits the rest of the world had never heard about, about crime scenes so clean they seemed hopeless until the searchers found the single bit of dust, the fingernail, the dot of spit, the hair or fiber that revealed who the perp was or where he lived – well, revealed these facts to *Rhyme,* not necessarily anyone else. No, his mind never stopped. She knew that before the injury he'd roam the streets of New York looking for samples of soil or glass or plants or rocks – anything that might help him solve cases. It was as if that restlessness had moved from his useless legs into his mind, which roamed the city – in his imagination – well into the night.

But tonight was different. Rhyme was distracted. She didn't mind him ornery – which was good because he was ornery a lot. But she didn't like him being elsewhere. She sat on the edge of the bed.

He began to say what he'd apparently asked her here for. 'Sachs . . . Lon told me. About what happened at the airport.'

She shrugged.

'There's nothing you could've done except gotten yourself killed. You did the right thing, going for cover. He fired one for range and would've gotten you with the second shot.'

'I had two, three seconds. I could've hit him. I *know* I could've.'

'Don't be reckless, Sachs. That bomb—'

The fervent look in her eyes silenced him. 'I want to get him, whatever it takes. And I have a feeling you want to get him just as much. I think you'd take chances too.' She added with cryptic significance, 'Maybe you *are* taking chances.'

This had a greater reaction than she'd expected. He blinked, looked away. But he said nothing else, sipped his scotch.

On impulse she asked, 'Can I ask something? If you don't want me to, you can tell me to clam up.'

'Come on, Sachs. We've got secrets, you and me? I don't think so.'

Eyes on the floor, she said, 'I remember once I was telling you about Nick. How I felt about him and so on. How what happened between us was so hard.'

He nodded.

'And I asked you if you'd felt that way about anyone, maybe your wife. And you said yes, but not Blaine.' She looked up at him.

He recovered fast, though not fast enough. And she realized she'd blown cold air on an exposed nerve.

'I remember,' he answered.

'Who was she? Look, if you don't want to talk about it . . .'

'I don't mind. Her name was Claire. Claire Trilling. How's that for a last name?'

'Probably put up with the same crap in school I had to. Amelia Sex. Amelia Sucks . . . How'd you meet her?'

'Well . . .' He laughed at his own reluctance to continue. 'In the department.'

'She was a cop?' Sachs was surprised.

'Yep.'

'What happened?'

'It was a . . . difficult relationship.' Rhyme shook his head ruefully. 'I was married, she was married. Just not to each other.'

'Kids?'

'She had a daughter.'

'So you broke up?'

'It wouldn't have worked, Sachs. Oh, Blaine and I were destined to get divorced – or kill each other. It was only a matter of time. But Claire ... she was worried about her daughter – about her husband taking the little girl if she got divorced. She didn't love him, but he was a good man. Loved the girl a lot.'

'You meet her?'

'The daughter? Yes.'

'You ever see her now? Claire?'

'No. That was the past. She's not on the force anymore.'

'You broke up after your accident?'

'No, no, before.'

'She knows you were hurt, though, right?'

'No,' Rhyme said after another hesitation.

'Why didn't you tell her?'

A pause. 'There were reasons ... Funny you bring her up. Haven't thought about her for years.'

He offered a casual smile, and Sachs felt the pain course through her – actual pain like the blow that left the bruise in the shape of the Show Me State. Because what he was saying was a lie. Oh, he'd been thinking about this woman. Sachs didn't believe in woman's intuition, but she did believe in cop's intuition; she'd walked a beat for far too long to discount insights like these. She *knew* Rhyme'd been thinking about Ms Trilling.

Her feelings were ridiculous, of course. She had no patience for jealousy. Hadn't been jealous of Nick's job – he was undercover and spent weeks on the street. Hadn't been jealous of the hookers and blond ornaments he'd drink with on assignments.

And beyond jealousy, what could she possibly hope for with Rhyme? She'd talked about him to her mother many times. And the cagey old woman would usually say something like 'It's good to be nice to a cripple like that.'

Which just about summed up all that their relationship should be. All that it *could* be.

It was *more* than ridiculous.

But jealous she was. And it wasn't of Claire.

It was of Percey Clay.

Sachs couldn't forget how they'd looked together when she'd seen them sitting next to each other in his room, earlier today.

More scotch. Thinking of the nights she and Rhyme had spent here, talking about cases, drinking this very good liquor.

Oh, great. Now I'm maudlin. That's a mature feeling. I'm gonna group a cluster right in its chest and kill it dead.

But instead she offered the sentiment a little more liquor.

Percey wasn't an attractive woman, but that meant nothing; it had taken Sachs all of one week at Chantelle, the modeling agency on Madison Avenue where she'd worked for several years, to understand the fallacy of the beautiful. Men love to look at gorgeous women, but nothing intimidates them more.

'You want another hit?' she asked.

'No,' he said.

Without thinking now, she reclined, laid her head on his pillow. It was funny how we adjust to things, she thought. Rhyme couldn't, of course, pull her to his chest and slip his arm around her. But the comparable gesture was his tilting his head to hers. In this way they'd fallen asleep a number of times.

Tonight, though, she sensed a stiffness, a caution.

She felt she was losing him. And all she could think about was trying to be closer. As close as possible.

Sachs had once confided with her friend Amy, her god-daughter's mother, about Rhyme, about her feelings for him. The woman had wondered what the attraction was and speculated, 'Maybe it's that, you know, he can't move. He's a man but he doesn't have any control over you. Maybe that's a turn-on.'

But Sachs knew it was just the opposite. The turn-on was

that he was a man who had complete control, *despite* the fact he couldn't move.

Fragments of his words floated past as he spoke about Claire, then about the Dancer. She tilted her head back and looked at his thin lips.

Her hands started roving.

He couldn't feel, of course, but he could see her perfect fingers with their damaged nails slide over his chest, down his smooth body. Thom exercised him daily with a passive range of motion exercises and though Rhyme wasn't muscular he had a body of a young man. It was as if the ageing process had stopped the day of the accident.

'Sachs?'

Her hand moved lower.

Her breathing was coming faster now. She tugged the blanket down. Thom had dressed Rhyme in a T-shirt. She tugged it up, moved her hands over his chest. Then she pulled her own shirt off, unhooked her bra, pressed her flushed skin against his pallid. She expected it to be cold but it wasn't. It was hotter than hers. She rubbed harder.

She kissed him once on the cheek, then the corner of the mouth, then squarely on the mouth.

'Sachs, no . . . Listen to me. No.'

But she didn't listen.

She'd never told Rhyme, but some months ago she'd bought a book called *The Disabled Lover*. Sachs was surprised to learn that even quadriplegics can make love and father children. A man's perplexing organ literally has a mind of its own, and severing the spinal cord eliminates only one type of stimulus. Handicapped men were capable of perfectly normal erections. True, he'd have no sensation, but – for her – the physical thrill was only a part of the event, often a minor part. It was the closeness that counted; that was a high that a million phony movie orgasms would never approach. She suspected that Rhyme might feel the same way.

She kissed him again. Harder.

After a moment's hesitation he kissed her back. She was not surprised that he was good at it. After his dark eyes, his perfect lips were the first thing she'd noticed about him.

Then he pulled his face away.

'No, Sachs, don't . . .'

'Shhh, quiet . . .' She worked her hand under the blankets, began rubbing, touching.

'It's just that . . .'

It was *what*? she wondered. That things might not work out?

But things were working out fine. She felt him growing hard under her hand, more responsive than some of the most macho lovers she'd had.

She slid on top of him, kicked the sheets and blanket back, bent down and kissed him again. Oh, how she wanted to be here, face-to-face – as close as they could be. To make him understand that she saw he was her perfect man. He was whole as he was.

She unpinned her hair, let it fall over him. Leaned down, kissed him again.

Rhyme kissed back. They pressed their lips together for what seemed like a full minute.

Then suddenly he shook his head, so violently that she thought he might have been having an attack of dysreflexia.

'No!' he whispered.

She'd expected playful, she'd expected passionate, at worst a flirtatious *Oh-oh, not a good idea* . . . But he sounded weak. The hollow sound of his voice cut into her soul. She rolled off, clutching a pillow to her breasts.

'No, Amelia. I'm sorry. No.'

Her face burned with shame. All she could think was how

many times she'd been out with a man who was a friend or a casual date and suddenly been horrified to feel him start to grope her like a teenager. Her voice had registered the same dismay that she now heard in Rhyme's.

So this was all that she was to him, she understood at last. A partner. A colleague. A capital *F* Friend.

'I'm sorry, Sachs . . . I can't. There're complications.'

Complications? None that she could see, except, of course, for the fact that he didn't love her.

'No, *I'm* sorry,' she said brusquely. 'Stupid. Too much of that damn single-malt. I never could hold the stuff. You know that.'

'Sachs.'

She kept a terse smile on her face as she dressed.

'Sachs, let me say something.'

'No.' She didn't want to hear another word.

'Sachs . . .'

'I should go. I'll be back early.'

'I want to say something.'

But Rhyme never got a chance to say anything, whether it was an explanation or apology or a confession. Or a lecture.

They were interrupted by a huge pounding on the door. Before Rhyme could ask who it was, Lon Sellitto burst into the room.

He glanced at Sachs without judgment, then back to Rhyme and announced, 'Just heard from Bo's guys over at the Twentieth. The Dancer was there, staking out the place. The son of a bitch's taken the bait! We're gonna get him, Lincoln. This time we're gonna get him.'

'Couple hours ago,' the detective continued his story, 'some of the S&S boys saw a white male taking a stroll around the Twentieth Precinct house. He ducked into an alley and it looked like he was checking out guards. And then they saw him scoping out the gas pump next to the station house.'

'Gas pump? For the RMPs?' Radio mobile patrols – Squad cars.

'Right.'

'They follow him?'

'Tried. But he vanished 'fore they got close.'

Rhyme was aware of Sachs's discreetly fixing the top button of her blouse . . . He had to have a talk with her about what had happened. He *had* to make her understand. But considering what Sellitto was now saying, it would have to wait.

'Gets better. Half hour ago, we got a report of a truck hijacking. Rollins Distributing. Upper West Side near the river. They deliver gas to independent service stations. Some guy cuts through the chain-link. The guard hears and goes to investigate. He gets blindsided. Gets the absolute crap beat out of him. And the guy gets away with one of the trucks.'

'Is Rollins the company the department uses for gas?'

'Naw, but who'd know? The Dancer pulls up to the Twentieth in a tanker, the guards there don't think anything of it, they wave him through, next thing—'

Sachs interrupted. 'The truck blows.'

This brought Sellitto up short. 'I was just thinking he'd use it as a way to get inside. You're thinking a bomb?'

Rhyme nodded gravely. Angry with himself. Sachs was right. 'Outsmarted ourselves here. Never occurred to me he'd try anything like this. Jesus, a tanker truck goes up in that neighborhood . . .'

'A fertilizer bomb?'

'No,' Rhyme said. 'I don't think he'd have time to put that together. But all he needs is an AP charge on the side of a small tanker and he's got a super gas-enhanced device. Burn the precinct to the ground. We've got to evacuate everyone. Quietly.'

'Quietly,' Sellitto muttered. 'That'll be easy.'

'How's the guard from the gas distributor? Can he talk?'

'Can, but he got hit from behind. Didn't see a thing.'

'Well, I want his clothes at least. Sachs' – she caught his eye – 'could you get over to the hospital and bring them back? You'll know how to pack them to save the trace. And then work the scene where he stole the truck.'

He wondered what her response would be. He wouldn't have been surprised if she'd quit cold and walked out the door. But he saw in her still, beautiful face that she was feeling exactly what he was: ironically, relief that the Dancer had intervened to change the disastrous course of their evening.

Finally, finally, some of the luck Rhyme had hoped for.

An hour later Amelia Sachs was back. She held up a plastic bag containing a pair of wire cutters.

'Found them near the chain-link. The guard must've surprised the Dancer and he dropped them.'

'Yes!' Rhyme shouted. 'I've never known him to make a mistake like that. Maybe he *is* getting careless . . . I wonder what's spooking him.'

Rhyme glanced at the cutters. Please, he prayed silently, let there be a print.

But a groggy Mel Cooper – he'd been sleeping in one of the smaller bedrooms upstairs – went over every square millimeter of the tool. Not a print to be found.

'Does it tell us *anything*?' Rhyme asked.

'It's a Craftsman model, top of the line, sold in every Sears around the country. And you can pick them up in garage sales and junkyards for a couple bucks.'

Rhyme wheezed in disgust. He gazed at the clippers for a moment then asked, 'Tool marks?'

Cooper looked at him curiously. Tool marks are distinctive impressions left at crime scenes by the tools criminals used – screwdrivers, pliers, lock picks, crowbars, slim jims, and the like. Rhyme had once linked a burglar to a crime scene solely on the basis of a tiny V notch on a brass lock plate. The notch matched an imperfection in a chisel found on the man's workbench. Here, though, they had the *tool*, not any marks it might have made. Cooper didn't understand what tool marks Rhyme might be referring to.

'I'm talking about marks *on* the blade,' he said impatiently. 'Maybe the Dancer's been cutting something distinctive, something that might tell us where he's holing up.'

'Oh.' Cooper examined it closely. 'It's nicked, but take a look . . . Do you see anything unusual?'

Rhyme didn't. 'Scrape the blade and handle. See if there's any residue.'

Cooper ran the scrapings through the gas-chromatograph.

'Phew,' he muttered as he read the results. 'Listen to this. Residue of RDX, asphalt, and rayon.'

'Detonating cord,' Rhyme said.

'He cut it with clippers?' Sachs asked. 'You can do that?'

'Oh, it's stable as clothesline,' Rhyme said absently, picturing what a thousand gallons of flaming gasoline would do to the neighborhood around the Twentieth Precinct.

I should've made them leave, he was thinking, Percey and Brit Hale. Put them into protective custody and sent them to Montana until the grand jury. This is damn nuts what I'm doing, this trap idea.

'Lincoln?' Sellitto asked. 'We've got to find that truck.'

'We've got a little time,' Rhyme said. 'He's not going to try to get in until the morning. He needs the cover story of a delivery. Anything else, Mel? Anything in the trace?'

Cooper scanned the vacuum filter. 'Dirt and brick. Wait . . . here're some fibers. Should I GC them?'

'Yes.'

The tech hunched over the screen as the results came up. 'Okay, okay, it's vegetable fiber. Consistent with paper. And I'm reading a compound . . . NH four OH.'

'Ammonium hydroxide,' Rhyme said.

'Ammonia?' Sellitto asked. 'Maybe you're wrong about the fertilizer bomb.'

'Any oil?' Rhyme asked.

'None.'

Rhyme asked, 'The fiber with the ammonia – was it from the handle of the clipper?'

'No. It was on the clothes of the guard he beat up.'

Ammonia? Rhyme wondered. He asked Cooper to look at one of the fibers through the scanning electron microscope. 'High magnification. How's the ammonia attached?'

The screen clicked on. The strand of fiber appeared like a tree trunk.

'Heat fused, I'd guess.'

Another mystery. Paper and ammonia . . .

Rhyme looked at the clock. It was 2:40 A.M.

Suddenly he realized Sellitto had asked him a question. He cocked his head.

'I said,' the detective repeated, 'should we start evacuating everybody around the precinct? I mean, better now than wait till it's closer to the time he might attack.'

For a long moment Rhyme gazed at the bluish tree trunk of fiber on the screen of the SEM. Then he said abruptly, 'Yes. We have to get everybody out. Evacuate the buildings around the station house. Let's think – the four apartments on either side and across the street.'

'That many?' Sellitto asked, giving a faint laugh. 'You think we really gotta do that?'

Rhyme looked up at the detective and said, 'No, I've changed my mind. The whole block. We've got to evacuate the whole block. Immediately. And get Haumann and Dellray over here. I don't care where they are. I want them now.'

# Chapter
# SEVENTEEN

Some of them had slept.

Sellitto in an armchair, waking more rumpled than ever, his hair askew. Cooper downstairs.

Sachs had apparently spent the night on a couch downstairs or in the other bedroom on the first floor. No interest in the Clinitron anymore.

Thom, himself bleary, was hovering, a dear busybody, taking Rhyme's blood pressure. The smell of coffee filled the town house.

It was just after dawn and Rhyme was staring at the evidence charts. They'd been up till four, planning their strategy for snagging the Dancer – and responding to the legion of complaints about the evacuation.

Would this work? Would the Dancer step into their trap? Rhyme believed so. But there was another question, one that Rhyme didn't like to think about but couldn't avoid. How bad would springing the trap be? The Dancer was deadly enough on his own territory. What would he be like when he was cornered?

Thom brought coffee around and they looked over Dellray's tactical map. Rhyme, back in the Storm Arrow, rolled into position and studied it too.

'Everybody in place?' he asked Sellitto and Dellray.

Both Haumann's 32-E teams and Dellray's federal pickup band of Southern and Eastern District FBI SWAT officers were ready. They'd moved in under cover of night, through sewers and basements and over rooftops, in full urban camouflage; Rhyme was convinced that the Dancer was maintaining surveillance of his target.

'He won't be sleeping tonight,' Rhyme had said.

'You sure he's going in this way, Linc?' Sellitto'd asked uncertainly.

Sure? he thought testily. Who can be sure about anything with the Coffin Dancer?

*His deadliest weapon is deception* . . .

Rhyme said wryly, 'Ninety-two point seven percent sure.'

Sellitto snorted a sour laugh.

It was then that the doorbell rang. A moment later a stocky, middle-aged man Rhyme didn't recognize appeared in the doorway of the living room.

The sigh from Dellray suggested trouble brewing. Sellitto knew the man too, it seemed, and nodded cautiously.

He identified himself as Reginald Eliopolos, assistant U.S. attorney in the Southern District. Rhyme recalled he was the prosecutor handling the Phillip Hansen case.

'You're Lincoln Rhyme? Hear good things about you. Uh-huh. Uh-huh.' He started forward, automatically offering his hand. Then he realized that the extended arm was wasted on Rhyme, so he simply pointed it toward Dellray, who shook it reluctantly. Eliopolos's cheerful 'Fred, good to see you' meant just the opposite and Rhyme wondered what was the source of the cold fusion between them.

The attorney ignored Sellitto and Mel Cooper. Thom instinctively sensed what was what and didn't offer the visitor coffee.

'Uh-huh, uh-huh. Hear you've got quite an operation

together. Not checking too much with the boys upstairs, but, hell, I know all about improvising. Sometimes you just can't spend time waiting for signatures in triplicate.' Eliopolos walked up to a compound 'scope, peered through the eyepiece. 'Uh-huh,' he said, though what he might be seeing was a mystery to Rhyme since the stage light was off.

'Maybe—' Rhyme began.

'The chase? Cut to the chase?' Eliopolos swung around. 'Sure. Here it is. There's an armored van at the Federal Building downtown. I want the witnesses in the Hansen case in it within the hour. Percey Clay and Brit Hale. They'll be taken to the Shoreham federal protective reserve, on Long Island. They'll be kept there until their grand jury testimony late on Monday. Period. End of chase. How's that?'

'You think that's a wise idea?'

'Uh-huh, we do. We think it's wiser than using them as bait for some kind of personal vendetta by the NYPD.'

Sellitto sighed.

Dellray said, 'Open your eyes little bit here, Reggie. You're not exactly out of the loop. Do I see a joint operation? Do I see *task-forced* operation?'

'And a good thing too,' Eliopolos said absently. His full attention was on Rhyme. 'Tell me, did you really think that nobody downtown would remember that this was the perp who killed your techs five years ago?'

Well, *uh-huh*, Rhyme *had* hoped that nobody would remember. And now that somebody had, he and the team were swimming in the soup pot.

'But, hey, hey,' the attorney said with jolly cheer, 'I don't want a turf war. Do I want that? Why would I want that? What I want is Phillip Hansen. What *everybody* wants is Hansen. Remember? He's the big fish.'

As a matter of fact Rhyme had largely forgotten about Phillip Hansen, and now that he'd been reminded he understood exactly what Eliopolos was doing. And the insight troubled him a great deal.

Rhyme snuck around Eliopolos like a coyote. 'You've got yourself some good agents out there, do you,' he asked innocently, 'who'll protect the witnesses?'

'At Shoreham?' the attorney responded uncertainly. 'Well, you bet we do. Uh-huh.'

'You've briefed them about security? About how dangerous the Dancer is?' Innocent as a babe.

A pause. 'I've briefed them.'

'And what exactly are their orders?'

'Orders?' Eliopolos asked lamely. He wasn't a stupid man. He knew that he'd been caught.

Rhyme laughed. He glanced at Sellitto and Dellray. 'See, our U.S. attorney friend here has *three* witnesses he hopes can nail Hansen.'

'Three?'

'Percey, Hale . . . and the Dancer himself.' Rhyme scoffed. 'He wants to capture him so he'll turn evidence.' He looked at Eliopolos. 'So *you're* using Percey as bait too.'

'Only,' Dellray chuckled, 'he's putting her in a Havaheart trap. Got it, got it.'

'You're thinking,' Rhyme said, 'that your case against Hansen's not so good, whatever Percey and Hale saw.'

Mr Uh-huh tried sincerity. 'They saw him ditch some goddamn evidence. Hell, they didn't even actually *see* him do that. If we find the duffel bags and it links him to the killings of those two soldiers last spring, fine, we've got a case. Maybe. But, A, we might not find the bags, and, B, the evidence inside them might be damaged.'

Then, C, call *me*, Rhyme thought. I can find evidence in the clear night wind.

Sellitto said, 'But you get Hansen's hit man alive, he can dime his boss.'

'Exactly.' Eliopolos crossed his arms the way he must have done in court, when he was delivering closing statements.

Sachs had been listening from the doorway. She asked the question Rhyme had just been about to. 'And what would you plea the Dancer out to?'

Eliopolos asked, 'Who're you?'

'Officer Sachs. IRD.'

'It's not really a crime scene tech's place to question—'

'Then *I'm* asking the fuckin' question,' Sellitto barked, 'and if I don't get an answer, the mayor's gonna be asking it too.'

Eliopolos had a political career ahead of him, Rhyme supposed. And a successful one, most likely. Eliopolos said, 'It's important that we successfully prosecute Hansen. He's the greater of the two evils. The more potential for harm.'

'That's a pretty answer,' Dellray said, scrunching up his face. 'But it don't do a thing for the question. What're you gonna agree to give the Dancer if he snitches on Hansen?'

'I don't know,' the attorney said evasively. 'That hasn't been discussed.'

'Ten years in medium security?' Sachs muttered.

'It hasn't been *discussed*.'

Rhyme was thinking about the trap that they'd planned so carefully until 4 A.M. If Percey and Hale were moved now, the Dancer would learn of it. He'd regroup. He'd find out they were at Shoreham and, against guards with orders to take him alive, he'd waltz in, kill Percey and Hale – and a half dozen U.S. marshals – and leave.

The attorney began, 'We don't have much time—'

Rhyme interrupted with, 'You have paper?'

'I was hoping you'd be willing to cooperate.'

'We aren't.'

'You're a civilian.'

'*I'm* not,' echoed Sellitto.

'Uh-huh. I see.' He looked at Dellray but didn't even bother asking the agent whose side he was on. The attorney said, 'I can get an order to show cause for protective custody in three or four hours.'

On Sunday morning? Rhyme thought. *Uh-uh.* 'We're not releasing them,' he said. 'Do what you have to do.'

Eliopolos smiled a smile in his round bureaucratic face. 'I should tell you that if this perp dies in any attempt to collar him I will personally be reviewing the shooting committee report, and it is a distinct possibility that I'll conclude that proper orders on the use of deadly force in an arrest situation were not given by supervisory personnel.' He looked at Rhyme. 'There could also be issues of interference by civilians with federal law enforcement activity. That could lead to major civil litigation. I just want you to be forewarned.'

'Thanks,' Rhyme said breezily. 'Appreciate it.'

When he was gone, Sellitto crossed himself. 'Jesus, Linc, you hear him. He said *major* civil litigation.'

'My my my . . . Speaking for myself, *minor* litigation woulda scared this boy plenty,' Dellray chimed in.

They laughed.

Then Dellray stretched and said, 'A pisser what's going round. You hear 'bout it, Lincoln? That bug?'

'What's that?'

'Been infecting a lotta folk lately. My SWAT boys and me're out on some operation or other and what happens but they come down with this nasty twitch in their trigger fingers.'

Sellitto, a much worse actor than the agent, said broadly, 'You too? I thought it was just our folks at ESU.'

'But listen,' said Fred Dellray, the Alec Guinness of street cops. 'I got a cure. All you gotta do is kill yourself a mean asshole, like this Dancer fella, he so much as looks cross-eyed at you. That always works.' He flipped open his phone. 'Think I'll call in and make sure my boys and girls remember 'bout that medicine. I'm gonna do that right now.'

## Chapter
# EIGHTEEN

Waking in the gloomy safe house at dawn, Percey Clay rose from her bed and walked to the window. She drew aside the curtain and looked out at the gray monotonous sky. A slight mist was in the air.

Close to minimums, she estimated. Wind 090 at five knots. Quarter mile visibility. She hoped the weather cleared for the flight tonight. Oh, she could fly in any weather – and had. Anyone with an IFR ticket – instrument flight rules rating – could take off, fly, and land in dense overcast. (In fact, with their computers, transponders, radar, and collision avoidance systems, most commercial airliners could fly themselves – even setting down for a perfect, hands-free landing.) But Percey liked to fly in clear weather. She liked to see the ground pass by beneath her. The lights at night. The clouds. And above her the stars.

*All the stars of evening . . .*

She thought again of Ed and her call to his mother in New Jersey last night. They'd made plans for his memorial service. She wanted to think some more about it, work on the guest list, plan the reception.

But she couldn't. Her mind was preoccupied with Lincoln Rhyme.

Recalling the conversation they'd had yesterday behind closed doors in his bedroom – after the fight with that officer, Amelia Sachs.

She'd sat next to Rhyme in an old armchair. He'd studied her for a moment, looking her up and down. A curious sensation came over her. It wasn't personal perusal – not the way men looked over some women (not her, of course) in bars or on the street. It was the way a senior pilot might study her before their first flight together. Checking her authority, her demeanor, her quickness of thought. Her courage.

She'd pulled her flask from her pocket but Rhyme had shaken his head and suggested eighteen-year-old scotch. 'Thom thinks I drink too much,' he'd said. 'Which I do. But what's life without vices, right?'

She gave a wan laugh. 'My father's a purveyor.'

'Of booze? Or vice in general?'

'Cigarettes. Executive with U.S. Tobacco in Richmond. Excuse me. They're not called that anymore. It's U.S. Consumer Products or something like that.'

There was a flutter of wings outside the window.

'Oh.' She'd laughed. 'It's a tiercel.'

Rhyme had followed her gaze out the window. 'A what?'

'A male peregrine. Why's his aerie down here? They nest higher in the city.'

'I don't know. I woke up one morning and there they were. You know falcons?'

'Sure.'

'Hunt with them?' he asked.

'I used to. I had a tiercel I used for hunting partridge. I got him as an eyas.'

'What's that?'

'A young bird in the nest. They're easier to train.' She'd examined the nest carefully, a faint smile on her face. 'But my best hunter was a haggard – a mature goshawk. Female.

They're bigger than the males, better killers. Hard to work with. But she'd take anything – rabbit, hare, pheasant.'

'You still have her?'

'Oh, no. One day, she was waiting on – that means hovering, looking for prey. Then she just changed her mind. Let a big fat pheasant get away. Flew into a thermal that took her hundreds of feet up. Disappeared into the sun. I staked bait for a month but she never came back.'

'She just vanished?'

'Happens with haggards,' she'd said, shrugging unsentimentally. 'Hey, they're wild animals. But we had a good six months together.' It was this Falcon that had been the inspiration for the Hudson Air logo. Nodding toward the window. 'You're lucky for the company. Have you named them?'

Rhyme'd given a scornful laugh. 'Not the kind of thing I'd do. Thom tried. I laughed him out of the room.'

'Is that officer Sachs really going to arrest me?'

'Oh, I think I can persuade her not to. Say, I have to tell you something.'

'Go ahead.'

'You have a choice to make, you and Hale. That's what I wanted to talk to you about.'

'Choice?'

'We can get you out of town. To a witness protection facility. With the right evasive maneuvers I'm pretty sure we can lose the Dancer and keep you safe for the grand jury.'

'But?' she'd asked.

'But he'll keep after you. And even after the grand jury you'll still be a threat to Phillip Hansen because you'll have to testify at trial. That could be months away.'

'The grand jury might not indict him, no matter what we say,' Percey'd pointed out. 'Then there's no point in killing us.'

'It doesn't matter. Once the Dancer's been hired to kill someone he doesn't stop until they're dead. Besides, the prosecutors'll go after Hansen for killing your husband and you'll be a witness in that case too. Hansen needs you gone.'

'I think I see where you're heading.'

He'd cocked an eyebrow.

'Worm on a hook,' she'd said.

His eyes had crinkled and he'd laughed. 'Well, I'm not going to parade you around in public, just put you into a safe house here in town. Fully guarded. State-of-the-art security. But we'll dig in and keep you there. The Dancer'll surface and we'll stop him, once and for all. It's a crazy idea, but I don't think we have much choice.'

Another tipple of the scotch. It wasn't bad. For a product not bottled in Kentucky. 'Crazy?' she'd repeated. 'Let me ask you a question. You have your role models, Detective? Somebody you admire?'

'Sure. Criminalists. August Vollmer, Edmond Locard.'

'Do you know Beryl Markham?'

'No.'

'Aviatrix in the thirties and forties. She – not Amelia Earhart – was an idol of mine. She led a very dashing life. British upper class. The *Out of Africa* crowd. She was the first person – not first *woman*, the first person – to fly solo across the Atlantic the hard way, east to west. Lindbergh used tailwinds.' She laughed. 'Everybody thought *she* was crazy. Newspapers were running editorials begging her not to try the flight. She did, of course.'

'And made it?'

'Crash-landed short of the airport, but, yeah, she made it. Well, I don't know if that was brave or crazy. Sometimes I don't think there's any difference.'

Rhyme continued. 'You'll be pretty safe, but you won't be completely safe.'

'Let me tell you something. You know that spooky name? That you call the killer?'

'The Dancer.'

'The *Coffin* Dancer. Well, there's a phrase we use in flying jets. The "coffin corner".'

'What's that?'

'It's the margin between the speed your plane stalls at and the speed it starts to break apart from Mach turbulence – when you approach the speed of sound. At sea level you've got a couple hundred miles per hour to play with, but at fifty or sixty thousand feet, your stall speed's maybe five hundred knots per hour and your Mach buffet's about five forty. You don't stay within that forty-knots-per-hour margin, you turn the coffin corner and you've had it. Any planes that fly that high have to have autopilots to keep the speed inside the margin. Well, I'll just say that I fly that high all the time and I hardly ever use an autopilot. Completely safe isn't a concept I'm familiar with.'

'Then you'll do it.'

But Percey didn't answer right away. She scrutinized him for a moment. 'There's more to this, isn't there?'

'More?' Rhyme had asked, but the innocence in his voice had been a thin patina.

'I read the *Times* Metro section. You cops don't go all out like this for just any murderer. What'd Hansen do? He killed a couple of soldiers, and my husband, but you're after him like he's Al Capone.'

'I don't give a damn about Hansen,' quiet Lincoln Rhyme had said, sitting in his motorized throne, with a body that didn't move and eyes that flickered like dark flames, exactly like the eyes of her hawk. She hadn't told Rhyme that she, like him, would never name a hunting bird, that she'd called the haggard merely, 'the falcon'.

Rhyme had continued. 'I want to get the Dancer. He's killed cops, including two who worked for me. I'm *going* to get him.'

Still, she'd sensed there was more. But she hadn't pushed it. 'You'll have to ask Brit too.'

'Of course.'

Finally, she'd said, 'All right, I'll do it.'

'Thank you. I—'

'But,' she interrupted.

'What?'

'There's a condition.'

'What's that?' Rhyme lifted an eyebrow, and Percey had been struck by this thought: once you overlooked his damaged body you saw what a handsome man he was. And, yes, yes, realizing that, she felt her old enemy – the familiar cringe of being in the presence of a good-looking man. Hey, Troll Face, Pug Face, Troll, Trollie, Frog Girl, gotta date for Saturday night? Betcha don't . . .

Percey'd said, 'That I fly the U.S. Medical charter tomorrow night.'

'Oh, I don't think that would be a very good idea.'

'It's a deal breaker,' she'd said, recalling a phrase Ron and Ed used occasionally.

'Why do *you* have to fly?'

'Hudson Air needs this contract. Desperately. It's a narrow-margin flight and we need the best pilot in the company. That's me.'

'What do you mean, narrow margin?'

'Everything's planned out to the nth degree. We're going with minimum fuel. I can't have a pilot wasting time making go-arounds because he's blown the approach or declaring alternates because of minimum conditions.' She'd paused, then added, 'I am *not* letting my company go down the tubes.'

Percey'd said this with an intensity that matched his, but she'd been surprised when he nodded without any protest. 'All right,' Rhyme said. 'I'll agree.'

'Then we have a deal.' She instinctively reached forward to shake his hand but caught herself.

He'd laughed. 'I stick to solely verbal agreements these days.' They sipped the scotch to seal the bargain.

Now, early on Sunday morning, she rested her head against the glass of the safe house. There was so much to do. Getting *Foxtrot Bravo* repaired. Preparing the nav log and the flight plan – which alone would take hours. But still, despite her uneasiness, despite her sorrow about Ed, she felt that indescribable sense of pleasure; she'd be flying tonight.

'Hey,' a friendly voice drawled.

She turned to see Roland Bell in the doorway.

'Morning,' she said.

He walked forward quickly. 'You have those curtains open you better be keepin' low as a bedbaby.' He tugged the drapes shut.

'Oh. I heard Detective Rhyme was springing some trap. Guaranteed to catch him.'

'Well, word is Lincoln Rhyme is all the time right. But I wouldn't trust this particular killer behind a dime. You sleep decent?'

'No,' she said. 'You?'

'I dozed a couple hours aback,' Bell said, peering with sharp eyes out through the curtain. 'But I don't need much sleep. Wake up full of git most days. Havin' youngsters does that to you. Now, just you keep that curtain closed. Remember, this *is* New York City, and think what'd happen to my career if you got yourself winged by some gangsta shootin' stray bullets in the air. I'd have the dry grins for a week, that happened. Now how about some coffee?'

Here were a dozen punchy clouds reflected in the windows of the old town house this Sunday morning.

Here was a hint of rain.

Here was the Wife standing in a bathrobe at the window, her white face surrounded by dark curly hair mussed from just waking.

And here was Stephen Kall, one block away from the Justice Department's safe house on Thirty-fifth Street, blending into the shadows beneath a water tower on the top of an old apartment building, watching her through his Leica binoculars, the reflection of the clouds swimming across her thin body.

He knew that the glass would be bulletproof and would certainly deflect the first shot. He could place another round within four seconds, but she'd stumble backward in reaction to the shattering glass even if she didn't realize she was being fired at. The odds were he couldn't inflict a mortal wound.

Sir, I will stick to my original plan, sir.

A man appeared beside her and the curtain fell back. Then his face peered through the crack, eyes scanning the rooftops where a sniper would logically be positioned. He looked efficient and dangerous. Stephen memorized his appearance.

Then he ducked behind the facade of the building before he was seen.

The police trick – he guessed it was Lincoln the Worm's idea – about moving the Wife and the Friend into the police precinct building on the West Side hadn't fooled him for more than ten minutes. After listening to the Wife and Ron over the tapped line, he'd simply run a renegade software program – a remote star-69 – he'd downloaded from the warez newsgroup on the Internet. It returned a 212 phone number. Manhattan.

What he'd done next was a long shot.

But how are victories won, Soldier?

By considering every possibility, however improbable, sir.

He logged on to the Net and a moment later was typing

the phone number into a reverse phone book, which gave you the address and name of the subscriber. It didn't work with unlisted numbers and Stephen was certain that no one in the federal government would be so stupid as to use a listed number for a safe house.

He was wrong.

The name *James L. Johnson, 258 East 35th Street* popped onto the screen.

Impossible . . .

He then called the Manhattan Federal Building and asked to speak to Mr Johnson. 'That'd be James Johnson.'

'Hold please, I'll put you through.'

'Excuse me,' Stephen interrupted. 'What department is he in again?'

'That'd be the Justice Department. Facilities Management Office.'

Stephen hung up as the call was being transferred.

Once he knew the Wife and Friend were in a safe house on Thirty-fifth Street, he'd stolen some official city maps of the block to plan his assault. Then he'd taken his stroll around the Twentieth Precinct building on the West Side and let himself be seen gazing at the gas pump. After that he'd boosted a gas delivery truck and left plenty of evidence behind so that they'd think he'd be using the truck as a giant gas bomb to take out the witnesses.

And so here was Stephen Kall now, within small-arms range of the Wife and the Friend.

Thinking of the job, trying not to think about the obvious parallel: the face in the window, looking for him.

A little cringey, not too bad. A little wormy.

The curtain closed. Stephen now examined the safe house again.

It was a three-story building unattached to adjacent buildings, the alley like a dark mote around the structure. The walls were brownstone – the hardest building material other than granite or marble to tunnel or blast through – and the windows were blocked with bars that looked like old iron but that Stephen knew were really case-hardened steel and would be wired with motion or decibel sensors or both.

The fire escape was real, but if you looked closely you could see that behind the curtained windows was darkness. Probably sheet steel bolted to the inside frame. He'd found the real fire door – behind a large theatrical poster pasted to the brick. (Why would anyone put up an ad in an alley unless it was to disguise a door?) The alley itself looked like any other in midtown, cobblestone and asphalt, but he could see the glass eyes of security cameras recessed into the walls. Still, there were trash bags and several Dumpsters in the alley that would provide pretty good cover. He could climb into the alley from a window in the office building next door and use the Dumpsters for cover to get to the fire door.

In fact, there was an open window on the first floor of the office building, a curtain blowing in and out. Whoever was monitoring the security screens would have seen the motion and become used to it. Stephen could drop through the window, six feet to the ground, and then move behind the Dumpster and crawl to the fire door.

He also knew they wouldn't be expecting him here – he'd heard the reports of an evacuation of all the buildings near the Twentieth Precinct, so they'd really believed that he'd try to get a gas truck bomb close to the station house.

*Evaluate, Soldier.*

*Sir, my evaluation is that the enemy is relying on both physical structure and anonymity of the premises for defense. I note the absence of large numbers of tactical personnel and I have concluded that a single-person assault on the premises has a good likelihood of success in eliminating one or both of the targets, sir.*

Despite the confidence, though, he felt momentarily cringey.

Picturing Lincoln searching for him. Lincoln the Worm. A big lumpy thing, a larva, moist with worm moisture, looking everywhere, seeing through walls, oozing up through cracks.

Looking through windows . . .

Crawling up his leg.

Chewing on his flesh.

Wash 'em off. Wash them off!

Wash what off, Soldier? You still harping on those fucking worms?

Sir, I am . . . Sir, no, sir.

Are you going soft on me, Soldier? Are you feeling like a little pussy *schoolgirl*?

Sir, no sir. I am a knife blade, sir. I am pure death. I have a hard-on to kill, sir!

Breathed deeply. Slowly calmed.

He hid the guitar case containing the Model 40 on the roof, under a wooden water tower. The rest of the equipment he transferred to a large book bag, and then pulled on the Columbia University windbreaker and his baseball cap.

He climbed down the fire escape and disappeared into the alley, feeling ashamed, even scared – not of his enemy's bullets but of the piercing hot gaze of Lincoln the Worm, moving closer, easing slowly but relentlessly through the city, looking for him.

Stephen had planned on an invasive entry, but he didn't have to kill a soul. The office building next to the safe house was empty.

The lobby was deserted and there were no security cameras inside. The main door was wedged partly open with a rubber doorstop and he saw dollies and furniture pads stacked beside it. It was tempting, but he didn't want to run into any movers or tenants, so he stepped outside again and slipped around the corner, away from the safe house. He eased behind a potted pine tree, which hid him from the sidewalk. With his elbow he broke the narrow window leading into a darkened office – of a psychiatrist, it turned out – and climbed in. He stood completely still for five minutes, pistol in hand. Nothing. He then eased silently out the door and into the first-floor corridor of the building.

He paused outside the office he believed was the one with the window opening onto the alley – the one with the blowing curtain. Stephen reached for the doorknob.

But instinct told him to change his plans. He decided to try the basement. He found the stairs and descended into the musty warren of basement rooms.

Stephen worked his way silently toward the side of the building closest to the safe house and pushed open a steel door. He walked into a dimly lit twenty-by-twenty room filled with boxes and old appliances. He found a head-high window that opened onto the alley.

It'd be a tight fit. He'd have to remove the glass and the frame. But once he was out he could slip directly behind a pile of trash bags and in a sniper's low crawl make his way to the fire door of the safe house. Much safer than the window upstairs.

Stephen thought: I've done it.

He'd fooled them all.

Fooled Lincoln the Worm! This gave him as much pleasure as killing the two victims would.

He took a screwdriver from his book bag and began to work the glazier's putty out of the window. The gray wads came away slowly and he was so absorbed in his task that by the time he dropped the screwdriver and got his hand on the butt of his Beretta, the man was on top of him, shoving a pistol into Stephen's neck and telling him in a whisper, 'You move an inch and you're dead.'

# CRAFTSMANSHIP

[The falcon] began to fly. To fly: the horrible aerial toad, the silent-feathered owl, the hump-backed aviating Richard III, he made toward me close to the ground. His wings beat with a measured purpose, the two eyes of his low-held head fixed me with a ghoulish concentration.

*THE GOSHAWK*, T. H. WHITE

## Chapter
# NINETEEN

Short-barrel, probably Colt or Smittie or Dago knockoff, not fired recently. Or oiled.

I smell rust.

And what does a rusty gun tell us, Soldier?

Plenty, sir.

Stephen Kall lifted his hands.

The high, unsteady voice said, 'Drop your gun over there. And your walkie-talkie.'

*Walkie-talkie?*

'Come on, do it. I'll blow your brains out.' The voice crackled with desperation. He sniffled wetly.

Soldier, do professionals threaten?

Sir, they do not. This man is an amateur. Should we immobilize him?

Not yet. He still represents a threat.

Sir, yessir.

Stephen dropped his gun on a cardboard box.

'Where . . . ? Come on, where's your radio?'

'I don't have a radio,' Stephen said.

'Turn around. And don't try anything.'

Stephen eased around and found himself looking at a

skinny man with darting eyes. He was filthy and looked sick. His nose ran and his eyes were an alarming red. His thick brown hair was matted. And he stank. Homeless, probably. A wino, his stepfather would have called him. Or a hophead.

The old battered snub-nose Colt was thrust forward at Stephen's belly and the hammer was back. It wouldn't take much for the cams to slip, especially if it was old. Stephen smiled a benign smile. He didn't move a muscle. 'Look,' he said, 'I don't want any trouble.'

'Where's your radio?!' the man blurted.

'I don't *have* a radio.'

The man nervously patted his captive's chest. Stephen could have killed him easily – the man's attention kept wandering. He felt the skittering fingers glide over his body, probing. Finally the man stepped back. 'Where's your partner?'

'Who?'

'Don't give me any shit. You know.'

Suddenly cringey again. Wormy . . . Something was wrong. 'I really don't know what you mean.'

'The cop who was just here.'

'Cop?' Stephen whispered. 'In *this* building?'

The man's rheumy eyes flickered with uncertainty. 'Yeah. Aren't you his partner?'

Stephen walked to the window and looked out.

'Hold it. I'll shoot.'

'Point that someplace else,' Stephen commanded, glancing over his shoulder. No longer worried about slipping cams. He was beginning to see the extent of his mistake. He felt sick to his stomach.

The man's voice cracked as he threatened, 'Stop. Right there. I fucking mean it.'

'Are they in the alley too?' Stephen asked calmly.

A moment of confused silence. 'You really aren't a cop?'

'Are they in the alley too?' Stephen repeated firmly.

The man looked uneasily around the room. 'A bunch of them were a while ago. They're the ones put those trash bags there. I don't know 'bout now.'

Stephen stared into the alley. The trash bags . . . They'd been left there to lure me out. False cover.

'If you signal anybody, I swear—'

'Oh, be quiet.' Stephen scanned the alley slowly, patient as a boa, and finally he saw a faint shadow on the cobblestones – behind a Dumpster. It moved an inch or two.

And on top of the building behind the safe house – on the elevator tower – he saw a ripple of shadow. They were too good to let their gun muzzles show but not good enough to think about blocking the light reflecting upward from the standing water that covered the roof of the building.

Jesus, Lord . . . Somehow Lincoln the Fucking Worm had known that Stephen wouldn't buy the setup about the Twentieth Precinct. They'd been expecting him *here* all along. Lincoln had even figured out his strategy – that Stephen would try to get through the alley from *this* very building.

The face in the window . . .

Stephen suddenly had the absurd idea that it had been Lincoln the Worm in Alexandria, Virginia, standing in the window, lit with rosy light, looking at him. He couldn't have been the one, of course. Still, that impossibility didn't stop the cringey, pukey nausea from unfurling in Stephen's gut.

The chocked door, the open window, and the fluttering curtain . . . a fucking welcome mat. And the alley: a perfect kill zone.

The only thing that had saved him was his instinct.

Lincoln the Worm had set him up.

Who the hell *is* he?

Rage boiled in him. A wave of heat swept over his body. If they were expecting him they'd be following S&S procedures – search and surveillance. Which meant the cop this little shit had seen would be coming back soon to check this room. Stephen spun around to the thin man. 'When was the last time the cop checked in here?'

The man's apprehensive eyes flickered, then blossomed with fear.

'Answer me,' Stephen snapped, despite the black bore of the Colt pointed at him.

'Ten minutes ago.'

'What kind of weapon does he have?'

'I don't know. I guess one of those fancy ones. Like a machine gun.'

'Who *are* you?' Stephen asked.

'I don't have to answer your fucking questions,' the man said defiantly. He wiped his runny nose on his sleeve. And made the mistake of doing this with his gun hand. In a flash Stephen lifted the gun away from him and shoved the little man to the floor.

'No! Don't hurt me.'

'Shut up,' Stephen barked. Instinctively he opened the little Colt to see how many rounds were in the cylinder. There were none. 'It's empty?' he asked, incredulous.

The man shrugged. 'I—'

'You were threatening me with an unloaded weapon?'

'Well . . . See, if they catch you and it's not loaded, they don't put you away for as long.'

Stephen didn't understand the point. He thought he might just kill the man for the stupidity of carrying an unloaded gun. 'What're you doing here?'

'Just go away and leave me alone,' the man whimpered, struggling to climb to his feet.

Stephen dropped the Colt into his pocket then snagged his Beretta and trained it at the man's head. 'What are you doing here?'

He wiped his face again. 'There're doctors' offices upstairs.

And nobody's here on Sunday so I hit 'em for, you know, samples.'

'Samples?'

'Doctors get all these free samples of drugs and shit and there's no record, so you can steal as much as you want and nobody knows. Percodan, Fiorinol, diet pills, stuff like that.'

But Stephen wasn't listening. He felt the chill of the Worm again. Lincoln was very close.

'Hey, you all right?' the man asked, looking at Stephen's face.

Oddly, the worms went away.

'What's your name?' Stephen asked.

'Jodie. Well, Joe D'Oforio. But everybody, like, calls me Jodie. What's yours?'

Stephen didn't answer. Staring out the window. Another shadow moved on top of the building behind the safe house.

'Okay, Jodie. Listen up. You want to make some money?'

'Well?' Rhyme asked impatiently. 'What's going *on*?'

'He's still in the building to the east of the safe house. He hasn't gone into the alley yet.' Sellitto reported.

'Why not? He *has* to. There's no reason for him not to. What's the problem?'

'They're checking every floor. He's not in the office we thought he'd go for.'

The one with the open window. Damn! Rhyme had debated about leaving the window open, letting the curtain blow in and out, tempting him. But it was too obvious. The Dancer'd become suspicious.

'Everybody's loaded and locked?' Rhyme asked.

'Of course. Relax.'

But he couldn't relax. Rhyme hadn't known exactly how the Dancer would try his assault on the safe house. He'd been sure, though, it would be through the alley. He'd hoped that the trash bags and Dumpsters would lull him into thinking there was enough cover to make his approach from that direction. Dellray's agents and Haumann's 32-E teams were surrounding the alley, in the office building itself, and on the buildings around the safe house. Sachs was with Haumann, Sellitto, and Dellray in a fake UPS van parked up the block from the house.

Rhyme had been temporarily fooled by the feint with the supposed gas truck bomb. That the Dancer would drop a tool at a crime scene was improbable but somewhat credible. But then Rhyme grew suspicious about the quantity of detonating cord residue on the clippers. It suggested that the Dancer had smeared the blade with explosive to make sure the police thought he'd try an assault on the precinct house with a bomb. He decided that, no, the Dancer hadn't been losing his touch – as he and Sachs had originally thought. Being spotted surveying his intended route of attack and then leaving a guard alive so that the man could call the police and tell them about the theft of the truck – those were intentional.

The final gram tipping the scales, though, was physical evidence. Ammonia bound to a paper fiber. There are only two sources for that combination – old architectural blueprints and land plat maps, which were reproduced by large-sheet ammonia printers. Rhyme had had Sellitto call Police Plaza and ask about break-ins at architectural firms or the county deeds office. A report came back that the recorder's office had been broken into. Rhyme asked them to check East Thirty-fifth Street, amazing the city guards, who reported that, yes, those plats were missing.

Though how the Dancer'd found out that Percey and Brit were at the safe house and what its address was remained a mystery.

Five minutes ago two ESU officers had found a broken window on the first floor of the office building. The Dancer'd shunned the open front door but had still moved in for the assault on the safe house through the alley just as Rhyme had predicted. But something had spooked him. He was loose in the building and they had no idea where. A poisonous snake in a dark room. Where was he, what was he planning?

*Too many ways to die . . .*

'He wouldn't wait,' Rhyme muttered. 'It's too risky.' He was growing frantic.

An agent called in, 'Nothing on the first floor. We're still making our rounds.'

Five minutes passed. Guards checked in with negative reports but all Rhyme really heard was the static rustling in his headset.

Jodie answered, 'Who doesn't wanna make money? But I don't know doing what.'

'Help me get out of here.'

'I mean, what're you doing here? Are they looking for *you*?'

Stephen looked the sad little man up and down. A loser, but not crazy or stupid. Stephen decided it was best tactically to be honest. Besides, the man'd be dead in a few hours anyway.

He said, 'I've come here to kill somebody.'

'Whoa. Like, are you in the Mafia or something? Who're you gonna kill?'

'Jodie, be quiet. We're in a tough situation here.'

'*We?* I didn't do anything.'

'Except you're at the wrong place at the wrong time,' Stephen said. 'And that's too bad, but you're in the same situation I am because they want me and they aren't going to believe you're not with me. Now, you gonna help me or not? All I've got time for is yes or no.'

Jodie tried not to look scared, but his eyes betrayed him.

'Yes. Or. No.'

'I don't want to get hurt.'

'If you're on my side you'll never get hurt. One thing I'm good at is making sure who gets hurt and who doesn't.'

'And you'll pay me? Money? Not a check.'

Stephen had to laugh. 'Not a check. No. Cash.'

The jelly beans of eyes were considering something. 'How much?'

The little crud was negotiating.

'Five thousand.'

The fear remained in the eyes but it was pushed aside by shock. 'For real? You're not shitting me?'

'No.'

'What if I get you out and you kill me so you don't have to pay?'

Stephen laughed again. 'I'm getting paid a lot more than that. Five's nothing to me. Anyway, if we get out of here I could use your help again.'

'I—'

A sound in the distance. Footsteps coming closer.

It was the S&S cop, looking for him.

Just one, Stephen could tell, listening to the steps. Made sense. They'd be expecting him to go for the first floor office with the open window, where Lincoln the Worm would've stationed most of the troopers.

Stephen replaced the pistol in his book bag and pulled out his knife. 'You going to help me?'

A no-brainer, of course. If Jodie didn't help he'd be dead in sixty seconds. And he knew it.

'Okay.' He extended his hand.

Stephen ignored it and asked, 'How do we get out?'

'See those cinder blocks there. You can pull 'em out. See, there? It leads to an old tunnel. There're these delivery tunnels going underneath the city. Nobody knows about them.'

'There are?' Stephen wished he'd known it before.

'I can get us to the subway. That's where I live. This old subway station.'

It was two years since Stephen had worked with a partner. Sometimes he wished he hadn't killed the man.

Jodie started toward the concrete blocks.

'No,' Stephen whispered. 'Here's what I want you to do. You stand against that wall. There.' He pointed to a wall opposite the doorway.

'But he'll see me. He checks in here with his flashlight and I'll be the first thing he'll see!'

'Just stand there and put your hands up.'

'He'll shoot me,' Jodie whimpered.

'No, he won't. You've got to trust me.'

'But . . .' His eyes darted toward the door. He wiped his face.

Is this man going to buckle, Soldier?

That is a risk, sir, but I've considered the odds and I think he won't. This is a man who wants money badly.

'You'll have to trust me.'

Jodie sighed. 'Okay, okay . . .'

'Make sure your hands are up or he *will* shoot.'

'Like this?' He lifted his arms.

'Step back so your face is in the shadows. Yeah, like that. I don't want him to see your face . . . Good. Perfect.'

The footsteps were coming closer now. Walking softly. Hesitating.

Stephen touched his fingers to his lips and went prone, disappearing into the floor.

The footsteps grew soft and then paused. The figure appeared in the doorway. He was in body armor and wore an FBI windbreaker.

He pushed into the room, scanning with the flashlight attached to the end of his H&K. When the beam caught Jodie's midriff he did something that astonished Stephen.

He started to pull the trigger.

It was very subtle. But Stephen had shot so many animals and so many people that he knew the ripple of muscles, the tension of stance, just before you fired your weapon.

Stephen moved fast. He leapt up, lifting the machine gun away and breaking off the agent's stalk microphone. Then he drove his k-bar knife up under the agent's triceps, paralyzing his right arm. The man cried out in pain.

They're green-lighted to kill! Stephen thought. No surrender pitch. They see me, they shoot. Armed or not.

Jodie cried, 'Oh, my God!' He stepped forward uncertainly, hands still airborne – almost comically.

Stephen knocked the agent to his knees and pulled his Kevlar helmet over his eyes, gagged him with a rag.

'Oh, God, you stabbed him,' Jodie said, lowering his arms and walking forward.

'Shut up,' Stephen said. 'What we talked about. The exit.'

'But—'

'Now.'

Jodie just stared.

'Now!' Stephen raged.

Jodie ran to the hole in the wall as Stephen pulled the agent to his feet and led him into the the corridor.

Green-lighted to kill . . .

Lincoln the Worm had decided he'd die. Stephen was furious.

'Wait there,' he ordered Jodie.

Stephen plugged the headset back into the man's transceiver and listened. They were on the Special Operations channel and there must have been a dozen or so cops and agents, calling in as they searched different parts of the building.

He didn't have much time, but he had to slow them up.

Stephen led the dazed agent out into the yellow hallway.

He pulled out his knife again.

## Chapter
# TWENTY

'Damn. *Damn!*' Rhyme snapped, flecking his chin with spittle. Thom stepped up to the chair and wiped it, but Rhyme angrily shook him away.

'Bo?' he called into his microphone.

'Go ahead,' Haumann said from the command van.

'I think somehow he made us and's going to fight his way out. Tell your agents to form defensive teams. I don't want anybody alone. Move everybody into the building. I think—'

'Hold on . . . Hold on. Oh, no . . .'

'Bo? Sachs? . . . Anybody?'

But nobody answered.

Rhyme heard shouting voices through the radio. The transmission was cut off. Then staccato bursts: '. . . assistance. We've got a blood trail . . . In the office building. Right, right . . . no . . . downstairs . . . Basement. Innelman's not reporting in. He was . . . basement. All units move, move. Come on, *move!* . . .'

Rhyme called, 'Bell, you hear me? Double up on the principals. Do not, repeat, do not leave them unguarded. The Dancer's loose and we don't know where he is.'

Roland Bell's calm voice came over the line. 'Got 'em under our wing. Nobody's getting in here.'

An infuriating wait. Unbearable. Rhyme wanted to scream with frustration.

Where was he?

*A snake in a dark room* . . .

Then one by one the troopers and agents called in, telling Haumann and Dellray that they'd secured one floor after another.

Finally, Rhyme heard: 'Basement's secure. But Jesus Lord there's a lot of blood down here. And Innelman's gone. We can't find him! Jesus, all this blood!'

'Rhyme, can you hear me?'

'Go ahead.'

'I'm in the basement of the office building,' Amelia Sachs said into her stalk mike, looking around her.

The walls were filthy yellow concrete and the floors were painted battleship gray. But you hardly noticed the decor of the dank place; blood spatter was everywhere, like a horrific Jackson Pollock painting.

The poor agent, she thought. Innelman. Better find him fast. Someone bleeding this much couldn't last more than fifteen minutes.

'You have the kit?' Rhyme asked her.

'We don't have time! All the blood, we've got to find him!'

'Steady, Sachs. The kit. Open the kit.'

She sighed. 'All right! Got it.'

The crime scene blood kit contained a ruler, protractor with string attached, tape measure, the Kastle-Meyer Reagent presumptive field test. Luminol too – which detects iron oxide residue of blood even when a perp scrubs away all visual trace.

'It's just a mess, Rhyme,' she said. 'I'm not going to be able to figure out anything.'

'Oh, the scene'll tell us more than you think, Sachs. It'll tell us plenty.'

Well, if anybody could make sense of this macabre setting, it would be Rhyme; she knew that he and Mel Cooper were long-standing members of the International Association of Blood Pattern Analysts. (She didn't know which was more disturbing – the gruesome blood spatter at crime scenes or the fact that there was a group of people who specialized in the subject.) But this seemed hopeless.

'We've got to *find* him . . .'

'Sachs, calm down . . . You with me?'

After a moment she said, 'Okay.'

'All you need for now is the ruler,' he said. 'First, tell me what you see.'

'There're drips all over the place here.'

'Blood spatter's very revealing. But it's meaningless unless the surface it's on is uniform. What's the floor like?'

'Smooth concrete.'

'Good. How big are the drops? Measure them.'

'He's *dying*, Rhyme.'

'How *big*?' he snapped.

'All different sizes. There're hundreds of them about three-quarters of an inch. Some are bigger. About an inch and a quarter. Thousands of very little ones. Like a spray.'

'Forget the little ones. They're "overcast" drops, satellites of the others. Describe the biggest ones. Shape?'

'Mostly round.'

'Scalloped edges?'

'Yes,' she muttered. 'But there are some that just have smooth edges. Here're some in front of me. They're a little smaller, though.'

Where *is* he? she wondered. Innelman. A man she'd never met. Missing and bleeding like a fountain.

'Sachs?'

'What?' she snapped.

'What about the smaller drops? Tell me about them.'

'We don't have time to do this!'

'We don't have time *not* to,' he said calmly.

God damn you, Rhyme, she thought, then said, 'All right.' She measured. 'They're about a half inch. Perfectly round. No scalloped edges . . .'

'Where are those?' he asked urgently. 'At one end of the corridor, or the other?'

'Mostly in the middle. There's a storeroom at the end of the hall. Inside there and near it they're bigger and have ragged or scalloped edges. At the other end of the corridor, they're smaller.'

'Okay, okay,' Rhyme said absently, then he announced, 'Here's the story . . . What's the agent's name?'

'Innelman. John Innelman. He's a friend of Dellray's.'

'The Dancer got Innelman in the storeroom, stabbed him once, high. Debilitated him, probably arm or neck. Those are the big, uneven drops. Then he led him down the corridor, stabbing him again, lower. Those are the smaller, rounder ones. The shorter the distance blood falls, the more even the edges.'

'Why'd he do that?' she gasped.

'To slow us down. He knows we'll look for a wounded agent before we start after him.'

He's right, she thought, but we're not looking *fast* enough!

'How long's the corridor?'

She sighed, looked down it. 'About fifty feet, give or take, and the blood trail covers the whole thing.'

'Any footprints in the blood?'

'Dozens. They go everywhere. Wait . . . There's a service elevator. I didn't see it at first. That's where the trail leads! He must be inside. We have to—'

'No, Sachs, wait. That's too obvious.'

'We have to get the elevator door open. I'm calling the Fire Department for somebody with a Halligan tool or an elevator key. They can—'

Calmly Rhyme said, 'Listen to me. Do the drops leading to the elevator look like teardrops? With the tails pointing in different directions?'

'He's got to be in the elevator! There's smears on the door. He's dying, Rhyme! Will you listen to me!'

'Teardrops, Sachs?' he asked soothingly. 'Do they look like tadpoles?'

She looked down. They did. Perfect tadpoles, with the tails pointing in a dozen different directions.

'Yeah, Rhyme. They do.'

'Backtrack until those stop.'

This was crazy. Innelman was bleeding out in the elevator shaft. She gazed at the metal door for a moment, thought about ignoring Rhyme, but then trotted back down the corridor.

To the place where they stopped.

'Here, Rhyme. They stop here.'

'It's at a closet or door?'

'Yes, how'd you know?'

'And it's bolted from the outside?'

'That's right.'

How the hell does he *do* it?

'So the search team'd see the bolt and pass it by – the Dancer couldn't very well bolt himself inside. Well, Innelman's in there. Open the door, Sachs. Use the pliers on the handle, not the knob itself. There's a chance we can lift a print. And Sachs?'

'Yes?'

'I don't think he left a bomb. He hardly had time. But whatever shape the agent's in, and it won't be good, ignore him for a minute and look for any traps first.'

'Okay.'

'Promise?'

'Yes.'

Pliers out . . . unbolt the latch . . . twist the knob.

Glock up. Apply poundage. Now!

The door flew outward.

But there was no bomb or other trap. Just the pale, blood-slicked body of John Innelman, unconscious, tumbling to her feet.

She barked a soft scream. 'He's here. Need medics! He's cut bad.'

Sachs bent over him. Two EMS techs and more agents ran up, Dellray with them, grim faced.

'What'd he do to you, John? Oh, man.' The lanky agent stood back while the medics went to work. They cut off much of his clothing and examined the stab wounds. Innelman's eyes were half open, glazed.

'Is he . . . ?' Dellray asked.

'Alive, just barely.'

The medics slapped pads on the slashes, put a tourniquet on his leg and arm, and then ran a plasma line. 'Get him in the bus. We gotta move. I mean, move!'

They placed the agent on a gurney and hurried down the corridor, Dellray with him, head down, muttering to himself and squeezing his dead cigarette between his fingers.

'Could he talk?' Rhyme asked. 'Any clue where the Dancer went?'

'No. He was unconscious. I don't know if they can save him. Jesus.'

'Don't get rattled, Sachs. We've got a crime scene to analyze. We *have* to find out where the Dancer is, if he's still around. Go back to the storeroom. See if there are exterior doors or windows.'

As she walked to it she asked, 'How'd you know about the closet?'

'Because of the direction of the drops. He shoved Innelman inside and soaked a rag in the cop's blood. He walked to the elevator, swinging the rag. The drops were moving in different directions when they fell. So they had a teardrop appearance. And since he tried leading us to the elevator, we should look in the opposite direction for his escape route. The storeroom. Are you there?'

'Yes.'

'Describe it.'

'There's a window looking out on the alley. Looks like he started to open it. But it's puttied shut. No doors.' She looked out the window. 'I can't see any of the troopers' positions, though. I don't know what tipped him.'

'*You* can't see any of the troopers,' Rhyme said cynically. 'He could. Now, walk the grid and let's see what we find.'

She searched the scene carefully, walking the grid, then vacuumed for trace and carefully bagged the filters.

'What do you see? Anything?'

She shone her light on the walls and she found two mismatched blocks. A tight squeeze, but someone limber could have fit through there.

'Got his exit route, Rhyme. He went through the wall. Some loose concrete blocks.'

'Don't open it. Get SWAT there.'

She called several agents down to the room and they pulled the blocks out, sweeping the inner chamber with flashlights mounted on the barrels of their H&K submachine guns.

'Clear,' one agent called. Sachs drew her weapon and slipped into the cool, dank space.

It was a narrow declining ramp filled with rubble, leading through a hole in the foundation. Water dripped. She was careful to step on large chunks of concrete and leave the damp earth untouched.

'What do you see, Sachs? Tell me!'

She waved the PoliLight wand over the places where the Dancer would logically have gripped with his hands and stepped with his feet. 'Whoa, Rhyme.'

'What?'

'Fingerprints. Fresh latents . . . Wait. But here're the glove prints too. In blood. From holding the rag. I don't get it. It's like a cave . . . Maybe he took the gloves off for some reason. Maybe he thought he was safe in the tunnel.'

Then she looked down and shone the eerie glow of yellow-green light at her feet. 'Oh.'

'What?'

'They're not his prints. He's with somebody else.'

'Somebody else? How do you know?'

'There's another set of footprints too. They're both fresh. One bigger than the other. They go off in the same direction, running. Jesus, Rhyme.'

'What's the matter?'

'It means he's got a partner.'

'Come on, Sachs. The glass is half full.' Rhyme added cheerfully, 'It means we'll have twice as much evidence to help us track him down.'

'I was thinking,' she said darkly, 'that it meant he'd be twice as dangerous.'

'What've you got?' Lincoln Rhyme asked.

Sachs had returned to his town house and she and Mel Cooper were looking over the evidence collected at the scene. Sachs and SWAT had followed the footsteps into a Con Ed access tunnel, where they lost track of both the Dancer and his companion. It looked as if the men had climbed to the street and escaped through a manhole.

She gave Cooper the print she'd found in the entrance to the tunnel. He scanned it into the computer and sent it off to the feds for an AFIS search.

Then she held up two electrostatic prints for Rhyme to examine. 'These're the footprints in the tunnel. This one's the Dancer's.' She lifted one of the prints – transparent, like an X ray. 'It matches a print in the shrink's office he broke into on the first floor.'

'Wearing average ordinary factory shoes,' Rhyme said.

'You'd think he'd be in combat boots,' Sellitto muttered.

'No, those'd be too obvious. Work shoes have rubber soles for gripping and steel caps in the toes. They're as good as boots if you don't need ankle support. Hold the other one closer, Sachs.'

The smaller shoes were very worn at the heel and the ball of the foot. There was a large hole in the right shoes and through it you could see a lattice of skin wrinkles.

'No socks. Could be his friend's homeless.'

'Why's he got somebody with him?' Cooper asked.

'Don't know,' Sellitto said. 'Word is he always works alone. He uses people but he doesn't trust them.'

Just what I've been accused of, Rhyme thought. He said, 'And leaving fingerprints at the scene? This guy's no pro. He must have something the Dancer needs.'

'A way out of the building, for one thing,' Sachs suggested.

'That could be it.'

'And's probably dead now,' she suggested.

Probably, Rhyme agreed silently.

'The prints,' Cooper said. 'They're pretty small. I'd guess size eight male.'

The size of the sole doesn't necessarily correspond to shoe size and provides even less insight into the stature of the person wearing them, but it was reasonable to conclude the Dancer's partner had a slight build.

Turning to the trace evidence, Cooper mounted samples onto a slide and slipped it under the compound 'scope. He patched the image through to Rhyme's computer.

'Command mode, cursor left,' Rhyme ordered into his microphone. 'Stop. Double click.' He examined the computer monitor. 'More of the mortar from the cinder block. Dirt and dust . . . Where'd you get this, Sachs?'

'I scraped it from around the cinder blocks and vacuumed the floor of the tunnel. I also found a nest behind some boxes where it looked like somebody'd been hiding.'

'Good. Okay, Mel, gas it. There's a lot of stuff here I don't recognize.'

The chromatograph rumbled, separating the compounds, and sent the resulting vapors to the spectrometer for identification. Cooper examined the screen.

He exhaled a surprised breath. 'I'm surprised his friend's able to walk at all.'

'Little more specific there, Mel.'

'He's a drug store, Lincoln. We've got secobarbital, phenobarbital, Dexedrine, amobarbital, meprobamate, chlordiazepoxide, diazepam.'

'Jesus,' Sellitto muttered. 'Reds, dexies, blue devils . . .'

Cooper continued, 'Lactose and sucrose too. Calcium, vitamins, enzymes consistent with dairy products.'

'Baby formula,' Rhyme muttered. 'Dealers use it to cut drugs.'

'So the Dancer's got himself a cluckhead for a sidekick. Go figure.'

Sachs said, 'All those doctors' offices there . . . This guy must've been boosting pills.'

'Log onto FINEST,' Rhyme said. 'Get a list of every drugstore cowboy they've got.'

Sellitto laughed. 'It's gonna be big as the White Pages, Lincoln.'

'Nobody says it's easy, Lon.'

But before he could make the call, Cooper received an E-mail. 'Don't bother.'

'Huh?'

'The AFIS report on the fingerprints?' The tech tapped the screen. 'Whoever the guy is, he doesn't have a record in New York City or State or NCIC.'

'Hell!' Rhyme snapped. He felt cursed. Couldn't it be just a little easier? He muttered, 'Any other trace?'

'Something here,' Cooper said. 'A bit of blue tile, grouted on the back, attached to what looks like concrete.'

'Let's see it.'

Cooper mounted the specimen onto the 'scope's stage.

His neck quivering, almost breaking into a spasm, Rhyme leaned forward and studied it carefully. 'Okay. Old mosaic tile. Porcelain, crackle finish, lead based. Sixty, seventy years old, I'd guess.' But he could make no cunning deductions from the sample. 'Anything else?' he muttered.

'Some hairs.' Cooper mounted them to do a visual. He bent over the 'scope.

Rhyme too examined the thin shafts.

'Animal,' he announced.

'More cats?' Sachs asked.

'Let's see,' Cooper said, head down.

But these hairs weren't feline. They were rodent. 'Rat,' Rhyme announced. '*Rattus norvegicus*. Your basic sewer rat.'

'Keep going. What's in that bag, Sachs?' Rhyme asked like a hungry boy looking over chocolates in a candy store display case. 'No, no. There. Yes, that one.'

Inside the evidence bag was a square of paper towel smeared with a faint brown stain.

'I found that on the cinder block, the one he moved. I think it was on his hands. There were no prints but the pattern could've been made by a palm.'

'Why do you think that?'

'Because I rubbed my hand in some dirt and pushed on another cinder block. The mark was the same.'

That's my Amelia, he thought. For an instant his thoughts

returned to last night – the two of them lying in bed together. He pushed the thought away.

'What is it, Mel?'

'Looks like it's grease. Impregnated with dust, dirt, fragments of wood, bits of organic material. Animal flesh, I think. All very old. And look there in the upper corner.'

Rhyme examined some silvery flecks on his computer screen. 'Metal. Ground or shaved off of something. Gas it. Let's find out for certain.'

Cooper did.

'Petrochemical,' he answered. 'Crudely refined, no additives . . . . There's iron with traces of manganese, silicon, and carbon.'

'Wait,' Rhyme called. 'Any other elements – chromium, cobalt, copper, nickel, tungsten?'

'No.'

Rhyme gazed at the ceiling. 'The metal? It's old steel, made from pig iron in a Bessemer furnace. If it were modern it'd have some of those other materials in it.'

'And here's something else. Coal tar.'

'Creosote!' Rhyme cried. 'I've got it. The Dancer's first big mistake. His partner's a walking road map.'

'To where?' Sachs asked.

'To the subway. That grease is old, the steel's from old fixtures and tie spikes, the creosote's from the ties. Oh, and the fragment of tile is from a mosaic. A lot of the old stations were tiled – they had pictures of something that related to the neighborhood.'

Sachs said, 'Sure – the Astor Place station's got mosaics of the animals that John Jacob Astor traded.'

'Grouted porcelain tile. So that's what the Dancer wanted him for. A place to hide out. The Dancer's friend's probably a homeless druggie living in an abandoned siding or tunnel or station somewhere.'

Rhyme realized that everyone was looking at a man's shadow in the doorway. He stopped speaking.

'Dellray?' Sellitto said uncertainly.

The dark, somber face of Fred Dellray was focused out the window.

'What is it?' Rhyme asked.

'Innelman's what it is. They stitched him up. Three hundred stitches they gave him. But it was too late. Lost too much blood. He just died.'

'I'm sorry,' Sachs said.

The agent lifted his hands, long sticklike fingers raised like spikes.

Everyone in the room knew about Dellray's long-time partner – the one killed in the Oklahoma City federal building bombing. And Rhyme thought too of Tony Panelli – 'napped downtown a few days ago. Probably dead by now, the only clue to his whereabouts the grains of curious sand.

And now another of Dellray's friends was gone.

The agent paced in a threatening lope.

'You know why he got cut, don't you – Innelman?'

Everyone knew; no one answered.

'A diversion. That's the only reason in the world. To keep us off the scent. Can you believe that? A fuckin' di-version.' He stopped pacing abruptly. He looked at Rhyme with his frightening black eyes. 'You got any leads at all, Lincoln?'

'Not much.' He explained about the Dancer's homeless friend, the drugs, the hidey-hole in the subway. Somewhere.

'That's it?'

'Afraid so. But we still have some more evidence to look at.'

'Evidence,' Dellray whispered contemptuously. He walked to the door, paused. 'A distraction. That's no fucking reason for a good man to die. No reason at all.'

'Fred, wait . . . we need you.'

But the agent didn't hear, or he ignored Rhyme if he did. He stalked out of the room.

A moment later the door downstairs closed with a sharp click.

# Chapter
# TWENTY-ONE

'Home, sweet home,' Jodie said.

A mattress and two boxes of old clothes, canned food. Magazines – *Playboy* and *Penthouse* and some cheap hardcore porn, which Stephen glanced at distastefully. A book or two. The fetid subway station where Jodie lived, somewhere downtown, had been closed decades ago and replaced by one up the street.

A good place for worms, Stephen thought grimly, then pried the image from his mind.

They'd entered the small station from the platform below. They'd made their way here – probably two or three miles from the safe house – completely underground, moving through the basements of buildings, tunnels, huge sewer pipes, and small sewer pipes. Leaving a false lead – an open manhole cover. Finally they'd entered the subway tunnel and made good time, though Jodie was pathetically out of shape and gasped for breath trying to keep up with Stephen's frantic pace.

There was a door leading out to the street, barred from the inside. Slanting lines of dusty light fell through the slats in the boards. Stephen peered outside into the grim spring overcast. It was a poor part of town. Derelicts sat on street corners, bottles of Thunderbird and Colt 44 were strewn on the sidewalk, and the polka dots of crack vial caps were everywhere. A huge rat chewed something gray in the alley.

Stephen heard a clatter behind him and turned to see Jodie dropping a handful of stolen pills into coffee cans. He was hunched over, carefully organizing them. Stephen dug through his book bag and found his cell phone. He made a call to Sheila's apartment. He was expecting to hear her answering machine, but a recording came on that said the line was out of order.

Oh, no . . .

He was stunned.

It meant that the antipersonnel satchel had gone off in Sheila's apartment. And *that* meant they'd found out he'd been there. How the hell had they done that?

'You all right?' Jodie asked.

*How?*

Lincoln, King of the Worms. That's how!

Lincoln, the white, wormy face peering out the window . . .

Stephen's palms began to sweat.

'Hey?'

Stephen looked up.

'You seem—'

'I'm fine,' Stephen answered shortly.

Stop worrying, he told himself. If it blew, the explosion was big enough to hose the apartment and destroy any trace of him. It's all right. You're safe. They'll never find you, never tie you down. The worms won't get you . . .

He looked at Jodie's easy smile of curiosity. The cringe went away. 'Nothing,' he said. 'Just a change of plans.' He hung up.

Stephen opened his book bag again, counted out $5,000. 'Here's the money.'

Jodie was transfixed by the cash. His eyes flipped back and forth between the bills and Stephen's face. The thin hand reached out, shaking, and took the five thousand carefully, as if it might crumble if he held it too hard.

As he gripped the bills Jodie's hand touched Stephen's. Even through the glove the killer felt a huge jolt – like the time he'd been stabbed in the gut with a razor knife – stunning but painless. Stephen let go of the money and, looking away, said, 'If you'll help me again I'll pay you another ten.'

The man's red, puffy face broke into a cautious smile. He took a deep breath, and poked through one of his coffee cans. 'I get . . . I don't know . . . nervous, sort of.' He found a pill, swallowed it. 'It's a blue devil. Makes you feel nice. Makes you feel all comfy. Want one?'

'Uhm . . .'

Soldier, do men take a drink occasionally?

Sir, I don't know, sir.

Well, they do. Here, have one.

'I don't think I—'

Take a drink, Soldier. That's an order.

Well, sir—

You're not a pussy girl, are you, Soldier? You have titties?

I . . . Sir, I do not, sir.

Then drink, Soldier.

Sir, yessir.

Jodie repeated, 'You want one?'

'No,' Stephen whispered.

Jodie closed his eyes and lay back. 'Ten . . . thousand . . .' After a moment he asked, 'You killed him, didn't you?'

'Who?' Stephen asked.

'Back there, that cop? Hey, you want some orange juice?'

'That agent in the basement? *Maybe* I killed him. I don't know. That wasn't the point.'

'Was it hard to do? Like, I don't mean anything, I'm just

curious. Orange juice? I drink a lot of it. Pills make you thirsty. Your mouth gets all dry.'

'No.' The can looked dirty. Maybe worms had crawled on it. Maybe crawled *inside*. You could drink a worm and never know it . . . He shivered. 'Do you have running water here?'

'No. But I have some bottles. Poland Spring. I stole a case from A&P.'

Cringey.

'I need to wash my hands.'

'You do?'

'To get the blood off them. It soaked through the gloves.'

'Oh. It's right there. Why do you wear gloves all the time? Fingerprints?'

'That's right.'

'You were in the army, right? I knew it.'

Stephen was about to lie, changed his mind suddenly. He said, 'No. I was almost in the army. Well, the marines. I was going to join. My stepfather was a marine and I was going in like him.'

'*Semper Fi.*'

'Right.'

There was silence and Jodie was looking at him expectantly. 'What happened?'

'I tried to enlist but they wouldn't let me in.'

'That's stupid. Wouldn't *let* you? You'd make a great soldier.' Jodie was looking Stephen up and down, nodding. 'You're strong. Great muscles. I' – he laughed – 'I don't hardly get any exercise, 'cept running from niggers or kids want to mug me. And they always catch me anyway. You're handsome too. Like soldiers ought to be. Like the soldiers in movies.'

Stephen felt the wormy feeling going away and, my God, he started blushing. He stared at the floor. 'Well, I don't know about that.'

'Come on. Your girlfriend thinks you're handsome, bet.'

Little cringey here. Worms starting to move.

'Well, I—'

'Don't you have a girlfriend?'

Stephen asked, 'You got that water?'

Jodie pointed to the box of Poland Spring. Stephen opened two bottles and began washing his hands. Normally he hated people watching him do this. When people watched him wash he kept being cringey and the worms never went away. But for some reason he didn't mind Jodie watching.

'No girlfriend, huh?'

'Not right now,' Stephen explained carefully. 'It's not like I'm a homo or anything, if you were wondering.'

'I wasn't.'

'I don't believe in that cult. Now, I don't think my step-father was right – that AIDS is God's way of getting rid of homosexual people. Because if that's what God wanted to do he'd be smart and just get rid of them, the faggots, I mean. Not make there be a risk that normal people might get sick too.'

'That makes sense,' Jodie said from his hazy plateau. 'I don't have one either, a girlfriend.' He laughed bitterly. 'Well, how could I? Right? What've I got? I'm not good-looking like you, I don't have any money . . . I'm just a fucking junkie is all.'

Stephen felt his face burn hot and he washed harder.

Scrub that skin, yes, yes, yes . . .

Worms, worms, go away . . .

Looking at his hands Stephen continued. 'The fact is I've been in a situation lately where I haven't really . . . where I haven't been as interested in women as most men are. But it's just a temporary condition.'

'Temporary,' Jodie repeated.

Eyes watching the bar of soap, as if it were a prisoner trying to escape.

'Temporary. Owing to my necessary vigilance. In my work, I mean.'

'Sure. Your vigilance.'

Scrub, scrub, the soap lathered like thunderheads.

'Have you ever killed a faggot?' Jodie asked, curious.

'I don't know. I'll tell you I've never killed anybody *because* he's a homosexual. That would make no sense.' Stephen's hands tingled and buzzed. He scrubbed harder, not looking at Jodie. He suddenly felt swollen with an odd feeling – of talking to someone who might just understand him. 'See, I don't kill people just to kill them.'

'Okay,' Jodie said. 'But what if some drunk came up to you on the street and pushed you around and called you, I don't know, a motherfucking faggot? You'd kill him, right? Say you could get away with it.'

'But . . . well, a faggot wouldn't want to have sex with his mother now, would he?'

Jodie blinked then laughed. 'That's pretty good.'

Did I just make a joke? Stephen wondered. He smiled, pleased that Jodie'd been impressed.

Jodie continued, 'Okay, let's say he just called you a motherfucker.'

'Of course I wouldn't kill him. And I'll tell you this, if you're talking about faggots let's talk about Negroes and Jewish people too. I wouldn't kill a Negro unless I'd been hired to kill somebody who happened to be a Negro. There are probably reasons why Negroes shouldn't live, or at least shouldn't live here in this country. My stepfather had a lot of reasons for that. I'm pretty much in accord with him. He felt the same about Jewish people, but there I disagree. Jewish people make very good soldiers. I respect them.'

He continued. 'See, killing's a business, that's all it is. Look at Kent State. I was just a kid then, but my stepfather told me about it. You know Kent State? Those students got shot by the National Guard?'

'Sure. I know.'

'Now, come on, nobody really cared that those students died, right? But to me it was stupid shooting them. Because what purpose did it serve? None. If you wanted to stop the movement, or whatever it was, you should've targeted the leaders and taken them out. It would've been so easy. Infiltrate, evaluate, delegate, isolate, eliminate.'

'That's how you kill people?'

'You infiltrate the area. Evaluate the difficulty of the kill and the defenses. You delegate the job of diverting everyone's attention from the victim – make it look like you're coming at them from one way but it turns out that it's just a delivery boy or shoe shine boy or something, and meanwhile you've come up behind the victim. Then you isolate him, and eliminate him.'

Jodie sipped his orange juice. There were dozens of empty orange juice cans piled in the corner. It seemed to be all he lived on. 'You know,' he said, wiping his mouth on his sleeve, 'you think professional killers'd be crazy. But you don't seem crazy.'

'I don't think I'm crazy,' Stephen said matter-of-factly.

'The people you kill, are they bad? Like crooks and Mafia people and things?'

'Well, they've done something bad to people who pay me to kill them.'

'Which means they're bad?'

'Sure.'

Jodie laughed dopily, eyelids half closed. 'Well, some people'd say that's not exactly how you, you know, figure out what's good or bad.'

'Okay, what *is* good and bad?' Stephen responded. 'I don't do anything different than God does. Good people die and bad people die in a train wreck and nobody gets on God's case because of it. Some professional killers call their victims "targets" or "subjects", One guy I heard about calls them "corpses". Even before he kills them. Like, "The corpse is leaving his car. I'm targeting him." It's easier for him to think of the victims that way, I guess. Me, I don't care. I call 'em what they are. Who I'm after now are the Wife and the Friend. I already killed the Husband. That's how I think of them. They're people I kill, is all. No big deal.'

Jodie considered what he'd heard and said, 'You know something? I don't think you're evil. You know why?'

'Why's that?'

'Because evil is something that looks innocent but turns out to be bad. The thing about you is you're exactly what you are. I think that's good.'

Stephen flicked his scrubbed fingernails with a click. He felt himself blushing again. Hadn't done that for years. Finally, he asked, 'I scare you, don't I?'

'No,' Jodie said. 'I wouldn't want to have you against me. No sir, I wouldn't want that. But I feel like we're friends. I don't think you'd hurt me.'

'No,' Stephen said. 'We're partners.'

'You talked about your stepfather. He still alive?'

'No, he died.'

'I'm sorry. When you mentioned him I was thinking about my father – he's dead too. He said the thing he respected most in the world was craftsmanship. He liked watching a talented man do what he did best. That's kind of like you.'

'Craftsmanship,' Stephen repeated, feeling swollen with inexplicable feelings. He watched Jodie hide the cash in a slit in his filthy mattress. 'What're you going to do with the money?'

Jodie sat up and looked at Stephen with dumb but earnest

eyes. 'Can I show you something?' The drugs made his voice slurred.

'Sure.'

He lifted a book out of his pocket. The title was *Dependent No More*.

'I stole it from this bookstore on Saint Marks Place. It's for people who don't want to be, you know, alcoholics or drug addicts anymore. It's pretty good. It mentions these clinics you can go to. I found this place in New Jersey. You go in there and you spend a month – a whole month – but you come out and you're clean. They say it really works.'

'That's good of you,' Stephen said. 'I approve of that.'

'Yeah, well,' Jodie curled up his face. 'It costs fourteen thousand.'

'No shit.'

'For *one* month. Can you believe that?'

'Somebody's making some bucks there.' Stephen made $150,000 for a hit, but he didn't share this information with Jodie, his newfound friend and partner.

Jodie sighed, wiped his eyes. The drugs had made him weepy, it seemed. Like Stephen's stepfather when he drank. 'My whole life's been so messed up,' he said. 'I went to college. Oh, yeah. Didn't do too bad either. I taught for a while. Worked for a company. Then I lost my job. Everything went bad. Lost my apartment . . . I'd always had a pill problem. Started stealing . . . Oh, hell . . .'

Stephen sat down next to him. 'You'll get your money and go into that clinic there. Get your life turned around.'

Jodie smiled blearily at him. 'My father had this thing he said, you know? When there was something you had to do that was hard. He said don't think about the hard part as a problem, just think about it as a factor. Like something to consider. He'd look me in the eye and say, "It's not a problem, it's just a factor." I keep trying to remember that.'

'Not a problem, just a factor,' Stephen repeated. 'I like that.'

Stephen put his hand on Jodie's leg to prove that he really did like it.

Soldier, what the fuck are you doing?

Sir, busy at the moment, sir. Will report in later.

Soldier—

Later, *sir*!

'Here's to you,' Jodie said.

'No, to you,' Stephen said.

And they toasted, mineral water and orange juice, to their strange alliance.

# Chapter
# TWENTY-TWO

A labyrinth.

The New York City subway system extends for over 250 miles and incorporates more than a dozen separate tunnels that crisscross four of the five boroughs (Staten Island only being excluded, though the islanders, of course, have a famous ferry of their very own).

A satellite could find a sailboat adrift in the North Atlantic quicker than Lincoln Rhyme's team could locate two men hiding in the New York subway.

The criminalist, Sellitto, Sachs, and Cooper were poring over a map of the system taped inelegantly to Lincoln Rhyme's wall. Rhyme's eyes scanned the different-colored lines representing the various routes, blue for Eighth Avenue, green for Lex, red for Broadway.

Rhyme had a special relationship with the cantankerous system. It was in the pit of a subway construction site that an oak beam had split and crushed Rhyme's spine – just as he'd said, 'Ah,' and leaned forward to lift a fiber, golden as an angel's hair, from the body of a murder victim.

Yet even before the accident, subways played an important role in NYPD forensics. Rhyme'd studied them diligently when he was running IRD: because they covered so much terrain and incorporated so many different kinds of building materials over the years, you could often link a perp to a particular subway line, if not his neighborhood and station, on the basis of good trace evidence alone. Rhyme had collected subway exemplars for years – some of the samples dating to the prior century. (It had been in the 1860s that Alfred Beach, the publisher of the *New York Sun* and *Scientific American*, decided to adapt his idea of transmitting mail via small pneumatic tubes to moving people in large ones.)

Rhyme now ordered his computer to dial a number and in a few moments was connected with Sam Hoddleston, chief of the Transit Authority Police. Like the Housing Police, they were regular New York City cops, no different from NYPD, merely assigned to the transportation system. Hoddleston knew Rhyme from the old days and the criminalist could hear in the silence after he identified himself some fast mental tap-dancing; Hoddleston, like many of Rhyme's former colleagues, didn't know that Rhyme had returned from the near dead.

'Should we power-off any of the lines?' Hoddleston asked after Rhyme briefed him about the Dancer and his partner. 'Do a field search?'

Sellitto heard the question on the speakerphone and shook his head.

Rhyme agreed. 'No, we don't want to tip our hand. Anyway, I think he's in an abandoned area.'

'There aren't many empty stations,' Hoddleston said. 'But there're a hundred deserted spurs and yards, work areas. Say, Lincoln, how're you doing? I—'

'Fine, Sam. I'm fine,' Rhyme said briskly, deflecting the question as he always did. Then added, 'We were talking – we think they're probably going to stick to foot. Stay off the trains themselves. So we're guessing they're in Manhattan.

We've got a map here and we're going to need your help in narrowing it down some.'

'Whatever I can do,' the chief said. Rhyme couldn't remember what he looked like. From his voice he sounded fit and athletic, but then Rhyme supposed he himself might seem like an Olympian to someone who couldn't see his destroyed body.

Rhyme now considered the rest of the evidence that Sachs had found in the building next to the safe house – the evidence left by the Dancer's partner.

He said to Hoddleston, 'The dirt has a high moisture content and's loaded with feldspar and quartz sand.'

'I remember you always like your dirt, Lincoln.'

'Useful, soil is,' he said, then continued. 'Very little rock and none of it blasted or chipped, no limestone or Manhattan mica schist. So we're looking at downtown. And from the amount of old wood particles, probably closer to Canal Street.'

North of Twenty-seventh Street the bedrock lies close to the surface of Manhattan. South of that, the ground is dirt, sand, and clay, and it's very damp. When the sandhogs were digging the subways years ago the soupy ground around Canal Street would flood the shaft. Twice a day all work had to cease while the tunnel was pumped out and the walls shored up with timber, which over the years had rotted away into the soil.

Hoddleston wasn't optimistic. Although Rhyme's information limited the geographic area, he explained, there were dozens of connecting tunnels, transfer platforms, and portions of stations themselves that had been closed off over the years. Some of them were as sealed and forgotten as Egyptian tombs. Years after Alfred Beach died workmen building another subway line broke through a wall and discovered his original tunnel, long abandoned, with its opulent waiting room, which had included murals, a grand piano, and a goldfish tank.

'Any chance he's just sleeping in active stations or between stations in a cutout?' Hoddleston asked.

Sellitto shook his head. 'Not his profile. He's a druggie. He'd be worried about his stash.'

Rhyme then told Hoddleston about the turquoise mosaic.

'Impossible to say where that came from, Lincoln. We've done so much work retiling, there's tile dust and grout everywhere. Who knows where he could've picked it up.'

'So give me a number, chief,' Rhyme said. 'How many spots we looking at?'

'I'd guess twenty locations,' Hoddleston's athletic voice said. 'Maybe a few less.'

'Ouch,' Rhyme muttered. 'Well, fax us a list of the most likely ones.'

'Sure. When do you need it?' But before Rhyme could answer, Hoddleston said, 'Never mind. I remember you from the old days, Lincoln. You want it yesterday.'

'Last week,' Rhyme joked, impatient the chief was bantering and not writing.

Five minutes later the fax machine buzzed. Thom set the piece of paper in front of Rhyme. It listed fifteen locations in the subway system. 'Okay, Sachs, get going.'

She nodded as Sellitto called Haumann and Dellray to have the S&S teams get started. Rhyme added emphatically, 'Amelia, you stay in the rear now, okay? You're Crime Scene, remember? Only Crime Scene.'

On a curb in downtown Manhattan sat Leon the Shill. Beside him was the Bear Man – so named because he wheeled around a shopping cart filled with dozens of stuffed animals, supposedly for sale, though only the most psychotic of parents would buy one of the tattered, licey little toys for their child.

Leon and the Bear Man lived together – that is, they

shared an alley near Chinatown – and survived on bottle deposits and handouts and a little harmless petty larceny.

'He dying, man,' Leon said.

'Naw, bad dream's what it is,' Bear Man responded, rocking his shopping cart as if trying to put the bears to sleep.

'Oughta spenda dime, get a ambulance here.'

Leon and the Bear Man were looking across the street, into an alley. There lay another homeless man, black and sick looking, with a twitchy and mean – though currently unconscious – face. His clothes were in tatters.

'Oughta call somebody.'

'Les take a look.'

They crossed the street, skittish as mice.

The man was skinny – AIDS, probably, which told them he probably used smack – and filthy. Even Leon and Bear Man bathed occasionally in the Washington Square Park fountain or the lagoon in Central Park, despite the turtles. He wore ragged jeans, caked socks, no shoes, and a torn, filthy jacket that said, *Cats . . . The Musical* on it.

They stared at him for a moment. When Leon tentatively touched Cats's leg the man jerked awake and sat up, freezing them with a weird glare. 'The fuck're you? The fuck're you?'

'Hey, man, you okay?' They backed away a few feet.

Cats shivered, clutching his abdomen. He coughed long and Leon whispered, 'Looks too fucking mean to be sick, you know?'

'He's scary. Les go.' Bear Man wanted to get back to his A&P baby carriage.

'I need help,' Cats muttered. 'I hurt, man.'

'There's a clinic over on—'

'Can't go to no *clinic*,' Cats snapped, as if they'd insulted him.

So he had a record, and on the street refusing to go to a clinic when you were this sick meant you had a *serious* record. Felony warrants outstanding. Yeah, this mutt was trouble.

'I need medicine. You got some? I pay you. I got money.'

Which they normally wouldn't've believed except that Cats was a can picker. And fucking good at it, they could see. Beside him was a huge bag of soda and beer cans he'd culled from the trash. Leon eyed it enviously. Must've taken two days to get that many. Worth thirty bucks, forty.

'We don't got nothing. We don't do that. Stuff, I mean.'

'Pills, he means.'

'You wanna bottle? T-bird. I got some nice T-bird, yessir. Trade you a bottle fo' them cans . . .'

Cats struggled up on one arm. 'I don't want no fuckin' bottle. I got beat up. Some kids, they beat me up. They busted something in me. It don't feel right. I need medicine. Not crack or smack or fucking T-bird. I need something stop me hurtin'. I need pills!' He climbed to his feet and teetered, swaying toward Bear Man.

'Nothing, man. We don't got nothing.'

'I'ma ask you a las' time, you gonna give me somethin'?' He groaned and held his side. They knew how crazy strong some crackheads were. And this guy was *big*. He could easily break both of them in half.

Leon whispered to Bear Man, 'That guy, th'other day?'

Bear Man was nodding avidly, though it was a fear reflex. He didn't know who the hell Leon was talking about.

Leon continued, 'There's this guy, okay? Was trying to sell us some shit yesterday. Pills. Pleased as could be.'

'Yeah, pleased as could be,' Bear Man said quickly, as if confirming the story might calm Cats down.

'Didn't care who saw him. Just selling pills. No crack, no smack, no Jane. But uppers, downers, you name it.'

'Yeah, you name it.'

'I got money.' Cats fumbled in his filthy pocket and pulled out two or three crumpled twenties. 'See? So where this motherfucker be?'

'Over near City Hall. Old subway station . . .'

'I'm sick, man. I got beat up. Why somebody beat me up? What I do? I's pickin' some cans's all. And look what happen. Fuck. What his name?'

'I don't know,' Bear Man said quickly, squiggling up his forehead as if he were thinking fiercely. 'No, wait. He said something.'

'I don't remember.'

'You remember . . . He was looking at your bears.'

'An' he said something. Yeah, yeah. Said his name was Joe or something. Maybe Jodie.'

'Yeah, that was it. I'm sure.'

'Jodie,' Cats repeated, then wiped his forehead. 'I'ma see him. Man, I need somethin'. I'm sick, man. Fuck you. I'm sick. Fuck you too.'

When Cats had staggered off, moaning and muttering to himself, dragging his bag of cans behind him, Leon and Bear Man returned to the curb and sat down. Leon cracked a Voodoo ale and they started drinking.

'Shouldn'ta done that to that fella,' he said.

'Who?'

'Jodie or whatever his name was.'

'You want that motherfucker round here?' Bear Man asked. 'He dangerous. He scare me. You want him to hang round here?'

'Course I don't. But, man, you know.'

'Yeah, but—'

'You know, man.'

'Yeah, I know. Gimme the bottle.'

# Chapter
# TWENTY-THREE

Sitting next to Jodie on the mattress, Stephen was listening through the tap box to the Hudson Air phone line.

He was listening to Ron's phone. Talbot was his last name, Stephen had learned. He wasn't exactly sure what Ron's job was but he seemed to be an executive with the charter company and Stephen believed he'd get the most information about the Wife and Friend by listening to this line.

He heard the man arguing with someone from the distributor who handled parts for Garrett turbines. Because it was Sunday they were having trouble getting the final items for the repairs – a fire extinguisher cartridge and something called the annular.

'You promised it by three,' Ron grumbled. 'I want it by three.'

After some bargaining – and bitching – the company agreed to fly the parts into their Connecticut office from Boston. They'd be trucked to the Hudson Air office and arrive by three or four. They hung up.

Stephen listened for a few minutes longer but there were no other calls.

He clicked the phone off, frustrated.

He didn't have a clue as to where the Wife and Friend were. Still in the safe house? Had they been moved?

What was wormy Lincoln thinking now? How clever was he?

And *who* was he? Stephen tried to picture him, tried to picture him as a target through the Redfield telescope. He couldn't. All he saw was a mass of worms and a face looking at him calmly through a greasy window.

He realized that Jodie'd said something to him.

'What?'

'What'd he do? Your stepfather?'

'Just odd jobs mostly. Hunted and fished a lot. He was a hero in Vietnam. He went behind enemy lines and killed fifty-four people. Politicians and people like that, not just soldiers.'

'He taught you all this, about . . . what you do?' The drugs had worn off and Jodie's green eyes were brighter now.

'I got most of my practice in Africa and South America, but he started me. I called him "WGS". The World's Greatest Soldier. He laughed at that.'

At ages eight and nine and ten Stephen would walk behind Lou as they trooped through the hills of West Virginia, hot drops of sweat falling down their noses and into the crooks of their index fingers, which curled around the ribbed triggers of their Winchesters or Rugers. They'd lie in the grass for hours and be quiet, be still. The sweat glistened on Lou's scalp just below the bristly crew cut, both eyes open as they sighted on their targets.

Don't you squint that left eye, Soldier.

Sir, never, sir.

Squirels, wild turkeys, deer in season or out, bear when they could find them, dogs on slow days.

'Make 'em dead, Soldier. Watch me.'

*Ka-rack.* The thud against the shoulder, the bewildered eyes of an animal dying.

Or on steaming August Sundays they'd slip the $CO_2$ cartridges into their paint-ball guns and strip down to their shorts, stalking each other and raising molehills of welts on their chests and thighs with the marble-sized balls that hissed through the air at three hundred feet per second, young Stephen struggling to keep from crying at the awful sting. The paint balls came in every color, but Lou insisted on loading with red. Like blood.

And at night, sitting in front of a fire in the backyard as the smoke curled toward the sky and into the open window where his mother stood cleaning the supper dishes with a toothbrush, the taut little man – Stephen at fifteen was as tall as Lou – would sip from the newly opened bottle of Jack Daniel's and talk and talk and talk, whether Stephen was listening or not, as they watched the sparks flying into the sky like orange lightning bugs.

'Tomorrow I want you to bring down a deer with just a knife.'

'Well . . .'

'Can you do that, Soldier?'

'Yessir, I can.'

'Now look here.' He'd take another sip. 'Where d'you think the neck vein is?'

'I—'

'Don't be afraid to say you don't know. A good soldier admits his ignorance. But then he does something to correct it.'

'I don't know where the vein is, sir.'

'I'll show it on you. It's right here. Feel that? Right there. Feel it?'

'Yessir. I feel it.'

'Now, what you do is you find a family – doe and calves. You come up close. That's the hard part, getting up close. To kill the doe, you endanger the calf. You move for her baby. You threaten the calf and then the mother won't run off. She'll come after you. Then, swick! Cut through her neck. Not side-ways, but at an angle. Okay? A V-shape. You feel that? Good, good. Hey, boy, aren't we having a high old time!'

Then Lou would go inside to inspect the plates and bowls and make sure they were lined up on the checkered table-cloth, four squares from the edge, and sometimes when they were only three and a half squares from the edge or there was still a dot of grease on the rim of a melamine plate Stephen would listen to the slaps and the whimpers from inside the house as he lay on his back beside the fire and watched the sparks fly toward the dead moon.

'You gotta be good at something,' the man would say later, his wife in bed and he outside again with his bottle. 'Otherwise there's no point in being alive.'

Craftsmanship. He was talking about *craftsmanship*.

Jodie now asked, 'How come you couldn't be in the marines? You never told me.'

'Well, it was stupid,' Stephen said, then paused and added, 'I got into some trouble when I was a kid. D'you ever do that?'

'Get into trouble? Not much. I was scared to. I didn't want to upset my mother, stealing and shit. What'd you do?'

'Something that wasn't real bright. There was this man lived up the road in our town. He was, you know, a bully. I saw him twisting this woman's arm. She was sick, and what was he doing hurting her? So I went up to him and said if he didn't stop I'd kill him.'

'You said that?'

'Oh, and another thing my stepfather taught me. You don't threaten. You either kill someone or let them be, but you don't threaten. Well, he kept on hassling this woman and I had to teach him a lesson. I started hitting him. It got out of hand. I grabbed a rock and hit him. I wasn't thinking. I did a couple years for manslaughter. I was just a kid. Fifteen.

But it was a criminal record. And that was enough to keep me out of the marines.'

'I thought I read somewhere that even if you've got a record you can go into the service. If you go to some special boot camp.'

'I guess maybe 'cause it was manslaughter.'

Jodie's hand pressed Stephen's shoulder. 'That's not fair. Not one *bit* fair.'

'I didn't think so.'

'I'm real sorry,' Jodie said.

Stephen, who never had any trouble looking any man in the eye, glanced at Jodie once then down immediately. And from somewhere, totally weird, this image came to mind. Jodie and Stephen living together in the cabin, going hunting and fishing. Cooking dinner over a campfire.

'What happened to him? Your stepfather?'

'Died in an accident. He was hunting and fell off a cliff.'

Jodie said, 'Sounds like it was probably the way he'd've wanted to go.'

After a moment Stephen said, 'Maybe it was.'

He felt Jodie's leg brush his. Another electric jolt. Stephen stood quickly and looked out the window again. A police car cruised past but the cops inside were drinking soda and talking.

The street was deserted except for a clutch of homeless men, four or five whites and one Negro.

Stephen squinted. The Negro, lugging a big garbage bag full of soda and beer cans, was arguing, looking around, gesturing, offering the bag to one of the white guys, who kept shaking his head. He had a crazy look in his eyes and the whites were scared. Stephen watched them argue for a few minutes, then he returned to the mattress, sat down next to Jodie.

Stephen put his hand on Jodie's shoulder.

'I want to talk to you about what we're going to do.'

'Okay, all right. I'm listening, partner.'

'There's somebody out there looking for me.'

Jodie laughed. He said, 'Seems to me after what happened back at that building there's a buncha people looking for you.'

Stephen didn't smile. 'But there's one person in particular. His name's Lincoln.'

Jodie nodded. 'That's his first name?'

Stephen shrugged. 'I don't know . . . I've never met anyone like him.'

'Who is he?'

A worm . . .

'Maybe a cop. FBI. A consultant or something. I don't know exactly.' Stephen remembered the Wife describing him to Ron – the way somebody'd talk about a guru, or a ghost. He felt cringey again. He slid his hand down Jodie's back. It rested at the base of his spine. The bad feeling went away.

'This is the second time he's stopped me. And he almost got me caught. I'm trying to figure him out and I can't.'

'What do you have to figure out?'

'What he's going to do next. So I can stay ahead of him.'

Another squeeze to the spine. Jodie didn't seem to mind. He didn't look away either. He wasn't timid anymore. And the look he gave Stephen was odd. Was it a look of . . . ? Well, he didn't know. Admiration maybe . . .

Stephen realized that it was the way Sheila had looked at him in Starbucks when he was saying all the right things. Except that, with her, he hadn't been Stephen, he was somebody else. Somebody who didn't exist. Jodie was now looking at him this way even though he knew exactly who Stephen was, that he was a killer.

Leaving his hand on the man's back, Stephen said, 'What I can't figure out is if he's going to move them out of their safe house. The one next to the building where I met you.'

'Move who? The people you're trying to kill?'

'Yeah. He's going to try to outguess me. He's thinking . . .' Stephen's voice faded.

Thinking . . .

And what *was* Lincoln the Worm thinking? Would he move the Wife and the Friend, guessing I'll try the safe house again? Or would he leave them, thinking I'll wait and try for them at a new location? And even if he thinks I'll try the safe house again, will he leave them there as bait, trying to sucker me back for another ambush? Will he move two decoys to a new safe house? And try to take me when I follow them?

The thin man said, almost whispering, 'You seem, I don't know, shook up or something.'

'I can't *see* him . . . I can't see what he's going to do. Everybody else's ever been after me I can see. I can figure them out. Him, I can't.'

'What do you want me to do?' Jodie asked, swaying against Stephen. Their shoulders brushed.

Stephen Kall, craftsman extraordinaire, stepson of a man who never had a moment's hesitation in anything he did – killing deer or inspecting plates cleaned with a toothbrush – was now confounded, staring at the floor, then looking up into Jodie's eyes.

Hand on the man's back. Shoulders touching too.

Stephen made up his mind.

He bent forward and rummaged through his backpack. He found a black cell phone, looked at it for a moment, then handed it to Jodie.

'Whatsis?' the man asked.

'A phone. For you to use.'

'A cell phone! Cool.' He examined it as if he'd never seen one, flipped it open, studying all the buttons.

Stephen asked, 'You know what a spotter is?'

'No.'

'The best snipers don't work alone. They always have a spotter with them. He locates the target and figures out how far away it is, looks for defensive troops, things like that.'

'You want me to do that for you?'

'Yep. See, I think Lincoln's going to move them.'

'Why, you figure?' Jodie asked.

'I can't explain it. I just have this feeling.' He looked at his watch. 'Okay, here's the thing. At twelve-thirty this afternoon, what I want you to do is walk down the street like a . . . homeless person.'

'You can say "bum", you want.'

'And watch the safe house. Maybe you could look through trash cans or something.'

'For bottles. I do that. All the time.'

'You find out what kind of car they get into, then call and tell me. I'll be on the street around the corner, in a car, waiting. But you'll have to watch out for decoys.'

An image of the red-haired woman cop came to mind. She could hardly be a decoy for the Wife. Too tall, too pretty. He wondered why he disliked her so much . . . He regretted not judging that shot at her better.

'Okay. I can do that. You'll shoot them in the street?'

'It depends. I might follow them to the new safe house and do it there. I'll be ready to improvise.'

Jodie studied the phone like a kid at Christmas. 'I don't know how it works.'

Stephen showed him. 'You call me on it when you're in position.'

'"In position." That sounds professional.' Then Jodie looked up from the phone. 'You know, after this's over and I go through the rehab thing, why don't we get together sometime? We could have some juice or coffee or something. Huh? You wanta do that?'

'Sure,' Stephen said. 'We could—'

But suddenly a huge pounding shook the door. Spinning around like a dervish, whipping his gun from his pocket, Stephen dropped into a two-handed shooting position.

'Open the fuckin' door,' a voice from outside shouted. 'Now!'

'Quiet,' Stephen whispered to Jodie. Heart racing.

'You in there, booger?' the voice persisted. 'Jo-die. Where the fuck're you?'

Stephen stepped to the boarded-over window and looked out again. The Negro homeless guy from across the street. He wore a tattered jacket that read, *Cats . . . The Musical*. The Negro didn't see him.

'Where'sa little man?' the Negro said. 'I needa little man. I gotta have some pills! Jodie Joe? Where you be?'

Stephen said, 'You know him?'

Jodie looked out, shrugged, and whispered, 'I don't know. Maybe. Looks like a lota people on the street.'

Stephen studied the man for a long moment, thumbing the plastic grip of his pistol.

The homeless man called, 'I know you here, man.' His voice dissolved into a gargle of disgusting cough. 'Jo-die. Jo-die! It cos' me, man. As' wha' it cos' me. Cos' me a fuckin' weeka pickin' cans's what it cos' me. They *tole* me you here. Ever-bod-y told me. Jodie, Jodie!'

'He'll just go away,' Jodie said.

Stephen said, 'Wait. Maybe we can use him.'

'How?'

'Remember what I told you? *Delegate*. This is good . . .' Stephen was nodding. 'He looks scary. They'll focus on him, not you.'

'You mean take him along with me? To that safe house place?'

'Yes,' Stephen said.

'I need some *stuff*, man,' the Negro moaned. 'Come on. I'm fucked-up, man. Please. I got the wobblies. You *fuck*!' He kicked the door hard. 'Please, man. You in there, Jodie? The fuck you at? You booger! Help me.' It sounded like he was crying.

'Go on out,' Stephen said. 'Tell him you'll give him something if he goes along with you. Just have him go through the trash or something across the street from the safe house, while you're watching the traffic. It'll be perfect.'

Jodie looked at him. 'You mean now. Just go talk to him?'

'Yeah. Now. Tell him.'

'You want him to come in?'

'No, I don't want him to see me. Just go talk to him.'

'Well . . . Okay.' Jodie pried the front door open. 'What if he stabs me or something?'

'Look at him. He's almost dead. You could beat the crap out of him with one hand.'

'Looks like he has AIDS.'

'Go on.'

'What if he touches—'

'Go!'

Jodie took a deep breath then stepped outside. 'Hey, keep it down,' he said to the man. 'What the hell you want?'

Stephen watched the Negro look over Jodie with his crazed eyes. 'Word up you selling shit, man. I got money. I got sixty bucks. I need pills. Look, I'm sick.'

'Whatta you want?'

'Whatchu got, man?'

'Reds, bennies, dexies, yellow jackets, demmies.'

'Yeah, demmies're good shit, man. I pay you. Fuck. I got money. I'm hurting inside. Got beat up. Where my money?' He slapped his pockets several times before realizing he was clutching the precious twenties in his left hand.

'But,' Jodie said, 'you gotta do something for me first.'

'Yeah, whatta I gotta do that? You wanna blow job?'

'No,' Jodie snapped, horrified. 'I want you to help me go through some trash.'

'Why I gotta do that shit?'

'Picking some cans.'

'Cans?' the man roared, scratching his nose compulsively. 'The fuck you need a nickel for? I just give away a hunnered cans find out where yo' ass be. Fuck cans. I pay you money, man.'

'I give you the demmies for free, only you gotta help me get some bottles.'

'Free?' The man didn't seem to understand this. 'You mean, free like I don't gotta pay?'

'Yeah.'

The Negro looked around as if he was trying to find somebody to explain this.

'Wait here,' Jodie said.

'Where I gotta look for bottles?'

'Just wait . . .'

'Where?' he demanded.

Jodie stepped back inside. He said to Stephen, 'He's gonna do it.'

'Good job.' Stephen smiled.

Jodie grinned back. He started to turn back to the door but Stephen said, 'Hey.'

The little man paused.

Stephen blurted suddenly, 'It's good I met you.'

'I'm glad I met you too.' Jodie hesitated for a minute. 'Partner.' He stuck his hand out.

'Partner,' Stephen echoed. He had a fierce urge to take his glove off, so he could feel Jodie's skin on his. But he didn't.

Craftsmanship had to come first.

# Chapter
# TWENTY-FOUR

The debate was feverish.

'I think you're wrong, Lincoln,' Lon Sellitto said. 'We gotta move 'em. He'll hit the safe house again, we leave 'em there.'

They weren't the only ones considering the dilemma. Prosecutor Reg Eliopolos hadn't checked in – not yet – but Thomas Perkins, the FBI special agent in charge of the Manhattan office, was here in person, representing the federal side of the debate. Rhyme wished Dellray were here – and Sachs too, though she was with the joint city/federal tactical force searching abandoned subway locations. So far they hadn't found any trace of the Dancer or his compatriot.

'I'm being completely proactive in my take on the situation,' said earnest Perkins. 'We have other facilities.' He was appalled that it had taken the Dancer only eight hours to find out where the witnesses were being held and to get within five yards of the disguised fire door of the safe house. '*Better* facilities,' he added quickly. 'I think we should expedite immediate transferal. I've gotten a heads-up from high levels. Washington itself. They want the witnesses immunized.'

Meaning, Rhyme assumed, move 'em and move 'em now.

'No,' the criminalist said adamantly. 'We have to leave them where they are.'

'Prioritizing the variables,' Perkins said, 'I think the answer's pretty clear. Move them.'

But Rhyme said, 'He'll come after them wherever they are, a new safe house or the existing one. We know the turf there, we know something about his approach. We've got good ambush coverage.'

'That's a good point,' Sellitto conceded.

'It'll also throw him off stride.'

'How so?' Perkins asked.

'He's debating right now too, you know.'

'He is?'

'Oh, you bet,' Rhyme said. 'He's trying to figure out what *we're* going to do. If we decide to keep them where they are, he'll do one thing. If we move them – which I think is what he's guessing we'll do – he'll try for a transport hit. And however good security is on the road, it's always worse than fixed premises. No, we have to keep them where they are and be prepared for the next attempt. Anticipate it and be ready to move in. The last time—'

'The last time, an agent got killed.'

Rhyme snapped back to the SAC, 'If Innelman had had a backup, it would've gone different.'

Perkins of the perfect suit was a self-protecting bureaucrat, but he was reasonable. He nodded his concession.

But *am* I right? Rhyme wondered.

What *is* the Dancer thinking? Do I really know?

Oh, I can look over a silent bedroom or filthy alleyway and read perfectly the story that turned them into crime scenes. I can see, in the Rorschach of blood pasted to carpet and tile, how close the victim came to escaping or how little chance he had and what kind of death he died. I can look at the dust the killer leaves behind and know immediately where he comes from.

I can answer who, I can answer why.

But what's the Dancer *going* to do?

That I can guess at but I can't say for certain.

A figure appeared in the doorway, one of the officers from the front door. He handed Thom an envelope and stepped back to his guard post.

'What's that?' Rhyme eyed it carefully. He wasn't expecting any lab reports and he was all too conscious of the Dancer's predilection for bombs. The package was no more than a sheet of paper thick, however, and was from the FBI.

Thom opened it and read.

'It's from PERT. They tracked down a sand expert.'

Rhyme explained to Perkins, 'It's not for this case. It's about that agent who disappeared the other night.'

'Tony?' the SAC asked. 'We haven't had a single lead so far.'

Rhyme glanced at the report.

*Substance submitted for analysis is not technically sand. It is coral rubble from reef formations and contains spicules, cross sections of marine worm tubes, gastropod shells and foraminifers. Most likely source is the northern Caribbean: Cuba, the Bahamas.*

Caribbean . . . Interesting. Well, he'd have to put the evidence on hold for the time being. After the Dancer was bagged and tagged he and Sachs would get back—

His headset crinkled.

'Rhyme, you there?' Sachs's voice snapped.

'Yes! Where are you, Sachs? What do you have?'

'We're outside an old subway station near City Hall. All boarded up. S&S says there's somebody inside. At least one, maybe two.'

'Okay, Sachs,' he said, heart racing at the thought they

might be close to the Dancer. 'Report back.' Then he looked up at Sellitto and Perkins. 'Looks like we may not have to decide about moving them from the safe house after all.'

'They found him?' the detective asked.

But the criminalist – a scientist foremost – refused to give voice to his hopes. Afraid he might jinx the operation – well, jinx *Sachs*, he was thinking. He muttered, 'Let's keep our fingers crossed.'

Silently the ESU troops surrounded the subway station.

This was probably the place where the Dancer's new partner lived, Amelia Sachs concluded. S&S had found several locals who'd reported a druggie selling pills out of the place. He was a slightly built man – in line with a size-eight shoe.

The station was, almost literally, a hole in the wall, supplanted years ago by the fancier City Hall stop a few blocks away.

The 32-E team went into position, while S&S began to set up their microphones and infrareds, and other officers cleared the street of traffic and the homeless men sitting on curbs or in doorways.

The commander moved Sachs away from the main entrance, out of the line of fire. They gave her the demeaning job of guarding a subway exit that had been barred and padlocked for years. She actually wondered if Rhyme had cut a deal with Haumann to keep her safe. Her anger from last night, in abeyance in their search for the Dancer, now bubbled up again.

Sachs nodded toward the rusty lock. 'Hmm. He probably won't be getting out this way,' she'd offered brightly.

'Gotta guard all entrances,' the masked ESU officer muttered, missing or ignoring her sarcasm, and returned to his comrades.

Rain fell around her, a chill rain, dropping straight down

from a dirty gray sky, tapping loudly on the refuse banked in front of the iron bars.

Was the Dancer inside? If so, there'd be a firefight. Absolutely. She couldn't imagine he'd give it up without a violent struggle.

And it infuriated her that she wouldn't be part of it.

You're a slick dick when you've got a rifle and a quarter mile of protection, she thought to the killer. But tell me, asshole, how're you with a handgun at close range? How'd you like to face me down? On her mantel at home were a dozen trophies of gold-plated shooters aiming pistols. (The gilt figures were all men, which for some reason tickled Amelia Sachs immensely.)

She stepped farther down the stairs, to the bars, then flattened against the wall.

Sachs, the criminalist, examined the squalid spot carefully, smelling garbage, rot, urine, the salty smell of the subway. She examined the bars and the chain and padlock. She peered inside the dim tunnel and could see nothing, hear nothing.

Where is he?

And what are the cops and agents doing? What's the delay?

She heard the answer a moment later in her earphone: they were waiting for backup. Haumann had decided to call in another twenty ESU officers and the second 32-E team.

No, no, no, she thought. That was all wrong! All the Dancer has to do is take one peek outside and see that not a single car or taxi or pedestrian is going by and he'll know instantly there's a tactical operation under way. There'll be a bloodbath . . . Don't they get it?

Sachs left the crime scene kit at the foot of the stairs and climbed back to street level. A few doors away was a drugstore. She went inside. She bought two large cans of butane and borrowed the storekeeper's awning rod – a five-foot-long piece of steel.

Back at the gated subway exit, Sachs slipped the awning rod through one of the chain links that was partially sawn through, and twisted until the chain was taut. She pulled on a Nomex glove and emptied the contents of butane cans on the metal, watching it grow frosty from the freezing gas. (Amelia Sachs hadn't walked a beat along the Deuce in Times Square – Forty-second Street – for nothing; she knew enough about breaking and entering to take up a second line of work.)

When the second can was empty she gripped the rod in both hands and began to twist. The icy gas had made the metal very brittle. With a soft *snap* the link cracked in half. She caught the chain before it fell to the ground and set it quietly in a pile of leaves.

The hinges were wet with rainwater but she spit on them for good measure to keep them from squeaking and pushed inside, sweeping her Glock from its holster, thinking: I missed you at three hundred yards. I won't at thirty.

Rhyme wouldn't have approved of this, of course, but Rhyme didn't know. She thought momentarily about him, about last night, lying in his bed. But the image of his face vanished quickly. Like driving at a hundred and fifty miles an hour, her mission now left no time for ruing the disaster of her personal life.

She disappeared into the dim corridor, leapt over the ancient wooden turnstile, and started along the platform toward the station.

She heard the voices before she got more than twenty feet.

'I have to leave . . . understand . . . I'm saying? Go away.'

White, male.

Was it the Dancer?

Heart slamming in her chest.

Breathe slow, she told herself. Shooting is breathing.

(But she hadn't been breathing slow at the airport. She'd been gasping in fear.)

'Yo, whatchu sayin'?' Another voice. Black male. Something about it scared her. Something dangerous. 'I can get money, I can. I can get a shitload a money. I got sixty, I tell you that? But I can get mo'. I can get as much's you want. I ha' me a good job. Fuckers took it away. I knew too much.'

The weapon is merely an extension of your arm. Aim your-self, not the weapon.

(But she hadn't been aiming at all when she'd been at the airport. She'd been on her belly like a scared rabbit, shooting blind – the most pointless and dangerous of practices with a firearm.)

'You understand me? I changed my mind, okay? Let me . . . and just leave. I'll give . . . demmies.'

'You ain' tole me where we goin'. Where this place we gotta look through? You tell me that first. Where? Tell me!'

'You're not going anywhere. I want you to go away.'

Sachs started up the stairs slowly.

Thinking: Draw your target, check your background, squeeze three. Return to cover. Draw, squeeze three more if you have to. Cover. Don't get rattled.

(But she had been rattled at the airport. That terrible bullet snapping past her face . . .)

Forget it. Concentrate.

Up a few more stairs.

'An' now you sayin' I don't get 'em fo' free, right? Now you sayin' I gotta pay. You motherfuck!'

Stairs were the worst. Knees, her weak spot. Fucking arthritis . . .

'Here. Here's a dozen demmies. Take 'em and go!'

'A dozen. And I ain' gotta pay you?' He brayed a laugh. 'A dozen?'

Approaching the top of the stairs.

She could almost peer into the station itself. She was ready to shoot. He moves any direction more than six inches, girl, take him out. Forget the rules. Three head shots. Pop, pop, pop. Forget the chest. Forget—

Suddenly the stairs vanished.

'Ugh.' A grunt from deep in her throat as she fell.

The step she'd placed her foot on was a trap. The riser had been removed and the step rested only on two shoe boxes. They collapsed under her weight and the concrete slab pitched downward, sending her backward down the stairs. The Glock flew from her hand and as she started to shout, 'Ten-thirteen!' she realized that the cord linking her headset to her Motorola had been yanked out of the radio.

Sachs fell with a thud onto the concrete-and-steel landing. Her head slammed into a pole supporting the handrail. She rolled onto her stomach, stunned.

'Oh, great,' the white guy's voice muttered from the top of the stairs.

'Who the fuck that?' the black voice asked.

She lifted her head and caught a glimpse of two men standing at the top of the stairs, gazing down at her.

'Shit,' the black man muttered. 'Fuck. What the fuck goin' on here?'

The white guy snagged a baseball bat and started down the stairs.

I'm dead, she thought. I'm dead.

The switchblade rested in her pocket. It took every ounce of energy to get her right arm out from underneath her. She rolled onto her back, fishing for the knife. But it was too late. He stepped on her arm, pinning it to the ground, and he gazed down at her.

Oh, man, Rhyme, blew it bad. Wish we'd had a better farewell night . . . I'm sorry . . . I'm sorry . . .

She lifted her hands defensively to deflect the blow to her head, glanced for her Glock. It was too far away.

With a tendony hand tough as a bird claw, the small man pulled the knife from her pocket. He tossed it away.

Then he stood and gripped the club.

Pop, she spoke to her deceased father, how bad d'I blow this one? How many rules d'I break? Recalling that he'd told her all it took to get killed on the street was a one-second lapse.

'Now, you're gonna tell me what you're doing here,' he muttered, swinging the club absently, as if he couldn't decide what to break first. 'Who the hell're you?'

'Her name's Mizz Amelia Sachs,' said the homeless guy, suddenly sounding a lot less homeless. He stepped off the bottom stair and moved up to the white guy quickly, pulling the bat away. 'And unless I'm most mistaken, she's come here to bust your little ass, my friend. Just like me.' Sachs squinted to see the homeless guy straighten up and turn into Fred Dellray. He was pointing a very large Sig-Sauer automatic pistol at the astonished man.

'You're a cop?' he sputtered.

'FBI.'

'Shit!' he spat out, closing his eyes in disgust. 'This is just my fucking luck.'

'Nup,' Dellray said. 'Luck didn't have a bitsy thing to do with it. Now, I'm gonna cuff you and you're gonna let me. You don't, you gonna hurt for months and months. We all together on that?'

'How'd you do it, Fred?'

''Seasy,' the lanky FBI agent said to Sachs as they stood in front of the deserted subway station. He still was dressed homeless and was filthy with the mud he'd smeared on his face and hands to simulate weeks of living on the street. 'Rhyme was tellin' me 'bout the Dancer's friend being a junkie and living downtown in the subways, knew just where I hadta come. Bought a bag of empties and talked to who I knew I oughta talk to. Just 'bout got di-rections t'his livin' room.' He nodded toward the subway. They glanced at a squad car, where Jodie sat, cuffed and miserable, in the backseat.

'Why didn't you tell us what you were doing?'

Dellray's answer was a laugh and Sachs knew the question was pointless; undercover cops rarely told anyone – fellow cops included, and especially supervisors – what they were doing. Nick, her ex, had been undercover too and there'd been a hell of a lot he hadn't told her.

She massaged her side where she'd fallen. It hurt like a son of a bitch, and the medics said she ought to have X rays. Sachs reached up and squeezed Dellray's biceps. She felt uneasy *receiving* gratitude – she was truly Lincoln Rhyme's protégée there – but she now had no problem saying, 'You saved my life. My ass'd be capped now if it wasn't for you. What can I say?'

Dellray shrugged, deflecting the thanks, and bummed a cigarette from one of the uniformed cops standing in front of the station. He sniffed the Marlboro and slipped it behind his ear. He looked toward a blacked-out window in the station. 'Please,' he said to no one, sighing. "Bout time we had some luck here.'

When they'd arrested Joe D'Oforio and flung him into the back of a car, he'd told them that the Dancer had left only ten minutes before, climbing down the stairs and vanishing along a spur line. Jodie – the mutt's nickname – didn't know which direction he'd gone, only that he'd disappeared suddenly with his gun and his backpack. Haumann and Dellray sent their troopers to scour the station, the tracks, and the nearby City Hall station. They were now waiting for the results of the sweep.

'Come on . . .'

Ten minutes later a SWAT officer pushed through the

doorway. Sachs and Dellray both looked at him hopefully. But he shook his head. 'Lost his prints a hundred feet down the tracks. Don't have a clue where he went.'

Sachs sighed and reluctantly relayed the message to Rhyme and asked if she should do a search of the tracks and the nearby station.

He took the news as acerbically as she'd guessed he would. 'Dammit,' the criminalist muttered. 'No, just the station itself. Pointless to grid the others. Shit, how does he *do* it? It's like he's got some kind of fucking second sight.'

'Well,' she said, 'at least we've got a witness.'

And regretted immediately that she'd said that.

'Witness?' Rhyme spat out. 'A witness? I don't *need* witnesses. I need evidence! Well, get him down here anyway. Let's hear what he has to say. But, Sachs, I want that station swept like you've never swept a scene before. You hear me? Are you there, Sachs? Do you hear me?'

# Chapter
# TWENTY-FIVE

'And what do we have here?' Rhyme asked, giving a soft puff into the Storm Arrow control straw to scoot forward.

'An itsy piece of garbage,' offered Fred Dellray, cleaned up and back in uniform – if you could call an Irish green suit a uniform. 'Uh, uh, uh. Don't say a word. Not till we ask fo' it.' He turned his alarming stare on Jodie.

'You fooled me!'

'Quiet, you little skel.'

Rhyme wasn't pleased that Dellray had gone out on his own, but that was the nature of undercover work, and even if the criminalist didn't understand it exactly, he couldn't dispute that – as the agent's skills just proved – it could get results.

Besides, he'd saved Amelia Sachs's hide.

She'd be here soon. The medics had taken her to the emergency room for a rib X ray. She was bruised from the fall down the stairs, but nothing was broken. He'd been dismayed to learn that his talk the other night had had no effect; she'd gone into the subway after the Dancer alone.

Damn it, he thought, she's as pigheaded as me.

'I wasn't going to hurt anybody,' Jodie protested.

'Hard o' hearing? I said don't say a word.'

'I didn't know who she was!'

'No,' Dellray said, 'that pretty silver badge of hers didn't give nuthin' away.' Then remembered he didn't want to hear from the man.

Sellitto walked up close and bent over Jodie. 'Tell us some more about your friend.'

'I'm not his friend. He kidnapped me. I was in that building on Thirty-fifth because—'

'Because you were boosting pills. We know, we know.'

Jodie blinked. 'How'd you—'

'But we don't care about that. Not yet, at least. Keep going.'

'I thought he was a cop but then he said he was there to kill some people. I thought he was going to kill me too. He needed to escape so he told me to stand still and I did, and this cop or somebody came to the door and he stabbed him—'

'And killed him,' Dellray spat out.

Jodie sighed and looked miserable. 'I didn't know he was going to kill him. I thought he was just going to knock him out or something.'

'Well, asshole,' Dellray spat out, 'he *did* kill him. Killed him dead as a rock.'

Sellitto looked over the evidence bags from the subway, containing scuzzy porn magazines, hundreds of pills, clothes. A new cellular phone. A stack of money. He turned his attention back to Jodie. 'Keep going.'

'He said he'd pay me to get him out of there and I led him through this tunnel to the subway. How'd you *find* me, man?' He looked at Dellray.

''Cause you were skipping 'long the street hawking your be-bops to everybody you came across. I even knew your *name*. Jee-sus, you *are* a mutt. I oughta squeeze your neck till you're blue.'

'You can't hurt me,' he said, struggling to be defiant. 'I have rights.'

'Who hired him?' Sellitto asked Jodie. 'He mention the name Hansen?'

'He didn't say.' Jodie's voice quavered. 'Look, I only agreed to help him 'cause I knew he'd kill me if I didn't. I wasn't going to do it.' He turned to Dellray. 'He wanted me to get you to help. But soon as he left I wanted you to leave. I was going to the police and telling them. I *was*. He's a scary guy. I'm afraid of him!'

'Fred?' Rhyme asked.

'Yeah, yeah,' the agent conceded, 'he did have a change of tune. Wanted me gone. Didn't say anything about going to the police, though.'

'Where's he going? What were you supposed to do?'

'I was supposed to go through the trash bins in front of that town house and watch the cars. He told me to look for a man and a woman getting into a car and leaving. I was supposed to tell him what kind of car. I was going to call on that phone there. Then he was going to follow.'

'You were right, Lincoln,' Sellitto said. 'About keeping them in the safe house. He's going for a transport hit.'

Jodie continued, 'I was going to come to you—'

'Man, you're useless when you lie. Don't you have any dignity?'

'Look, I was *going* to,' he said, calmer now. He smiled. 'I figured there was a reward.'

Rhyme glanced at the greedy eyes and tended to believe him. He looked at Sellitto, who nodded in agreement.

'You cooperate now,' Sellitto grumbled, 'and we might just keep your ass out of jail. I don't know about money. Maybe.'

'I've never hurt anybody. I wouldn't. I—'

'Cool that tongue,' Dellray said. 'We all together on that?'

Jodie rolled his eyes.

'Together?' the agent whispered maliciously.

'Yeah, yeah, yeah.'

Sellitto said, 'We've got to move fast here. When were you supposed to be at the town house?'

'At twelve-thirty.'

They had fifty minutes left.

'What kind of car's he driving?'

'I don't know.'

'What's he look like?'

'In his early, mid-thirties, I guess. Not tall. But he was strong. Man, he had muscles. Crew-cut black hair. Round face. Look, I'll do one of those drawings . . . The police sketch thing.'

'Did he give you a name? Anything? Where he's from?'

'I don't know. He has kind of a Southern accent. Oh, and one thing – he said he wears gloves all the time because he's got a record.'

Rhyme asked, 'Where and for what?'

'I don't know where. But it's for manslaughter. He said he killed this guy in his town. When he was a teenager.'

'What else?' Dellray barked.

'Look,' Jodie said, crossing his arms and looking up at the agent, 'I've done some bad shit but I've never hurt anybody in my life. This guy kidnaps me and he's got all these guns and is one crazy fucked-up guy and I was scared to death. I think you woulda done the same thing I did. So I'm not putting up with this crap anymore. You want to arrest me, do it and, like, take me to detention. But I'm not gonna say anything else. Okay?'

Dellray's gangly face suddenly broke into a grin. 'Well, the rock cracks.'

Amelia Sachs appeared in the doorway and she walked in, glancing at Jodie.

'Tell them!' he said. 'I didn't hurt you. Tell 'em.'

She looked at him the way you'd look at a wad of used chewing gum. 'He was going to brain me with a Louisville Slugger.'

'Not so, not so!'

'You okay, Sachs?'

'Another bruise is all. On my back. Bookends.'

Sellitto, Sachs, and Dellray huddled with Rhyme, who told Sachs what Jodie'd reported.

The detective asked Rhyme in a whisper, 'We believe him?'

'Little skel,' Dellray muttered. 'But I gotta say I think he's telling the God-ugly truth.'

Sachs nodded too. 'I guess. But I think we have to keep him on a tight leash, whatever we do.'

Sellitto agreed. 'Oh, we'll keep him close.'

Rhyme reluctantly agreed too. It seemed impossible to get ahead of the Dancer without this man's help. He'd been adamant about keeping Percey and Hale in the safe house but in fact he hadn't *known* that the Dancer was going for a transport hit. He was only leaning toward that conclusion. He might easily have decided to move Percey and Hale and they might have been killed as they drove to the new safe house.

The tension gripped his jaw.

'How do you think we should handle it, Lincoln?' Sellitto asked.

This was tactical, not evidentiary. Rhyme looked at Dellray, who tugged his unlit cigarette out from behind his ear and smelled it for a moment. He finally said, 'Have the mutt make the call and try to get whatever dope he can from the Dancer. We'll set up a decoy car, send the Dancer after it. Have it full of our folks. Stop it fast, sandwich him in with a couple unmarkeds, and take him down.'

Rhyme nodded reluctantly. He knew how dangerous a tactical assault on a city street would be. 'Can we get him out of midtown?'

'We could lead him over to the East River,' Sellitto suggested. 'There's plenty of room there for a takedown. Some of those old parking lots. We could make it look like we're transferring them to another van. Doin' a round-robin.'

They agreed this would be the least dangerous approach.

Sellitto nodded toward Jodie, whispered, 'He's diming the Coffin Dancer . . . what're we gonna give him? Gotta be good to make it worth his while.'

'Waive conspiracy and aiding and abetting,' Rhyme said. 'Give him some money.'

'Fuck,' said Dellray, though he was generally known for his generosity with the undercover CIs who worked for him. But finally he nodded. 'Hokay, hokay. We'll split the bill. Depending on how greedy the rodent is.'

Sellitto called him over.

'All right, here's the deal. You help us, you make the call like he wanted *and* we get him, then we'll drop all charges and get you some reward money.'

'How much?' Jodie asked.

'Yo, mutt, you're not in any way, shape, or form to negotiate here.'

'I need money for a drug rehab program. I need another ten thousand. Is there any way?'

Sellitto looked at Dellray. 'What's your snitch fund look like?'

'We could go there,' the agent said, 'if you do halvsies. Yeah.'

'Really?' Jodie repressed a smile. 'Then I'll do whatever you want.'

Rhyme, Sellitto, and Dellray hashed out a plan. They'd set up a command post on the top floor of the safe house, where Jodie would be with the phone. Percey and Brit would be on the main floor, with troopers protecting them. Jodie would call the Dancer and tell him that the couple had just gotten into a van and were leaving. The van would move slowly through traffic to a deserted parking lot on the East Side. The Dancer'd follow. They'd take him in the lot.

'All right, let's put it together,' Sellitto said.

'Wait,' Rhyme ordered. They stopped and looked at him. 'We're forgetting the most important part of all.'

'Which is?'

'Amelia searched the scene at the subway. I want to analyze what she found. It might tell us how he's coming at us.'

'We *know* how he's coming at us, Linc,' Sellitto said, nodding at Jodie.

'Humor an old crip, will you? Now, Sachs, let's see what we've got.'

The Worm.

Stephen was moving through alleys, riding on buses, dodging the cops he saw and the Worm he couldn't see.

The Worm, watching him through every window on every street. The Worm, getting closer and closer.

He thought about the Wife and the Friend, he thought about the job, about how many bullets he had left, about whether the targets would be wearing body armor, what range he would shoot from, whether this time he should use a suppressor or not.

But these were automatic thoughts. He didn't control them any more than he controlled his breathing or heartbeat or the speed of the blood coursing through his body.

What his conscious thoughts were consumed with was Jodie.

What was there about him that was so fascinating?

Stephen couldn't say for certain. Maybe it was the way he lived by himself and didn't seem to be lonely. Maybe the way he carried that little self-help book around with him and truly wanted to crawl out of the hole he was in. Or the way he hadn't balked when Stephen told him to stand in the doorway and risk getting shot.

Stephen felt funny. He—

You feel what, Soldier?

Sir, I—

Funny, Soldier? What the fuck does 'funny' mean? You going soft on me?

No, sir, I am not.

It wasn't too late to change the plans. There were still alternatives. Plenty of alternatives.

Thinking about Jodie. About what he'd said to Stephen. Hell, maybe they *could* get coffee after the job was over.

They could go to Starbucks. It would be like when he was talking to Sheila, only this would be real. And he wouldn't have to drink that pissy little tea but he'd have real coffee, double strong like the kind Stephen's mother made in the morning for his stepfather, water at a rolling boil for exactly sixty seconds, exactly two and three-quarters level tablespoons per cup, not a single black ground spilled *anywhere*.

And was fishing or hunting totally out of the question?

Or the campfire . . .

He could tell Jodie to abort the mission. He could take the Wife and the Friend on his own.

Abort, Soldier? What're you *talking* about?

Sir, nothing, sir. I am considering all eventualities regarding the assault, as I have been instructed, sir.

Stephen climbed off the bus and slipped into the alley behind the fire station on Lexington. He rested the book bag behind a Dumpster, slipped his knife from the sheath under his jacket.

Jodie. Joe D . . .

He pictured the thin arms again, the way the man had looked at him.

I'm glad I met you too, partner.

Then Stephen shivered suddenly. Like the time in Bosnia when he'd had to jump into a stream to avoid being caught by guerrillas. The month was March and the water just above freezing.

He closed his eyes and pressed up against the brick wall, smelled the wet stone.

Jodie was—

Soldier, what the fuck is going on there?

Sir, I—

*What?*

Sir, uhm . . .

Spit it out. Now, Soldier!

Sir, I have ascertained that the enemy was trying psychological warfare. His attempts have proved unsuccessful, sir. I am ready to proceed as planned.

Very good, Soldier. But watch your fucking step.

And Stephen realized, as he opened the back door to the firehouse and slipped inside, that there'd be no changing the plans now. This was a perfect setup and he couldn't waste it, particularly when there was a chance not only of killing the Wife and the Friend but of killing Lincoln the Worm and the redheaded woman cop too.

Stephen glanced at his watch. Jodie would be in position in fifteen minutes. He'd call Stephen's phone. Stephen would answer and hear the man's high-pitched voice one last time.

And he'd push the transmit button that would detonate the twelve ounces of RDX in Jodie's cell phone.

Delegate . . . isolate . . . eliminate.

He really had no choice.

Besides, he thought, what would we ever have to talk about? What would we ever have to do after we'd finished our coffee?

# MONKEY SKILLS

[Falcons'] capacity for aerial acrobatics and foolery is matched only by the clowning of ravens, and they seem to fly for the pure hell of it.

*A RAGE FOR FALCONS*, STEPHEN BODIO

# Chapter
# TWENTY-SIX

Waiting.

Rhyme was now alone in his bed upstairs, listening in to the Special Ops frequency. He was dead tired. It was noon on Sunday and he'd had virtually no sleep. And he was exhausted from the most arduous effort of all – of trying to outthink the Dancer. It was taking its toll on his body.

Cooper was downstairs in the lab, running tests to confirm Rhyme's conclusions about the Dancer's latest tactic. Everyone else was at the safe house, Amelia Sachs too. Once Rhyme, Sellitto, and Dellray had decided how to counter what they believed would be the Dancer's next effort to kill Percey Clay and Brit Hale, Thom had checked Rhyme's blood pressure and asserted his virtual parental authority and ordered his boss into bed, no arguments, reasonable or otherwise, accepted. They'd ridden up in the elevator, Rhyme oddly silent, uneasy, wondering if he'd guessed right again.

'What's the matter?' Thom asked.

'Nothing. Why?'

'You're not complaining about anything. No grousing means something's wrong.'

'Ha. Very funny,' Rhyme grumbled.

After a sitting transfer to get him in bed, some bodily functions taken care of, Rhyme was now leaning back into his luxurious down pillow. Thom had slipped the voice recognition headset over his head and, despite his fatigue, Rhyme himself had gone through the steps of talking to the computer and having it patch into the Special Ops frequency.

This system *was* an amazing invention. Yes, he'd downplayed it to Sellitto and Banks. Yes, he'd *groused*. But the device, more than any other of his aids, made him feel differently about himself. For years he'd been resigned to never leading a life that approached normal. Yet with this machine and software he *did* feel normal.

He rolled his head in a circle and let it ease back into the pillow.

Waiting. Trying not to think of the debacle with Sachs last night.

Motion nearby. The falcon strutted into view. Rhyme saw a flash of white breast, then the bird turned his blue-gray back to Rhyme and looked out over Central Park. It was the male. The tiercel, he remembered Percey Clay telling him. Smaller and less ruthless than the female. He remembered something else about peregrines. They'd come back from the dead. Not too many years ago the entire population in eastern North America grew sterile from chemical pesticides and the birds nearly became extinct. Only through captive breeding efforts and control of pesticides had the creatures thrived.

*Back from the dead . . .*

The radio clattered. It was Amelia Sachs calling in. She sounded tense as she told him that everything was set up at the safe house.

'We're all on the top floor with Jodie,' she said. 'Wait . . . Here's the truck.'

An armored 4x4 with mirrored windows, filled with four officers from the tactical team, was being used as the bait.

It would be followed by a single unmarked van, containing – apparently – two plumbing supply contractors. In fact they were 32-E troopers in street clothes. In the back of the van were four others.

'The decoys're downstairs. Okay . . . okay.'

They were using two officers from Haumann's unit for decoys.

Sachs said, 'Here they go.'

Rhyme was pretty sure that given the Dancer's new plans, he wouldn't try a sniper shot from the street. Still, he found himself holding his breath.

'On the run . . .'

A click as the radio went dead.

Another click. Static. Sellitto broadcast, 'They made it. Looks good. Starting to drive. The tail cars're ready.'

'All right,' Rhyme said. 'Jodie's there?'

'Right here. In the safe house with us.'

'Tell him to make the call.'

'Okay, Linc. Here we go.'

The radio clicked off.

Waiting.

To see if this time the Dancer had faltered. To see if this time Rhyme had outthought the cold brilliance of the man's mind.

Waiting.

Stephen's cell phone brayed. He flipped it open.

''Lo.'

'Hi. It's me. It's—'

'I know,' Stephen said. 'Don't use names.'

'Right, sure.' Jodie sounded nervous as a cornered 'coon. A pause, then the little man said, 'Well, I'm here.'

'Good. You got that Negro to help you?'

'Uhm, yeah. He's here.'

'And where are you? Exactly?'

'Across the street from that town house. Man, there're a lot of cops. But nobody's paying any attention to me. There's a van just pulled up a minute ago. One of those four-by-fours. A big one. A Yukon. It's blue and it's easy to spot.' In his discomfort he was rambling. 'It's really, really neat. It has mirrored windows.'

'That means they're bulletproof.'

'Oh. Really. It's neat how you know all this stuff.'

You're going to die, Stephen said to him silently.

'This man and a woman just ran out of the alley with, like, ten cops. I'm sure it's them.'

'Not decoys?'

'Well, they didn't look like cops and they were looking pretty freaked out. Are you on Lexington?'

'Yeah.'

'In a car?' Jodie asked.

'Of course in a car,' Stephen said. 'I stole some little shit Jap thing. I'm going to follow them. Then wait 'till they get to some deserted areas and do it.'

'How?'

'How what?'

'How're you going to do it? Like a grenade or a machine gun?'

Stephen thought, Wouldn't you like to know?

He said, 'I'm not sure. It depends.'

'You see 'em?' Jodie asked, sounding uncomfortable.

'I see them,' Stephen said. 'I'm behind them. I'm pulling into traffic now.'

'A Jap car, huh?' Jodie said. 'Like a Toyota or something?'

Why, you little asshole traitor, Stephen thought bitterly, stung deeply by the betrayal even though he'd known it was probably inevitable.

Stephen was in fact watching the Yukon and backup vans

speed past him. He wasn't, however, in any Japanese car, shitty or otherwise. He wasn't in any car at all. Wearing the fireman's uniform he'd just stolen, he was standing on the street corner exactly one hundred feet from the safe house, watching the real version of the events Jodie was fictionalizing. He knew they were decoys in the Yukon. He knew the Wife and the Friend were still in the safe house.

Stephen picked up the gray remote-det transmitter. It looked like a walkie-talkie but had no speaker or microphone. He set the frequency to the bomb in Jodie's phone and armed the device.

'Stand by,' he said to Jodie.

'Heh,' Jodie laughed. 'Will do, sir.'

Lincoln Rhyme, just a spectator now, a voyeur.

Listening through his headset. Praying that he was right.

'Where's the van?' Rhyme heard Sellitto ask.

'Two blocks away,' Haumann said. 'We're on it. It's moving slowly up Lex. Getting near traffic. He . . . wait.' A long pause. 'What?'

'We've got a couple cars, a Nissan, a Subaru. An Accord too, but that's got three people in it. The Nissan's getting close to the van. That might be it. Can't see inside.'

Lincoln Rhyme closed his eyes. He felt his left ring finger, his only extant digit, flick nervously on the comforter covering the bed.

'Hello?' Stephen said into the phone.

'Yeah,' Jodie responded. 'I'm still here.'

'Directly across from the safe house?'

'That's right.'

Stephen was looking at the building directly across from the safe house. No Jodie, no Negro.

'I want to say something to you.'

'What's that?' the little man asked.

Stephen remembered the electric sizzle as his knee touched the man's.

I can't do it . . .

Soldier . . .

Stephen gripped the remote-det box in his left hand. He said, 'Listen carefully.'

'I'm listening. I—'

Stephen pushed the transmit button.

The explosion was astonishingly loud. Louder than even Stephen expected. It rattled panes and sent a million pigeons reeling into the sky. Stephen saw the glass and wood from the top floor of the safe house go spraying into the alley beside the building.

Which was even better than he hoped. He'd expected Jodie to be *near* the safe house. Maybe in a police van in front. Maybe in the alley. But he couldn't believe his good fortune that Jodie'd actually been inside. It was perfect!

He wondered who else had died in the blast.

Lincoln the Worm, he prayed.

The redheaded cop?

He looked over at the safe house and saw the smoke curling from the top window.

Now, just a few more minutes, until the rest of his team joined him.


The telephone rang and Rhyme ordered the computer to shut off the radio and answer the phone.

'Yes,' he said.

'Lincoln.' It was Lon Sellitto. 'I'm landline,' he said, referring to the phone. 'Want to keep Special Ops free for the chase.'

'Okay. Go ahead.'

'He blew the bomb.'

'I know.' Rhyme had heard it; the safe house was a mile or two from his bedroom, but his windows had rattled and the peregrines outside his window had taken off and flown a slow circle, angry at the disturbance.

'Everybody okay?'

'The mutt's freaking out, Jodie. But 'side from that everything's okay. 'Cept for the feds're looking at more damage to the safe house than they'd planned on. Already bitching about it.'

'Tell 'em we'll pay our taxes early this year.'

What had tipped Rhyme to the cell phone bomb had been tiny fingernails of polystyrene that Sachs had found in the trace at the subway station. That and more residue of plastic explosive, a slightly different formula from that of the AP bomb in Sheila Horowitz's apartment. Rhyme had simply matched the polystyrene fragments to the phone the Dancer'd given to Jodie and realized that somebody had unscrewed the casing.

Why? Rhyme had wondered. There was only one logical reason that he could see and so he'd called the bomb squad down at the Sixth Precinct. Two detectives had rendered the phone safe, removed the large wad of plastic explosive and the firing circuit from the phone, then mounted a much smaller bit of explosive and the same circuit in an oil drum near one of the windows, pointed into the alley like a mortar. They'd filled the room with bomb blankets and stepped into the corridor, handing the harmless phone back to Jodie, who held it with shaking hands, demanding that they prove to him all the explosive had been taken out.

Rhyme had guessed that the Dancer's tactic was to use the bomb to divert attention away from the van and give him a better chance to assault it. The killer had also probably guessed that Jodie would turn and, when he made the call, that the little man would be close to the cops who were mounting the operation. If he took out the leaders the Dancer would have an even better chance of success.

*Deception . . .*

There was no perp Rhyme hated more than the Coffin Dancer, no one he wanted more to run to ground and skewer through his hot heart. Still, Rhyme was a criminalist before anything else and he had a secret admiration for the man's brilliance.

Sellitto explained, 'We've got two tail cars behind the Nissan. We're going to—'

There was a long pause.

'Stupid,' Sellitto muttered.

'What?'

'Oh, nothing. It's just nobody called Central. We've got fire trucks coming in. Nobody called to tell 'em to ignore the reports of the blast.'

Rhyme had forgotten about that too.

Sellitto continued. 'Just got word. The decoy van's turning east, Linc. The Nissan's following. Maybe forty yards behind the van. It's about four blocks to the parking lot by the FDR.'

'Okay, Lon. Is Amelia there? I want to talk to her.'

'Jesus,' he heard someone call in the background. Bo Haumann, Rhyme thought. 'We got fire trucks all over the place here.'

'Didn't somebody . . . ?' another voice began to ask, then faded.

No, somebody didn't, Rhyme thought. You can't think of—

'Have to call you back, Lincoln,' Sellitto said. 'We gotta do something. There're fire trucks up on the goddamn sidewalks.'

'I'll call Amelia myself,' Rhyme said.

Sellitto hung up.

\*     \*     \*

The room darkened, curtains drawn.

Percey Clay was afraid.

Thinking of her haggard, the falcon, captured by the snare, flapping her muscular wings. The talons and beaks slicing the air like honed blades, the mad screech. But the most horrifying of all to Percey, the bird's frightened eyes. Denied her sky, the bird was lost in terror. Vulnerable.

Percey felt the same. She detested it here in the safe house. Closed in. Looking at – hating – the foolish pictures on the wall. Crap from Woolworth or J. C. Penney. The limp rug. The cheap water basin and pitcher. A ratty pink chenille bedspread, a dozen threads pulled out in long hoops from a particular corner; maybe a mob informant had sat there, tugging compulsively on the pink knobby cloth.

Another sip from the flask. Rhyme had told her about the trap. That the Dancer would be following the van he believed Percey and Hale were in. They'd stop his car and arrest or kill him. Her sacrifice was now going to pay off. In ten minutes they'd have him, the man who killed Ed. The man who'd changed her life forever.

She trusted Lincoln Rhyme, and believed him. But she believed him the same way she believed Air Traffic Control when they reported no wind shear and you suddenly found your aircraft dropping at three thousand feet a minute when you were only two thousand feet in the air.

Percey tossed her flask on the bed, stood up and paced. She wanted to be flying, where it was safe, where she had control. Roland Bell had ordered her lights out, had ordered her to stay locked in her room. Everyone was upstairs on the top floor. She'd heard the bang of the explosion. She'd been expecting it. But she hadn't been expecting the fear that it brought. Unbearable. She'd have given anything to look out the window.

She walked to the door, unlocked it, stepped into the corridor.

It too was dark. Like the night . . . *All the stars of evening*.

She smelled a pungent chemical scent. From whatever had made the bang, she guessed. The hallway was deserted. There was slight motion at the end of the hall. A shadow from the stairwell. She looked at it. It wasn't repeated.

Brit Hale's room was only ten feet away. She wanted badly to talk to him, but she didn't want him to see her this way, pale, hands shaking. Eyes watering in fear . . . My God, she'd pulled a seven three seven out of a wing-ice nosedive more calmly than this: looking into that dark corridor.

She stepped back into her room.

Did she hear footsteps?

She closed the door, returned to the bed.

More footsteps.

'Command mode,' Lincoln Rhyme instructed. The box dutifully came up on-screen.

He heard a faint siren in the distance.

And it was then that Rhyme realized his mistake.

Fire trucks . . .

No! I didn't think about that.

But the Dancer did. Of course! He'd have stolen a fireman's or medic's uniform and was strolling into the safe house at this moment!

'Oh, no,' he muttered. 'No! How could I be so far off?'

And the computer heard the last word of Rhyme's sentence and dutifully shut off his communications program.

'No!' Rhyme cried. 'No!'

But the system couldn't understand his loud, frantic voice and with a silent flash the message came up, *Do you really want to shut off your computer?*

'No,' he whispered desperately.

For a moment nothing happened, but the system didn't shut down. A message popped up. *What would you like to do now?*

'Thom!' he shouted. 'Somebody . . . please. Mel!'

But the door was closed; there was no response from downstairs.

Rhyme's left ring finger twitched dramatically. At one time he'd had a mechanical ECU controller and he could use his one working finger to dial the phone. The computer system had replaced that and he now *had* to use the dictation program to call the safe house and tell them that the Dancer was on his way there, dressed as a fireman or rescue worker.

'Command mode,' he said into the microphone. Fighting to stay calm.

*I did not understand what you just said. Please try again.*

Where was the Dancer now? Was he inside already? Was he just about to shoot Percey Clay or Brit Hale?

Or Amelia Sachs?

'Thom! Mel!'

*I did not understand . . .*

Why wasn't I thinking better?

'Command mode,' he said breathlessly, trying to master the panic.

The command mode message box popped up. The cursor arrow sat at the top of the screen and, a continent away, at the bottom, was the communications program icon.

'Cursor down,' he gasped.

Nothing happened.

'Cursor down,' he called, louder.

The message came back: *I did not understand what you just said. Please try again.*

'Oh, goddamn . . .'

*I did not understand . . .*

Softer, forcing himself to speak in a normal tone, he said, 'Cursor down.'

The glowing white arrow began its leisurely trip down the screen.

We've still got time, he told himself. And it wasn't as though the people in the safe house were unprotected or unarmed.

'Cursor left,' he gasped.

*I did not understand . . .*

'Oh, come on!'

*I did not understand . . .*

'Cursor up . . . cursor left.'

The cursor moved like a snail over the screen until it came to the icon.

Calm, calm . . .

'Cursor stop. Double click.'

Dutifully, an icon of a walkie-talkie popped up on the screen.

He pictured the faceless Dancer moving up behind Percey Clay with a knife or garrote.

In as calm a voice as he could muster he ordered the cursor to the set-frequency box.

It seated itself perfectly.

'Four,' Rhyme said, pronouncing the word so very carefully.

A 4 popped up into the box. Then he said, 'Eight.'

The letter *A* appeared in the second box.

Lord in heaven!

'Delete left.'

*I did not understand . . .*

No, no!

He thought he heard footsteps. 'Hello?' he cried. 'Is someone there? Thom? Mel?'

No answer except from his friend the computer, which placidly offered its contrarian response once again.

'Eight,' he said slowly.

The number appeared. His next attempt, 'Three,' popped into the box without a problem.

'Point.'

The word *point* appeared.

Goddamn!

'Delete left.' Then, 'Decimal.'

The period popped up.

'Four.'

One space left. Remember, it's *zero* not *oh*. Sweat streaming down his face, he added the final number of the Secure Ops frequency without a glitch.

The radio clicked on.

Yes!

But before he could transmit, static clattered harshly and, with a frozen heart, he heard a man's frantic voice crying, 'Ten-thirteen, need assistance, federal protection location six.'

The safe house.

He recognized the voice as Roland Bell's. 'Two down and . . . Oh, Jesus, he's still here. He's got us, he's hit us! We need—'

There were two gunshots. Then others. A dozen. A huge firefight. It sounded like Macy's fireworks on the fourth of July.

'We need—'

The transmission ended.

'Percey!' Rhyme cried. 'Percey . . .'

On the screen came the message in simple type: *I did not understand what you just said. Please try again*.


A nightmare.

Stephen Kall, in ski mask and wearing the bulky fireman's coat, lay pinned down in the corridor of the safe house, behind the body of one of the two U.S. marshals he'd just killed.

Another shot, closer, digging a piece out of the floor near his head. Fired by the detective with the thinning brown hair – the one he'd seen in the window of the safe house that morning. He crouched in a doorway, presenting a fair target, but Stephen couldn't get a clean shot at him. The detective held automatic pistols in both his hands and was an excellent shot.

Stephen crawled forward another yard, toward one of the open doorways.

Panicked, cringey, coated with worms . . .

He fired again and the brown-haired detective ducked back into the room, called something on his radio, but came right back, firing coolly.

Wearing a fireman's long, black coat – the same as thirty or forty other men and women in front of the safe house – Stephen had blown open the alley door with a cutting charge and run inside, expecting to find the interior a fiery shambles and the Wife and Friend – as well as half the other people inside – blown to pieces or badly wounded. But Lincoln the Worm had fooled him again. He'd figured out that the phone was booby-trapped. The only thing they hadn't expected was that he'd hit the safe house again; they believed he was going for a transport hit. Still, when he burst inside he was met by the frantic fire from the two marshals. But they'd been stunned by the cutting charge and he'd managed to kill them.

Then the brown-haired detective charged around the corner firing both-handed, skimming two off Stephen's vest, while Stephen himself danced one round off the detective's and they fell backward simultaneously. More shooting, more near misses. The cop was almost as good a shot as he was.

A minute at the most. He had no more time than that.

He felt so wormy he wanted to cry . . . He'd thought his plan out as best he could. He couldn't get any smarter than he'd been and Lincoln the Worm had *still* outthought him. Was this him? The balding detective with the two guns?

Another volley from Stephen's gun. And . . . damn . . . the brown-haired detective dove right into it, kept coming forward. Every other cop in the world would've run for cover. But not him. He struggled another two feet forward, then three. Stephen reloaded, fired again, crawling about the same distance toward the door of his target's room.

You disappear into the ground, boy. You can make yourself invisible, you want to.

I want to, sir. I want to be invisible . . .

Another yard, almost to the doorway.

'This's Roland Bell again!' the cop shouted into his microphone. 'We need backup immediately!'

*Bell*, Stephen noted the name. So he's not Lincoln the Worm.

The cop reloaded and continued to fire. A dozen shots, two dozen . . . Stephen could only admire his technique. This Bell would keep track of how many shots he'd fired from each gun and alternate reloading so he was never without a loaded weapon.

The cop parked a slug in the wall an inch from Stephen's face, and Stephen returned a shot that landed just as close.

Crawling forward another two feet.

Bell glanced up and saw that Stephen had finally made it to the doorway of the darkened bedroom. Their eyes locked and, mock soldier though he was, Stephen Kall had seen enough combat to know that the string of rationality within this cop had snapped and he'd become the most dangerous thing there was – a skillful soldier with no regard for his own safety. Bell rose to his feet and started forward, firing from both guns.

That's why they used .45s in the Pacific Theater, boy. Big slugs to stop those crazy little Japs. When they came at you they didn't care about getting killed; they just didn't want to get stopped.

Stephen lowered his head, tossed the one-second-delay flash bang at Bell and closed his eyes. The grenade detonated with an astonishingly loud explosion. He heard the cop cry out and saw him stumble to his knees, hands over his face.

Stephen had guessed that because of the guards and Bell's furious effort to stop him, either the Wife or the Friend was in this room. Stephen had also guessed that whoever it was would be hiding in the closet or under the bed.

He was wrong.

As he glanced into the doorway he saw the figure come charging at him, holding a lamp as a weapon and uttering a wail of fear and anger.

Five fast shots from Stephen's gun. Head and chest hits, well grouped. The body spun around fast and flew backward to the floor

Good job, Soldier.

Then more footsteps on the floor coming down the stairs. A woman's voice. And more voices too. No time to finish Bell, no time to look for the other target.

Evacuate . . .

He ran to the back door and stuck his head outside, shouting for more firemen.

A half dozen of them ran up cautiously.

Stephen nodded them inside. 'Gas line just blew. I'd get everybody out. Now!'

And he disappeared into the alley, then stepped into the street, dodging the Mack and Seagrave fire trucks, the ambulances, the police cars.

Shaken, yes.

But satisfied. His job was now two-thirds finished.

*     *     *

Amelia Sachs was the first to respond to the bang of the entry charge and the shouts.

Then Roland Bell's voice from the first floor: 'Backup! Backup! Officer down!'

And gunfire. A dozen sharp cracks, a dozen more.

She didn't know how the Dancer'd done it and she didn't care. She wanted only a fair glimpse of target and two seconds to sink half a clip of nine-millimeter hollow-points into him.

The light Glock in her hand, she pushed into the second floor corridor. Behind her were Sellitto and Dellray and a young uniform, whose credentials under fire she wished she'd taken the time to learn. Jodie cowered on the floor, painfully aware he'd betrayed a very dangerous man who was armed and no more than thirty feet away.

Sachs's knees screamed as she took the stairs fast, the arthritis again, and she winced as she leapt down the last three steps to the first floor.

In her headset she heard Bell's repeated request for assistance.

Down the dark corridor, pistol close to the body, where it couldn't be knocked aside (only TV cops and movie gangsters stick a gun out in front of them phallically before turning corners, or tilt a weapon on its side). Fast glance into each of the rooms she passed, crouching, below chest height, where a muzzle would be pointed.

'I'll take the front,' Dellray called and vanished down the hallway behind her, his big Sig-Sauer in hand.

'Watch our backs,' Sachs ordered Sellitto and the uniform, caring not a bit about rank.

'Yes'm,' the young man answered. 'I'm watching. Our backs.'

Puffing Sellitto was too, his head swiveling back and forth.

Static crinkled in her ear but she heard no voices. She

tugged the headset off – no distractions – and continued cautiously down the corridor.

At her feet two U.S. marshals lay dead on the floor.

The smell of chemical explosive was strong and she glanced toward the back door of the safe house. It was steel but he'd blown it open with a powerful cutting charge as if it had been paper.

'Jesus,' Sellitto said, too professional to bend down over the fallen marshals but too human not to glance in horror at their riddled bodies.

Sachs came to one room, paused at the door. Two of Haumann's troops entered from the destroyed doorway.

'Cover,' she called and before anyone had a chance to stop her she leapt through the doorway fast.

Glock up, scanning the room.

Nothing.

No cordite smell either. There'd been no shooting here.

Back into the corridor. Heading toward the next doorway.

She pointed to herself and then into the room. The 32-E officers nodded.

Sachs spun around the doorway, ready to fire, the troopers right behind. She froze at the sight of the gun muzzle aimed at her chest.

'Lord,' Roland Bell muttered and lowered his weapon. His hair was mussed and his face was sooty. Two bullets had torn his shirt and streaked over his body armor.

Then her eyes took in the terrible sight on the floor.

'Oh, no . . .'

'Building's clear,' a patrolman called from the corridor. 'They saw him leave. He was wearing a fireman's uniform. He's gone. Lost in the crowd out front.'

Amelia Sachs, once again a criminalist and not a tactical officer, observed the blood spatter, the astringent scent of gunshot residue, the fallen chair, which might indicate a struggle and therefore would be a logical transfer point for trace evidence. The bullet casings, which she immediately noticed were from a 7.62 millimeter automatic.

She observed too the way the body had fallen, which told her that the victim had been attacking the attacker, apparently with a lamp. There were other stories the crime scene would tell and, for that reason, she knew she should help Percey Clay to her feet and lead her away from the body of her slain friend. But Sachs couldn't do that. All she could do was watch the small woman with the squat unpretty face cradle Brit Hale's bloody head, muttering, 'Oh, no, oh, no . . .'

Her face was a mask, unmoving, untouched by tears.

Finally Sachs nodded to Roland Bell, who slipped his arms around Percey and led her out into the corridor, still vigilant, still clutching his own weapon.

Two hundred and thirty yards from the safe house.

Red and blue lights from the dozens of emergency vehicles flashed and tried to blind him but he was sighting through the Redfield telescope and was oblivious to anything but the reticles. He scanned back and forth over the kill zone.

Stephen had stripped off the fireman's uniform and was dressed again as a late-blooming college student. He'd recovered the Model 40 from under the water tank, where he'd hidden it that morning. The weapon was loaded and locked. The sling was around his arm and he was ready to murder.

At the moment it wasn't the Wife he was after.

And it wasn't Jodie, the little faggot Judas.

He was looking for Lincoln the Worm. The man who'd outthought him once again.

Who was he? Which of them?

Cringey.

Lincoln . . . Prince of Worms.

Where are you? Are you right in front of me now? In that crowd standing around the smoking building?

Was he that large lump of a cop, sweating like a hog?

The tall, thin Negro in the green suit? He looked familiar. Where had Stephen seen him before?

An unmarked car streaked up and several men in suits climbed out.

Maybe Lincoln was one of *them*.

The red-haired policewoman stepped outside. She was wearing latex gloves. Crime Scene, are you? Well, I treat my casings and slugs, darling, he said to her silently as the reticles of the telescope picked out a pretty target on her neck. And you'll have to fly to Singapore before you pick up a lead to my gun.

He figured he had time to fire just one shot and then be driven into the alley by the fusillade that would follow.

*Who are you?*

Lincoln? Lincoln?

But he had no clue.

Then the front door swung open and Jodie appeared, stepping out the door uneasily. He looked around, squinted, shrank back against the building.

You . . .

The electric sizzle again. Even at this distance.

Stephen easily moved the reticles onto his chest.

Go ahead, Soldier, fire your weapon. He's a logical target; he can identify you.

Sir, I am adjusting for tracking and windage.

Stephen upped the poundage on his trigger.

Jodie . . .

He betrayed you, Soldier. Take . . . him . . . out.

Sir, yessir. He is ice cold. He is dead meat. Sir, vultures are already hovering.

Soldier, the USMC sniper's manual dictates that you

increase poundage on the trigger of your Model 40 imperceptibly so that you are not aware of the exact moment your weapon will discharge. Is that correct, Soldier?

Sir, yessir.

Then why the fuck aren't you doing it?

He squeezed harder.

Slowly, slowly . . .

But the gun wasn't firing. He lifted the sights to Jodie's head. And as it happened, Jodie's eyes, which had been scanning the rooftops, saw him.

He'd waited too long.

Shoot, Soldier. Shoot!

A whisper of a pause . . .

Then he jerked the trigger like a boy on the .22 rifle range at summer camp.

Just as Jodie leapt out of the way, pushing the cops with him aside.

How the fuck d'you miss that shot, Soldier? Repeat fire!

Sir, yessir.

He got off two more rounds but Jodie and everyone else was under cover or crawling fast along the sidewalk and street.

And then the return fire began. First a dozen guns, then a dozen more. Mostly pistols but some H&Ks too, spewing the bullets so fast they sounded like unmuffled car engines.

Bullets were striking the elevator tower behind him, showering him with bits of brick and concrete and lead and sharp, craggy copper jackets from the slugs, cutting his forearms and the backs of his hands.

Stephen fell backward, covering his face with his hands. He felt the cuts and saw tiny drops of his blood fall on the tar paper roof.

Why did I wait? Why? I could have shot him and been gone.

Why?

The sound of a helicopter speeding toward the building. More sirens.

Evacuate, Soldier! Evacuate!

He glanced down to see Jodie scrambling to safety behind a car. Stephen threw the Model 40 into the case, slung the backpack over his shoulder, and slid down the fire escape into the alley.

The second tragedy.

Percey Clay had changed her clothes and stepped into the corridor, slumped against the strong figure of Roland Bell. He put his arm around her.

The second of three. It hadn't been their mechanic quitting or problems with the charter. It had been the death of her dear friend.

Oh, Brit . . .

Imagining him, eyes wide, mouth open in a soundless shout, charge toward the terrible man. Trying to stop him, appalled that someone would actually be trying to kill him, to kill Percey. More indignant and betrayed than scared. Your life was so precise, she thought to him. Even your risks were calculated. The inverted flight at fifty feet, the tailspins, the skydiving. To spectators, it looked impossible. But you knew what you were doing and if you thought about the chance of an early death, you believed it would be from a bum linkage or a clogged fuel line or some careless student who intruded into your airspace.

The great aviation writer Ernest K. Gann wrote that fate was a hunter. Percey'd always thought he meant nature or circumstance – the fickle elements, the faulty mechanisms that conspire to send airplanes hurtling into the ground. But fate was more complicated than that. Fate was as complicated as the human mind. As complicated as evil.

Tragedies came in threes . . . And what would the last one be? Her death? The Company's? Someone else's?

Huddling against Roland Bell, she shivered with anger at the coincidence of it all. Thinking back: she and Ed and Hale, groggy from lack of sleep, standing in the glare of the hangar lights around Learjet *Charlie Juliet*, hoping desperately they'd win the U.S. Medical contract, shivering in the damp night as they tried to figure out how best to outfit the jet for the job.

Late, a misty night. The airport deserted and dark. Like the final scene in *Casablanca*.

Hearing the squeal of brakes and glancing outside.

The man lugging the huge duffle bags out of the car on the tarmac, flinging them inside, and firing up the Beachcraft. The distinctive whine of a piston engine starting.

She remembered Ed saying, incredulous, 'What's he doing? The airport's closed.'

Fate.

That they happened to be there that night.

That Phillip Hansen had chosen that exact moment to get rid of his damaging evidence.

That Hansen was a man who would kill to keep that flight a secret.

*Fate* . . .

Then she jumped – at a knocking on the door of the safe house.

Two men stood there. Bell recognized them. They were from the NYPD Witness Protection Division. 'We're here to transport you to the Shoreham facility on Long Island, Mrs Clay.'

'No, no,' she said. 'There's a mistake. I have to go to Mamaroneck Airport.'

'Percey,' Roland Bell said.

'I *have* to.'

'I don't know about that, ma'am,' one of the officers said. 'We've got orders to take you to Shoreham and keep you in protective confinement until a grand jury appearance on Monday.'

'No, no, no. Call Lincoln Rhyme. He knows about it.'

'Well . . .' One of the officers looked to the other.

'Please,' she said, 'call him. He'll tell you.'

'Actually, Mrs Clay, it was Lincoln Rhyme who ordered you moved. If you'll come with us, please. Don't you worry. We'll take good care of you, ma'am.'

# Chapter
# TWENTY-SEVEN

'It's not pleasant,' Thom told Amelia Sachs.

From behind the bedroom door she heard, 'I want that bottle and I want it now.'

'What's going on?'

The handsome young man grimaced. 'Oh, he can be such a prick sometimes. He got one of the patrol officers to pour him some scotch. For the pain, he said. He said he's got a prescription for single-malt. Can you believe it? Oh, he's insufferable when he drinks.'

A howl of rage from his room.

Sachs knew the only reason he wasn't throwing things was that he couldn't.

She reached for the doorknob.

'You might want to wait a little,' Thom warned.

'We can't wait.'

'*Goddamnit!*' Rhyme snarled. 'I want that fucking bottle!'

She opened the door. Thom whispered, 'Don't say I didn't warn you.'

Inside, Sachs paused in the doorway. Rhyme was a sight. His hair was disheveled, there was spittle on his chin, and his eyes were red.

The Macallan bottle was on the floor. He must have tried to grab it with his teeth and knocked it over.

He noticed Sachs but all he said was a brisk 'Pick it up.'

'We've got work to do, Rhyme.'

'Pick. Up. That. Bottle.'

She did. And placed it on the shelf.

He raged, 'You know what I mean. I want a drink.'

'You've had more than enough, sounds like.'

'Pour some whiskey in my goddamn glass. Thom! Get the hell in here . . . Coward.'

'Rhyme,' she snapped, 'we've got evidence to look at.'

'Hell with the evidence.'

'How much did you drink?'

'The Dancer got inside, didn't he? Fox in the henhouse. Fox in the henhouse.'

'I've got a vacuum filter full of trace, I've got a slug, I've got samples of his blood . . .'

'Blood? Well, that's fair. He's got plenty of ours.'

She snapped back, 'You oughta be like a kid on his birthday, all the evidence I've got. Quit feeling sorry for yourself, and let's get to work.'

He didn't respond. As she looked at him she saw his bleary eyes focused past her on the doorway. She turned. There was Percey Clay.

Immediately, Rhyme's eyes dropped to the floor. He fell silent.

Sure, Sachs thought. Doesn't want to misbehave in front of his new love.

She walked into the room, looked at the mess that was Lincoln Rhyme.

'Lincoln, what's going on?' Sellitto had accompanied Percey here, she guessed. He stepped into the room.

'Three dead, Lon. He got three more. Fox in the henhouse.'

'Lincoln,' Sachs blurted. 'Stop it. You're embarrassing yourself.'

Wrong thing to say. Rhyme slapped a bewildered gaze on his face. 'I'm not embarrassed. Do I look embarrassed? Anyone? Am I embarrassed? *Am I fucking embarrassed?*'

'We've got—'

'No, we've got zip! It's over with. It's done. It's finished. Duck 'n' cover. We're heading for the hills. Are you going to join us, Amelia? Suggest you do.'

He finally looked at Percey. 'What are you doing here? You're supposed to be on Long Island.'

'I want to talk to you.'

He said nothing at first, then, 'Give me a drink, at least.'

Percey glanced at Sachs and stepped forward to the shelf, poured herself and Rhyme both glasses. Sachs glared at her and she noticed, didn't respond.

'Here's a classy lady,' Rhyme said. 'I kill her partner and she still shares a drink with me. *You* didn't do that, Sachs.'

'Oh, Rhyme, you can be such an asshole,' Sachs spat out. 'Where's Mel?'

'Sent him home. Nothing more to do . . . We're bundling her up and shipping her off to Long Island, where she'll be safe.'

'What?' Sachs asked.

'Doing what we should've done at the beginning. Hit me again.'

Percey began to. Sachs said, 'He's had enough.'

'Don't listen to her,' Rhyme blurted. 'She's mad at me. I don't do what she wants and so she gets mad.'

Oh, thank you, Rhyme. Let's air linen in public, why don't we? She turned her beautiful, cold eyes on him. He didn't even notice; he was gazing at Percey Clay.

Who said, 'You made a deal with me. The next thing I know there're two agents about to take me off to Long Island. I thought I could trust you.'

'But if you *trust* me, you'll die.'

'It was a risk,' Percey said. 'You told us there was a chance he'd get into the safe house.'

'Sure, but you didn't know that I figured it out.'

'You . . . what?'

Sachs frowned, listened.

Rhyme continued, 'I figured out he was going to hit the safe house. I figured out he was in a fireman's uniform. I fucking figured out he'd use a cutting charge on the back door. I'll bet it was an Accuracy Systems Five Twenty-one or Five Twenty-two with an Instadet firing system. Am I right?'

'I—'

'*Am I right?*'

'A Five Twenty-one,' Sachs said.

'See? I figured all that out. I knew it five minutes before he got in. It's just that I couldn't fucking call anyone and tell them! I couldn't . . . pick up . . . the fucking phone and tell anybody what was going to happen. And your friend died. Because of me.'

Sachs felt pity for him and it was sour. She was torn apart by his pain, yet she didn't have a clue what she might say to comfort him.

There was moisture on his chin. Thom stepped forward with a tissue, but he waved the aide away with a furious nod of his handsome jaw. He nodded toward the computer. 'Oh, I got cocky. I got to thinking I was pretty normal. Driving around like a race car driver in the Storm Arrow, flipping on lights and changing CDs . . . What bullshit!' He closed his eyes and pressed his head back in the pillow.

A sharp laugh, surprising everyone, filled the room.

Percey Clay poured some more scotch into her glass. Then a little more for Rhyme too. 'There's bullshit here, that's for sure. But it's only what I'm hearing from you.'

Rhyme opened his eyes, glaring.

Percey laughed again.

'Don't,' Rhyme warned ambiguously.

'Oh, please,' she muttered dismissingly. 'Don't what?'

Sachs watched Percey's eyes narrow. 'What're you saying?' Percey began. 'That somebody's dead because of . . . technical failure?'

Sachs realized that Rhyme had been expecting her to say something else. He was caught off guard. After a moment he said, 'Yes. That's exactly what I'm saying. If I'd been able to pick up the phone—'

She cut him off. 'And, what? That gives you the right to have a goddamn tantrum? To renege on your promises?' She tossed back her liquor and gave an exasperated sigh. 'Oh, for God's sake . . . Do you have any idea what I do for a living?'

To her astonishment Sachs saw that Rhyme was calm now. He started to speak, but Percey cut him off. 'Think about this.' Her drawl was back. 'I sit in a little aluminum tube going four hundred knots an hour, six miles above the ground. It's sixty below zero outside and the winds are a hundred miles an hour. I'm not even talking about lightning, wind sheer, and ice. Jesus Christ, I'm only alive *because* of machines.' Another laugh. 'How's that different from you?'

'You don't understand,' he said snippily.

'You're not answering my question. How?' she demanded, unrelenting. 'How's it different?'

'You can walk around, you can pick up the phone—'

'I can walk around? I'm at fifty thousand feet. I open that door and my blood boils in seconds.'

For the first time since she'd known him, Sachs thought, Rhyme's met his match. He's speechless.

Percey continued, 'I'm sorry, Detective, but I don't see a lick of difference between us. We're products of twentieth-century science. Goddamn it, if I had wings I'd be flying on my own. But I don't and never will. To do what we have to do, both of us . . . we *rely*.'

'Okay . . .' He grinned devilishly.

Come on, Rhyme, Sachs thought. Let her have it! How badly Sachs wanted him to win, to boot this woman off to Long Island, have done with her forever.

The criminalist said, 'But if *I* screw up, people die.'

'Oh? And what happens if my deicer fails? What happens if my yaw damper goes? What if a pigeon flies into my pitot tube on an ILS approach? I . . . am . . . dead. Flameouts, hydraulic failures, mechanics who forget to replace bum circuit breakers . . . Redundant systems fail. In *your* case they might get a chance to recover from their gunshots. But my aircraft hits the ground at three hundred miles an hour, there ain't nothing left.'

Rhyme seemed completely sober now. His eyes were swiveling around the room as if looking for an infallible bit of evidence to refute Percey's argument.

'Now,' Percey said evenly, 'I understand Amelia here has some evidence she found back at the safe house. My suggestion is you start looking at it and stop this asshole once and for all. Because I am on my way to Mamaroneck right now to finish repairing my aircraft and then I'm flying that job tonight. Now, I'll ask you point-blank: You going to let me go to the airport, like you agreed? Or do I have to call my lawyer?'

He was still speechless.

A moment passed.

Sachs jumped when Rhyme called in his booming baritone, 'Thom! *Thom!* Get in here.'

The aide peered around the doorway suspiciously.

'I've made a mess here. Look, I knocked my glass over. And my hair's mussed. Would you mind straightening up a little? Please?'

'Are you fooling with us, Lincoln?' he asked dubiously.

'And Mel Cooper? Could you call him, Lon? He must have taken me seriously. I was kidding. He's such a goddamn scientist. No sense of humor. We'll need him back here.'

Amelia Sachs wanted to flee. To bolt out of here, get into her car, and tear up the roads in New Jersey or Nassau County at 120 miles an hour. She couldn't stand to be in the same room with this woman a moment longer.

'All right, Percey,' Rhyme said, 'take Detective Bell with you and we'll make sure plenty of Bo's troopers are with you too. Get up to your airport. Do what you have to do.'

'Thank you, Lincoln.' She nodded, and offered a smile.

Just enough of one to make Amelia Sachs wonder if part of Percey Clay's speech wasn't meant for Sachs's benefit too, to make clear who the undisputed winner in this contest was. Well, some sports Sachs believed she was doomed to lose. Champion shooter, decorated cop, a demon of a driver, and pretty good criminalist, Sachs nonetheless possessed an unjacketed heart. Her father had sensed this about her; he'd been a romantic too. After she'd gone through a bad affair some years ago he'd said to her, 'They oughta make body armor for the soul, Amie. They oughta do that.'

Good-bye, Rhyme, she thought. Good-bye.

And his response to this tacit farewell? A minuscule glance and the gruff words 'Let's look at that evidence, Sachs. Time's a-wasting.'

# Chapter
# TWENTY-EIGHT

Individuation is the goal of the criminalist.

It's the process of tracing a piece of evidence back to a single source, to the exclusion of all other sources.

Lincoln Rhyme now gazed at the most individuated evidence there was: blood from the Dancer's body. A restriction fragment length polymorphism DNA test could eliminate virtually any possibility that the blood had come from anyone else.

Yet there was little that this evidence could tell him. CODIS – the Computer-Based DNA Information System – contained profiles of some convicted felons, but it was a small database, made up primarily of sex offenders and a limited number of violent criminals. Rhyme wasn't surprised when the search of the Dancer's blood came back negative.

Still, Rhyme harbored a faint pleasure that they now had a piece of the killer himself, swabbed and stuck into a test tube. For most criminalists, the perps were usually 'out there'; he rarely met them face-to-face, often never saw them at all unless it was at trial. So he felt a deep stirring to be in the presence of the man who'd caused so many people, himself included, so much pain.

'What else did you find?' he asked Sachs.

She'd vacuumed Brit Hale's room for trace but she and Cooper, donning magnifiers, had been through it all and found nothing except gunshot residue and fragments of bullets and brick and plaster from the shoot-outs.

She'd found casings from the semiautomatic pistol he'd used. His weapon was a 7.62-millimeter Beretta. It was probably old; it showed breach spread. The casings, all of which Sachs had recovered, had been dipped in cleansers to eliminate even the prints of the employees of the ammunition company – so no one could trace the purchase back to a certain shift at one of the Remington plants and then forward to a shipment that ended up in a particular location. And the Dancer had apparently loaded them with his knuckles to avoid prints. An old trick.

'Keep going,' Rhyme said to Sachs.

'Pistol slugs.'

Cooper looked over the bullets. Three flattened. And one in pretty good shape. Two were covered with Brit Hale's black, cauterized blood.

'Scan them for prints,' Rhyme ordered.

'I did,' she said, her voice clipped.

'Try the laser.'

Cooper did.

'Nothing, Lincoln.' The tech looked at a piece of cotton in a plastic bag. He asked, 'What's that?'

Sachs said, 'Oh, I got one of his rifle slugs too.'

'What?'

'He took a couple shots at Jodie. Two of them hit the wall and exploded. This one hit dirt – a bed of flowers – and didn't go off. I found a hole in one of the geraniums and—'

'Wait.' Cooper blinked. 'That's one of the *explosive* rounds?'

Sachs said, 'Right, but it didn't go off.'

He gingerly set the bag on the table and stepped back,

pulling Sachs – two inches taller than he was – along with him.

'What's the matter?'

'Explosive bullets're very unstable. Powder grains could be smouldering right now . . . It could go off at any minute. A piece of shrapnel could kill you.'

'You saw the fragments of the other ones, Mel,' Rhyme said. 'How's it made?'

'It's nasty, Lincoln,' the tech said uneasily, his bald crown dotted with sweat. 'A PETN filling, smokeless powder as the primary. That makes it unstable.'

Sachs asked, 'Why didn't it go off?'

'The dirt'd be soft impact. And he makes them himself. Maybe his quality control wasn't so good for that one.'

'He makes them himself?' Rhyme asked. 'How?'

Eye fixed on the plastic bag, the tech said, 'Well, the usual way is to tap a hole from the point almost through the base. Drop in a BB and some black or smokeless powder. You roll a thread of plastic and feed it inside. Then seal it up again – in his case with a ceramic nose cone. When it hits, the BB slams into the powder. That sets off the PETN.'

'Rolls the plastic?' Rhyme asked. 'Between his fingers?'

'Usually.'

Rhyme looked at Sachs and for a moment the rift between them vanished. They smiled and said simultaneously, 'Fingerprints!'

Mel Cooper said, 'Maybe. But how're you going to find out? You'd have to take it apart.'

'Then,' Sachs said, 'we'll take it apart.'

'No, no, no, Sachs,' Rhyme said curtly. 'Not you. We'll wait for the bomb squad.'

'We don't have time.'

She bent over the bag, started to open it.

'Sachs, what the hell're you trying to prove?'

'Not trying to prove anything,' she responded coolly. 'I'm trying to catch the killer.'

Cooper stood by helplessly.

'Are you trying to save Jerry Banks? Well, it's too late for that. Give him up. Get on with your job.'

'This *is* my job.'

'Sachs, it wasn't your fault!' Rhyme shouted. 'Forget it. Give up the dead. I've told you that a dozen times.'

Calmly she said, 'I'll put my vest on top of it, work from behind it.' She stripped her blouse off and ripped the Velcro straps of her American Body Armor. She set this up like a tent over the plastic bag containing the bullet.

Cooper said, 'You're behind the armor but your hands won't be.'

'Bombs suits don't have hand protection either,' she pointed out, and pulled her shooting earplugs from her pocket, screwed them into her ears. 'You'll have to shout,' she said to Cooper. 'What do I do?'

No, Sachs, no, Rhyme thought.

'If you don't tell me I'll just cut it apart.' She picked up a forensic razor saw. The blade hovered over the bag. She paused.

Rhyme sighed, nodded to Cooper. 'Tell her what to do.'

The tech swallowed. 'All right. Unwrap it. But carefully. Here, put it on this towel. Don't jar it. That's the worst thing you can do.'

She exposed the bullet, a surprisingly tiny piece of metal with an off-white tip.

'That cone?' Cooper continued. 'If the bullet goes off the cone'll go right through the body armor and at least one or two walls. It's Teflon-coated.'

'Okay.' She turned it aside, toward the wall.

'Sachs,' Rhyme said soothingly. 'Use forceps, not your fingers.'

'It won't make any difference if it blows, Rhyme. And I need the control.'

'Please.'

She hesitated and took the hemostat that Cooper offered her. She gripped the base of the slug.

'How do I open it up? Cut it?'

'You can't cut through the lead,' Cooper called. 'The heat from the friction'll set off the black powder. You'll have to work the cone off and pull the wad of plastic out.'

Sweat was rolling down her face. 'Okay. With pliers?'

Cooper picked up a pair of needle-nose pliers from the worktable and walked to her side. He put them in her right hand, then retreated.

'You'll have to grip it and twist hard. He glued it on with epoxy. That doesn't bond well with lead, so it should just pop off. But don't squeeze too hard. If it fractures you'll never get it off without drilling. And that'll set it off.'

'Hard but not too hard,' she muttered.

'Think of all those cars you worked on, Sachs,' Rhyme said.

'What?'

'Trying to get those old spark plugs out. Hard enough to unseat them, not so hard you broke the ceramic.'

She nodded absently and he didn't know if she'd heard him. Sachs lowered her head behind the tepee of her body armor.

Rhyme saw her eyes squinting shut.

Oh, Sachs . . .

He never saw any motion. He just heard a very faint snap. She froze for a moment, then looked over the armor. 'It came off. It's open.'

Cooper said, 'Do you see the explosive?'

She looked inside. 'Yes.'

He handed her a can of light machine oil. 'Drip some of

this inside then tilt it. The plastic should fall out. We can't pull it or the fingerprints'll be ruined.'

She added the oil, then tilted the slug, open end down, toward the towel.

Nothing happened.

'Damn,' she muttered.

'Don't—'

She shook it. Hard.

'—shake it!' Cooper shouted.

'Sachs!' Rhyme gasped.

She shook harder. 'Damn it.'

'No!'

A tiny white thread fell out, followed by some grains of black powder.

'Okay,' Cooper said, exhaling. 'It's safe.'

He walked over and, using a needle probe, rolled the plastic onto a glass slide. He walked in the smooth gait of criminalists around the world – back straight, hand buoyed and carrying the sample rock steady – to the microscope. He mounted the explosive.

'Magna-Brush?' Cooper asked, referring to a fine gray fingerprint powder.

'No,' Rhyme responded. 'Use gentian violet. It's a plastic print. We just need a little contrast.'

Cooper sprayed it, then mounted the slide in the 'scope.

The image popped onto the screen of Rhyme's computer simultaneously.

'Yes!' he shouted. 'There it is.'

The whorls and bifurcations were very visible.

'You nailed it, Sachs. Good job.'

As Cooper slowly rotated the plug of explosive, Rhyme made progressive screen captures – bitmap images – and saved them on the hard drive. He then assembled them and printed out a single, two-dimensional sliver of print.

But when the tech examined it he sighed.

'What?' Rhyme asked.

'Still not enough for a match. Only a quarter inch by a five eighths. No AFIS in the world could pick up anything from this.'

'Jesus,' Rhyme spat out. All that effort . . . wasted.

A sudden laugh.

From Amelia Sachs. She was staring at the wall, the evidence charts. CS-1, CS-2 . . .

'Put them together,' she said.

'What?'

'We've got three partials,' she explained. 'They're probably all from his index finger. Can't you fit them together?'

Cooper looked at Rhyme. 'I've never heard of doing that.'

Neither had Rhyme. The bulk of forensic work was analyzing evidence for presentation at trial – 'forensic' *means* 'relating to legal proceedings' – and a defense lawyer'd go to town if cops started assembling fragments of perps' fingerprints.

But their priority was *finding* the Dancer, not making a case against him.

'Sure,' Rhyme said. 'Do it!'

Cooper grabbed the other pictures of the Dancer's prints from the wall and rested them on the table in front of him.

They started to work, Sachs and the tech. Cooper made photocopies of the prints, reducing two so they were all the same size. Then he and Sachs began fitting them together like a jigsaw puzzle. They were like children, trying variations, rearranging, arguing playfully. Sachs went so far as to take out a pen and connect several lines over a gap in the print.

'Cheating,' Cooper joked.

'But it fits,' she said triumphantly.

Finally they cut and pasted a print together. It represented about three-quarters of a friction ridge print, probably the right index finger.

Cooper held it up. 'I have my doubts about this, Lincoln.'

But Rhyme said, 'It's art, Mel. It's beautiful!'

'Don't tell anyone at the identification association or they'll drum us out.'

'Put it through AFIS. Authorize a priority search. All states.'

'Oooo,' Cooper said. 'That'll cost my annual salary.'

He scanned the print into the computer.

'It could take a half hour,' said Cooper, more realistic than pessimistic.

But it didn't take that long at all. Five minutes later – long enough only for Rhyme to speculate who'd be more willing to pour him a drink, Sachs or Cooper – the screen fluttered and a new image came up.

*Your request has found . . . 1 match. 14 points of comparison. Statistical probability of identity: 97%.*

'Oh, my God,' Sachs muttered. 'We've got him.'

'Who is he, Mel?' Rhyme asked softly, as if he were afraid the words would blow the fragile electrons off the computer screen.

'He's not the Dancer anymore,' Cooper said. 'He's Stephen Robert Kall. Thirty-six. Present whereabouts unknown. LKA, fifteen years ago, an RFD number in Cumberland, West Virginia.'

Such a mundane name. Rhyme found himself experiencing an unreasonable tug of disappointment. Kall.

'Why was he on file?'

Cooper read. 'What he was telling Jodie . . . He did twenty months for manslaughter when he was fifteen.' A faint laugh. 'Apparently the Dancer *didn't* bother to tell him that the victim was his stepfather.'

'Stepfather, hm?'

'Tough reading,' Cooper said, poring over the screen. 'Man.'

'What?' Sachs asked.

'Notes from the police reports. Here's what happened.

Seems like there'd been a history of domestic disputes. The boy's mother was dying of cancer and her husband – Kall's stepfather – hit her for doing something or another. She fell and broke her arm. She died a few months later and Kall got it into his head her death was Lou's fault.'

Cooper continued to read and he actually seemed to shiver. 'Want to hear what happened?'

'Go ahead.'

'A couple months after she died Stephen and his stepfather were out hunting. The kid knocked him out, stripped him naked, and tied him to a tree in the woods. Left him there for a few days. Just wanted to scare him, his lawyer said. By the time the police got to him, well, let's just say the infestation was pretty bad. Maggots, mostly. Lived for two days after that. Delirious.'

'Man,' Sachs whispered.

'When they found him, the boy was there, just sitting next to him, watching.' Cooper read, '"The suspect surrendered without resistance. Appeared in a disoriented state. Kept repeating, 'Anything can kill, anything can kill . . .' Taken to Cumberland Regional Mental Health Center for evaluation."'

The psychological makeup didn't interest Rhyme very much. He trusted his forensic profiling techniques far more than the behavioral law enforcers'. He knew the Dancer was a sociopath – all professional killers were – and the sorrows and traumas that made him who he was weren't much help at the moment. He asked, 'Picture?'

'No pictures in juvie.'

'Right. Hell. How 'bout military?'

'Nope. But there's another conviction,' Cooper said. 'He tried to enlist in the marines but the psych profile got him rejected. He hounded the recruiting officers in D.C. for a couple months and finally assaulted a sergeant. Pled a suspended.'

Sellitto said, 'We'll run the name through FINEST, the alias list, and NCIC.'

'Have Dellray get some people to Cumberland and start tracing him,' Rhyme ordered.

'Will do.'

Stephen Kall . . .

After all these years. It was like finally visiting a shrine you'd read about all your life but never seen in person.

There was a startling knock on the door. Sachs and Sellitto's hands both twitched impulsively toward their weapons.

But the visitor was just one of the cops from downstairs. He had a large satchel. 'Delivery.'

'What is it?' Rhyme asked.

'A trooper from Illinois. Said this was from Du Page County Fire and Rescue.'

'What is it?'

The cop shrugged. 'He *said* it was shit from some truck treads. But that's nuts. Must've been kidding.'

'No,' Rhyme said, 'that's exactly what it is.' He glanced at Cooper. 'Tire scrapings from the crash site.'

The cop blinked. 'You wanted that? Flown in from Chicago?'

'We've been waiting with bated breath.'

'Well. Life's funny sometimes, ain't it?'

And Lincoln Rhyme could only agree.

Professional flying is only partly about flying.

Flying is also about paperwork.

Littering the back of the van transporting Percey Clay to Mamaroneck Airport was a huge stack of books and charts and documents: NOS's *Airport/Facility Directory*, the *Airman's Information Manual*, the FAA's NOTAMs – 'Notices to Airmen' – and advisory circulars, and the Jeppesen 'J-Aids', the *Airport and Information Directory*. Thousands of pages. Mountains of information. Percey, like most pilots, knew much of it by heart. But she also wouldn't think about driving an aircraft without going back to the original materials and studying them, literally, from the ground up.

With this information and her calculator she was filling out the two basic pre-flight documents: the navigation log and the flight plan. On the log she'd mark their altitude, calculate the course variations due to wind and the variance between true course and magnetic course, determine their ETE – estimated time en route – and come up with the Godhead number: the amount of fuel they'd need for the flight. Six cities, six different logs, dozens of checkpoints in between . . .

Then there was the FAA flight plan itself, on the reverse side of the navigation log. Once airborne, the copilot would activate the plan by calling the Flight Service Station at Mamaroneck, which would in turn call ahead to Chicago with *Foxtrot Bravo*'s estimated time of arrival. If the aircraft didn't arrive at its destination within a half hour after ETA, it would be declared overdue and search-and-rescue procedures would start.

These were complicated documents and had to be calculated perfectly. If aircraft had unlimited fuel supplies they could rely on radio navigation and spend as much time as they wanted cruising from destination to destination at whatever altitudes they wanted. But not only was fuel expensive to begin with (and the twin Garrett turbofans burned an astonishing amount of it); it was also extremely heavy and cost a lot – in extra fuel charges – just to carry. On a long flight, especially with a number of fuel-hungry take-offs, carrying too much gas could drastically erode the profit the Company was making on the flight. The FAA dictated that each flight have enough fuel to make it to the point of destination, plus a reserve, in the case of a night flight, of forty-five minutes' flying time.

Fingers tapping over the calculators, Percey Clay filled in the forms in her precise handwriting. Careless about so much else in her life, she was meticulous about flying. The merest act of filling in ATIS frequencies or the magnetic heading variations gave her pleasure. She never scrimped, never estimated when accurate calculations were called for. Today, she submerged herself in the work.

Roland Bell was beside her. He was haggard and sullen. The good ole boy was long gone. She grieved for him, as much as for herself; it seemed that Brit Hale was the first witness he'd lost. She felt an unreasonable urge to touch his arm, to reassure him, as he'd done for her. But he seemed to be one of those men who, when faced with loss, disappear into themselves; any sympathy would jar. He was much like herself, she believed. Bell gazed out the window of the van, his hand frequently touching the checkered black grip of the pistol in his shoulder holster.

Just as she finished the last flight plan card, the van turned the corner and entered the airport, stopping for the armed guards, who examined their IDs and waved them through.

Percey directed them to the hangar but she noticed that the lights were still on in the office. She told the cars to stop and she climbed out, as Bell and her other bodyguards walked with her, vigilant and tense, into the main part of the office.

Ron Talbot, grease-stained and exhausted, sat in the office, wiping his sweating forehead. His face was an alarming red.

'Ron . . .' She hurried forward. 'Are you all right?'

They embraced.

'Brit,' he said, shaking his head, gasping. 'He got Brit too. Percey, you shouldn't be here. Go someplace safe. Forget about the flight. It isn't worth it.'

She stepped back. 'What's wrong? You sick?'

'Just tired.'

She took the cigarette out of his hand and stubbed it out. 'You did the work yourself? On *Foxtrot Bravo*?'

'I—'

'Ron?'

'Most of it. It's almost finished. The guy from Northeast delivered the fire extinguisher cartridge and the annular about an hour ago. I started to mount them. Just got a little tired.'

'Chest pains?'

'No, not really.'

'Ron, go home.'

'I can—'

'Ron,' she snapped. 'I've lost two dear people in the last two days. I'm not going to lose a third . . . I can mount an annular. It's a piece of cake.'

Talbot looked like he couldn't even lift a wrench, much less a heavy combustor.

Percey asked, 'Where's Brad?' The FO for the flight.

'On his way. Be here in an hour.'

She kissed his sweaty forehead. 'You get home. And lay off the weeds, for God's sake. You crazy?'

He hugged her. 'Percey, about Brit . . .'

She hushed him with a finger to her lips. 'Home. Get some sleep. When you wake up I'll be in Erie and we'll have ourselves that contract. Signed, sealed, and delivered.'

He struggled to his feet, stood for a moment looking out the window at *Foxtrot Bravo*. His face revealed an acrid bitterness. It was the same look she'd remembered in his milky eyes when he'd told her that he'd flunked his physical and could no longer fly for a living. Talbot headed out the door.

It was time to get to work. She rolled up her sleeves, motioned Bell over to her. He lowered his head to her in a way she found charming. The same pose Ed fell into when she was speaking softly. She said, 'I'm going to need a few hours in the hangar. Can you keep that son of a bitch off me until then?'

No down-home aphorisms, no done deals. Roland Bell, the man with two guns, nodded solemnly, his eyes moving quickly from shadow to shadow.

They had a mystery on their hands.

Cooper and Sachs had examined all the trace found in the treads of the Chicago fire trucks and police cars that had been at the scene of the Ed Carney crash. There was the useless dirt, dog shit, grass, oil, and garbage that Rhyme had expected to find. But they made one discovery that he felt was important.

He just didn't have a clue what it meant.

The only batch of trace exhibiting indications of bomb residue were tiny fragments of a pliable beige substance. The gas chromatograph/mass spectrometer reported it was $C_5H_8$.

'Isoprene,' Cooper reflected.

'What's that?' Sachs had asked.

'Rubber,' Rhyme answered.

Cooper continued. 'I'm also reading fatty acids. Dyes, talcum.'

'Any hardening agents?' Rhyme asked. 'Clay? Magnesium carbonate? Zinc oxide?'

'None.'

'It's soft rubber. Like latex.'

'And little fragments of rubber cement too,' Cooper added, peering at a sample in the compound microscope. 'Bingo,' he said.

'Don't tease, Mel,' Rhyme grumbled.

'Bits of soldering and tiny pieces of plastic embedded in the rubber. Circuit boards.'

'Part of the timer?' Sachs wondered aloud.

'No, that was intact,' Rhyme reminded.

He felt they were onto something here. If this was another part of the bomb, it might give them a clue as to the source of the explosive or another component.

'We have to know for sure whether this's from the bomb or from the plane itself. Sachs, I want you to go up to the airport.'

'The—'

'Mamaroneck. Find Percey and have her give you samples of anything with latex, rubber, or circuit boards that would be in the belly of a plane like the one Carney was flying. Near the seat of the explosion. And, Mel, send the info off to the Bureau's Explosives Reference Collection and check army CID – maybe there's a latex waterproof coating of some kind the army uses for explosives. Maybe we can trace it that way.'

Cooper began typing the request on his computer, but Rhyme noticed Sachs wasn't pleased with her assignment.

'You want me to go talk to her?' she asked. 'To Percey?'

'Yes. That's what I'm saying.'

'Okay.' She sighed. 'All right.'

'And don't give her any crap like you've been doing. We need her cooperation.'

Rhyme didn't have a clue why she pulled on her vest so angrily and stalked out the door without saying good-bye.

# Chapter
# TWENTY-NINE

At Mamaroneck Airport Amelia Sachs saw Roland Bell lurking outside the hangar. Another six officers stood guard around the huge building. She supposed there were snipers nearby too.

Her eye caught the hillock where she'd dropped to the ground under fire. She remembered, with a disgusted twist in her belly, the smell of the dirt mingling with the sweet cordite scent from her own impotent pistol shots.

Turned to Bell. 'Detective.'

His eyes glanced at her once. 'Hey.' Then he returned to scanning the airport. His easy Southern demeanor was gone. He'd changed. Sachs realized that they shared something notorious now. They'd both had a shot at the Coffin Dancer and missed.

They both had also been in his kill zone and survived. Bell, though, with more glory than she. *His* body armor, she noticed, bore stigmata: the streaks from the two slugs that had glanced off him during the safe house attack. He'd stood *his* ground.

'Where's Percey?' Sachs asked.

'Inside. Finishing up the repairs.'

'By herself?'

'Think so. She's something, she is. You wouldn't think a woman that wasn't so, well, attractive'd have quite the draw she does. You know?'

Ugh. Don't get me started.

'Anybody else here? From the Company?' She nodded toward the Hudson Air office. There was a light on inside.

'Percey sent 'most everybody home. Fellow's going to be her copilot's due here anytime. And somebody from Operations's inside. Needs to be on duty when there's a flight going on, I guess. I checked him out. He's okay.'

'So she's really going to fly?' Sachs asked.

'Looks that way.'

'The plane's been guarded the whole time?'

'Yep, since yesterday. What're you doing here?'

'Need some samples for analysis.'

'That Rhyme, he's something too.'

'Uh-huh.'

'All two of you go back a ways?'

'We've worked a few cases,' she said dismissingly. 'He saved me from Public Affairs.'

'That's his good deed. Say, I hear you can really drive a nail.'

'I can . . . ?'

'Shoot. Sidearms. You're on a team.'

And here I am at the site of my latest competition, she thought bitterly. 'Just weekend sport,' she muttered.

'I do some pistol work myself, but I'll tell you, even on a good day, with a nice, long barrel and firing single-action, fifty, sixty yards is all the far I can shoot.'

She appreciated his comments but recognized that they were just an attempt to reassure her about yesterday's fiasco; the words meant nothing to her. .

'Better talk to Percey now.'

'Right through there, Officer.'

Sachs pushed into the huge hangar. She walked slowly, looking at all the places the Dancer could hide. Sachs paused behind a tall row of boxes; Percey didn't see her.

The woman was standing on a small scaffolding, hands on her hips, as she gazed at the complicated network of pipes and tubes of the open engine. She'd rolled her sleeves up and her hands were covered with grease. She nodded to herself then reached forward into the compartment.

Sachs was fascinated, watching the woman's hands fly over the machinery, adjusting, probing, seating metal to metal, and tightening the fixtures down with judicious swipes of her thin arms. She mounted a large red cylinder, a fire extinguisher, Sachs guessed, in about ten seconds flat.

But one part – it looked like a big metal inner tube – wouldn't fit correctly.

Percey climbed off the scaffolding, selected a socket wrench, and climbed up again. She loosened bolts, removed another part to give her more room to maneuver, and tried again to push the big ring into place.

Wouldn't budge.

She shouldered it. Didn't move an inch. She removed yet another part, meticulously setting each screw and bolt in a plastic tray at her feet. Percey's face turned bright red as she struggled to mount the metal ring. Her chest heaved as she fought the part. Suddenly it slipped, dropping completely out of position, and knocked her backward off the scaffolding. She landed on her hands and knees. The tools and bolts that she'd arranged so carefully in the tray spilled to the floor beneath the plane's tail.

'No!' Percey cried. 'No!'

Sachs stepped forward to see if she was hurt, but noticed immediately that the outburst had nothing to do with pain –

Percey grabbed a large wrench and slammed it furiously into the floor of the hangar. The policewoman stopped, stepped into the shadow beside a large carton.

'No, no, no . . .' Percey cried, hammering the smooth concrete.

Sachs remained where she was.

'Oh, Ed . . .' She dropped the wrench. 'I can't do it alone.' Gasping for breath, she rolled into a ball. 'Ed . . . oh, Ed . . . I miss you so much!' She lay, curled like a frail leaf, on the shiny floor and wept.

Then, suddenly, the attack was over. Percey rolled upright, took a deep breath, and climbed to her feet, wiped the tears from her face. The aviatrix within her took charge once again and she picked up the bolts and tools and climbed back up onto the scaffolding. She stared at the troublesome ring for a moment. She examined the fittings carefully but couldn't see where the metal pieces were binding.

Sachs retreated to the door, slammed it hard, and then started back into the hangar, walking with loud steps.

Percey swung around, saw her, then turned back to the engine. She gave a few swipes to her face with her sleeve and continued to work.

Sachs walked up to the base of the scaffolding and watched as Percey struggled with the ring.

Neither woman said anything for a long moment.

Finally Sachs said, 'Try a jack.'

Percey glanced back at her, said nothing.

'It's just that the tolerance is close,' Sachs continued. 'All you need is more muscle. The old coercion technique. They don't teach it in mechanics school.'

Percey looked carefully at the mounting brackets on the pieces of metal. 'I don't know.'

'I do. You're talking to an expert.'

The flier asked, 'You've mounted a combustor in a Lear?'

'Nope. Spark plugs in a Chevy Monza. You have to jack up the engine to reach them. Well, only in the V-eight. But who'd buy a four-cylinder car? I mean, what's the point?'

Percey looked back at the engine.

'So?' Sachs persisted. 'A jack?'

'It'll bend the outer housing.'

'Not if you put it there.' Sachs pointed to a structural member connecting the engine to the support that went to the fuselage.

Percey studied the fitting. 'I don't have a jack. Not one small enough to fit.'

'I do. I'll get it.'

Sachs stepped outside to the RRV and returned with the accordion jack. She climbed up on the scaffolding, her knees protesting the effort.

'Try right there.' She touched the base of the engine. 'That's I-beam steel.'

As Percey positioned the jack, Sachs admired the intricacies of the engine. 'How much horsepower?'

Percey laughed. 'We don't rate in horsepower. We rate in pounds of thrust. These're Garrett TFE Seven Three Ones. They give up about thirty-five hundred pounds each.'

'Incredible.' Sachs laughed. 'Brother.' She hooked the handle into the jack, then felt the familiar resistance as she started turning the crank. 'I've never been this close to a turbine engine,' she said. 'Was always a dream of mine to take a jet car out to the salt flats.'

'This isn't a pure turbine. There aren't many of those left anymore. Just the Concorde. Military jets, of course. These're turbofans. Like the airliners. Look in the front – see those blades? That's nothing more than a fixed-pitch propeller. Pure jets are inefficient at low altitudes. These're about forty percent more fuel efficient.'

Sachs breathed hard as she struggled to turn the jack

handle. Percey put her shoulder against the ring again and shoved. The part didn't seem large but it was very heavy.

'You know cars, huh?' Percey asked, also gasping.

'My father. He loved them. We'd spend the afternoon taking 'em apart and putting 'em back together. When he wasn't walking a beat.'

'A beat?'

'He was a cop too.'

'And you got the mechanic bug?' Percey asked.

'Naw, I got the *speed* bug. And when you get that you better get the suspension bug and the transmission bug and the engine bug or you ain't going anywhere fast.'

Percey asked, 'You ever driven an aircraft?'

'"Driven"?' Sachs smiled at the word. 'No. But maybe I'll think about it, knowing you've got that much oomph under the hood.'

She cranked some more, her muscles aching. The ring groaned slightly and scraped as it rose into its fittings.

'I don't know,' Percey said uncertainly.

'Almost there!'

With a loud metallic clang the ring popped onto the mounts perfectly. Percey's squat face broke into a faint smile.

'You torque 'em?' Sachs asked, fitting bolts into the slots on the ring and looking for a wrench.

'Yeah,' Percey said. 'The poundage I use is "Till there's no way in hell they'll come loose."'

Sachs tightened the bolts down with a ratcheting socket. The clicking of the tool took her back to high school, cool Saturday afternoons with her father. The smells of gasoline, of fall air, of meaty casseroles cooking in the kitchen of their Brooklyn attached house.

Percey checked Sachs's handiwork then said, 'I'll do the rest.' She started reconnecting wires and electronic components. Sachs was mystified but fascinated. Percey paused.

She added a soft 'Thanks.' A few moments later: 'What're you doing here?'

'We found some other materials we think might be from the bomb, but Lincoln didn't know if it was part of the plane or not. Bits of beige latex, circuit board? Sound familiar?'

Percey shrugged. 'There're thousands of gaskets in a Lear. They could be latex, I don't have any idea. And circuit boards? There're probably another thousand of them.' She nodded to a corner, toward a closet and workbench. 'The boards are special orders, depending on the component. But there should be a good stock of gaskets over there. Take samples of whatever you need.'

Sachs walked over to the bench, began slipping all the beige-colored bits of rubber she could find into an evidence bag.

Without glancing at Sachs, Percey said, 'I thought you were here to arrest me. Haul me back to jail.'

I ought to, the policewoman thought. But she said, 'Just collecting exemplars.' Then, after a moment: 'What other work needs to be done? On the plane?'

'Just recalibration. Then a run-up to check the power settings. I have to take a look at the window too, the one Ron replaced. You don't want to lose a window at four hundred miles an hour. Could you hand me that hex set? No, the metric one.'

'I lost one at a hundred once,' Sachs said, passing over the tools.

'A what?'

'A window. A perp I was chasing had a shotgun. Double-ought buckshot. I ducked in time. But it blew the windshield clean out . . . I'll tell you, I caught a few bugs in my teeth before I collared him.'

'And I thought *I* lived an adventurous life,' Percey said.

'Most of it's dull. They pay you for the five percent that's adrenaline.'

'I hear that,' Percey said. She hooked up a laptop computer to components in the engine itself. She typed on the keyboard, read the screen. Without looking down she asked, 'So, what is it?'

Eyes on the computer, the numbers flicking past, Sachs asked, 'What do you mean?'

'This, uhm, tension. Between us. You and me.'

'You nearly got a friend of mine killed.'

Percey shook her head. She said reasonably, 'That's not it. There's risks in your job. You decide if you're going to assume them or not. Jerry Banks wasn't a rookie. It's something else – I felt it before Jerry got shot. When I first saw you, in Lincoln Rhyme's room.'

Sachs said nothing. She lifted the jack out of the engine compartment and set it on a table, absently wound it closed.

Three pieces of metal slipped into place around the engine and Percey applied her screwdriver like a conductor's baton. Her hands were truly magic. Finally she said, 'It's about him, isn't it?'

'Who?'

'You know who I mean. Lincoln Rhyme.'

'You think I'm jealous?' Sachs laughed.

'Yes, I do.'

'Ridiculous.'

'It's more than just work between you. I think you're in love with him.'

'Of course I'm not. That's crazy.'

Percey offered a telling glance and then carefully twined excess wire into a bundle and nestled it into a cutout in the engine compartment. 'Whatever you saw is just respect for his talent, that's all.' She lifted a grease-stained hand toward herself. 'Come on, Amelia, look at me. I'd make a lousy lover. I'm short, I'm bossy, I'm not good looking.'

'You're—' Sachs began.

Percey interrupted. 'The ugly duckling story? You know, the bird that everybody thought was ugly until it turned out to be a swan? I read that a million times when I was little. But I never turned into a swan. Maybe I learned to fly like one,' she said with a cool smile, 'but it isn't the same. Besides,' Percey continued, 'I'm a widow. I just lost my husband. I'm not the least interested in anyone else.'

'I'm sorry,' Sachs began slowly, feeling unwillingly drawn into this conversation, 'but I've got to say . . . well, you don't really seem to be in mourning.'

'Why? Because I'm trying my hardest to keep my company going?'

'No, there's more than that,' Sachs replied cautiously. 'Isn't there?'

Percey examined Sachs's face. 'Ed and I were incredibly close. We were husband and wife and friends and business partners . . . And yes, he was seeing someone else.'

Sachs's eyes swiveled toward the Hudson Air office.

'That's right,' Percey said. 'It's Lauren. You met her yesterday.'

The brunette who'd been crying so hard.

'It tore me apart. Hell, it tore Ed apart too. He loved me but he needed his beautiful lovers. Always did. And, you know, I think it was harder on them. Because he always came home to me.' She paused for a moment and fought the tears. 'That's what love is, I think. Who you come home to.'

'And you?'

'Was I faithful?' Percey asked. She gave another of her wry laughs – the laugh of someone who has keen self-awareness but who doesn't like all the insights. 'I didn't have a lot of opportunities. I'm hardly the kind of girl gets picked up walking down the street.' She examined a socket wrench absently. 'But, yeah, after I found out about Ed and his girlfriends, a few years ago, I was mad. It hurt a lot. I saw some other men. Ron and I – Ron Talbot – spent some time together, a few months.' She smiled. 'He even proposed to me. Said I deserved better than Ed. And I supposed I did. But even with those other women in his life, Ed was the man I had to be with. That never changed.'

Percey's eyes grew distant for a moment. 'We met in the navy, Ed and I. Both fighter pilots. When he proposed . . . See, the traditional way to propose in the military is you say, "You want to become my dependent?" Sort of a joke. But we were both lieutenants j.g., so Ed said, "Let's you and me become each other's dependents." He wanted to get me a ring but my father'd disowned me—'

'For real?'

'Yep. Real soap opera, which I won't go into now. Anyway, Ed and I were saving every penny to open our own charter company after we were discharged and we were completely broke. But one night he said, "Let's go up." So we borrowed this old Norseman they had on the field. Tough plane. Big air-cooled rotary engine . . . You could do anything with that aircraft. Well, I was in the left-hand seat. I'd taken off and'd got us up to about six thousand feet. Suddenly he kissed me and wobbled the yoke, which meant he was taking over. I let him. He said, "I got you a diamond after all, Perce."'

'He did?' Sachs asked.

Percey smiled. 'He throttled up, all the way to the fire wall, and pulled the yoke back. The nose went straight up in the air.' Tears were coming fast now to Percey Clay's eyes. 'For a moment, before he kicked rudder and we started down out of the stall, we were looking straight up into the night sky. He leaned over and said, "Take your pick. All the stars of evening – you can have any one you want."' Percey lowered her head, caught her breath. All the stars of evening . . .

After a moment she wiped her eyes with her sleeve, then turned back to the engine. 'Believe me, you don't have anything to worry about. Lincoln's a fascinating man, but Ed was all I ever wanted.'

'There's more to it than you know.' Sachs sighed. 'You remind him of someone. Someone he was in love with. You show up and all of a sudden it's like he's with her again.'

Percey shrugged. 'We have some things in common. We understand each other. But so what? That doesn't mean anything. Take a look, Amelia. Rhyme loves you.'

Sachs laughed. 'Oh, I don't think so.'

Percey gave her another look that said, *Whatever* . . . and began replacing the equipment in boxes as meticulously as she'd worked with the tools and computers.

Roland Bell ambled inside, checking windows and scanning the shadows.

'All quiet?' he asked.

'Not a peep.'

'Got a message to pass on. The folk from U.S. Medical just left Westchester Hospital. The shipment'll be here in an hour. I've got a car of my people behind them just to be on the safe side. But don't worry that it'll spook 'em and be bad for business – my guys're top-notch. The driver'll never know he's being followed.'

Percey looked at her watch. 'Okay.' She glanced at Bell, who was looking uncertainly at the open engine compartment, like a snake at a mongoose. She asked, 'We don't need baby-sitters on the flight, do we?'

Bell's sigh was loud. 'After what happened at the safe house,' he said in a low, solemn voice, 'I'm not letting you outa my sight.' He shook his head and, already looking airsick, he walked back to the front door and disappeared into the cool late afternoon air.

Her head in the engine compartment, studying her work carefully, Percey said in a reverberating voice, 'Looking at Rhyme and looking at you, I wouldn't give it much more than fifty-fifty, I've got to say.' She turned and looked down at Sachs. 'But you know, I had this flight instructor a long time ago.'

'And?'

'When we'd fly multi-engine he had this game of throttling back one engine to idle and feathering the prop, then telling us to land. Lot of instructors'll cut power for a few minutes, with altitude, just to see how you can handle it. But they always throttled up again before landing. This instructor, though – uh-uh. He'd make us land on one engine. Students'd always be asking him, "Isn't that risky?" His answer was, "God don't give out certain. Sometimes you just gotta play the odds."'

Percey lowered the flap of the engine cowl and clamped it into place. 'All right, this's done. Damn aircraft may actually fly.' She swatted the glossy skin like a cowgirl patting a rodeo rider's butt.

# Chapter
# THIRTY

At 6 P.M. on Sunday they summoned Jodie from Rhyme's downstairs bedroom, where he'd been under lock and key.

He trotted up the stairs reluctantly, clutching his silly book, *Dependent No More*, like a Bible. Rhyme remembered the title. It had been on the *Times* best-seller list for months. In a black mood at the time, he'd noticed the book and thought cynically, about himself, dependent forever.

A team of federal agents was flying from Quantico to Cumberland, West Virginia, Stephen Kall's old residence, to pick up whatever leads they could, hoping they might track him to his present whereabouts from there. But Rhyme had seen how carefully he'd scoured his crime scenes and he had no reason to think the man would have been any less careful in covering his other tracks.

'You told us some things about him,' Rhyme said to Jodie. 'Some *facts*, some *nutritional* information. I want to know more.'

'I—'

'Think hard.'

Jodie squinted. Rhyme supposed he was considering what he could say to mollify them, superficial impressions. But he was surprised when Jodie said, 'Well, for one thing, he's afraid of you.'

'Us?' Rhyme asked.

'No. Just you.'

'Me?' he asked, astonished. 'He knows about me?'

'He knows your name's Lincoln. And that you're out to get him.'

'How?'

'I don't know,' the man said, then added. 'You know, he made a couple of calls on that cell phone. And he listened for a long time. I was thinking—'

'Oh, hellfire,' Dellray sang out. 'He's tapping somebody's line.'

'Of course!' Rhyme cried. 'Probably the Hudson Air office. That's how he found out about the safe house. Why didn't we think about that?'

Dellray said, 'We gotta sweep the office. But the bug might be in a relay box somewheres. We'll find it. We'll find it.' He placed a call to the Bureau's tech services.

To Jodie, Rhyme said, 'Go on. What else does he know about me?'

'He knows you're a detective. I don't think he knows where you live, or your last name. But you scare the hell out of him.'

If Rhyme's belly had been able to register the lub-dub of excitement – and pride – he'd have felt that now.

Let's see, Stephen Kall, if we can't give you a little more to be afraid of.

'You helped us once, Jodie. I need you to help us again.'

'Are you crazy?'

'Shut the fuck up,' Dellray barked. 'And listen t'what the man's sayin', hokay? *Hokay?*'

'I did what I said I would. I'm not doing anything more.' The whine really was too much. Rhyme glanced at Sellitto. This called for people skills.

'It's in your interest,' Sellitto said reasonably, 'to help us.'

'Gettin' shot in the *back*'s in my interest? Gettin' shot in the *head*'s in my interest? Uh-huh. I see. You wanna explain that?'

'Sure, I'll fucking explain it,' Sellitto grumbled. 'The Dancer knows you dimed him. He didn't *have* to target you back there at the safe house, right? Am I right?'

Always get the mutts to talk. To *participate*. Sellitto had often explained the ways of interrogation to Lincoln Rhyme.

'Yeah. I guess.'

Sellitto motioned Jodie closer with a crooked finger. 'It woulda been the smart thing for him just to take off. But he went to the trouble to take up a sniper position and try to cap your ass. Now, what's that tell us?'

'I—'

'It tells us that he ain't gonna rest till he clips you.'

Dellray, happy to play straight man for a change, said, 'And he's the sort I don't think you wanna have knocking on yo' door at three in the morning – this week, next month, or next year. We all together on that?'

'So,' Sellitto resumed snappily, 'agreed that it's in your *interest* to help us?'

'But you'll give me, like, witness protection?'

Sellitto shrugged. 'Yes and no.'

'Huh?'

'If you help us, yes. If you don't, no.'

Jodie's eyes were red and watery. He seemed so afraid. In the years since his accident Rhyme had been fearful for others – Amelia and Thom and Lon Sellitto. But he himself didn't believe he'd ever been afraid to die, certainly not since the accident. He wondered what it must be like to live so timidly. A mouse's life.

*Too many ways to die . . .*

Sellitto, slipping into his good-cop persona, offered a faint smile to Jodie. 'You were there when he killed that agent, in the basement, right?'

'I was there, yeah.'

'That man could be alive now. And Brit Hale could be alive now. A lot of other people could too . . . *if* somebody'd helped us stop this asshole a coupla years ago. Well, you can help us stop him now. You can keep Percey alive, maybe dozens of others. *You* can do that.'

This was Sellitto's genius at work. Rhyme would have bullied and coerced and, in a pinch, bribed the little man. But it never occurred to him to appeal to the splinter of decency that the detective, at least, could see within him.

Jodie absently rifled the pages in his book with a filthy thumb. Finally he looked up and – with surprising sobriety – said, 'When I was taking him to my place, in the subway, a couple times I thought I'd maybe push him into a sewer interceptor pipe. The water goes real fast there. Wash him right down to the Hudson. Or I know where they have these piles of tie spikes in the subway. I could grab one and hit him over the head when he wasn't looking. I really, really thought about doing that. But I got scared.' He held up the book. '"Chapter Three. Confronting your Demons." I've always run, you know. I never stood up to anything. I thought maybe I could stand up to him, but I couldn't.'

'Hey, now's your chance to,' Sellitto said.

Flipping through the tattered pages again. Sighing. 'Whatta I gotta do?'

Dellray pointed an alarmingly long thumb toward the ceiling. His mark of approval.

'We'll get to that in a minute,' Rhyme said, looking around the room. Suddenly he shouted, 'Thom! Thom! Come *here*. I need you.'

The handsome, exasperated face of the aide poked around the corner. 'Yessss?'

'I'm feeling vain,' Rhyme announced dramatically.

'What?'

'I'm feeling vain. I need a mirror.'

'You want a mirror?'

'A big one. And would you please comb my hair. I keep asking you and you keep forgetting.'

The U.S. Medical and Healthcare van pulled onto the tarmac. If the two white-jacketed employees, carting a quarter million dollars' worth of human organs, were concerned about the machine-gun-armed cops ringing the field, they gave no indication of it.

The only time they flinched was when King, the bomb squad German shepherd, sniffed the cargo cases for explosives.

'Uhm, I'd watch that dog there,' one of the deliverymen said uneasily. 'I imagine to them liver's liver and heart's heart.'

But King behaved like a thorough professional and signed off on the cargo without sampling any. The men carried the containers on board, loaded them into the refrigeration units. Percey returned to the cockpit where Brad Torgeson, a sandy-haired young pilot who flew occasional freelance jobs for Hudson Air, was going through the pre-flight check.

They'd both already done the walkaround, accompanied by Bell, three troopers, and King. There was no way the Dancer could have gotten to the plane in the first place, but the killer now had a reputation of materializing out of thin air; this was the most meticulous pre-flight visual in the history of aviation.

Looking back into the passenger compartment, Percey could see the lights of the refrigeration units. She felt that tug of satisfaction she always felt when inanimate machinery, built and honed by humans, came to life. The proof of God, for Percey Clay, could be found in the hum of servomotors and the buoyancy of a sleek metal wing at that instant when the airfoil creates negative top pressure and you become weightless.

Continuing with the pre-flight checklist, Percey was startled by the sound of heavy breathing next to her.

'Whoa,' Brad said as King decided there were no explosives in his crotch and continued his examination of the inside of the plane.

Rhyme had spoken to Percey not long ago and told her that he and Amelia Sachs had examined the gaskets and tubing and found no match for the latex discovered at the crash site in Chicago. Rhyme got the idea that he might have used the rubber to seal the explosives so that the dogs couldn't smell it. So he had Percey and Brad stand down for a few minutes while Tech Services went through the entire plane, inside and out, with hypersensitive microphones, listening for a detonator timer.

Clean.

When the plane rolled out, the taxiway would be guarded by uniformed patrolmen. Fred Dellray had contacted the FAA to arrange that the flight plan be sealed so that the Dancer couldn't learn where the plane was going – if he even knew that Percey was at the helm. The agent had also contacted the FBI field offices in each of the arrival cities and arranged for tactical agents to be on the tarmac when the shipments were delivered.

Now, engines started, Brad in the right-hand seat and Roland Bell shifting uneasily in one of the two remaining passenger seats, Percey Clay spoke to the tower, 'Lear Six Niner Five *Foxtrot Bravo* at Hudson Air. Ready for taxi.'

'Roger, Niner Five *Foxtrot Bravo*. Cleared onto taxiway zero nine right.'

'Zero nine right, Niner Five *Foxtrot Bravo*.'

A touch to the smooth throttles and the spritely plane turned onto the taxiway and proceeded through the gray, early spring evening. Percey was driving. Copilots have flight authority but only the pilot can steer the plane on the ground.

'You having fun, Officer?' she called back to Bell.

'I'm just tickled,' he said, looking sourly out the large round window. 'You know, you can see straight down. I mean, the windows go so far round. Why'd they make it that way?'

Percey laughed. She called out, 'On airliners, they try to keep you from realizing you're flying. Movies, food, small windows. Where's the fun? What's the point?'

'I can see a point or two,' he said, chewing his Wrigley's with energetic teeth. He closed the curtain.

Percey's eyes were on the taxiway, checking left and right, always vigilant. To Brad she said, 'I'll do the briefing now. Okay?'

'Yes'm.'

'This'll be a rolling takeoff with flaps set to 15 degrees,' Percey said. 'I'll advance the throttles. You call airspeed, eighty knots, cross-check, V one, rotate, V two, and positive rate. I'll command gear up and you raise it. Got that?'

'Airspeed, eighty, V one, rotate, V two, positive rate. Gear.'

'Good. You'll monitor all instruments and the annunciator panel. Now, if we get a red panel light or there's an engine malfunction before V one, sing out "Abort" loud and clear and I'll make a go/no-go decision. If there's a malfunction at or after V one, we will continue the takeoff and we'll treat the situation as an in-flight emergency. We will continue on heading and you'll request VFR clearance for an immediate return to the airport. Understood?'

'Understood.'

'Good. Let's do some flying . . . You ready, Roland?'

'*I'm* ready. Hope you are. Don't drop your candy.'

Percey laughed again. Their housekeeper in Richmond had used that expression. It meant, don't screw up.

She wobbled the throttles a little closer to the firewall.

The engines gave a grinding sound and the Learjet sped forward. They continued to the hold position, where the killer had placed the bomb on Ed's plane. She looked out the window and saw two cops standing guard.

'Lear Niner Five *Foxtrot Bravo*,' Ground Control called through the radio, 'proceed to and hold short of runway five left.'

'*Foxtrot Bravo*. Hold short of zero five left.'

She steered onto the taxiway.

The Lear was a ground hugger, yet whenever Percey Clay sat in the left-hand seat, whether in the air or on the ground, she felt that she was a mile high. It was a powerful place to be. All the decisions would be hers, followed unquestioningly. All the responsibility was on her shoulders. She was the captain.

Eyes scanning the instruments.

'Flaps fifteen, fifteen, green,' she said, repeating the degree setting.

Doubling the redundancy, Brad said, 'Flaps fifteen, fifteen, green.'

ATC called, 'Lear Niner Five *Foxtrot Bravo*, turn into position. Cleared for takeoff, runway five left.'

'Five left, *Foxtrot Bravo*. Cleared for takeoff.'

Brad concluded the takeoff checklist. 'Pressurization, normal. Temperature select is in auto. Transponder and exterior lights on. Ignition, pitot heat, and strobes, your side.'

Percey checked those controls, said, 'Ignition, pitot heat, and strobes on.'

She turned the Lear onto the runway, straightened the nosewheel, and lined up with centerline. She glanced at the compass. 'All heading indicators check zero five. Runway five L. I'm setting power.'

She pushed the throttles forward. They began racing down the middle of the concrete strip. She felt his hand grip the throttles just below hers.

'Power set.' Then Brad called, 'Airspeed alive,' as the airspeed indicators jumped off the peg and started to move upward, twenty knots, forty knots . . .

The throttles nearly to the fire wall, the plane shot forward. She heard a 'wayl . . .' from Roland Bell and repressed a smile.

Fifty knots, sixty knots, seventy . . .

'Eighty knots,' Brad called out, 'cross-check.'

'Check,' she called after a glance at the airspeed indicator.

'V one,' Brad sang out. 'Rotate.'

Percey removed her right hand from the throttles and took the yoke. Wobbly until now, the plastic control suddenly grew firm with air resistance. She eased back, rotating the Lear upward to the standard seven-and-a-half-degree incline. The engines continued to roar smoothly and so she pulled back slightly more, increasing the climb to ten degrees.

'Positive rate,' Brad called.

'Gear up. Flaps up. Yaw damp on.'

Through the headphone came the voice of ATC. 'Lear Niner Five *Foxtrot Bravo*, turn left heading two eight oh. Contact departure control.'

'Two eight oh, Niner Five *Foxtrot Bravo*. Thank you, sir.'

'Good evening.'

Tugging the yoke a bit more, eleven degrees, twelve, fourteen . . . Leaving the power settings at takeoff level, higher than normal, for a few minutes. Hearing the sweet grind of the turbofans behind her, the slipstream.

And in this sleek silver needle, Percey Clay felt herself flying into the heart of the sky, leaving behind the cumbersome, the heavy, the painful. Leaving behind Ed's death and Brit's, leaving behind even that terrible man, the devil, the Coffin Dancer. All of the hurt, all of the uncertainty, all of the ugliness were trapped far below her, and she was free. It seemed unfair that she should escape these stifling burdens so easily but that was the fact of it. For the Percey Clay who sat in the left-hand seat of Lear N695FB was not Percey Clay the short girl with the squat face, or Percey Clay the girl whose only sex appeal was the lure of Daddy's chopped-tobacco money. It wasn't Per-ceee Pug, Percey the Mug, Percey the Troll, the awkward brunette struggling with the ill-fitting gloves at her cotillion, on the arm of her mortified cousin, surrounded by willowy blondes who nodded at her with pleasant smiles and stored up the sight for a gossip fest later.

That wasn't the real Percey Clay.

*This* was.

Another gasp from Roland Bell. He must have peeked through the window curtain during their alarming bank.

'Mamaroneck Departure, Lear Niner Five *Foxtrot Bravo* with you out of two thousand.'

'Evening, Five *Foxtrot Bravo*. Climb and maintain six thousand.'

And then they began the mundane tasks of setting nav com for the VOR frequencies that would guide them to Chicago as straight as a samurai's arrow.

At six thousand feet they broke through the cloud cover into a sky that was as spectacular as any sunset Percey had ever seen. Not really an outdoor person, she never grew tired of the sight of beautiful skies. Percey allowed herself a single sentimental thought – that it would have been a very good thing if Ed's last sight had been as beautiful as this.

At twenty-one thousand feet she said, 'Your aircraft.'

Brad responded, 'Got it.'

'Coffee?'

'Love some.'

She stepped into the back of the plane, poured three cups, took one to Brad, and then sat down next to Roland Bell, who took the cup in shaking hands.

'How you doing?' she asked.

'It's not like I get airsick. It's just I get' – his face folded – 'well, nervous as a . . .' There were probably a thousand good Tarheel similes to choose from, but for once his Southern talk failed him. 'Just nervous,' he concluded.

'Take a look,' she said, pointing out the cockpit window.

He eased forward in the seat and looked out the windshield. She watched his craggy face blossom in surprise as they stared into the maw of the sunset.

Bell whistled. 'Well, now. Lookit that . . . Say, that was a real rush, takeoff.'

'She's a sweet bird. You ever hear of Brooke Knapp?'

'Don't believe so.'

'Businesswoman in California. Set an around-the-world speed record in a Lear thirty-five A – what we're in right now. Took her a hair over fifty hours. I'm going to break that someday.'

'I don't doubt you are.' Calmer now. Eyes on the controls. 'Looks awful complicated.'

She sipped the coffee. 'There's a trick to flying we don't tell people. Sort of a trade secret. It's a lot simpler than you'd think.'

'What's that?' he asked eagerly. 'The trick?'

'Well, look outside. You see those colored lights on the wing tips?'

He didn't want to look, but he did. 'Okay, got it.'

'There's one on the tail too.'

'Uh-huh. Remember seeing that, I think.'

'All we have to do is make sure we keep the plane in between those lights and everything'll go fine.'

'In between . . .' It took a moment for the joke to register. He gazed at her deadpan face for a minute, then smiled. 'You get a lotta people with that one?'

'A few.'

But the joke didn't really amuse him. His eyes were still

on the carpet. After a long moment of silence she said, 'Brit Hale could've said no, Roland. He knew the risks.'

'No, he didn't,' Bell answered. 'Nope. He went along with what we had in mind, not knowing much of anything. I should've thought better. I should've guessed about the fire trucks. Should've guessed that the killer'd know where your rooms were. I could've put you in the basement, or some-place. And I could've shot better too.'

Bell seemed so despondent that Percey could think of nothing to say. She rested her veiny hand on his forearm. He seemed thin, but he was really quite strong.

He gave a soft laugh. 'You wanta know something?'

'What?'

'This is the first time I've seen you looking halfway comfort-able since I met you.'

'Only place I feel really at home,' she said.

'We're going two hundred miles an hour a mile up in the air and you feel safe.' Bell sighed.

'No, we're going four hundred miles an hour, four miles up.'

'Uh. Thanks for sharing that.'

'There's an old pilot's saying,' Percey said. '"Saint Peter doesn't count the time spent flying, and he doubles the hours you spend on the ground."'

'Funny,' Bell said. 'My uncle said something like that too. Only he used it talking about fishing. I'd vote for his version over yours any day. Nothing personal.'

# Chapter
# THIRTY-ONE

Worms . . .

Stephen Kall, sweating, stood in a filthy bathroom in the back of a Cuban Chinese restaurant.

Scrubbing to save his soul.

Worms gnawing, worms eating, worms swarming . . .

Clean 'em away . . . Clean them away!!!

Soldier—

Sir, I'm busy, sir.

Sol—

Scrub, scrub, scrub, scrub.

Lincoln the Worm is looking for me.

Everywhere Lincoln the Worm looks, worms appear.

Go away!!!

The brush moved whisk, whisk, back and forth until his cuticles bled.

Soldier, that blood is evidence. You can't—

Go away!!!!

He dried his hands then grabbed the Fender guitar case and the book bag, pushed into the restaurant.

Soldier, your gloves—

The alarmed patrons stared at his bloody hands, his crazed

expression. 'Worms,' he muttered in explanation to the entire restaurant, 'fucking worms,' then burst outside onto the street.

Hurrying down the sidewalk, calming. He was thinking about what he had to do. He *had* to kill Jodie, of course. Have to kill him have to kill him have to ... Not because he was a traitor, but because he'd given away so much information—

And why the fuck d'you do that, Soldier?

—about himself to the man. And he had to kill Lincoln the Worm because ... because the worms would get him if he didn't.

Have to kill have to have to have ...

Are you *listening* to me, Soldier? Are you?

That was all there was left to do.

Then he'd leave this city. Head back to West Virginia. Back to the hills.

Lincoln, dead.

Jodie, dead.

Have to kill have to have to have to ...

Nothing more to keep him here.

As for the Wife – he looked at his watch. Just after 7 P.M. Well, she was probably dead already.


''Sbulletproof.'

'Against *those* bullets?' Jodie asked. 'You said they blow up!'

Dellray assured him it was effective. The vest was thick Kevlar on top of a steel sheet. It weighed forty-two pounds and Rhyme didn't know a cop in the city who wore a vest like this, or ever would.

'But what if he shoots my head?'

'He wants me a lot more than he wants *you*,' Rhyme said.

'And how's he gonna know I'm staying here?'

'How d'ya think, mutt?' Dellray snapped. 'I'ma tell him.'

The agent cinched up the little man tight in the vest and tossed him a windbreaker. He'd showered – after protesting – and had been given a set of clean clothes. The large navy blue jacket, covering the bulletproof vest, was a little lopsided but actually gave him a muscular physique. He caught sight of himself in the mirror – his scrubbed and newly attired self – and smiled for the first time since he'd been here.

'Okay,' Sellitto said to two undercover officers, 'take him downtown.'

The officers ushered him out the door.

After he'd left, Dellray looked at Rhyme, who nodded. The lanky agent sighed and flicked open his cell phone, placed a call to Hudson Air Charters, where another agent was waiting to pick up the phone. The fed's tech group had found a remote tap on a relay box near the airport, clipped into the Hudson Air phone lines. The agents hadn't removed it, though; in fact at Rhyme's insistence they checked to make sure it was working and had replaced the weak batteries. The criminalist was relying on the device for the new trap.

On the speakerphone, several rings then a click.

'Agent Mondale,' came the deep voice. Mondale wasn't Mondale and he was speaking according to a prewritten script.

'Mondale,' Dellray said, sounding lily white, to a Connecticut manor born. 'Agent Wilson here, we're at Lincoln's now.' (Not 'Rhyme'; the Dancer knew him as 'Lincoln'.)

'How's the airport?'

'Still secure.'

'Good. Listen, got a question. We've got a CI working for us, Joe D'Oforio.'

'He was the one—'

'Right.'

'—turned. You're working with him?'

'Yeah,' said Wilson, AKA Fred Dellray. 'Bit of a mutt, but

he's cooperating. We're going to run him down to his hidey-
hole and back here.'

'Where's "here"? You mean, back to Lincoln's?'

'Right. He wants his stuff.'

'Fuck you doing that for?'

'He cut a deal. He dimes this killer and Lincoln agreed
he could have some stuff from his place. This old subway
station . . . Anyway, we're not doing a convoy. Just one car.
Reason I called, we need a good driver. You worked with somebody you liked, right?'

'Driver?'

'On the Gambino thing?'

'Oh, yeah . . . Lemme think.'

They stretched it out. Rhyme was, as always, impressed
with Dellray's performance. Whoever he wanted to be, he was.

The phony agent Mondale – who deserved a best-
supporting award himself – said, 'I remember. Tony Glidden.
No, Tommy. The blond guy, right?'

'That's him. I want to use him. He around?'

'Naw. He's in Phillie. That carjacking sting.'

'Phillie. Too bad. We're going in about twenty minutes.
Can't wait any longer than that. Well, I'll just do it myself
then. But that Tommy. He—'

'Fucker could drive a car! He could lose a tail in two
blocks. Man was amazing.'

'Sure could use him now. Listen, thanks, Mondale.'

'Later.'

Rhyme winked, a quad's equivalent of applause. Dellray
hung up, exhaled long and slow. 'We'll see. We'll see.'

Sellitto uttered an optimistic 'The third time we're baiting
him. This should be it.'

Lincoln Rhyme didn't believe that was a rule of law
enforcement, but he said, 'Let's hope.'

\*     \*     \*

Sitting in a stolen car not far from Jodie's subway station, Stephen Kall watched a government-issue sedan pull up.

Jodie and two uniformed cops climbed out, scanning the rooftops. Jodie ran inside and, five minutes later, escaped back to the car with two bundles under his arm.

Stephen could see no backup, no tail cars. What he'd heard on the tap was accurate. They pulled into traffic and he started after them, thinking there was no place in the world like Manhattan for following and not being seen. He couldn't be doing this in Iowa or Virginia.

The unmarked car drove fast, but Stephen was a good driver too and he stayed with it as they made their way uptown. The sedan slowed when they got to Central Park West and drove past a town house in the Seventies. There were two men in front of it, wearing street clothes, but they were obviously cops. A signal – probably 'All clear' – passed between them and the driver of the unmarked sedan.

So that's it. That's Lincoln the Worm's house.

The car continued north. Stephen did too for a little ways, then parked suddenly and climbed out, hurrying into the trees with the guitar case. He knew there'd be some surveillance around the apartment and he moved quietly.

Like a deer, Soldier.

Yessir.

He vanished into a stand of brush and crawled back toward the town house, finding a good nest on a stony ledge under a budding lilac tree. He opened the case. The car containing Jodie, now going south, screeched up to the town house. Standard evasive practice, Stephen recognized – it had made an abrupt U-turn in heavy traffic and sped back here.

He was watching the two cops climb out of the sedan, look around, and escort a very scared Jodie along the sidewalk.

Stephen flipped the covers off the telescope and took careful aim on the traitor's back.

Suddenly a black car drove past and Jodie spooked. His eyes went wide and he pulled away from the cops, running into the alley beside the town house.

His escorts spun around, hands on their weapons, staring at the car that had startled him. They looked at the quartet of Latino girls inside and realized it was just a false alarm. The cops laughed. One of them called to Jodie.

But Stephen wasn't interested in the little man right now. He couldn't get both the Worm and Jodie, and Lincoln was the one he had to kill now. He could taste it. It was a hunger, a need as great as scrubbing his hands.

To shoot the face in the window, to kill the worm.

Have to have to have to have to . . .

He was looking through the telescope, scanning the building's windows. And there he was. Lincoln the Worm.

A shiver rippled through Stephen's entire body.

Like the electricity he felt when his leg rubbed against Jodie's . . . only a thousand times greater. He actually gasped in excitement.

For some reason Stephen wasn't the least surprised to see that the Worm was crippled. In fact, this was how he knew the handsome man in a fancy motorized wheelchair *was* Lincoln. Because Stephen believed it would take an extraordinary man to catch him. Someone who wasn't distracted by everyday life. Someone whose essence was his mind.

Worms could crawl over Lincoln all day long and he'd never even feel them. They could crawl into his skin and he'd never know. He was immune. And Stephen hated him all the more for his invulnerability.

So the face in the window during the Washington, D.C., hit . . . it hadn't been Lincoln.

Or had it?

Stop thinking about it! Stop! The worms'll get you if you don't.

The explosive rounds were in the clip. He chambered one, and scanned the room again.

Lincoln the Worm was speaking to someone Stephen couldn't see. The room, on the first floor, seemed to be a laboratory. He saw a computer screen and some other equipment.

Stephen wrapped the sling around him, spot-welded the rifle butt to his cheek. It was a cool, damp evening. The air was heavy; it would sustain the explosive bullet easily. There was no need to correct; the target was only eighty yards away. Safety off, breathe, breathe . . .

Go for a head shot. It would be easy from here.

Breathe . . .

In, out, in, out.

He looked through the reticles, centered them on Lincoln the Worm's ear as he stared at the computer screen.

The pressure on the trigger began to build.

Breathe. Like sex, like coming, like touching firm skin . . .

Harder.

Harder . . .

Then Stephen saw it.

Very faint – a slight unevenness on Lincoln the Worm's sleeve. But not a wrinkle. It was a distortion.

He relaxed his trigger finger and studied the image through the telescope for a moment. Stephen clicked to a higher resolution on the Redfield telescope. He looked at the type on the computer screen. The letters were backwards.

A mirror! He was sighting on a mirror.

It was *another* trap!

Stephen closed his eyes. He'd almost given his position away. Cringey now. Smothering in worms, choking on worms. He looked around him. He knew there must be a dozen search-and-surveillance troopers in the park with Big Ears microphones just waiting to pinpoint the gunshot. They'd sight on him with M-16s mounted with Starlight scopes and nail him in a cross fire.

Green-lighted to kill. No surrender pitch.

Quickly but in absolute silence he removed the telescope with shaking hands and replaced it and the gun in the guitar case. Fighting down the nausea, the cringe.

Soldier . . .

Sir, go away, sir.

Soldier, what are you—

Sir, fuck you, sir!

Stephen slipped through the trees to a path and walked casually around the meadow, heading east.

Oh, yes, he was now even more certain than before that he had to kill Lincoln. A new plan. He needed an hour or two, to think, to consider what he was going to do.

He turned suddenly off the path, paused in the bushes for a long moment, listening, looking around him. They'd been so worried he'd be suspicious if he noticed that the park was deserted, so they hadn't closed the entrances.

That was their mistake.

Stephen saw a group of men about his age – yuppies, from the look of them, dressed in sweats or jogging outfits. They were carrying racquetball cases and backpacks and headed for the Upper East Side, talking loudly as they walked. Their hair glistened from the showers they'd just had at a nearby athletic club.

Stephen waited until they were just past, then fell in behind them, as if he were a part of the group. Offered one of them a big smile. Walking briskly, swinging the guitar case jauntily, he followed them toward the tunnel that led to the East Side.

# Chapter
# THIRTY-TWO

Dusk surrounded them.

Percey Clay, once again in the left-hand seat of the Learjet, saw the cusp of light that was Chicago in front of them.

Chicago Center cleared them down to twelve thousand feet.

'Starting descent,' she announced, easing back on the throttles. 'ATIS.'

Brad clicked his radio to the automated airport information system and repeated out loud what the recorded voice told him. 'Chicago information, Whiskey. Clear and forever. Wind two five oh at three. Temperature fifty-nine degrees. Altimeter thirty one one.'

Brad set the altimeter as Percey said into her microphone, 'Chicago Approach, this is Lear Niner Five *Foxtrot Bravo*. With you inbound at twelve thousand. Heading two eight zero.'

'Evening, *Foxtrot Bravo*. Descend and maintain one zero thousand. Expect vectors runway twenty-seven right.'

'Roger. Descend and maintain ten. Vectors, two seven right. Niner Five *Foxtrot Bravo*.'

Percey refused to look down. Somewhere below and ahead of them was the grave of her husband and his aircraft. She didn't know if he'd been cleared to land on O'Hare's runway

27 right, but it was likely that he had and, if so, ATC would've vectored Ed through exactly the same airspace she was now sailing through.

Maybe he'd started to call her right about here . . .

No! Don't think about it, she ordered herself. Fly the aircraft.

In a low, calm voice she said, 'Brad, this will be a visual approach to runway twenty-seven right. Monitor the approach and call all assigned altitudes. When we turn on final please monitor airspeed, altitude, and rate of descent. Warn me of a sink rate greater than one thousand fpm. Go-around will be at ninety-two percent.'

'Roger.'

'Flaps ten degrees.'

'Flaps, ten, ten, green.'

The radio crackled, 'Lear Niner Five *Foxtrot Bravo*, turn left heading two four zero, descend, and maintain four thousand.'

'Five *Foxtrot Bravo*, out of ten for four. Heading two four zero.'

She eased back on the throttle and the plane settled slightly, the grinding sound of the engines diminished, and she could hear the woosh of the air like a whisper of wind over bedsheets beside an open window at night.

Percey yelled back to Bell, 'You're about to have your first landing in a Lear. Let's see if I can set her down without rippling your coffee.'

'In one piece's all I'm asking for,' Bell said and cinched his seat belt tight as a bungee cord harness.

'Nothing, Rhyme.'

The criminalist closed his eyes in disgust. 'I don't believe it. I just don't believe it.'

'He's gone. He was there, they're pretty sure. But the mikes didn't pick up a sound.'

Rhyme glanced up at the big mirror he'd ordered Thom to prop up across the room. They'd been waiting for the explosive rounds to crash into it. Central Park was peppered with Haumann's and Dellray's tactical officers, just waiting for a gunshot.

'Where's Jodie?' Rhyme asked.

Dellray snickered. 'Hiding in the alley. Saw some car go by and spooked.'

'What car?' Rhyme asked.

The agent laughed. 'If it *was* the Dancer, then he turned hisself into four fat Puerto Rican girls. Little shit said he won't come out till somebody shuts off the streetlight in front of your building.'

'Leave him. He'll come back when he gets cold.'

'Or to get his money,' Sachs reminded.

Rhyme scowled. He was bitterly disappointed that this trick too hadn't worked.

Was it his failing? Or was there some uncanny instinct that the Dancer had? A sixth sense? The idea was repugnant to Lincoln Rhyme, the scientist, but he couldn't discount it completely. After all, even the NYPD used psychics from time to time.

Sachs started toward the window.

'No,' Rhyme said to her. 'We still don't know for certain he's gone.' Sellitto stood away from the glass as he drew the drapes shut.

Oddly, it was scarier not knowing exactly where the Dancer was than thinking he was pointing a large rifle through a window twenty feet away.

It was then that Cooper's phone rang. He took the call.

'Lincoln, it's the Bureau's bomb people. They've checked the Explosives Reference Collection. They say they've got a possible match on those bits of latex.'

'What do they say?'

Cooper listened to the agent for a moment.

'No leads on the specific type of rubber, but they say its not inconsistent with a material used in altimeter detonators. There's a latex balloon filled with air. It expands when the plane goes up because of the low pressure at higher altitudes, and at a certain height the balloon presses into a switch on the side of the bomb wall. Contact's completed. The bomb goes off.'

'But this bomb was detonated by a timer.'

'They're just telling me about the latex.'

Rhyme looked at the plastic bags containing components of the bomb. His eyes fell to the timer, and he thought: Why's it in such perfect shape?

Because it had been mounted behind the overhanging lip of steel.

But the Dancer could have mounted it anywhere, pressed it into the plastic explosive itself, which would have reduced it to microscopic pieces. Leaving the timer intact had seemed careless at first. But now he wondered.

'Tell him that the plane exploded as it was *descending*,' Sachs said.

Cooper relayed the comment, then listened. The tech reported, 'He says it could just be a point-of-construction variation. As the plane climbs, the expanding balloon trips a switch that arms the bomb; when the plane descends the balloon shrinks and closes the circuit. That detonates it.'

Rhyme whispered, 'The timer's a fake! He mounted it behind the piece of metal so it wouldn't be destroyed. So we'd *think* it was a time bomb, not an altitude bomb. How high was Carney's plane when it exploded?'

Sellitto raced through the NTSB report. 'It was just descending through five thousand feet.'

'So it armed when they climbed through five thousand outside of Mamaroneck and detonated when he went below it near Chicago,' Rhyme said.

'Why on descent?' the detective asked.

'So the plane would be farther away?' Sachs suggested.

'Right,' Rhyme said. 'It'd give the Dancer a better chance to get away from the airport before it blew.'

'But,' Cooper asked, 'why go to all the trouble to fool us into thinking it was one kind of bomb and not another?'

Rhyme saw that Sachs figured it out just as fast as he did. 'Oh, no!' she cried.

Sellitto still didn't get it. 'What?'

'Because,' she said, 'the bomb squad was looking for a *time* bomb when they searched Percey's plane tonight. Listening for the timer.'

'Which means,' Rhyme spat out, 'Percey and Bell've got an altitude bomb on board too.'

'Sink rate twelve hundred feet per minute,' Brad sang out.

Percey gentled the yoke of the Lear back slightly, slowing the descent. They passed through fifty-five hundred feet.

Then she heard it.

A strange chirping sound. She'd never heard any sound like it, not in a Lear 35A. It sounded like a warning buzzer of some kind, but distant. Percey scanned the panels but could see no red lights. It chirped again.

'Five three hundred feet,' Brad called. 'What's that noise?'

It stopped abruptly.

Percey shrugged.

An instant later, she heard a voice shouting beside her, 'Pull up! Go higher! Now!'

Roland Bell's hot breath was on her cheek. He was beside her, in a crouch, brandishing his cell phone.

'What?'

'There's a bomb on! Altitude bomb. It goes off when we hit five thousand feet.'

'But we're above—'

'I know! Pull up! Up!'

Percey shouted, 'Set power, ninety-eight percent. Call out altitude.'

Without a second's hesitation, Brad shoved the throttles forward. Percey pulled the Lear into a ten-degree rotation. Bell stumbled backward and landed with a crash on the floor.

Brad said, 'Five thousand two, five one five . . . five two, five thousand three, five four . . . Five eight. Six thousand feet.'

Percey Clay had never declared an emergency in all her years flying. Once, she'd declared a 'pan-pan' – indicating an urgency situation – when an unfortunate flock of pelicans decided to commit suicide in her number two engine and clog up her pitot tube to boot. But now, for the first time in her career, she said, 'May-day, may-day, Lear Six Niner Five *Foxtrot Bravo*.'

'Go ahead, *Foxtrot Bravo*.'

'Be advised, Chicago Approach. We have reports of a bomb on board. Need immediate clearance to one zero thousand feet and a heading for holding pattern over unpopulated area.'

'Roger, Niner Five *Foxtrot Bravo*,' the ATC controller said calmly. 'Uhm, maintain present heading of two four zero. Cleared to ten thousand feet. We are vectoring all aircraft around you . . . Change transponder code to seven seven zero zero and squawk.'

Brad glanced uneasily at Percey as he changed the transponder setting – to the code that automatically sent a warning signal to all radar facilities in the area that *Foxtrot Bravo* was in trouble. Squawking meant sending out a signal from the transponder to let everyone at ATC and other aircraft know exactly which blip was the Lear.

She heard Bell say into his phone, 'Th' only person got close to the plane, 'cept for me and Percey, was the business manager, Ron Talbot – and, nothing personal to him, but my boys or I watched him like a hawk while he was doing the work, stood over his shoulder the whole time. Oh, and that guy delivered some of the engine parts came by too. From Northeast Aircraft Distributors in Greenwich. But I checked him out good. Even got his home phone and called his wife, had them talk – to make sure he was legit.' Bell listened for a moment more then hung up. 'They'll call us back.'

Percey looked at Brad and at Bell, then returned to the task of piloting her aircraft.

'Fuel?' she asked her copilot. 'How much time?'

'We're under our estimated. Headwinds've been good.' He did the calculations. 'A hundred and five minutes.'

She thanked God, or fate, or her own intuition, for deciding not to refuel at Chicago, but to load enough to get them to Saint Louis, plus the FAA requirement for an additional forty-five minutes' flying time.

Bell's phone chirped again.

He listened, sighed, then asked Percey, 'Did that Northeast company deliver a fire extinguisher cartridge?'

'Shit, did he put it in *there*?' she asked bitterly.

'Looks like it. The delivery truck had a flat tire just after it left the warehouse on the way to make that delivery to you. Driver was busy for about twenty minutes. Connecticut trooper just found a mess of what looks like carbon dioxide foam in the bushes right near where it happened.'

'God*damn!*' Percey glanced involuntarily toward the engine. 'And I installed the fucker myself.'

Bell asked, 'Rhyme wants to know about heat. Wouldn't it blow the bomb?'

'Some parts are hot, some aren't. It's not that hot by the cartridge.'

Bell told this to Rhyme, then he said, 'He's going to call you directly.'

A moment later, through the radio, Percey heard the patch of a unicom call.

It was Lincoln Rhyme.

'Percey, can you hear me?'

'Loud and clear. That prick pulled a fast one, hmm?'

'Looks like it. How much flying time do you have?'

'Hour forty-five minutes. About.'

'Okay, okay,' the criminalist said. A pause. 'All right . . . Can you get to the engine from the inside?'

'No.'

Another pause. 'Could you somehow disconnect the whole engine? Unbolt it or something? Let it drop off?'

'Not from the inside.'

'Is there any way you could refuel in midair?'

'Refuel? Not with this plane.'

Rhyme asked, 'Could you fly high enough to freeze the bomb mechanism?'

She was amazed at how fast his mind worked. These were things that wouldn't have occurred to her. 'Maybe. But even at emergency descent rate – I'm talking nosedive – it'd still take eight, nine minutes to get down. I don't think any bomb parts'd stay very frozen for that long. And the Mach buffet would probably tear us apart.'

Rhyme continued, 'Okay, what about getting a plane in front of you and tethering some parachutes back?'

Her initial thought was that she would never abandon her aircraft. But the realistic answer – the one she gave him – was that given the stall speed of a Lear 35A and the configuration of door, wings, and engines, it was unlikely that anyone could leap from the aircraft without being struck and killed.

Rhyme was again silent for a moment. Brad swallowed and wiped his hands on his razor-creased slacks. 'Brother.'

Roland Bell rocked back and forth.

Hopeless, she thought, staring down at the murky blue dusk.

'Lincoln?' Percey asked. 'Are you there?'

She heard his voice. He was calling to someone in his lab – or bedroom. In a testy tone he was demanding, 'Not *that* map. You know which one I mean. Well, why would I want that one? No, no . . .'

Silence.

Oh, Ed, Percey thought. Our lives have always followed parallel paths. Maybe our deaths will too. She was most upset about Roland Bell, though. The thought of leaving his children orphans was unbearable.

Then she heard Rhyme asking, 'On the fuel you've got left, how far can you fly?'

'At the most efficient power settings . . .' She looked at Brad, who was punching in the figures.

He said, 'If we got some altitude, say, eight hundred miles.'

'Got an idea,' Rhyme said. 'Can you make it to Denver?'

# Chapter
# THIRTY-THREE

'Airport elevation's fifty-one eighty feet,' Brad said, reviewing the *Airman's Guide of Denver International*. 'We were about that outside of Chicago and the thing didn't blow.'

'How far?' Percey asked.

'From present location, nine oh two miles.'

Percey debated for no more than a few seconds, nodded. 'We go for it. Give me a dead-reckoning heading, just something to play with till we get VORs.' Then into the radio: 'We're going to try it, Lincoln. The gas'll be real close. We've got a lot to do. I'll get back to you.'

'We'll be here.'

Brad eyeballed the map and referred to the flight log. 'Turn left heading two six six.'

'Two six six,' she repeated, then called ATC. 'Chicago Center, Niner Five *Foxtrot Bravo*. We're heading for Denver International. Apparently it's a . . . we've got an altitude-sensitive bomb on board. We need to get on the ground at five thousand feet or higher. Request immediate VORs for vectoring to Denver.'

'Roger, *Foxtrot Bravo*. We'll have those in a minute.'

Brad asked, 'Please advise the weather en route, Chicago Center.'

'High pressure front moving through Denver right now. Headwinds vary from fifteen to forty at ten thousand, increasing to sixty, seventy knots at twenty-five.'

'Ouch,' Brad muttered then returned to his calculations. After a moment he said, 'Fuel depletion about fifty-five miles short of Denver.'

Bell asked, 'Can you set down on the highway?'

'In a big ball of flames we can,' Percey said.

ATC asked, *Foxtrot Bravo*, ready to copy VOR frequencies?'

While Brad took down the information, Percey stretched, pressed her head into the back of her seat. The gesture seemed familiar and she remembered she'd seen Lincoln Rhyme do the same in his elaborate bed. She thought about her little speech to him. She'd meant it, of course, but hadn't realized how true the words were. How dependent they were on fragile bits of metal and plastic.

And maybe about to die because of them.

*Fate is the hunter . . .*

Fifty-five miles short. What could they do?

Why wasn't her mind as far-ranging as Rhyme's? Wasn't there anything she could think of to conserve fuel?

Flying higher was more fuel efficient.

Flying lighter was too. Could they throw anything out of the aircraft?

The cargo? The U.S. Medical shipment weighed exactly 478 pounds. That would buy them some miles.

But even as she considered this, she knew she'd never do it. If there was any chance she could salvage the flight, salvage the Company, she would.

Come on, Lincoln Rhyme, she thought, give me an idea. Give me . . . Picturing his room, picturing sitting beside him, she remembered the tiercel – the male falcon – lording about on the window ledge.

'Brad,' she asked abruptly, 'what's our glide ratio?'

'A Lear thirty-five A? No idea.'

Percey had flown a Schweizer 2-32 sailplane. The first prototype was built in 1962 and it had set the standard for glider performance ever since. Its sink rate was a miraculous 120 feet per minute. It weighed about thirteen hundred pounds. The Lear she was flying was fourteen thousand pounds. Still, aircraft will glide, any aircraft. She remembered the incident of the Air Canada 767 a few years ago – pilots still talked about it. The jumbo jet ran out of fuel due to a combination of computer and human error. Both engines flamed out at forty-one thousand feet and the aircraft became a 143-ton glider. It crash-landed without a single death.

'Well, let's think. What'd the sink rate be at idle?'

'We could keep it twenty-three hundred, I think.'

Which meant a vertical drop of about thirty miles per hour.

'Now. Calculate if we burned fuel to take us to fifty-five thousand feet, when would we deplete?'

'Fifty-five?' Brad asked with some surprise.

'Roger.'

He punched in numbers. 'Maximum climb is forty-three hundred fpm; we'd burn a lot down here, but after thirty-five thousand the efficiency goes way up. We could power back . . .'

'Go to one engine?'

'Sure. We could do that.'

He tapped in more numbers. 'That scenario, we'd deplete about eighty-three miles short. But, of course, then we'd have altitude.'

Percey Clay, who got As in math and physics and could dead reckon without a calculator, saw the numbers stream past in her head. Flame out at fifty-five thousand, sink rate of twenty-three . . . They could cover a little over eighty miles before they touched down. Maybe more if the headwinds were kind.

Brad, with the help of a calculator and fast fingers, came up with the same conclusion. 'Be close, though.'

*God don't give out certain.*

She said, 'Chicago Center. Lear *Foxtrot Bravo* requesting immediate clearance to five five thousand feet.'

*Sometimes you play the odds.*

'Uh, say again, *Foxtrot Bravo.*'

'We need to go high. Five five thousand feet.'

The ATC controller's voice intruded: '*Foxtrot Bravo*, you're a Lear three five, is that correct?'

'Roger.'

'Maximum operating ceiling is forty-five thousand feet.'

'That's affirmative, but we need to go higher.'

'Your seals've been checked lately?'

Pressure seals. Doors and windows. What kept the aircraft from exploding.

'They're fine,' she said, neglecting to mention that *Foxtrot Bravo* had been shot full of holes and jerry-rigged back together just that afternoon.

ATC answered, 'Roger, you're cleared to five five thousand feet, *Foxtrot Bravo.*'

And Percey said something that few, if any, Lear pilots had ever said, 'Roger, out of ten for fifty-five thousand.'

Percey commanded, 'Power to eighty-eight percent. Call out rate of climb and altitude at forty, fifty, and fifty-five thousand.'

'Roger,' Brad said placidly.

She rotated the plane and it began to rise.

They sailed upward.

*All the stars of evening . . .*

Ten minutes later Brad called out, 'Five five thousand.'

They leveled off. It seemed to Percey that she could actually hear the groaning of the aircraft's seams. She recalled her high-altitude physiology. If the window Ron had replaced were to blow out or any pressure seal burst – if it didn't tear the aircraft apart – hypoxia would knock them out in about five seconds. Even if they were wearing masks, the pressure difference would make their blood boil.

'Increase cabin pressure to ten thousand feet.'

'Pressure to ten thousand,' he said. This at least would relieve some of the terrible pressure on the fragile hull.

'Good idea,' Brad said. 'How'd you think of that?'

*Monkey skills* . . .

'Dunno,' she responded. 'Let's cut power in number two. Throttle closed, autothrottle disengaged.'

'Closed, disengaged,' Brad echoed.

'Fuel pumps off, ignition off.'

'Pumps off, ignition off.'

She felt the slight swerve as their right side thrust vanished. Percey compensated for the yaw with a slight adjustment to the rudder trim tabs. It didn't take much. Because the jets were mounted on the rear of the fuselage and not on the wings, losing one power plant didn't affect the stability of the aircraft much.

Brad asked, 'What do we do now?'

'I'm having a cup of coffee,' Percey said, climbing out of her seat like a tomboy jumping from a tree house. 'Hey, Roland, how d'you like yours again?'

For a tortuous forty minutes there was silence in Rhyme's room. No one's phone rang. No faxes came in. No computer voices reported, 'You've got mail.'

Then, at last, Dellray's phone brayed. He nodded as he spoke, but Rhyme could see the news wasn't good. He clicked the phone off.

'Cumberland?'

Dellray nodded. 'But it's a bust. Kall hasn't been there for years. Oh, the locals're still talking about the time the boy tied his stepdaddy up 'n' let the worms get him. Sorta a legend. But no family left in the area. And nobody knows nuthin'. Or's willing to say.'

It was then that Sellitto's phone chirped. The detective unfolded it and said, 'Yeah?'

A lead, Rhyme prayed, please let it be a lead. He looked at the cop's doughy, stoic face. He flipped the phone closed.

'That was Roland Bell,' he said. 'He just wanted us to know. They're outa gas.'

# Chapter
# THIRTY-FOUR

Three different warning buzzers went off simultaneously. Low fuel, low oil pressure, low engine temperature. Percey tried adjusting the attitude of the aircraft slightly to see if she could trick some fuel into the lines, but the tanks were bone dry.

With a faint clatter, number one engine quit coughing and went silent.

And the cockpit went completely dark. Black as a closet.

Oh, no . . .

She couldn't see a single instrument, a single control lever or knob. The only thing that kept her from slipping into blind-flight vertigo was the faint band of light that was Denver – in the far distance in front of them.

'What's this?' Brad asked.

'Jesus. I forgot the generators.'

The generators are run by the engines. No engines, no electricity.

'Drop the RAT,' she ordered.

Brad groped in the dark for the control and found it. He pulled the lever and the ram air turbine dropped out beneath the aircraft. It was a small propeller connected to a generator.

The slipstream turned the prop, which powered the generator. It provided basic power for the controls and lights. But not the flaps, gear, speed brakes.

A moment later some of the lights returned.

Percey was staring at the vertical speed indicator. It showed a decent rate of thirty-five hundred feet per minute. Far faster than they'd planned on. They were dropping at close to fifty miles an hour.

Why? she wondered. Why was the calculation so far off?

Because of the rarified air here! She was calculating sink rate based on denser atmosphere. And now that she considered this she remembered that the air around Denver would be rarified too. She'd never flown a sailplane more than a mile up.

She pulled back on the yoke to arrest the descent. It dropped to twenty-one hundred feet per minute. But the airspeed dropped too, fast. In this thin air the stall speed was about three hundred knots. The shaker stick began to vibrate and the controls went mushy. There'd be no recovery from a powerless stall in an aircraft like this.

*The coffin corner* . . .

Forward with the yoke. They dropped faster, but the airspeed picked up. For nearly fifty miles she played this game. Air Traffic Control told them where the headwinds were strongest and Percey tried to find the perfect combination of altitude and route – winds that were powerful enough to give the Lear optimal lift but not so fast that they slowed their ground speed too much.

Finally, Percey – her muscles aching from controlling the aircraft with brute force – wiped sweat from her face and said, 'Give 'em a call, Brad.'

'Denver Center, this is Lear Six Niner Five *Foxtrot Bravo*, with you out of one nine thousand feet. We are twenty-one miles from the airport. Airspeed two hundred twenty knots.

We're in a no-power situation here and requesting vectoring to longest available runway consistent with our present heading of two five zero.'

'Roger, *Foxtrot Bravo*. We've been expecting you. Altimeter thirty point nine five. Turn left heading two four zero. We're vectoring you to runway two eight left. You'll have eleven thousand feet to play with.'

'Roger, Denver Center.'

Something was nagging at her. That ping in the gut again. Like she'd felt recalling the black van.

What was it? Just superstition?

*Tragedies come in threes . . .*

Brad said, 'Nineteen miles from touchdown. One six thousand feet.'

'*Foxtrot Bravo*, contact Denver Approach.' He gave them the radio frequency, then added, 'They've been apprised of your situation. Good luck, ma'am. We're all thinking of you.'

'Goodnight, Denver. Thanks.'

Brad clicked the radio to the new frequency.

What's wrong? she wondered again. There's something I haven't thought of.

'Denver Approach, this is Lear Six Niner Five *Foxtrot Bravo*. With you at one three thousand feet, thirteen miles from touchdown.'

'We have you, *Foxtrot Bravo*. Come right heading two five zero. Understand you are power-free, is that correct?'

'We're the biggest damn glider you ever saw, Denver.'

'You have flaps and gear?'

'No flaps. We'll crank the gear down manually.'

'Roger. You want trucks?'

Meaning emergency vehicles.

'We think we've got a bomb on board. We want everything you've got.'

'Roger that.'

Then, with a shudder of horror, it occurred to her: the air pressure!

'Denver Approach,' she asked, 'what's the altimeter?'

'Uhm, we have three oh point nine six, *Foxtrot Bravo*.'

It had gone up a hundredth of an inch of mercury in the last minute.

'It's rising?'

'That's affirmative, *Foxtrot Bravo*. Major high-pressure front moving in.'

No! That would increase the ambient pressure around the bomb, which would shrink the balloon, as if they were lower than they actually were.

'Shit on the street,' she muttered.

Brad looked at her.

She said to him, 'What was the mercury at Mamaroneck?'

He looked it up in the log. 'Twenty-nine point six.'

'Calculate five thousand feet altitude at that pressure reading compared with thirty-one point oh.'

'Thirty-one? That's awful high.'

'That's what we're moving into.'

He stared at her. 'But the bomb . . .'

Percey nodded. 'Calculate it.'

The young man punched numbers with a steady hand.

He sighed, his first visible display of emotion. 'Five thousand feet at Mamaroneck translates to forty-eight five here.'

She called Bell forward again. 'Here's the situation. There's a pressure front coming in. By the time we get to the runway, the bomb may be reading the atmosphere as below five thousand feet. It may blow when were're fifty to a hundred feet above the ground.'

'Okay.' He nodded calmly. 'Okay.'

'We don't have flaps, so we're going to be landing fast, close to two hundred miles an hour. If it blows we'll lose control and crash. There won't be much fire 'cause the tanks are dry. And depending on what's in front of us, if we're low enough we may skid a ways before we start tumbling. There's nothing to do but keep the seat belts tight and keep your head down.'

'All right,' he said, nodding, looking out the window.

She glanced at his face. 'Can I ask you something, Roland?'

'You bet.'

'This isn't your first airplane flight, is it?'

He sighed. 'You know, you live mosta your born days in North Carolina, you just don't have much of a chance to travel. And coming to New York, well, those Amtraks're nice and comfy.' He paused. 'Fact is, I've never been higher than an elevator'll take me.'

'They're not all like this,' she said.

He squeezed her on the shoulder, whispered, 'Don't drop your candy.' He returned to his seat.

'Okay,' Percey said, looking over the *Airman's Guide* information on Denver International. 'Brad, this'll be a nighttime visual approach to runway two eight left. I'll have command of the aircraft. You'll lower the gear manually and call out rate of descent, distance to runway, and altitude – give me true altitude above ground, not sea level – and airspeed.' She tried to think of something else. No power, no flaps, no speed brakes. There was nothing else to say; it was the shortest prelanding briefing in the history of her flying career. She added, 'One last thing. When we stop, just get the fuck out as fast as you can.'

'Ten miles to runway,' he called. 'Speed two hundred knots. Altitude nine thousand feet. We need to slow descent.'

She pulled up on the yoke slightly and the speed dropped dramatically. The shaker stick vibrated again. Stall now and they died.

Forward again.

Nine miles . . . Eight . . .

Sweating like a rainstorm. She wiped her face. Blisters on the soft skin between her thumbs and index fingers.

Seven . . . Six . . .

'Five miles from touchdown, forty-five hundred feet. Airspeed two hundred ten knots.'

'Gear down,' Percey commanded.

Brad spun the wheel that manually lowered the heavy gear. He had gravity helping him, but it was nonetheless a major effort. Still, he kept his eyes glued to the instruments and recited, calm as an accountant reading a balance sheet, 'Four miles from touchdown, thirty-nine hundred feet . . .'

She fought the buffeting of the lower altitude and the harsh winds.

'Gear down,' Brad called, panting, 'three green.'

The airspeed dropped to one hundred eighty knots – about two hundred miles an hour. It was too fast. Way too fast. Without their reverse thrusters they'd burn up even the longest runway in a streak.

'Denver Approach, what's the altimeter?'

'Three oh nine eight,' the unflappable ATC controller said.

Rising. Higher and higher.

She took a deep breath. According to the bomb, the runway was slightly less than five thousand feet above sea level. How accurate had the Coffin Dancer been when he'd made the detonator?

'The gear's dragging. Sink rate's twenty-six hundred.'

Which meant a vertical speed of about thirty-eight miles per hour. 'We're dropping too fast, Percey,' Brad called. 'We'll hit in front of the approach lights. A hundred yards short. Two, maybe.'

ATC's voice had noticed this too: '*Foxtrot Bravo*, you have to get some altitude. You're coming in too low.'

Back on the stick. The speed dropped. Stall warning. Forward on the stick.

'Two and a half miles from touchdown, altitude nineteen hundred feet.'

'Too low, *Foxtrot Bravo!*' the ATC controller warned again.

She looked out over the silver nose. There were all the lights – the strobes of the approach lights beckoning them forward, the blue dots of the taxiway, the orange-red of the runway . . . And lights that Percey'd never seen before on approach. Hundreds of flashing lights. White and red. All the emergency vehicles.

Lights everywhere.

*All the stars of evening . . .*

'Still low,' Brad called. 'We're going to impact two hundred yards short.'

Hands sweating, straining forward, Percey thought again of Lincoln Rhyme, strapped to his seat, himself leaning forward, examining something in the computer screen.

'Too low, *Foxtrot Bravo,*' ATC repeated. 'I'm moving emergency vehicles to the field in front of the runway.'

'Negative that,' Percey said adamantly.

Brad called, 'Altitude thirteen hundred feet. One and a half miles from touchdown.'

We've got thirty seconds! What do I do?

Ed? Tell me? Brit? Somebody . . .

Come on, monkey skills . . . What the hell do I do?

She looked out the cockpit window. In the light of the moon she could see suburbs and towns and some farmland but also, to the left, large patches of desert.

Colorado's a desert state . . . Of course!

Suddenly she banked sharply to the left.

Brad, without a clue as to what she was doing, called out, 'Rate of descent thirty-two hundred, altitude one thousand feet, nine hundred feet, eight five . . . '

Banking a powerless aircraft sheds altitude in a hurry.

ATC called, '*Foxtrot Bravo*, do *not* turn. Repeat, do not turn! You don't have enough altitude as is.'

She leveled out over the patch of desert.

Brad gave a fast laugh. 'Altitude steady . . . Altitude rising, we're at nine hundred feet, one thousand feet, twelve hundred feet. Thirteen hundred feet . . . I don't get it.'

'A thermal,' she said. 'Desert soaks up heat during the day and releases it all night.'

ATC had figured it out too. 'Good, *Foxtrot Bravo*! Good. You just bought yourself about three hundred yards. Come right two nine oh . . . good, now left two eight oh. Good. On course. Listen, *Foxtrot Bravo*, you want to take out those approach lights, you go right ahead.'

'Thanks for the offer, Denver, but I think I'll set her down a thousand past the numbers.'

'That's all right too, ma'am.'

They had another problem now. They could reach the runway, but the airspeed was way too high. Flaps were what decreased the stall speed of an aircraft so it could land more slowly. The Lear 35A's normal stall speed was about 110 miles an hour. Without flaps it was closer to 180. At that speed even a two-mile-long runway vanishes in an instant.

So Percey sideslipped.

This is a simple maneuver in a private plane, used in crosswind landings. You bank to the left and hit the right rudder pedal. It slows the aircraft considerably. Percey didn't know if anyone had ever used this technique in a seven-ton jet, but she couldn't think of anything else to do. 'Need your help here,' she called to Brad, gasping at the effort and the pain shooting through her raw hands. He gripped the yoke and shoved on the pedal too. This had the effect of slowing the aircraft, though it dropped the left wing precipitously.

She'd straighten it out just before contact with the runway. She hoped.

'Airspeed?' she called.

'One fifty knots.'

'Looking good, *Foxtrot Bravo*.'

'Two hundred yards from runway, altitude two hundred eighty feet,' Brad called. 'Approach lights, twelve o'clock.'

'Sink rate?' she asked.

'Twenty-six hundred.'

Too fast. Landing at that sink rate could destroy the undercarriage. And might very well set off the bomb too.

There were the approach strobes right in front of her – guiding them forward . . .

Down, down, down . . .

Just as they hurtled toward the scaffolding of the lights, Percey shouted, 'My aircraft!'

Brad released the yoke.

Percey straightened from the sideslip and brought the nose up. The plane flared beautifully and grabbed air, halting the precipitous descent right over the numbers at the end of the runway.

Grabbed air so well, in fact, that it wouldn't land.

In the thicker air of the relatively lower atmosphere the speeding plane – lighter without fuel – refused to touch down.

She glimpsed the yellow-green of the emergency vehicles scattered along the side of the runway.

A thousand feet past the numbers, still thirty feet above the concrete.

Then two thousand feet past. Then three thousand.

Hell, fly her into the ground.

Percey eased the stick forward. The plane dipped dramatically and Percey yanked all the way back on the yoke. The silver bird shuddered then settled gently on the concrete. It was the smoothest landing she'd ever made.

'Full brakes!'

She and Brad jammed their feet down on the rudder pedals

and they heard the squealing of the pads, the fierce vibrations. Smoke filled the cabin.

They'd used well over half the runway already and were still speeding at a hundred miles an hour.

Grass, she thought, I'll veer into it if I have to. Wreck the undercarriage but I'll still save the cargo . . .

Seventy, sixty . . .

'Fire light, right wheel,' Brad called. Then: 'Fire light, nose-wheel.'

Fuck it, she thought, and pressed down on the brakes with all her weight.

The Lear began to skid and shudder. She compensated with the nosewheel. More smoke filling the cabin.

Sixty miles per hour, fifty, forty . . .

'The door,' she called to Bell.

In an instant the detective was up, pushing the door outward; it became a staircase.

The fire trucks were converging on the aircraft.

With a wild groan of the smoking brakes, Lear N695FB skidded to a stop ten feet from the end of the runway.

The first voice to fill the cabin was Bell's. 'Okay, Percey, out! Move.'

'I have to—'

'I'm taking over now!' the detective shouted. 'I have to drag you outa here, I'll do it. Now move!'

Bell hustled her and Brad out the door, then leapt to the concrete himself, led them away from the aircraft. He called to the rescue workers, who'd started shooting foam at the wheel wells, 'There's a bomb on board, could go any minute. In the engine. Don't get close.' One of his guns was in his hand and he surveyed the crowd of rescue workers circling the plane. At one time Percey would have thought he was being paranoid. No longer.

They paused about a hundred feet from the plane. The

Denver Police Bomb Squad truck pulled up. Bell waved it over.

A lanky cowboy of a cop got out of the truck and walked up to Bell. They flashed ID at each other and Bell explained about the bomb, where they thought it was.

'So,' the Denver cop said, 'you're not sure it's on board.'

'Nope. Not a hundred percent.'

Though as Percey happened to glance at *Foxtrot Bravo* – her beautiful silver skin flecked with foam and glistening under the fierce spotlights – there was a deafening bang. Everyone except Bell and Percey hit the ground fast as the rear half of the aircraft disintegrated in a huge flash of orange flame, strewing bits of metal into the air.

'Oh,' Percey gasped, her hand rising to her mouth.

There was no fuel left in the tanks, of course, but the interior of the aircraft – the seats, the wiring, the carpet, the plastic fittings, and the precious cargo – burned furiously as the fire trucks waited a prudent moment then streamed forward, pointlessly shooting more snowy foam on the ruined metallic corpse.

# DANCE MACABRE

I looked up to see a dot dropping, becoming an inverted heart, a diving bird. The wind screamed through her bells, making a sound like nothing else on earth as she fell a half mile through the clear autumn air. At the last moment she turned parallel to the chukar's line of flight and hit it from behind with the solid 'thwack' of a large-caliber bullet striking flesh.

A *RAGE FOR FALCONS*, STEPHEN BODIO

# Chapter
# THIRTY-FIVE

It was after 3 A.M., Rhyme noted. Percey Clay was flying back to the East Coast on an FBI jet and in just a few hours she'd be on her way to the courthouse to get ready for her grand jury appearance.

And he still had no idea where the Coffin Dancer was, what he was planning, what identity he was now assuming.

Sellitto's phone brayed. He listened. His face screwed up. 'Jesus. The Dancer just got somebody else. They found another body – ID-proofed – in a tunnel in Central Park. Near Fifth Avenue.'

'Completely ID-proofed?'

'Did it up right, sounds like. Removed the hands, teeth, jaw, and clothes. White male. Youngish. Late twenties, early thirties.' The detective listened again. 'Not a bum,' he reported. 'He's clean, in good shape. Athletic. Haumann thinks he's some yuppie from the East Side.'

'Okay,' Rhyme said. 'Bring him here. I want to go over it myself.'

'The body?'

'Right.'

'Well, okay.'

'So the Dancer's got a new identity,' Rhyme mused angrily. 'What the hell is it? How's he going to come at us next?'

Rhyme sighed, looked on the window. He said to Dellray, 'What safe house're you going to put them in?'

'I been thinking 'bout that,' the lanky agent said. 'Seems to me—'

'Ours,' a new voice said.

They looked at the heavyset man in the doorway.

'*Our* safe house,' Reggie Eliopolos said. 'We're taking custody.'

'Not unless you've got—' Rhyme began.

The prosecutor waved the paper too fast for Rhyme to read it, but they all knew the protective custody order would be legit.

'That's not a good idea,' Rhyme said.

'It's better than *your* idea of trying to get our last witness killed any way you can.'

Sachs stepped forward, angrily, but Rhyme shook his head.

'Believe me,' Rhyme said, 'the Dancer'll figure out that you're going to take them into custody. He's probably *already* figured it out. In fact,' he added ominously, 'he may be banking on it.'

'He'd have to be a mind reader.'

Rhyme tipped his head. 'You're catching on.'

Eliopolos snickered. He looked around the room, spotted Jodie. 'You're Joseph D'Oforio?'

The little man stared back. 'I – yes.'

'You're coming too.'

'Hey, hold on a minute, they said I'd get my money and I could—'

'This doesn't have anything to do with rewards. If you're entitled to it you'll get it. We're just going to make sure you're safe until the grand jury.'

'Grand jury! Nobody said anything about testifying!'

'Well,' Eliopolos said, 'you're a material witness.' A nod toward Rhyme. '*He* may have been intent on murdering some hit man. *We're* making a case against the man who hired him. Which is what most law enforcers do.'

'I'm not going to testify.'

'Then you're going to do time for contempt. In general population. And I'll bet you know how safe you'll be there.'

The little man tried to be angry but was just too scared. His face shriveled. 'Oh, Jesus.'

'You're not going to have enough protection,' Rhyme said to Eliopolos. 'We know him. Let *us* protect them.'

'Oh, and Rhyme?' Eliopolos turned to him. 'Because of the incident with the plane, I'm charging you with interference with criminal investigation.'

'The fuck you are,' Sellitto said.

'The fuck I am,' the round man snapped back. 'He could've ruined the case, letting her make that flight. I'm having the warrant served Monday. And I'm going to supervise the prosecution myself. He—'

Rhyme said softly, 'He's been here, you know.'

The assistant U.S. attorney stopped speaking. After a moment he asked, 'Who?'

Though he knew who.

'He was right outside that window not an hour ago, pointing a sniper rifle, loaded with explosive shells, into this room.' Rhyme's eyes dipped to the floor. 'Probably the very spot where you're standing.'

Eliopolos wouldn't have stepped back for the world. But his eyes flickered to the windows to make certain the shades were closed.

'Why . . . ?'

Rhyme finished the sentence. 'Didn't he shoot? Because he had a better idea.'

'What's that?'

'Ah,' Rhyme said. 'That's the million-dollar question. All we know is he's killed somebody else – some young man in Central Park – and stripped him. He's ID-proofed the body and taken over his identity. I don't doubt for one minute that he knows the bomb didn't kill Percey and that he's on his way to finish the job. And he'll make you a co-conspirator.'

'He doesn't even know I exist.'

'If that's what you want to believe.'

'Jesus, Reggie Boy,' Dellray said. 'Get with the picture!'

'Don't call me that.'

Sachs joined in. 'Aren't you figuring it out? You've never been up against anybody like him.'

Eyes on her, Eliopolos spoke to Sellitto. 'Guess you do things different on the city level. Federal, our people know their places.'

Rhyme snapped, 'You're a fool if you treat him like a gangsta or some has-been mafioso. Nobody can hide from him. The only way is to stop him.'

'Yeah, Rhyme, that's been your war cry all along. Well, we're not sacrificing any more troops because you've got a hard-on for a guy killed two of your techs five years ago. Assuming you can get a hard-on—'

Eliopolos was a large man and so he was surprised to find himself slammed so lithely to the floor, gasping for breath and staring up into Sellitto's purple face, the lieutenant's fist drawn back.

'Do that, Officer,' the attorney wheezed, 'and you'll be arraigned within a half hour.'

'Lon,' Rhyme said, 'let it go, let it go . . .'

The detective calmed, glared at the man, walked away. Eliopolos climbed to his feet.

The insult in fact meant nothing. He wasn't even thinking of Eliopolos. Or the Dancer for that matter. For he'd happened to glance at Amelia Sachs, at the hollowness in her eyes, the despair. And he knew what she was feeling: the desperation at losing her prey. Eliopolos was stealing away her chance to get the Dancer. As with Lincoln Rhyme, the killer had come to be the dark focus of her life.

All because of a single misstep – the incident at the airport, her going for cover. A small thing, minuscule to everyone but her. But what was the expression? A fool can throw a stone into a pond that a dozen wise men can't recover. And what was Rhyme's life now but the result of a piece of wood breaking a piece of bone? Sachs's life had been snapped in that single moment of what she saw as cowardice. But unlike Rhyme's case, there was – he believed – a chance for her to mend.

Oh, Sachs, how it hurts to do this, but I have no choice. He said to Eliopolos, 'All right, but you have to do one thing in exchange.'

'Or you'll what?' Eliopolos snickered.

'Or I won't tell you where Percey is,' Rhyme said simply. 'We're the only ones who know.'

Eliopolos's face, no longer flushed from his World Wrestling pin, gazed icily at Rhyme. 'What do you want?'

Rhyme inhaled deeply. 'The Dancer's shown an interest in targeting the people looking for him. If you're going to protect Percey, I want you to protect the chief forensic investigator in the case too.'

'You?' the lawyer asked.

'No, Amelia Sachs,' Rhyme replied.

'Rhyme, no,' she said, frowning.

Reckless Amelia Sachs . . . And I'm putting her square in the kill zone.

He motioned her over to him.

'I want to stay here,' she said. 'I want to find him.'

He whispered, 'Oh, don't worry about that, Sachs. He'll find *you*. We'll try to figure out his new identity, Mel and me. But if he makes a move out on Long Island, I want you there.

I want you with Percey. You're the only one who understands him. Well, you and me. And I won't be doing any shooting in the near future.'

'He could come back here—'

'I don't think so. There's a chance this is the first fish of his that's going to get away and he doesn't like that one bit. He's going after Percey. He's desperate to. I know it.'

She debated for a moment, then nodded.

'Okay,' Eliopolos said, 'you'll come with us. We've got a van waiting.'

Rhyme said, 'Sachs?'

She paused.

Eliopolos said, 'We really should move.'

'I'll be down in a minute.'

'We're under some time pressure here, Officer.'

'I said, a minute.' She handily won the staring contest and Eliopolos and his trooper escort led Jodie down the stairs. 'Wait,' the little man shouted from the hallway. He returned, grabbed his self-help book, and trotted down the stairs.

'Sachs . . .'

He thought of saying something about avoiding heroics, about Jerry Banks, about being too hard on herself.

About giving up the dead . . .

But he knew that any words of caution or encouragement would ring like lead.

And so he settled for 'Shoot first.'

She placed her right hand on his left. He closed his eyes and tried so very hard to feel the pressure of her skin on his. He believed he did, if just in his ring finger.

He looked up at her. She said, 'And you keep a minder handy, okay?' Nodding at Sellitto and Dellray.

Then an EMS medic appeared in the door, looking around the room at Rhyme, at the equipment, at the beautiful lady cop, trying to fathom why on earth he was doing what he'd been instructed to. 'Somebody wanted a body?' he asked uncertainly.

'In here!' Rhyme shouted. 'Now! We need it now!'

The van drove through a gate and then down a one-lane driveway. It extended for what seemed like miles.

'If this's the driveway,' Roland Bell muttered, 'can't wait to see the house.'

He and Amelia Sachs flanked Jodie, who irritated everybody to no end as he fidgeted nervously, his bulky bulletproof vest banging into them as he'd examined shadows and dark doorways and passing cars on the Long Island Expressway. In the back were two 32-E officers, armed with machine guns. Percey Clay was in the front passenger seat. When they'd picked up her and Bell at the Marine Air Terminal at LaGuardia on their way to Suffolk County, Sachs had been shocked at the sight of the woman.

Not exhaustion – though she was clearly tired. Not fear. No, it was Percey's complete resignation that troubled Sachs. As a Patrol officer, she'd seen plenty of tragedy on the street. She'd delivered her share of bad news, but she'd never seen someone who'd given up so completely as Percey Clay.

Percey was on the phone with Ron Talbot. Sachs deduced from the conversation that U.S. Medical hadn't even waited for the cinders of her airplane to cool before canceling the contract. When she hung up she stared at the passing scenery for a moment. She said absently to Bell, 'The insurance company isn't even going to pay for the cargo. They're saying I assumed a known risk. So, that's it. That's it.' She added briskly, 'We're bankrupt.'

Pine trees swept past, scrub oaks, patches of sand. Sachs, a city girl, had come to Nassau and Suffolk Counties when she was a teenager not for the beaches or the shopping malls but to pop the clutch of her Charger and goose the maroon car up to sixty within five point nine seconds in the renegade drag races that made Long Island famous. She appreciated trees and grass and cows but enjoyed nature best when she was streaking past it at 110 miles per hour.

Jodie crossed and uncrossed his arms and burrowed into the center seat, playing with the seat belt, knocking into Sachs again.

'Sorry,' he muttered.

She wanted to slug him.

The house didn't live up to the driveway.

It was a rambling split-level, a combination of logs and clapboard. A ramshackle place, added on to over the years with plenty of federal money and no inspiration.

The night was overcast, filled with dense patches of mist, but Sachs could see enough to note that the house was set in a tight ring of trees. The grounds around it had been cleared for two hundred yards. Good cover for the residents of the house and good groomed open areas to pick off anyone trying an assault. A grayish band in the distance suggested the resumption of the forest. There was a large, still lake behind the house.

Reggie Eliopolos climbed out of the lead van and motioned everyone out. He led them into the main entryway of the building. He handed them off to a round man, who seemed cheerful even though he never once smiled.

'Welcome,' he said. 'I'm U.S. Marshal David Franks. Want to tell you a little about your home away from home here. The most secure witness protection enclave in the country. We have weight and motion sensors built into the entire perimeter of the place. Can't be broken through without setting off all sorts of other alarms. The computer's programmed to sense human motion patterns, correlated to weight, so the alarm doesn't go off if a deer or dog happens to wander over the perimeter. Somebody – some *human* –

steps where he shouldn't, this whole place lights up like Times Square on Christmas Eve. What if somebody tries to ride a horse into the perimeter? We thought of that. The computer pick-ups a weight anomaly correlated to the distance between the animal's hooves, the alarm goes off. And any motion at all – racoon or squirrel – starts the infrared videos going.

'Oh, and we're covered by radar from the Hampton Regional Airport, so any aerial assault gets picked up plenty early. Anything happens, you'll hear a siren and maybe see the lights. Just stay where you are. Don't go outside.'

'What kind of guards do you have?' Sachs asked.

'We've got four marshals inside. Two outside at the front guard station, two in the back by the lake. And hit that panic button there and there'll be a Huey full of SWAT boys here in twenty minutes.'

Jodie's face said twenty minutes seemed like a very long time. Sachs had to agree with him.

Eliopolos looked at his watch. He said, 'We're going to have an armored van here at six to take you to the grand jury. Sorry you won't get much sleep.' He glanced at Percey. 'But if I'd had my way, you'd've been here all night, safe and sound.'

No one said a word of farewell as he walked out the door.

Franks continued, 'Few other things need mentioning. Don't look out windows. Don't go outside without an escort. That phone there' – he pointed to a beige phone in the corner of the living room – 'is secure. It's the only one you should use. Shut off your cell phones and don't use them under any circumstances. So. That's it. Any questions?'

Percey asked, 'Yeah, you got any booze?'

Franks bent to the cabinet beside him and pulled out a bottle of vodka and one of bourbon. 'We like to keep our guests happy.'

He set the bottles on the table, then walked to the front door, slipping his windbreaker on. 'I'm headed home. 'Night,

Tom,' he said to the marshal at the door and nodded to the quartet of guardees, standing incongruously in the middle of the varnished wood hunting lodge, two bottles of liquor between them and a dozen deer and elk heads staring down.

The phone rang, startling them all. One of the marshals got it on the third ring. 'Hello? . . .'

He glanced at the two women. 'Amelia Sachs?'

She nodded and took the receiver.

It was Rhyme. 'Sachs, how safe is it?'

'Pretty good,' she said. 'High tech. Any luck with the body?'

'Nothing so far. Four missing males reported in Manhattan in the last four hours. We're checking them all out. Is Jodie there?'

'Yes.'

'Ask him if the Dancer ever mentioned assuming a particular identity.'

She relayed the question.

Jodie thought back. 'Well, I remember him saying something once . . . I mean, nothing specific. He said if you're going to kill somebody you have to infiltrate, evaluate, delegate, then eliminate. Or something like that. I don't remember exactly. He meant delegate somebody else to do something, then when everybody's distracted, he'd move in. I think he mentioned like a delivery guy or shoe-shine boy.'

*Your deadliest weapon is deception . . .*

After she relayed this to Rhyme he said, 'We're thinking the body's a young businessman. Could be a lawyer. Ask Jodie if he ever mentioned trying to get into the courthouse for the grand jury.'

Jodie didn't think so.

Sachs told Rhyme this.

'Okay. Thanks.' She heard him calling something to Mel Cooper. 'I'll check in later, Sachs.'

After they hung up, Percey asked them, 'You want a nightcap?'

Sachs couldn't decide if she did or not. The memory of the scotch preceding her fiasco in Lincoln Rhyme's bed made her cringe. But on impulse she said, 'Sure.'

Roland Bell decided he could be off duty for a half hour.

Jodie opted for a fast, medicinal shot of whiskey, then headed off to bed, toting his self-help book under his arm and staring with a city boy's fascination at a mounted moose head.

Outside, in the thick spring air, cicadas chirped and bullfrogs belched their peculiar, unsettling calls.

As he looked out the window into the early morning darkness Jodie could see the starbursts of searchlights radiating through the fog. Shadows danced sideways – the mist moving through the trees.

He stepped away from his window and walked to the door of his room, looked out.

Two marshals guarded this corridor, sitting in a small security room twenty feet away. They seemed bored and only moderately vigilant.

He listened and heard nothing other than the snaps and ticks of an old house late in the evening.

Jodie returned to his bed and sat on the sagging mattress. He picked up his battered, stained copy of *Dependent No More*.

Let's get to work, he thought.

He opened the book wide, the glue cracking, and tore a small patch of tape off the bottom of the spine. A long knife slid onto the bed. It looked like black metal though it was made of ceramic-impregnated polymer and wouldn't register on a metal detector. It was stained and dull, sharp as a razor on one edge, serrated like a surgical saw on the other. The handle was taped. He'd designed and constructed it himself. Like most serious weapons it wasn't glitzy and it wasn't sexy and it did only one thing: it killed. And it did this very, very well.

He had no qualms about picking up the weapon – or touching doorknobs or windows – because he was the owner of new fingerprints. The skin on the pads of eight fingers and two thumbs had been burned away chemically last month by a surgeon in Berne, Switzerland, and a new set of prints etched into the scar tissue by a laser used for microsurgery. His own prints would regenerate, but not for some months.

Sitting on the edge of the bed, eyes closed, he pictured the common room and took a mental stroll through it, remembering the location of every door, every window, every piece of furniture, the bad landscapes on the walls, the elk antlers above the fireplace, ashtrays, weapons, and potential weapons. Jodie had such a good memory he would have been able to walk through the room blindfolded, never brushing a single chair or table.

Lost in this meditation, he steered his imaginary self to the telephone in the corner and spent a moment considering the safe house's communications system. He was completely familiar with how it worked (he spent much of his free time reading operating manuals of security and communications systems) and he knew that if he cut the line the drop in voltage would send a signal to the marshals' panel here and probably to a field office as well. So he'd have to leave it intact.

*Not a problem, just a factor.*

On with his mental stroll. Examining the common-room video cameras – which the marshal had 'forgotten' to tell them about. They were in the Y configuration that a budget-conscious security designer would use for a government safe house. He knew this system too and that it harbored a serious design flaw – all you had to do was tap the middle of the lens hard. This misaligned all the optics; the image in the security monitor would go black but there'd be no alarm, which would happen if the coaxial cable were cut.

Thinking about the lighting . . . He could shut out six – no, five – of eight lights he'd seen in the safe house but no more than that. Not until all the marshals were dead. He noted the location of each lamp and light switch, then moved on, more phantom walking. The TV room, the kitchen, the bedrooms. Thinking of distances, angles of view from outside.

*Not a problem . . .*

Noting the location of each of his victims. Considering the possibility that they might have moved in the past fifteen minutes.

*. . . just a factor.*

Now his eyes opened. He nodded to himself, slipped the knife in his pocket, and stepped to the door.

Silently he eased into the kitchen, stole a slotted spoon from a rack over the sink. Walked to the refrigerator and poured himself a glass of milk. Then he walked into the common room and meandered from bookshelf to bookshelf, pretending to look for something to read. As he passed each of the video surveillance cameras he reached up with the spoon and slapped the lenses. Then he set the milk and spoon on a table and headed into the security room.

'Hey, check out the monitors,' one marshal muttered, turning a knob on the TV screen in front of him.

'Yeah?' the other asked, not really interested.

Jodie walked past the first marshal, who looked up and started to ask, 'Hey, sir, how you doing?' when *swish, swish*, Jodie tidily opened the man's throat in a V, spraying his copious velvet blood in a high arc. His partner's eyes flashed wide and he reached for his gun, but Jodie pulled it from his hand and stabbed him once in the throat and once in the chest. He dropped to the floor and thrashed for a moment. It was a noisy death – as Jodie'd known it would be. But he couldn't do more knife work on the man; he needed the uniform and had to kill him with a minimum of blood.

As the marshal lay on the floor, shaking and dying, he gazed up at Jodie, who was stripping off his own blood-soaked clothes. The marshal's eyes flickered to Jodie's biceps. They focused on the tattoo.

As Jodie bent down and began to undress the marshal he noticed the man's gaze and said, 'It's called "Dance Macabre". See? Death's dancing with his next victim. That's her coffin behind them. Do you like it?'

He asked this with genuine curiosity, though he expected no answer. And received none.

# Chapter
# THIRTY-SIX

Mel Cooper, clad in latex gloves, was standing over the body of the young man they'd found in Central Park.

'I could try the plantars,' he suggested, discouraged.

The friction ridge prints on the feet were as unique as fingerprints but they were of marginal value until you had samples from a suspect; plantars weren't cataloged in AFIS databases.

'Don't bother,' Rhyme muttered.

Who the hell *is* this? Rhyme wondered, looking at the savaged body in front of him. He's the key to the Dancer's next move. Oh, this was the worst feeling in the world: an unreachable itch. To have a piece of evidence in front of you, to *know* it was the key to the case, and yet to be unable to decipher it.

Rhyme's eyes strayed to the evidence chart on the wall. The body was like the green fibers they'd found at the hangar – significant, Rhyme felt, but its meaning unknown.

'Anything else?' Rhyme asked the tour doctor from the medical examiner's office. He'd accompanied the body here. He was a young man, balding, with dots of sweat in constellations on his crown. The doctor said, 'He's gay or, to be accurate, he'd lived a gay lifestyle when he was young. He's had repeated anal intercourse though not for some years.'

Rhyme continued, 'What does that scar tell you? Surgery?'

'Well, it's a precise incision. But I don't know of any reason to operate there. Maybe some intestinal blockage. But even then I've never heard of a procedure in that quadrant of the abdomen.'

Rhyme regretted Sachs was not here. He wanted to throw around ideas with her. She'd think of *something* he'd overlooked.

Who could he be? Rhyme racked his brain. Identification was a complex science. He'd established a man's identity once with nothing more than a single tooth. But the procedure took time – usually weeks or months.

'Run blood type and DNA profile,' Rhyme said.

'Already ordered,' the tour doctor said. 'I sent the samples downtown already.'

If he were HIV positive that might help them ID him through doctors or clinics. But without anything else to go on, the blood work wouldn't be very helpful.

Fingerprint . . .

I'd give *anything* for a nice friction ridge print, Rhyme thought. Maybe—

'Wait!' Rhyme laughed out loud. 'His dick!'

'What?' Sellitto blurted.

Dellray lifted an arching brow.

'He doesn't have any hands. But what's the one part of his anatomy he'd be sure to touch?'

'Penis,' Cooper called out. 'If he peed in the last couple of hours we can probably get a print.'

'Who wants to do the honors?'

'No job too disgusting,' the tech said, donning a double layer of latex gloves. He went to work with Kromekote skin-printing cards. He lifted two excellent prints – a thumb from the top of the corpse's penis and an index finger from the bottom.

'Perfect, Mel.'

'Don't tell my girlfriend,' he said coyly. He fed the prints through the AFIS system.

The message came up on the screen: *Please Wait . . . Please Wait . . .*

Be on file, Rhyme thought desperately. Please be on file.

He was.

But when the results came back, Sellitto and Dellray, closest to Cooper's computer, stared at the screen in disbelief.

'What the hell?' the detective said.

'What?' Rhyme cried. 'Who is it?'

'It's Kall.'

'What?'

'It's Stephen Kall,' Cooper repeated. 'It's a twenty-point match. There's no doubt.' Cooper found the composite print they'd constructed earlier to find the Dancer's identity. He dropped it on the table next to the Kromekote. 'It's identical.'

How? Rhyme was wondering. How on earth?

'What if,' Sellitto said, 'it's Kall's prints on this guy's dick? What if Kall's a bone smoker?'

'We've got genetic markers from Kall's blood, right? From the water tower?'

'Right,' Cooper called.

'Compare them,' Rhyme called out. 'I want a profile of the corpse's markers. And I want it now.'

Poetry was not lost on him.

The 'Coffin Dancer' . . . I like that, he thought. Much better than 'Jodie' – the name he'd picked for this job because it was so unthreatening. A silly name, a diminutive name.

The Dancer . . .

Names were important, he knew. He read philosophy. The act of naming – of designating – is unique to humans. The Dancer now spoke silently to the late, dismembered, Stephen Kall: It was me you heard about. *I'm* the one who calls my victims 'corpses'. You call them Wives, Husbands, Friends, whatever you like.

But once I'm hired, they're corpses. That's all they are.

Wearing a U.S. marshal's uniform, he started down the dim hallway from the bodies of the two officers. He hadn't avoided the blood completely, of course, but in the murkiness of the enclave you couldn't see that the navy blue uniform had patches of red on it.

On his way to find Corpse three.

The Wife, if you will, Stephen. What a mixed-up, nervous creature you were. With your scrubbed hands and your confused dick. The Husband, the Wife, the Friend . . .

Infiltrate, Evaluate, Delegate, Eliminate . . .

Ah, Stephen . . . I could have taught you there's only one rule in this business: You stay one step ahead of every living soul.

He now had two pistols but wouldn't use them yet. He wouldn't think of acting prematurely. If he stumbled now he'd never have another chance to kill Percey Clay before the grand jury met later that morning.

Moving silently into a parlor where two more U.S. marshals sat, one reading a paper, one watching TV.

The first one glanced up at the Dancer, saw the uniform, and returned to the paper. Then looked up again.

'Wait,' the marshal said, suddenly realizing he didn't recognize the face.

But the Dancer didn't wait.

He answered with *swish, swish* to both carotid arteries. The man slid forward to die on page 6 of the *Daily News* so quietly that his partner never turned from the TV, where a blond woman wearing excessive gold jewelry was explaining how she met her boyfriend through a psychic.

'Wait? For what?' the second marshal asked, not looking away from the screen.

He died slightly more noisily than his partner, but no one in the compound seemed to notice. The Dancer dragged the bodies flat, stowed them under a table.

At the back door he made certain there were no sensors on the doorframe and then slipped outside. The two marshals in the front were vigilant, but their eyes were turned away from the house. One quickly glanced toward the Dancer, nodded a greeting, then turned back to their reconnaissance. The light of dawn was in the sky, but it was still dim enough so that the man didn't recognize him. They both died almost silently.

As for the two in the back, at the guard station overlooking the lake, the Dancer came up behind them. He tickled the heart of one marshal with a stab in the back and then, *swish*, *swish*, sliced apart the throat of the second guard. Lying on the ground, the first marshal gave a plaintive scream as he died. But once again no one seemed to notice; the sound, the Dancer decided, was very much like the call of a loon, waking to the beautiful pink and gray dawn.

Rhyme and Sellitto were deep in bureaucratic debt by the time the fax of the DNA profile arrived. The test had been the fast version, the polymerase chain reaction test, but it was still virtually conclusive; the odds were about six thousand to one that the body in front of them was Stephen Kall.

'Somebody killed *him*?' Sellitto muttered. His shirt was so wrinkled it looked like a fiber sample under five hundred times magnification. 'Why?'

But why was not a criminalist's question.

Evidence . . . Rhyme thought. Evidence was his only concern.

He glanced at the crime scene charts on his wall, scanning all the clues of the case. The fibers, the bullets, the broken glass . . .

Analyze! Think!

You know the procedure. You've done it a million times.

You identify the facts. You quantify and categorize them. You state your assumptions. And you draw your conclusions. Then you test—

Assumptions, Rhyme thought.

There was one glaring assumption that had been present in this case from the beginning. They'd based their entire investigation on the belief that Kall *was* the Coffin Dancer. But what if he weren't? What if *he* were the pawn and the Dancer'd been using him as a weapon?

*Deception* . . .

If so, there'd be some evidence that didn't fit. Something that pointed to the real Dancer.

He pored over the charts carefully.

But there was nothing unaccounted for except the green fiber. And that told him nothing.

'We don't have any of Kall's clothes, right?'

'No, he was buck naked when we found him,' the tour doctor said.

'We have anything he came in contact with?'

Sellitto shrugged. 'Well, Jodie.'

Rhyme asked, 'He changed clothes here, didn't he?'

'Right,' Sellitto said.

'Bring 'em here. Jodie's clothes. I want to look at them.'

'Uck,' Dellray said. 'They're excessively unpleasant.'

Cooper found and produced them. He brushed them out over sheets of clean newsprint. He mounted samples of the trace on slides and set them in the compound scope.

'What do we have?' Rhyme asked, looking over the computer screen, a copycat image of what Cooper was seeing in his microscope.

'What's that white stuff?' Cooper asked. 'Those grains. There's a lot of it. It was in the seams of his pants.'

Rhyme felt his face flush. Some of it was his erratic blood pressure from exhaustion, some of it was the phantom pain that still plagued him every now and then. But mostly it was the heat of the chase.

'Oh, my God,' he whispered.

'What, Lincoln?'

'It's oolite,' he announced.

'The fuck's that?' Sellitto asked.

'Eggstone. It's a wind-borne sand. You find it in the Bahamas.'

'Bahamas?' Cooper asked, frowning. 'What else did we just hear about the Bahamas?' He looked around the lab. 'I don't remember.'

But Rhyme did. His eyes were fixed on the bulletin board, where was pinned the FBI analyst's report on the sand Amelia Sachs had found last week in Tony Panelli's car, the missing agent downtown.

He read:

'*Substance submitted for analysis is not technically sand. It is coral rubble from reef formations and contains spicules, cross sections of marine worm tubes, gastropod shells and foraminifers. Most likely source is the northern Caribbean: Cuba, the Bahamas.*'

Dellray's agent, Rhyme reflected . . . A man who'd know where the most secure federal safe house in Manhattan was. Who'd tell whoever was torturing him the address.

So that the Dancer could wait there, wait for Stephen Kall to show up, befriend him, and then arrange to get captured and get close to the victims.

'The drugs!' Rhyme cried.

'What?' Sellitto asked.

'What was I thinking of? Dealers don't cut prescription drugs! It's too much trouble. Only street drugs!'

Cooper nodded. 'Jodie wasn't cutting them with the baby formula. He just dumped out the drugs. He was popping placebos, so we'd think he was a druggie.'

'Jodie's the Dancer,' Rhyme called. 'Get on the phone! Call the safe house now!'

Sellitto picked up the phone and dialed.

Was it too late?

Oh, Amelia, what've I done? Have I killed you?

The sky was turning a metallic rosy color.

A siren sounded far away.

The peregrine falcon – the *tiercel*, he reminded himself – was awake and about to go hunting.

Lon Sellitto looked up desperately from the phone. 'There's no answer,' he said.

# Chapter
# THIRTY-SEVEN

They'd talked for a while, the three of them, in Percey's room.

Talked about airplanes and cars and police work.

Then Bell went off to bed and Percey and Sachs had talked about men.

Finally Percey'd lain back on the bed, closed her eyes. Sachs lifted the bourbon glass from the sleeping woman's hand and shut out the lights. Decided to try to sleep herself.

She now paused in the corridor to look out at the dim dawn sky – pink and orange – when she realized that the phone in the compound's main hallway had been ringing for a long time.

Why wasn't anybody answering it?

She continued down the corridor.

She couldn't see the two guards nearby. The enclave seemed darker than before. Most of the lights had been shut off. A gloomy place, she thought. Spooky. Smelling of pine and mold. Something else? Another smell that was very familiar to her. What?

Something from crime scenes. In her exhaustion she couldn't place it.

The phone continued to chirp.

She passed Roland Bell's room. The door was partly open and she looked in. His back was to the door. He was sitting in an armchair that faced a curtained window, his head forward on his chest, arms crossed.

'Detective?' she asked.

He didn't answer.

Sound asleep. Just what *she* wanted to be. She closed his door softly and continued down the corridor, toward her room.

She thought about Rhyme. She hoped *he* was getting some sleep too. She'd seen one of his dysreflexia attacks. It had been terrifying and she didn't want him to go through another one.

The phone went quiet, cut off in the middle of a ring. She glanced toward where she'd heard it, wondering if it was for her. She couldn't hear whoever'd answered. She waited a moment, but no one summoned her.

Silence. Then a tap, a faint scrape. More silence.

She stepped into her room. It was dark. She turned to grope for the switch and found herself staring at two eyes that caught a sliver of reflected light from outside.

Right hand on the butt of her Glock, she swept her left up to the light switch. The eight-point buck stared at her with his shiny, false eyes.

'Dead animals,' she muttered. 'Great idea in a safe house . . .'

She pulled her blouse off and removed the bulky American Body Armor suit. Not as bulky as Jodie's of course. What a kick he was. The little . . . what was Dellray's street word? Skel. Short for skeleton. Scrawny little loser. What a mutt.

She reached under her mesh undershirt and scratched frantically. Her boobs, her back under the bra, her sides.

Ooooo, feels good.

Exhausted, sure, but could she sleep?

The bed looked pretty damn nice.

She pulled on her blouse again, buttoned it, and lay down on the comforter. Closed her eyes. Did she hear footsteps?

One of the guards making coffee, she supposed.

Sleep? Breathe deep . . .

No sleep.

Her eyes opened and she stared at the webby ceiling.

The Coffin Dancer, she mused. How would he come at them? What would his weapon be?

*His deadliest weapon is deception* . . .

Glancing out a crack in the curtain, she saw the beautiful fish-gray dawn. A haze of mist bleached the color from the distant trees.

Somewhere inside the compound she heard a thud. A footstep.

Sachs swung her feet around to the floor and sat up. May as well just give up and get some coffee. I'll sleep tonight.

She had a sudden urge to talk to Rhyme, to see if he'd found anything. She could hear him saying, *'If I'd found something I would've called you, wouldn't I? I said I'd check in.'*

No, she didn't want to wake him, but she doubted he was asleep. She pulled her cell phone out of her pocket and clicked it on before she remembered Marshal Franks's warning to use only the secure line in the living room.

As she was about to shut the phone off, it chirped loudly.

She shivered – not at the jarring sound, but at the thought that the Dancer had somehow found her number and wanted to confirm she was in the compound. For an instant she wondered if somehow he'd slipped explosives into her phone too.

Damnit, Rhyme, look how spooked I am!

Don't answer it, she told herself.

But instinct told her to, and while criminalists may shun instinct, Patrol cops, *street* cops, always listen to those inner voices. She pulled the antenna out of the phone.

'Lo?'

'Thank God . . .' The panicked tone of Lincoln Rhyme chilled her.

'Hey, Rhyme. What's—'

'Listen very carefully. Are you alone?'

'Yeah. What's going on?'

'Jodie's the Dancer.'

'What?'

'Stephen Kall was the diversion. Jodie killed him. It was his body in the park we found. Where's Percey?'

'In her room. Up the hall. But how—'

'No time. He's going for the kill right now. If the marshals're still alive, tell them to get into a defensive position in one of the rooms. If they're dead find Percey and Bell and get out. Dellray's scrambled SWAT but it'll be twenty or thirty minutes before they're there.'

'But there're eight guards. He can't've taken them all out . . .'

'Sachs,' he said sternly, 'remember who he is. Move! Call me when you're safe.'

Bell! she thought suddenly, recalling the detective's still posture, his head slumped forward.

She raced to her door, threw it open, drew her gun. The black living room and corridor gaped. Dark. Only faint dawn light filtering into the rooms. She listened. A shuffle. A clink of metal. But where were the sounds coming from?

Sachs turned toward Bell's room and trotted as quietly as she could.

He got her just before she got to his room.

As the figure stepped from the doorway she dropped into a crouch and swung the Glock toward him. He grunted and slapped the pistol from her hand. Without thinking, she shoved him forward, slamming his back into the wall.

Groping for her switchblade.

Roland Bell gasped, 'Hold up there. Hey, now . . .'

Sachs let go of his shirt.

'It's you!'

'You scared the everlivin' you-know-what outa me. What's—?'

'You're all right!' she said.

'Just dozed off for a minute. What's going on?'

'Jodie's the Dancer. Rhyme just called.'

'What? How?'

'I don't know.' She looked around, shivering in panic. 'Where're the guards?'

The hall was empty.

Then she recognized the smell she'd wondered about. It was blood! Like hot copper. And she knew then that all the guards were dead. Sachs went to retrieve her weapon, which was lying on the floor. She frowned, looking at the end of the grip. Where the clip should have been was an empty hole. She picked up the gun.

'No!'

'What?' Bell asked.

'My clip. It's gone.' She slapped her utility belt. The two clips in the keepers were gone too.

Bell drew his weapons – the Glock and the Browning. They too were clipless. The chambers of the guns were empty too.

'In the car!' she stammered. 'I'll bet he did it in the car. He was sitting between us. Fidgeting all the time. Bumping into us.'

Bell said, 'I saw a gun case in the living room. A couple of hunting rifles.'

Sachs remembered it. She pointed. 'There.' They could just make it out in the dim light of dawn. Bell looked around him and hurried to it, crouching, while Sachs ran to Percey's room and looked in. The woman was asleep on the bed.

Sachs stepped back to the corridor, flicked her knife open, and crouched, squinting. Bell returned a moment later. 'It's been broken into. All the rifles're gone. And no ammo for the sidearms.'

'Let's get Percey and get out of here.'

A footstep not far away. A click of a bolt-action rifle's safety going off.

She grabbed Bell's collar and pulled him to the floor.

The gunshot was deafening and the bullet broke the sound barrier directly over them. She smelled her own burning hair. Jodie must have had a sizable arsenal by now – all the sidearms of the marshals – but he was using the hunting rifle.

They sprinted for Percey's door. It opened just as they got there and she stepped out, saying, 'My God, what's—'

The full body tackle from Roland Bell shoved Percey back into her room. Sachs tumbled in on top of them. She slammed the door shut, locked it, and ran to the window, flung it open. 'Go, go, go, go . . .'

Bell lifted a stunned Percey Clay off the ground and dragged her toward the window as several high-powered deer slugs tore through the door around the lock.

None of them looked to see how successful the Coffin Dancer'd been. They rolled through the window into the dawn and ran and ran and ran through the dewy grass.

# Chapter
# THIRTY-EIGHT

Sachs stopped beside the lake. Mist, tinted red and pink, wafted in ghostly tatters over the still, gray water.

'Go on,' she shouted to Bell and Percey. 'Those trees.'

She was pointing to the nearest cover – a wide band of trees at the end of a field on the other side of the lake. It was more than a hundred yards away but was the closest cover.

Sachs glanced back at the cabin. There was no sign of Jodie. She dropped into a crouch over the body of one of the marshals. His holster was empty of course, his clip cases too. She'd known Jodie had taken those weapons, but she hoped there was one thing he hadn't thought of.

He *is* human, Rhyme . . .

And frisking the cool body she found what she was looking for. Tugging up the marshal's pants cuff she pulled his backup weapon out of his ankle holster. A silly gun. A tiny five-shot Colt revolver with a two-inch barrel.

She glanced at the cabin just as Jodie's face appeared in the window. He lifted the hunting rifle. Sachs spun and squeezed off a round. Glass broke inches from his face and he stumbled backward into the room.

Sachs sprinted around the lake after Bell and Percey. They ran fast, weaving sideways, through the dewy grass.

They got nearly a hundred yards from the house before they heard the first shot. It was a rolling sound, echoing off the trees. It kicked up dirt near Percey's leg.

'Down,' Sachs cried. 'There.' Pointing to a dip in the earth.

They rolled to the ground just as he fired again. If Bell had been upright the shot would have hit him directly between the shoulder blades.

They were still fifty feet from the nearest clump of trees that would give them protection. But to try for it now would be suicide. Jodie was apparently every bit the marksman that Stephen Kall had been.

Sachs lifted her head briefly.

She saw nothing but heard an explosion. An instant later the slug snapped through the air beside her. She felt the same draining terror as at the airport. She pressed her face into the cool spring grass, slick with dew and her sweat. Her hands shook.

Bell looked up fast and then down again.

Another shot. Dirt kicked up inches from his face.

'I think I saw him,' the detective drawled. 'There're some bushes to the right of the house. On that hill.'

Sachs breathed a trio of fast breaths. Then she rolled five feet to the right, poked her head up fast, ducked again.

Jodie chose not to shoot this time and she'd gotten a good look. Bell was right: The killer was on the side of a hill, targeting them with the telescopic deer rifle; she'd seen the faint glint from the scope. He couldn't quite hit them where they were if they stayed prone. But all he had to do was move up the hill. From its crest he could shoot down into the pit they were hiding in now – a perfect kill zone.

Five minutes passed without a shot. He'd be working his way up the hill, though cautiously – he knew Sachs was armed and he'd seen she was a good shot. Could they wait him out? When would the SWAT chopper get here?

Sachs squeezed her eyes closed, smelled the dirt, the grass.

She thought of Lincoln Rhyme.

*You know him better than anybody, Sachs . . .*

*You never really know a perp until you've walked where he's walked, until you've cleaned up after his evil . . .*

But, Rhyme, she thought, this isn't Stephen Kall. Jodie *isn't* the killer I know. It wasn't *his* crime scenes I walked through. It wasn't *his* mind I peered into . . .

She looked for a low spot in the ground that might lead them safely to the trees but there was nothing. If they moved five feet in either direction he'd have a clean shot.

Well, he'd have a clean shot at them any minute now, when he got to the crest of the hill.

Then something occurred to her. That the crime scenes she'd worked really *were* the Dancer's scenes. He may not have been the one who fired the bullet that killed Brit Hale or planted the bomb that blew up Ed Carney's plane or swung the knife that killed John Innelman in the basement of the office building.

But Jodie *was* a perpetrator.

Get into his mind, Sachs, she heard Lincoln Rhyme say. His deadliest – *my* deadliest weapon is deception.

'Both of you,' Sachs called, looking around. 'There.' She pointed toward a slight ravine.

Bell glanced at her. She saw how badly he wanted the Dancer too. But the look in her eyes told him that the killer was her prey and hers alone. No debate and no argument. Rhyme had given this chance to her and nothing in the world could stop her from doing what she was about to.

The detective nodded solemnly and he pulled Percey after him into the shallow notch in the earth.

Sachs checked the pistol. Four rounds left.

Plenty.

More than enough . . .

*If* I'm right.

Am I? she wondered, face against the wet, fragrant earth. And she decided that, yes, she was right . . . A frontal assault wasn't the Dancer's way. *Deception*.

And that's just what I'm going to give him.

'Stay down. Whatever happens, stay down.' She rose to her hands and knees, looking over the ridge. Getting ready, preparing herself. Breathing slowly.

'That's a hundred-yard shot, Amelia,' Bell whispered. 'With a snub-nose?'

She ignored him.

'Amelia,' Percey said. The flier held her eyes for a moment and the women shared a smile. 'Head down,' Sachs ordered and Percey complied, nestling into the grass.

Amelia Sachs stood up.

She didn't crouch, didn't turn sideways to present a more narrow target. She just slipped into the familiar two-hand target pistol stance. Facing the house, the lake, facing the prone figure halfway up the hill, who pointed the telescopic sight directly at her. The stubby pistol felt as light as a scotch glass in her hand.

She aimed at the glare of the telescopic sight, a football field away.

Sweat and mist forming on her face.

Breathe, breathe.

Take your time.

Wait . . .

A ripple passed through her back and arms and hands. She forced the panic away.

Breathe . . .

Listen, listen.

Breathe . . .

Now!

She spun around and dropped to her knees as the rifle jutting from the grove of trees behind her, fifty feet away, fired. The bullet split the air just over her head.

Sachs found herself staring at Jodie's astonished face, the hunting rifle still at his cheek. He realized that he hadn't fooled her after all. That she'd figured out his tactic. How he'd fired a few shots from the lake, then dragged one of the guards up the hill and propped him there with one of the hunting rifles to keep them pinned down while he jogged up the road and circled behind.

*Deception* . . .

For a moment neither of them moved.

The air was completely still. No tatters of mist floating past, no trees or grass bending in the wind.

A faint smile crossed Sachs's face as she lifted the pistol in both hands.

Frantic, he ejected the shell from the deer rifle and chambered another round. As he lifted the gun to his cheek again Sachs fired. Two shots.

Both clean hits. Saw him fly backward, the rifle sailing through the air like a majorette's baton.

'Stay with her, Detective!' Sachs called to Bell and sprinted toward Jodie.

She found him in the grass, lying on his back.

One of her bullets had shattered his left shoulder. The other had hit the telescopic sight straight on and blown metal and glass into the man's right eye. His face was a bloody mess.

She cocked her tiny gun, put a good ration of pressure on the trigger and pressed the muzzle against his temple. She frisked him. Lifted a single Glock and a long carbide knife out of his pocket. She found no other weapons.

'Clear,' she called.

As she stood, pulling her cuffs out of the case, the Dancer coughed and spit, wiped blood out of his good eye. Then he lifted his head and looked out over the field. He spotted Percey Clay as she slowly rose from the grass, staring at her attacker.

Jodie seemed to shiver as he gazed at her. Another cough then a deep moan. He startled Sachs by pushing against her leg with his uninjured arm. He was badly hurt— maybe mortally – and had little strength. It was a curious gesture, the way you'd push an irritating Pekinese out of your way.

She stepped back, keeping the gun trained squarely on his chest.

Amelia Sachs was no longer of any interest to the Coffin Dancer. Neither were his wounds or the terrible pain they must be radiating. There was only one thing on his mind. With superhuman effort he rolled onto his belly and, moaning and clawing dirt, he began muscling his way toward Percey Clay, toward the woman he'd been hired to kill.

Bell joined Sachs. She handed him the Glock and together they kept their weapons on the Dancer. They could easily have stopped him – or killed him. But they remained transfixed, watching this pitiable man so desperately absorbed in his task that he didn't even seem to know his face and shoulder had been destroyed.

He moved another few feet, pausing only to grab a sharp rock about the size of a grapefruit. And he continued on toward his prey. Never saying a word, drenched in blood and sweat, his face a knot of agony. Even Percey, who had every reason to hate this man, to sweep Sachs's pistol from her hand and end the killer's life right here, even she was mesmerized, watching this hopeless effort to finish what he'd started.

'That's enough,' Sachs said finally. She bent down and lifted the rock away.

'No,' he gasped. 'No . . .'

She cuffed him.

The Coffin Dancer gave a horrifying moan – which might have been from his pain but seemed to arise more out of unbearable loss and failure – and dropped his head to the ground.

He lay still. The trio stood around him, watching his blood soak the grass and innocent crocuses. Soon the heartrending call of the loons was lost in the *whup whup whup* of a helicopter skimming over the trees. Sachs noticed that Percey Clay's attention slipped immediately away from the man who'd caused her so much sorrow, and the flier watched in rapt attention as the cumbersome aircraft eased through the misty air and touched down lithely on the grass.

# Chapter
# THIRTY-NINE

'Ain't kosher, Lincoln. Can't do it.'

Lon Sellitto was insistent.

But so was Lincoln Rhyme. 'Give me a half hour with him.'

'They're not comfy with it.' Which really meant what the detective added: 'They shit when I suggested it. You're civilian.'

It was nearly ten on Monday morning. Percey's appearance before the grand jury had been postponed until tomorrow. The navy divers had found the duffle bags that Phillip Hansen had sunk deep in Long Island sound. They were being raced to an FBI PERT team in the Federal Building downtown for analysis. Eliopolos had delayed the grand jury to be able to present as much damning evidence against Hansen as possible.

'What're they worried about?' Rhyme asked petulantly. 'It's not as if I can beat him up.'

He thought about lowering his offer to twenty minutes. But that was a sign of weakness. And Lincoln Rhyme did not believe in showing weakness. So he said, 'I caught him. I deserve a chance to talk to him.'

And fell silent.

Blaine, his ex-wife, had told him in a moment of very uncharacteristic perception that Rhyme's eyes, dark as night, argued better than his words did. And so he stared at Sellitto until the detective sighed, then glanced at Dellray.

'Aw, give him a little time,' the agent said. 'What's it gonna hurt? Bring the billy-boy up here. And if he tries to run, hell, gimme a golden excuse for some target practice.'

Sellitto said, 'Oh, all right. I'll make the call. Only, don't fuck up this case.'

The criminalist barely heard the words. His eyes turned toward the doorway, as if the Coffin Dancer were about to materialize magically.

He wouldn't have been surprised if that had happened.

'What's your real name? Is it really Joe or Jodie?'

'Ah, what's it matter? You caught me. You can call me what you want.'

'How 'bout a first name?' Rhyme asked.

'How 'bout what *you* call me? The Dancer. I like that.'

The small man examined Rhyme carefully with his good eye. If he was in pain from the wounds, or groggy from medication, he didn't show it. His left arm was in a shoulder cast but he still wore thick cuffs attached to a waist shackle. His feet were chained too.

'Whatever you like,' Rhyme said pleasantly. And continued to study the man as if he were an unusual pollen spore picked up at a crime scene.

The Dancer smiled. Because of the damaged facial nerves and the bandages, his expression was grotesque. Tremors occasionally shook his body and his fingers twitched, his broken shoulder rose and fell involuntarily. Rhyme had a curious feeling – that he himself was healthy and it was the prisoner who was the cripple.

*In the valley of the blind, the one-eyed man is king.*

The Dancer smiled at him. 'You're just dying to know, aren't you?' he asked Rhyme.

'Know what?'

'To know all . . . That's why you brought me here. You were lucky – catching me, I mean – but you don't really have a clue as to how I did it.'

Rhyme clucked his tongue. 'Oh, but I know exactly how you did it.'

'Do you now?'

'I just asked you here to talk to you,' Rhyme replied. 'That's all. To talk to the man who almost outthought me.'

'"Almost."' The Dancer laughed. Another twisted smile. It was really quite eerie. 'Okay, then tell me.'

Rhyme sipped from his straw. It was fruit juice. He'd astonished Thom by asking him to dump out the scotch and replace it with Hawaiian Punch. Rhyme now said agreeably, 'All right. You were hired to kill Ed Carney, Brit Hale, and Percey Clay. You were paid a lot, I'd guess. Six figures.'

'Seven,' the Dancer said proudly.

Rhyme lifted an eyebrow. 'Lucrative line of work.'

'If you're good.'

'You deposited the money in the Bahamas. You'd gotten Stephen Kall's name from somewhere – I don't know where exactly. Probably a mercenary network—' the Dancer nodded '—and you hired him as a subcontractor. Anonymously, maybe by E-mail, maybe fax, using references he'd trust. You'd never meet him face-to-face of course. And I assume you tried him out?'

'Of course. A hit outside of Washington, D.C. I was hired to kill a congressional aide sneaking secrets out of Armed Services Committee files. It was an easy job, so I sub-contracted it to Stephen. Gave me a good chance to check him out. I watched him every step of the way. I checked the entrance wound on the body myself. Very professional. I think he saw me watching him and he came after me to take care of witnesses. That was good too.'

Rhyme continued. 'You left him his cash and the key to Phillip Hansen's hangar – where he waited to plant the bomb on Carney's plane. You knew he was good but you weren't sure he was good enough to kill all three of them. You probably thought he could get one at the most but would provide enough diversion for you to get close to the other two.'

The Dancer nodded, reluctantly impressed. 'Him killing Brit Hale surprised me. Oh, yes. And it surprised me even more that he got away afterward and got the second bomb onto Percey Clay's plane.'

'You guessed that you'd have to kill at least one of the victims yourself so last week you became Jodie, started hawking your drugs everywhere so that people on the street'd know about you. You kidnapped the agent in front of the federal building, found out which safe house they'd be in. You waited in the most logical place for Stephen to make his attack and let him kidnap you. You left plenty of clues to your subway hideout so we'd be sure to find you . . . and use you to get to Kall. We all trusted you. Sure, we did – Stephen didn't have a clue *you'd* hired him. All he knew was that you betrayed him and he wanted to kill you. Perfect cover for you. But risky.'

'But what's life without risk?' the Dancer asked playfully. 'Makes it all worthwhile, don't you think? Besides, when we were together I built in a few . . . let's call them countermeasures, so that he'd hesitate to shoot me. Latent homosexuality is *always* helpful.'

'But,' Rhyme added, piqued that his narrative had been interrupted, 'when Kall was in the park, you slipped out of the alley where you were hiding, found him, and killed him . . . You disposed of the hands, teeth, and clothes – and his guns – in the sewer interceptor pipes. And then we invited you out to Long Island . . . Fox in the henhouse.' Rhyme added flippantly, 'That's the schematic . . . That's the bare bones. But I think it tells the story.'

The man's good eye closed momentarily, then opened again. Red and wet, it stared at Rhyme. He gave a faint nod of concession, or perhaps admiration. 'What was it?' the Dancer finally asked. 'What tipped you?'

'Sand,' Rhyme answered. 'From the Bahamas.'

He nodded, winced at the pain. 'I turned my pockets out. I vacuumed.'

'In the folds of the seams. The drugs too. Residue and the baby formula.'

'Yes. Sure.' After a moment the Dancer added, 'He was right to be scared of you. Stephen, I mean.' The eye was still scanning Rhyme. Like a doctor looking for a tumor. He added, 'Poor man. What a sad creature. Who buggered him, d'you think? Stepdad or the boys in reform? Or all of the above?'

'I wouldn't know,' Rhyme said. On the windowsill the male falcon landed and folded his wings.

'Stephen got scared,' the Dancer mused. 'And when you get scared it's all over. He thought the worm was looking for him. Lincoln the Worm. I heard him whisper that a few times. He was scared of you.'

'But you weren't scared.'

'No,' the Dancer said. 'I don't get scared.' Suddenly he nodded, as if he'd finally noticed something that had been nagging him. 'Ah, listening carefully, are you? Trying to peg the accent?'

Rhyme had been.

'But, see, it changes. Mountain . . . Connecticut . . . Plains Southern and swamp Southern . . . Mizzura. Kayntuckeh. Why're you interrogating me? You're Crime Scene. I'm caught. Time for beddy-bye. End of story. Say, I like chess. I *love* chess. You ever play, Lincoln?'

He'd used to like it. He and Claire Trilling had played quite a bit. Thom had been after him to play on the computer and had bought him a good chess program, installed it. Rhyme had never loaded it. 'I haven't played for a long time.'

'You and I'll have to play a game of chess sometime. You'd be a good man to play against . . . You want to know a mistake some players make?'

'What's that?' Rhyme felt the man's hot gaze. He was suddenly uneasy.

'They get curious about their opponents. They try to learn things about their personal life. Things that aren't *useful*. Where they're from, where they were born, who their siblings are.'

'Is that right?'

'That may satisfy an itch. But it confuses them. It can be dangerous. See, the game is all on the board, Lincoln. It's all on the board.' A lopsided smile. 'You can't accept not knowing anything about me, can you?'

No, Rhyme thought, I can't.

The Dancer continued, 'Well, what exactly do you want? An address? A high school yearbook? How about a clue? "Rosebud." How's that? I'm surprised at you, Lincoln. You're a criminalist – the best I've ever seen. And here you are right now on some kind of pathetic sentimental journey. Well, who am I? The headless horseman. Beelzebub. I'm Queen Mab. I'm "them" as in "Look out for them; they're after you." I'm not your proverbial worst nightmare because nightmares aren't real and I am more real than anybody wants to admit. I'm a craftsman. I'm a businessman. You won't get my name, rank or serial number. I don't play according to the Geneva Convention.'

Rhyme could say nothing.

There was a knock on the door.

The transport had arrived.

'Can you take the shackles off my feet?' the Dancer asked the two officers in a pathetic voice, his good eye blinking and tearful. 'Oh, please. I hurt so much. And it's *so* hard to walk.'

One of the guards looked at him sympathetically then at Rhyme, who said matter-of-factly, 'You loosen so much as one restraint and you'll lose your job and never work in this city again.'

The trooper stared at Rhyme for a moment, then nodded at his partner. The Dancer laughed. 'Not a problem,' he said, eyes on Rhyme. 'Just a factor.'

The guards gripped him by his good arm and lifted him to his feet. He was dwarfed by the two tall men as they led him to the door. He looked back.

'Lincoln?'

'Yes?'

'You're going to miss me. Without me, you'll be bored.' His single eye burned into Rhyme's. 'Without me, you're going to die.'

An hour later the heavy footsteps announced the arrival of Lon Sellitto. He was accompanied by Sachs and Dellray.

Rhyme knew immediately there was trouble. For a moment he wondered if the Dancer had escaped.

But that wasn't the problem.

Sachs sighed.

Sellitto gave Dellray a look. The agent's lean face grimaced.

'Okay, tell me,' Rhyme snapped.

Sachs delivered the news. 'The duffle bags. PERT's been through 'em.'

'Guess what was inside,' Sellitto said.

Rhyme sighed, exhausted, and not in the mood for games. 'Detonators, plutonium, and Jimmy Hoffa's body.'

Sachs said, 'A bunch of Westchester County Yellow Pages and five pounds of rocks.'

'What?'

'There's nothing, Lincoln. Zip.'

'You're sure they were phone books, not encrypted business records?'

'Bureau cryptology looked 'em over good,' Dellray said. 'Fuckin' off-the-shelf Yellow Pages. And the rocks're nothin'. Just added 'em to make it sink.'

'They're gonna release Hansen's fat ass,' Sellitto muttered darkly. 'They're doin' the paperwork right now. They're not even presenting it to the grand jury. All those people died for nothing.'

'Tell him the rest,' Sachs added.

'Eliopolos is on his way here now,' Sellitto said. 'He's got paper.'

'A warrant?' Rhyme asked shortly. 'For what?'

'Oh. Like he said. To arrest you.'

# Chapter
# FORTY

Reginald Eliopolos appeared at the doorway, backed up by two large agents.

Rhyme had thought of the attorney as middle aged. But in the daylight he seemed to be in his early thirties. The agents were young too and dressed as well as he was, but they reminded Rhyme of pissed-off longshoremen.

What exactly did he need them for? Against a man flat on his back?

'Well, Lincoln, I guess you didn't believe me when I said there'd be repercussions. Uh-huh. You didn't believe me.'

'What the fuck're you bitchin' about, Reggie?' Sellitto asked. 'We caught him.'

'Uh-huh . . . uh-huh. I'll tell you what I'm—' he lifted his hands and made imaginary quotation marks in the air '—bitchin' for. The case against Hansen is kaput. No evidence in the duffle bags.'

'That's not our fault,' Sachs said. 'We kept your witness alive. And caught Hansen's hired killer.'

'Ah,' Rhyme said, 'but there's more to it than that, right, Reggie?'

The assistant U.S. attorney gazed at him coldly.

Rhyme continued, 'See, Jodie – I mean, the Dancer – is the only chance they have to make a case against Hansen now. Or that's what he thinks. But the Dancer'll never dime a client.'

'Oh, that a fact? Well, you don't know him as well as you think you do. I just had a long talk with him. He was more than willing to implicate Hansen. Except now he's stonewalling. Thanks to you.'

'Me?' Rhyme asked.

'He said you threatened him. During that little unauthorized meeting you had a few hours ago. Uh-huh. Heads are going to roll because of *that*. Rest assured.'

'Oh, for God's sake,' Rhyme spat out, laughing bitterly. 'Don't you see what he's doing? Let me guess . . . you told him that you'd arrest me, right? And he'd agree to testify if you did.'

The pendulum swing of Eliopolos's eyes told Rhyme that this was exactly what happened.

'Don't you get it?'

But Eliopolos didn't get a thing.

Rhyme said, 'Don't you think he'd like to get me in detention, maybe fifty, sixty feet from where he is?'

'Rhyme,' Sachs said, frowning with concern.

'What're you talking about?' the attorney said.

'He wants to *kill* me, Reggie. That's his point. I'm the only man who's ever stopped him. He can't very well go back to work knowing I'm out there.'

'But he's not going anywhere. Ever.'

*Uh-huh.*

Rhyme said, 'After I'm dead he'll recant. He'll never testify against Hansen. And what're you going to pressure him with? Threaten him with the needle? He won't care. He's not afraid of anything. Not a single thing.'

What was nagging? Rhyme wondered. Something seemed wrong here. Very wrong.

He decided it was the phone books . . .

Phone books and rocks.

Rhyme was lost in thought, staring at the evidence chart on the wall. He heard a jingle, glanced up. One of the agents with Eliopolos actually pulled out his handcuffs and was proceeding toward the Clinitron. Rhyme laughed to himself. Better shackle the old feet. Might run away.

'Come on, Reggie,' Sellitto said.

The green fiber, phone books, and rocks.

He remembered something the Dancer had told him. Sitting in the very chair Eliopolos stood beside now.

*A million dollars* . . .

Rhyme was vaguely aware of the agent trying to figure out how to best subdue a crip. And he was vaguely aware of Sachs stepping forward trying to figure out how to subdue the *agent*. Suddenly he barked, 'Wait,' in a voice commanding enough to freeze everyone in the room.

The green fiber . . .

He stared at it on the chart.

People were talking to him. The agent was still eyeing Rhyme's hands, brandishing the tinkling cuffs. But Rhyme ignored them all. He said to Eliopolos, 'Give me a half hour.'

'Why should I?'

'Come on, what's it going to hurt? It's not like I'm going anywhere.' And before the attorney could agree, or disagree, Rhyme was shouting, 'Thom! *Thom*, I need to make a phone call. Are you going to help me, or not? I don't know where he gets to sometimes. Lon, will you call for me?'

Percey Clay had just returned from burying her husband when Lon Sellitto tracked her down. Wearing black she sat in the crinkly wicker chair beside Lincoln Rhyme's bed. Standing nearby was Roland Bell, in a tan suit, badly cut – thanks to the size of the two guns he wore. He pushed his thinning brown hair straight back over the crown of his head.

Eliopolos was gone, though his two goons were outside, guarding the hallway. Apparently they actually *did* believe that, given a chance, Thom would try to wheel Rhyme out the door and he'd make a getaway in the Storm Arrow, top speed 7.5 mph.

Percey's outfit chafed at collar and waist, and Rhyme bet that it was the only dress she owned. She began to lift ankle to knee as she sat back, realized a skirt was wrong for this pose and sat up formally, knees together.

She eyed him with impatient curiosity and Rhyme realized that no one else – Sellitto and Sachs had fetched her – had delivered the news.

Cowards, he thought grumpily.

'Percey . . . They won't be presenting the case against Hansen to the grand jury.'

For an instant there was a flash of relief. Then she understood the implication. 'No!' she gasped.

'That flight Hansen made? To dump those duffle bags? The bags were fake. There was nothing in them.'

Her face grew pallid. 'They're letting him go?'

'They can't find any connection between the Dancer and Hansen. Until we do, he's free.'

Her hands rose to her face. 'It was all a waste then? Ed . . . And Brit? They died for nothing.'

He asked her, 'What's happening to your company now?'

Percey wasn't expecting the question. She wasn't sure she heard him. 'I'm sorry?'

'Your company? What's going to happen to Hudson Air now?'

'We'll sell it probably. We've had an offer from another company. They can carry the debt. We can't. Or maybe we'll just liquidate.' It was the first time he'd heard resignation in her voice. A Gypsy in defeat.

'What other company?'

'I frankly don't remember. Ron's been talking to them.'

'That's Ron Talbot, right?'

'Yes.'

'Would he know about the financial condition of the company?'

'Sure. As much as the lawyers and accountants. More than me.'

'Could you call him, ask him to come down here as soon as possible?'

'I suppose I could. He was at the cemetery. He's probably home by now. I'll call him.'

'And, Sachs?' he said, turning to her, 'we've got another crime scene. I need you to search it. As fast as possible.'

Rhyme looked over the big man coming through the doorway, wearing a dark blue suit. It was shiny and had the color and cut of a uniform about it. Rhyme supposed it was what he'd worn when he flew.

Percey introduced them.

'So you got that son of a bitch,' Talbot grumbled. 'Think he'll get the chair?'

'I collect the trash,' Rhyme said, pleased as always when he could think up a melodramatic line. 'What the DA does with it is up to him. Did Percey tell you we've had trouble with the evidence implicating Hansen?'

'Yeah, she said something about that. The evidence he dumped was fake? Why'd he do that?'

'I think I can answer that, but I need some more information. Percey tells me you know the Company pretty well. You're a partner, right?'

Talbot nodded, took out a pack of cigarettes, saw no one

else was smoking, replaced them in his pocket. He was even more rumpled than Sellitto and it looked as if it had been a long time since he'd been able to button his jacket around his ample belly.

'Let me try this out on you,' Rhyme said. 'What if Hansen didn't want to kill Ed and Percey because they were witnesses?'

'But then why?' Percey blurted.

Talbot asked, 'You mean, he had another motive? Like what?'

Rhyme didn't respond directly. 'Percey tells me the Company hasn't been doing well for a while.'

Talbot shrugged. 'Been a tough couple years. Deregulation, lots of small carriers. Fighting UPS and FedEx. Postal Service too. Margins've shrunk.'

'But you still have good – what is that, Fred? You did some white-collar crime work, right? Money that comes in. What's the word for it?'

Dellray snorted a laugh. 'Revy-nue, Lincoln.'

'You had good revenue.'

Talbot nodded. 'Oh, cash flow's never been a problem. It's just that more goes out than comes in.'

'What do you think about the theory that the Dancer was hired to murder Percey and Ed so that the killer could buy the Company at a discount?'

'What company? Ours?' Percey asked, frowning.

'Why would Hansen do that?' Talbot said, wheezing again.

Percey added, 'And why not just come to us with a big check? He never even approached us.'

'I didn't actually say Hansen,' Rhyme pointed out. 'The question I asked before was what if *Hansen* didn't want to kill Ed and Percey? What if it was somebody else?'

'Who?' Percey asked.

'I'm not sure. It's just . . . well, that green fiber.'

'Green fiber?' Talbot followed Rhyme's eyes to the evidence chart.

'Everyone seems to've forgotten about it. Except me.'

'Man never forgets a single thing. Do you, Lincoln?'

'Not too often, Fred. Not too often. That fiber. Sachs – my partner—'

'I remember you,' Talbot said, nodding toward her.

'She found it in the hangar that Hansen leased. It was in some trace materials near the window where Stephen Kall waited before he planted the bomb on Ed Carney's plane. She also found bits of brass and some white fibers and envelope glue. Which tells us that somebody left a key to the hangar in an envelope somewhere for Kall. But then I got to thinking – why did Kall need a key to break into an empty hangar? He was a pro. He could've broken into the place in his sleep. The only reason for the key was to make it look like Hansen had left it. To implicate him.'

'But the hijacking,' Talbot said, 'when he killed those soldiers and stole the guns. Everybody knows he's a murderer.'

'Oh, he probably is,' Rhyme agreed. 'But he didn't fly his airplane over Long Island sound and play bombardier with those phone books. Somebody else did.'

Percey stirred uneasily.

Rhyme continued, 'Somebody who never thought we'd find the duffle bags.'

'Who?' Talbot demanded.

'Sachs?'

She pulled three large evidence envelopes out of a canvas bag and rested them on the table.

Inside two of them were accounting books. The third contained a stack of white envelopes.

'Those came from your office, Talbot.'

He gave a weak laugh. 'I don't think you can just take those without a warrant.'

Percey Clay frowned. 'I gave them permission. I'm still head of the Company, Ron. But what're you saying, Lincoln?'

Rhyme regretted not sharing his suspicions with Percey before this; it was coming as a terrible shock. But he couldn't risk that she might tip their hand to Talbot. He'd covered his tracks so well until now.

Rhyme glanced at Mel Cooper, who said, 'The green fiber that we found with the particles of key came from a ledger sheet. The white ones from an envelope. There's no doubt they match.'

Rhyme continued, 'And all from your office, Talbot.'

'What do you mean, Lincoln?' Percey gasped.

Rhyme said to Talbot, 'Everybody at the airport knew Hansen was under investigation. You thought you'd use that fact. So you waited until one night when Percey and Ed and Brit Hale were working late. You stole Hansen's plane for the flight, you dumped the fake duffle bags. You hired the Dancer. I assume you'd heard about him on your jobs in Africa or the Far East. I made a few calls. You worked for the Botswana air force and the Burmese government advising them in buying used military airplanes. The Dancer told me he was paid a million for the hit.' Rhyme shook his head. 'That should have tipped me right there. Hansen could have had all three witnesses killed for a couple hundred thousand. Professional killing's definitely a buyer's market nowadays. A million told me that the man ordering the hit was an amateur. And that he had a lot of money at his disposal.'

The scream rose from Percey Clay's mouth and she leapt for him. Talbot stood, backed up. 'How could you?' she screamed. 'Why?'

Dellray said, 'My boys from financial crimes're looking over your books now. What we think we're gonna be finding is lots and lots of money that ain't where it oughta be.'

Rhyme continued, 'Hudson Air's a lot more successful than you were thinking, Percey. Only most of it was going into Talbot's pocket. He knew he was going to get caught some day and he needed to get you and Ed out of the way and buy the Company himself.'

'The stock purchase option,' she said. 'As a partner he had a right to buy our interest from our estates at a discount if we die.'

'This's bullshit. That guy was shooting at me too, remember.'

'But you didn't hire Kall,' Rhyme reminded. 'You hired Jodie – the Coffin Dancer – and he subcontracted the work with Kall. Who didn't know you from beans.'

'How could you?' Percey repeated in a hollow voice. 'Why? *Why?*'

Talbot raged, 'Because I loved you!'

'What?' Percey gasped.

Talbot continued. 'You laughed when I said I wanted to marry you.'

'Ron, no. I—'

'And you went back to him.' He sneered. 'Ed Carney, the handsome fighter pilot. Top gun . . . He treated you like shit and you still wanted him. Then . . .' His face was purple with fury. 'Then . . . then I lost the last thing I had – I was grounded. I couldn't fly anymore. I watched the two of you logging hundreds of hours a month while all I could do was sit at a desk and push papers. You had each other, you had flying . . . You don't have a clue what it's like to lose everything you love. You just don't have a clue!'

Sachs and Sellitto saw him tense. They anticipated his trying something but they hadn't guessed Talbot's strength. As Sachs stepped forward, unholstering her weapon, Talbot scooped the tall woman completely off her feet and flung her into the evidence table, scattering microscopes and equipment, knocking Mel Cooper back into the wall. Talbot pulled the Glock from her hand.

He swung it toward Bell, Sellitto and Dellray. 'All right, throw your guns on the floor. Do it now. Now!'

'Come on, man,' Dellray said, rolling his eyes. 'What're you gonna do? Climb out the window? You ain't going nowhere.'

He shoved the gun toward Dellray's face. 'I'm not going to say it again.'

His eyes were desperate. He reminded Rhyme of a cornered bear. The agent and the cops tossed their guns onto the ground. Bell dropped both of his.

'Where does that door lead?' He nodded to the wall. He'd have seen Eliopolos's guards outside and knew there was no escape that way.

'That's a closet,' Rhyme said quickly.

He opened it, eyed the tiny elevator.

'Fuck you,' Talbot whispered, pointing the gun at Rhyme.

'No,' Sachs shouted.

Talbot swung the weapon her way.

'Ron,' Percey cried, 'think about it. Please . . .'

Sachs, embarrassed but unhurt, was on her feet, looking at the pistols that lay on the floor ten feet away.

No, Sachs, Rhyme thought. Don't!

She'd survived the coolest professional killer in the country and now was about to get shot by a panicked amateur.

Talbot's eyes were flicking back and forth from Dellray and Sellitto to the elevator, trying to figure out the switchpad.

No, Sachs, don't do it.

Rhyme was trying to catch her attention but her eyes were judging distances and angles. She'd never make it in time.

Sellitto said, 'Let's just talk, Talbot. Come on, put the gun down.'

Please, Sachs, don't do it . . . He'll see you. He'll go for a head shot – amateurs always do – and you'll die.

She tensed, eyes on Dellray's Sig-Sauer.

No . . .

The instant Talbot looked back at the elevator Sachs leapt for the floor and snagged Dellray's weapon as she rolled. But

Talbot saw her. Before she could lift the large automatic he shoved the Glock at her face, squinting as he started to pull the trigger in panic.

'No!' Rhyme shouted.

The gunshot was deafening. Windows rattled and the falcons took off into the sky.

Sellitto scrambled for his weapon. The door burst open and Eliopolos's officers ran into the room, their own pistols drawn.

Ron Talbot, the tiny red hole in his temple, stood perfectly still for an instant, then dropped in a spiral to the ground.

'Oh, brother,' said Mel Cooper, frozen in position, holding an evidence bag and staring down at his skinny, little .38 Smith & Wesson, held in Roland Bell's steady hand, pointing out from beside the tech's elbow. 'Oh, my.' The detective had eased up behind Cooper and slipped the weapon off the narrow belt holster on the back of the tech's belt. Bell had fired from the hip – well, from Cooper's hip.

Sachs rose to her feet and lifted her Glock out of Talbot's hand. She felt for a pulse, shook her head.

The wailing filled the room as Percey Clay dropped to her knees over the body and, sobbing, pounded her fist into Talbot's dense shoulder again and again. No one moved for a long moment. Then both Amelia Sachs and Roland Bell started toward her. They paused and it was Sachs who backed away and let the lanky detective put his arm around the petite woman and lead her from the body of her friend and enemy.

# Chapter
# FORTY-ONE

A little thunder, a sprinkling of spring rain late at night. The window was open wide — not the falcon window of course; Rhyme didn't like them disturbed — and the room was filled with cool evening air.

Amelia Sachs popped the cork and poured Cakebread chardonnay into Rhyme's tumbler and her glass.

She looked down and gave a faint laugh.

'I don't believe it.'

On the computer beside the Clinitron was a chess program.

'You don't play games,' she said. 'I mean, I've *never* seen you play games.'

'Hold on,' he said to her.

On the screen: '*I did not understand what you said. Please say it again.*'

In a clear voice he said, 'Rook to queen's bishop four. Checkmate.'

A pause. The computer said, '*Congratulations.*' Followed by a digitized version of Sousa's *Washington Post* march.

'It's not for entertainment,' he said churlishly. 'Keeps the mind sharp. It's my Nautilus machine. You want to play sometime, Sachs?'

'I don't play chess,' she said after a swallow of the fine wine. 'Some damn knight goes for my king I'd rather blow him away than figure out how to outsmart him. How much did they find?'

'Money? That Talbot had hidden? Over five million.'

After the auditors had gone through the second set of books, the real books, they found that Hudson Air was an extremely profitable company. Losing the aircraft and the U.S. Medical contract would sting but there was plenty of cash to keep the company, as Percey told him, 'aloft'.

'Where's the Dancer?'

'In SD.'

Special Detention was a little known facility in the criminal courts building. Rhyme had never seen the place – few cops had – but in thirty-five years no one had ever broken out of it.

'Coped his talons pretty good,' Percey Clay had said when Rhyme told her this. Which meant, she explained, the filing down of a hunting falcon's claws.

Rhyme – given his special interest in the case – insisted on being informed about the Dancer's tenure in SP. He'd heard from the guards that he'd been asking about windows in the facility, what floor they were on, what part of town the facility was located in.

'Do I smell a service station nearby?' he'd asked cryptically.

When he'd heard this, Rhyme had immediately called Lon Sellitto and asked him to call the head of the detention center and double the guard.

Amelia Sachs took another fortifying sip of wine and whatever was coming was coming now.

She inhaled deeply then blurted, 'Rhyme, you should go for it.' Another sip. 'I wasn't sure I was going to say that.'

'Beg pardon?'

'She's right for you. It could be real good.'

They rarely had trouble looking at each other's eyes. But, rough water ahead, Sachs looked down at the floor.

What *was* this all about?

When she glanced up and saw her words weren't registering she said, 'I know how you feel about her. And she doesn't admit it but I know how she feels about you.'

'*Who?*'

'You know who. Percey Clay. You're thinking she's a widow, she's not going to want someone in her life right now. But . . . you heard what Talbot said – Carney had a girlfriend. A woman in the office. Percey knew about it. They stayed together because they were friends. And because of the company.'

'I never—'

'Go for it, Rhyme. Come on. I really mean that. You think it'd never work. But she doesn't care about your situation. Hell, look at what she said the other day. She was right – you're both real similar.'

There were times when you just needed to lift your hands and let them flop into your lap in frustration. Rhyme settled for nestling his head in his luxurious down pillow. 'Sachs, where on earth did you get this idea?'

'Oh, please. It's so obvious. I've seen how you've been since she showed up. How you look at her. How obsessed you've been to save her. I know what's going on.'

'What *is* going on?'

'She's like Claire Trilling, the woman who left you a few years ago. That's who you want.'

Oh . . . He nodded. So that's it.

He smiled. Said, 'Sure, Sachs, I have been thinking about Claire a lot the past few days. I lied when I said I hadn't been.'

'Whenever you mentioned her I could tell you were still

in love with her. I know that after the accident she never saw you again. I figured it was still an open book for you. Like me and Nick after he left me. You met Percey and she reminded you of Claire all over again. You realized that you could be with someone again. With her, I mean. Not . . . not with me. Hey, that's life.'

'Sachs,' he began, 'it's not Percey you should've been jealous of. She's not the one that booted you out of bed the other night.'

'No?'

'It was the Dancer.'

Another splash of wine in her glass. She swirled it and looked down at the pale liquid. 'I don't understand.'

'The other night?' He sighed. 'I had to draw the line between us, Sachs. I'm already too close to you for my own good. If we're going to keep working together, I had to keep that barrier up. Don't you see? I can't be close to you, not *that* close, and still send you in harm's way. I can't let it happen again.'

'*Again?*' She was frowning, then her face flooded with understanding.

Ah, that's my Amelia, he thought. A fine criminalist. A good shot. And she's quick as a fox.

'Oh, no, Lincoln, Claire was . . .'

He was nodding. 'She was the tech I assigned to search the crime scene in Wall Street after the Dancer's hit five years ago. She was the one who reached into the wastebasket and pulled out the paper that set off the bomb.'

Which is why he'd been so obsessed with the man. Why he'd wanted, so uncharacteristically, to debrief the killer. He wanted to catch the man who'd killed his lover. Wanted to know all about him.

It was revenge, undiluted revenge. When Lon Sellitto – who'd known about Claire – had wondered if it might not be better for Percey and Hale to leave town, he was asking if Rhyme's personal feelings weren't intruding into the case.

Well, yes, they were. But Lincoln Rhyme, for all the over-whelming stasis of his present life, was as much a hunter as the falcons on his window ledge. Every criminalist is. And when he scented his prey he wouldn't be stopped.

'So, that's it, Sachs. It has nothing to do with Percey. And as much as I wanted you to spend the night – to spend every night – I can't risk loving you any more than I do.'

It was so astonishing –bewildering – to Lincoln Rhyme to be having this conversation. After the accident he'd come to believe that the oak beam that had snapped his spine actually did its worst damage to his heart, killing all sensation within it. And his ability to love and be loved were as crushed as the thin fiber of his spinal cord. But the other night, Sachs close to him, he'd realized how wrong he was.

'You understand, don't you, Amelia?' Rhyme whispered.

'Last names only,' she said, smiling, walking close to the bed.

She bent down and kissed him on the mouth. He pressed back into his pillow for a moment then returned the kiss.

'No, no,' he persisted. But he kissed her hard once again.

Her purse dropped to the floor. Her jacket and watch went on the bedside table. Followed by the last of the fashion accessories to come off – her Glock 9.

They kissed again.

But he pulled away. 'Sachs . . . It's too risky!'

'God don't give out certain,' she said, their eyes locked on each other's. Then she stood and walked across the room to the light switch.

'Wait,' he said.

She paused, looked back. Her red hair fell over her face, obscuring one eye.

Into the microphone hanging on the bed frame Rhyme commanded, 'Lights out.'

The room went dark.

# Author's note

All writers know that their books are only partly products of their own efforts. Novels are molded by our loved ones and friends, sometimes directly, sometimes in more subtle but no less important ways. I'd like to say thanks to some of the people who've helped me with this book: To Madelyn Warcholik for keeping my characters true to themselves, for making sure my plots don't move so recklessly they get pulled over for speeding, and for being an unlimited source of inspiration. To editors David Rosenthal, Marysue Rucci, and Carolyn Mays for brilliantly and unflinchingly doing all the hard work. To agent Deborah Schneider for being the best in the business. And to my sister and fellow author, Julie Reece Deaver, for being there throughout it all.

## About the Author

A former journalist, folksinger and attorney, Jeffery Deaver is an international number one bestselling author. His novels have appeared on bestseller lists around the world, including the *New York Times*, *The Times* of London, Italy's *Corriere della Sera*, the *Sydney Morning Herald* and the *Los Angeles Times*. His books are sold in 150 countries and translated into twenty-five languages.

The author of thirty-one novels, two collections of short stories, and a non-fiction law book, he's received or been shortlisted for a number of awards around the world. *The Bodies Left Behind* was named Novel of the Year by the International Thriller Writers Association and Deaver's Lincoln Rhyme thriller, *The Broken Window,* and a stand-alone thriller, *Edge*, were also nominated for that prize. He has been awarded the Steel Dagger and the Short Story Dagger from the British Crime Writers' Association, and the Nero Wolfe Award, and he is a three-time recipient of the Ellery Queen Readers Award for Best Short Story of the Year, and a winner of the British Thumping Good Read Award. *The Cold Moon* was recently named the Book of the Year by the Mystery Writers Association of Japan, as well as by *Kono Mystery Wa Sugoi* magazine. In addition, the Japanese Adventure Fiction Association awarded the book their annual Grand Prix award; Deaver's *Carte Blanche* also received that honor.

Deaver has been nominated for seven Edgar Awards from the Mystery Writers of America, a Shamus award, an Anthony Award and a Gumshoe Award. He was recently shortlisted for the ITV3 Crime Thriller Award for Best International Author.

His latest novels are *The October List*, a reverse-time thriller, the Lincoln Rhyme novel *The Kill Room*, *XO*, featuring Kathryn Dance, and *Carte Blanche*, the 2011 James Bond continuation thriller.

His book *A Maiden's Grave* was made into an HBO movie starring James Garner and Marlee Matlin, and his novel *The Bone Collector* was a feature release from Universal Pictures, starring Denzel Washington and Angelina Jolie. And, yes, the rumors are true; he did appear as a corrupt reporter on his favorite soap opera, *As the World Turns*.

He was born outside Chicago and has a bachelor of journalism degree from the University of Missouri and a law degree from Fordham University.

Readers can visit his website at www.jefferydeaver.com.

In the best books, the ending often comes as a shock.
Not just because of that one last twist in the tale,
but because you have been so absorbed in their world,
that coming back to the harsh light of reality is a jolt.

If that describes you now, then perhaps you should track down
some new leads, and find new suspense in other worlds.

Join us at www.hodder.co.uk, or follow us on
Twitter @hodderbooks, and you can tap in to a
community of fellow thrill-seekers.

Whether you want to find out more about this book,
or a particular author, watch trailers and interviews, have
the chance to win early limited editions, or simply browse
our expert readers' selection of the very best books,
we think you'll find what you're looking for.

And if you don't, that's the place to tell us what's missing.

**We love what we do, and we'd love you to be part of it.**

www.hodder.co.uk

@hodderbooks

HodderBooks

HodderBooks